GIDEON . . .

Jamie was heartsick with longing for the quiet, handsome wrangler who'd somehow gone from her best friend to someone she couldn't live without. But she didn't regret it.

Why did he have to be so perfect? If only he was a jerk like every other guy she'd known, then she could flip him off and forget him.

Her face burned when she remembered the look on his face after she'd kissed him last Christmas. How deliberately he'd avoided her eyes, as if even that intimacy was too much. How carefully he'd chosen his tone, his words, as if afraid she would clasp them to her love-sick bosom and interpret even the slightest kindness as an admission of adoration.

Aw, James, no.

And he'd given her the old slug on the arm, like she was a buddy, a pal, a chum.

Okay, maybe he was a jerk after all.

So he was a little older than her, so they were different. She made him smile, loosened up that tight armor of his, made him laugh now and then, even. And his calm demeanor settled her somehow.

This was his fault. He'd made her fall in love with him. So one of two things had to happen now. Either she had to fall out of love with him.

Or he had to fall into love with her.

Books by Roxanne Snopek

The Sunset Bay Series

SUNSET BAY SANCTUARY

DRIFTWOOD CREEK

BLACKBERRY COVE
(coming in January 2019!)

Published by Kensington Publishing Corporation

DRIFTWOOD CREEK

ROXANNE SNOPEK

ZEBRA BOOKS
KENSINGTON PUBLISHING CORP.
http://www.kensingtonbooks.com

ZEBRA BOOKS are published by

Kensington Publishing Corp.
119 West 40th Street
New York, NY 10018

All Kensington titles, imprints, and distributed lines are available at special quantity discounts for bulk purchases for sales promotion, premiums, fund-raising, educational, or institutional use.

Special book excerpts or customized printings can also be created to fit specific needs. For details, write or phone the office of the Kensington Sales Manager: Attn.: Sales Department. Kensington Publishing Corp., 119 West 40th Street, New York, NY 10018. Phone: 1-800-221-2647.

Zebra and the Z logo Reg. U.S. Pat. & TM Off.

First Printing: July 2018
ISBN-13: 978-1-4201-4423-9
ISBN-10: 1-4201-4423-5

eISBN-13: 978-1-4201-4426-0
eISBN-10: 1-4201-4426-X

10 9 8 7 6 5 4 3 2 1

Printed in the United States of America

For Ray, forever and always

Chapter One

*The New Moon in Aries is a time of great
   beginnings.*

—Jamie's horoscope

Jamie Vaughn believed in signs. They were scattered across the universe like cosmic kitty litter, a nudge here, a suggestion there, a roadblock somewhere else. Or, if you weren't paying attention, the occasional punch to the gut.

Jamie meant to pay attention. She tried. But fortune favored the pigheaded, and decades of elbows-up, barge-in-and-take-it was proving tougher to shake than nicotine.

Her abs were rock-solid from all the gut-punches.

However, almost twenty-six seemed a good age for personal growth so she put on her toughest don't-care face, shoved her hands into the back pockets of her skinny jeans, and planted her boots squarely in the doorway of the kennel room, determined to get her way.

Haylee looked up from the grooming table where she was brushing Jewel, her Labrador-cross therapy dog. Pregnancy made her look round and cute and soft but Jamie knew that was an illusion.

"You're about to pop, Haylee."

As announcements went, it was worse than unnecessary.

The quick flare of Haylee's nostrils told Jamie it was also unwelcome and unappreciated. Not her best opening move.

"I've got eight weeks to go. That's nowhere near popping." She stuck out her lip and blew a blond curl off her face. "Grab a brush. How does this dog get so much junk in her coat on a thirty minute beach walk?"

"It's a mystery to all." Jamie joined her at the table, and began detangling the big dog's back end.

Determined.

Tough.

Strategic.

"I have a proposition, Haylee." She took a deep breath and dove in. "I want to take over the program while you're on maternity leave."

Haylee's hand stilled. "We've talked about this. Companions with Purpose is my baby."

Jamie had once dreamed of being a police K9 handler, but EX plus CON equalled a roadblock even Attila couldn't conquer. Training dogs at Sanctuary Ranch was her lifeline, her chance to get past the screw-ups she'd weaseled under, skated over, slipped around. To catch her breath from the gut-punch that kept on giving.

"I want more than hosing down kennels and exercising the boarders. I'm a good trainer. You said it yourself."

"You're a natural, but—"

"I understand suspending the classes." She didn't. "But at least continue the therapy visits. Jewel's slobbery kisses might be the only thing keeping some of those old geezers alive. Let me help. I've seen you getting in and out of a car. Juggling the leash, your purse, your keys, your emergency underwear. It's not pretty."

"No fair." Haylee pointed the slicker brush at her. "Let's see you watch *Bridesmaids* with a five-pound fetus dancing on your bladder."

Humor was a good sign.

Jamie switched to a wider-toothed comb, counted down from ten, then took fresh aim.

"Aiden thinks you're overworking yourself, you know. He told me. In fact, he kind of appointed me your guardian angel."

Truth was a fluid thing, Jamie believed, that the interpretation of facts changed according to the lens of the viewer. And what she'd said could have been true.

"Aiden thinks I need an angel?" Haylee met her eyes, gave a slow blink. "With Olivia and Daphne already vying for godmother, the last thing I need is more hovering."

Jewel yipped and Haylee dropped the comb. "Sorry, baby, that was a bad tangle."

"Mommy's mean, isn't she?" Jamie fished a piece of freeze-dried liver from the treat jar, fed it to Jewel, then stroked the greying muzzle.

"You'll miss your visiting, won't you, Ju-Jube? But it'll be okay. You're probably tired of all that helping anyway. You're an old dog, you've earned your retirement."

"Passive aggressive." Haylee flicked a chunk of bramble-laden fur into the trash. "Nice."

"Active aggressive isn't working so shit-hot. A girl's gotta do what a girl's gotta do."

The laugh she tagged onto the end sounded as fake as her boot-black hair. Pathetic. But she couldn't help herself.

Haylee ran one hand over Jewel's coat, checking for more burrs. "You were hired for the kitchen. I already take too much of your time."

"Wow, low blow." She handed Haylee a spray bottle of coat conditioner. "All those hormones must be poisoning your brain. You used to love me."

"I still love you. But I'm hot and fat and my back hurts." Haylee ran the back of her hand over her forehead. "Everything but the boarding kennel is on hold for now. Therapy visits. Rescues. Training. We'll revisit your role when I've figured out life with a new baby."

A scuffing noise sounded beyond them, and a long, tall shadow flickered through the sunshine.

Gideon.

Jamie's heart lurched like a newborn foal.

"Hi," she said. It came out like a gunshot and she felt blood rush into her cheeks. She'd been fine for a whole year. More than that. Then one day, that rough voice sent tremors to the pit of her stomach and just like that, she lost her mind. She didn't know where to put her hands or what to say. Her feet got big. Her mouth got bigger. She forgot how to breathe.

"Ladies," he said, tipping his hat and giving them that slow, narrow-eyed smile. "You're looking lovely today, Haylee."

"No ladies here. We're women." Jamie tossed her head, which felt like it weighed fifty pounds, and her hat fell off. "Oops."

Her conversation skills went straight down the drain when he was around.

"No disrespect intended." He turned to Haylee. "You, Haylee, look lovely. Glowing."

"You're such a liar. It's one of your best qualities." Haylee gave her dog a kiss, then helped her down the steps from the grooming table. "What's up?"

Jewel shook herself and ran to Gideon, who braced his muscular legs for the onslaught. She wriggled her big body, rubbing herself against him while he stroked and patted and murmured.

Jamie watched his hands roam over the dog's fur and her skin tingled, imagining.

"Wanted to let James know I don't need her for the trail ride tomorrow, after all," Gideon said. "Huck's coming instead."

The tingles evaporated. "Don't call me James."

"Daphne will be glad to hear that," Haylee said, running

a sticky roller over her pants to get rid of the dog hair. "Me too. She'll have time to feed the steers for me then, tomorrow."

"Gosh," Jamie said. "Did I forget to take off my secret invisibility cloak again? I'm right here. And can't I take an extra turn on barn-cleaning rather than feed Charley and his cohort? You know how I feel about them."

"We all told you not to name them." Gideon's smile faded. He glanced at Haylee. "She's not on the schedule, is she? For, you know."

"Again, right here!" She waved her hand in front of Gideon. "And no. I'm exempt from the final episode on religious grounds."

"Vegetarianism isn't a religion." But his smile was back.

"Buddhism is."

"You're not Buddhist."

"I could be Buddhist!"

"If I could interject," Haylee broke in, drawing Gideon's attention. "Jamie will be working elsewhere at slaughter time. And don't mind her. She's pissed because I'm not handing over the reins of Companions with Purpose to her while I'm . . . busy." She made a circular gesture toward her abdomen.

Gideon's eyebrows moved slightly. "Huh," he said.

"I don't want to take over. I just want to be a trainer." Jamie signalled for Jewel to sit, then gave her another treat. "I figured acting as Jewel's handler for a few weeks would be a good way to start, plus helping Haylee in her time of need. Win-win. And Jewel loves me. Look how well she responds to me."

Haylee put a hand to the small of her back and sighed. The skirmish was already lost.

"Look, I don't have the time or energy to argue. You get plenty of time away from the kitchen with Gideon and the horses already. And yes, I appreciate what you do around the kennels immensely. You've got a great heart." Haylee hesitated, and Jamie's guard went up. "But you're not ready for more, and I don't have time to teach you, even if you were. Sorry, James, it's just the way it is."

Ouch.

Haylee motioned to her dog and the two of them walked past Gideon and Jamie, leaving them alone in the grooming room.

Jamie began cleaning up, tossing equipment into the basket, sweeping fur off the table, moving too fast in hopes of distracting herself from what felt distressingly like an onslaught of tears.

Haylee was being unreasonable. Jamie could do so much more; she knew she could. All she needed was a chance. She swallowed, and her throat made an awkward, clicking sound.

Then the warm weight of Gideon's hand settled on her shoulder, stilling her. For a moment, she allowed it to seep into her, like seawater on sun-dried driftwood, making her feel dark and heavy and full of life.

"She knows how talented you are," he said quietly. "The timing's not right, that's all."

The comforting heat flowed over her like caramel over a ripe, red apple at the fair, taking a plain thing and making it better, sweeter, shinier. That's how it was with Gideon. He made people feel good about themselves. He made her believe she was more than a stray, more than unclaimed baggage, more than the flotsam and jetsam tossed onto the beach after a storm.

"Try not to take it personally, kiddo."

Kiddo.

The word hit like a rogue wave, snapping her back to reality, reminding her that no matter the hope he inspired, he still saw her as a girl who'd landed at Sanctuary Ranch with a lightweight backpack, a heavyweight past, and a big question mark for a future.

She shrugged out from beneath his hand and brushed her forearm over her eyes. "Glad you don't need me tomorrow.

I have to get out for a bit before supper. Tell Daphne I'll be back in time for prep." She shouldered past him through the door.

"Wait. Where're you going?"

"Riding." She headed for the corrals.

"Want some company?"

"No."

He continued to follow. "James? You okay?"

She gritted her teeth. "You betcha. I'm awesome."

She disappeared into the tack room and to her relief, he let her go.

Pigheaded persistence, she had it in spades. But her don't-care face only lasted so long. And all the signs in the world didn't matter if there was no way forward.

Jamie gave the bay gelding a solid nudge with her knee to move him farther up the wooded path. She had an hour before Daphne needed her for the dinner rush, and she had to get her act together.

The dense, heavy quiet of the coastal rainforest in summer was punctuated only by the rustlings and calls of the wildlife within it and the soft crush of hooves on humus. But instead of being soothing, the silence made the swirling maelstrom inside her head seem louder.

All she wanted was a chance. Haylee couldn't keep up with her schedule, not with the baby coming. And Jamie had more than proven herself in the kennel, with dogs Haylee herself had been iffy on. Like Hannibal, for instance. If not for Jamie, he'd be dead. Instead, the massive mastiff mix had raised the social capital of a cute, nerdy paraplegic kid who now had more girlfriends than he knew what to do with.

Nash pulled on the reins, reaching for a stand of juicy-looking grass.

She yanked his head up, then instantly regretted it.

"Sorry, buddy." She swallowed. "It's not you, it's me."

Her throat tightened. Talk about paying it forward. Or shit rolling downhill, which was more like it. Poor horse didn't deserve her today.

Nash whuffled softly through his nose, forgiving her. She gave him his head and listened to his hoofbeats as they thumped softly, rhythmically, hypnotically on the leaf-littered trail. Slowly, the thrashing of her heart and soul subsided.

Jamie could be a great trainer, she knew it. But Haylee was as territorial as any alpha and Jamie was just the new hire who helped out wherever needed—when she wasn't busy assisting the cook.

On a conscious level, Jamie knew she was overreacting. They were friends. Haylee valued her. The hurt was unintentional. She simply hadn't considered the idea that Jamie might have more to contribute.

She respected Haylee. To have her look through Jamie like she wasn't good enough or smart enough or . . . real, hurt.

But what bothered her the most was that Gideon had witnessed it. Heat twisted in her gut again as she recalled his expression. The lifted eyebrows, that surprised blink. Then the sigh, the slightly amused incredulity.

His touch, which she'd thought was so kind and understanding, had been nothing more than pity.

Of course, she knew Haylee's rejection wasn't personal. But it didn't matter.

It made no difference how tough she was on the outside because, on the inside, she was still the new kid, the foster kid, forgotten yet again at school pickup.

The invisibility cloak was real.

And there was no best-before date on humiliation, it seemed.

She reached down to stroke the horse. "You're a good boy, Nash."

He was exactly what she needed so she focused on her breath, the moment, the solid warmth of the animal beneath her. Nash was good on trails, energetic but not flighty, compliant without being passive, and most importantly for the ranch, he was reliable with guests. One of the perks of the job was that she could ride as much as she wanted in her off time.

She'd love to have a horse of her own one day, one she could train herself from a foal, really bond with, but second-hand was second nature for her, and working with other peoples' animals was better than nothing.

She wasn't complaining. She had it good at Sanctuary Ranch, and she knew it.

She inhaled deeply, bringing the green-drenched air into her lungs and holding it there, imagining bright white oxygen rushing in, healing cells from the insults of daily living. She let the breath out, loudly enough for Nash to glance backwards, braced for another outburst.

"Sorry, buddy." She reached down and patted his wide neck. "Just trying to live life in the now. No regrets, right?"

She was heartsick with longing for the quiet, handsome wrangler who'd somehow gone from her best friend to someone she couldn't live without. But she didn't regret it.

Gideon.

Why did he have to be so perfect? If only he were an asshole like every other guy she'd known, then she could flip him off and forget him.

Her face burned when she remembered the look on his face after she'd kissed him last Christmas. How deliberately he'd avoided her eyes, as if even that intimacy was too much. How carefully he'd chosen his tone, his words, as if afraid she would clasp them to her love-sick bosom and interpret even the slightest kindness as an admission of adoration.

Aw, James, no.

And he'd given her the old slug on the arm, like she was a buddy, a pal, a chum.

Okay, maybe he was an asshole after all.

"A gigantic asshole," she muttered, urging the horse into

a trot, dodging low-lying branches, welcoming the cold slap of damp leaves to her overheated skin.

So he was a little older than her, but she was an old soul, far older than her years. So they were different. She made him smile, loosened up that tight armor of his, made him laugh now and then, even. And his calm demeanor settled her somehow.

She whacked at a dead branch, hearing a satisfying crack as it twisted and broke.

This was his fault. He'd made her fall in love with him. So one of two things had to happen now. Either she had to fall out of love with him. Or he had to fall into love with her.

Pigheaded persistence, here we go again.

Suddenly the bay gelding's muscles tightened beneath her, alerting her to the present. He reared up with a shrill whinny, sidestepping on nervous hooves, an age-old instinct for self-preservation urging him to flee.

"Easy, boy." Jamie gathered the reins, gripping the saddle with her thighs, scanning the shadowy depths in front of them, her nerves jumping. Nash didn't freak out for no reason.

She squinted against the sunlight slanting through the canopy, and then she saw it.

Not a predator.

It was a chocolate-colored dog, skulking at the side of the path, half hidden by ferns, ears back, eyes wide. More frightened of them than they were of it, as the saying went.

She patted the horse's neck, her own heart pounding. "It's okay, Nash. It's just a dog." But the horse drummed a tattoo with his hooves, slipping on the rotting vegetation.

"Easy, easy, boy!"

She reined him in a tight circle, let him stomp and snort, hoping he wouldn't dump her and run. Though it would serve Gideon right if she broke her neck out here, wouldn't it? He'd be sorry then, wouldn't he?

"Listen to yourself," she muttered. No wonder he didn't take her seriously.

Nash quivered and rolled white eyes, more dramatic than necessary. The dog whined, took a few steps toward them, and Jamie got a better look. A Labrador retriever, female, old, unkempt. Scrawny. A leather collar hung loosely from her neck. When she walked, tags jingled.

"Hey, sweetie," Jamie called. "What are you doing out here alone?"

She pushed aside thoughts of Gideon and looked around for the dog's human.

"Hello?" she called.

No one answered.

"Is anyone there?"

The dog whined again and glanced up the path. A smell drifted in, nasty, like rotten garbage or manure, then just as quickly dissipated.

Unease lifted the hairs at the back of Jamie's neck.

"Talk to me, Lassie." She spoke loudly, glancing around her. "Is Timmy in the well?"

Or had someone abandoned the animal?

If so, they'd chosen a good spot. The tiny beach town of Sunset Bay was a couple of miles southwest of her current position. The ranch was a mile behind her by trail, three by road. It wouldn't be the first time some jerk had unloaded an unwanted dog or cat out here. Too lazy to find them a new home, too cheap to relinquish them to a shelter, wilfully ignorant enough to believe they were "setting them free."

Yeah, Jamie judged them.

"Be good, Nash." She slipped off the horse's back and tied the reins loosely to a branch.

"Hey, girl," she crooned, fishing a dog treat from her pocket. "You hungry?"

The dog's nose quivered, but she held back. Trust issues. Jamie knew about a few properties along the main road to town, but logging roads, most now abandoned, crisscrossed the area and beautiful, remote land always housed more inhabitants than met the eye.

With sufficient motivation, enough land between you and your neighbor, and the smarts to keep your nose clean and your fences mended, residents of the area were usually willing to live and let live. People came here for privacy. To start over. Sometimes to disappear.

The dog wagged her tail and began loping up the trail, favoring her right hind leg. And for a breed that should be stocky with muscle, this one barely had enough to cover her bony ribs.

Jamie leaped back onto Nash and nudged him with her heel, but the gelding tossed his head and tap-danced on the path. The ranch horses were well used to dogs, but something was definitely up Nash's butt today.

"Quit being a baby," she told him. "She's half the size of Hannibal and you're not scared of him."

The mastiff–pit bull cross was her success story, even though Haylee had done most of the training. He was the one that had given Jamie the itch. She wanted to do it again, channel that energy and intelligence, take that kernel of potential and nurture it into something amazing.

She could do with another Hannibal right now.

The bay gelding snorted and tossed his head again and obeyed, grudgingly.

"Ninety-nine bottles of beer on the wall," Jamie sang, glancing around her. "Ninety-nine bottles of beer." She paused, then switched to a conversational tone. "Why are they always on a wall? Shouldn't they be on a shelf? They're not posters. They're bottles."

They came to where the trail branched off into a lesser-used section leading farther up into the hills, or looped gently down to hug a series of inlets and eventually return to the ranch. The dog must be headed to a property in the hills somewhere.

"Where to now?" Jamie asked the dog. "If that's home, then good luck. Tell someone to look after that leg of yours. You probably smell like an appetizer out here."

But the dog didn't exit the downward trail. Instead, she continued to lead, picking up her limping pace enough that Jamie lost sight of her waving tail a few times. Each time, the dog doubled back, as if urging her to follow and hurry up about it.

Intriguing. What, or whom, was the dog heading for?

When the thick cedars and pines gave way to the lower scrub and rocky outcroppings, the Labrador sped up even more, whining. Now the dog veered off the main path, onto a smaller deer trail. Nash stopped, bobbing his head anxiously.

"Come on," said Jamie, urging him forward. "We've come this far."

A few yards in, the forest opened up and in front of them, framed by towering evergreens, was a small pool, carved into the basalt by the restless winter runoff from one of scores of creeks that cut through the palisade of mountains separating the ocean from the state's interior. Nurse trees, dead as the driftwood hurled inland by some long-ago tsunami, flanked the creek, green saplings spiking sunward from the rotting depths. With the gentle trickling of the mountain stream in the background, it was a mossy, haunting paradise.

"You," Jamie told the dog, "should be a tour guide."

Could it be a hot spring? A trail ride with this as a destination, plus Daphne's famous picnic lunch and an hour of swimming, would be a huge hit with ranch guests. She couldn't wait to tell Haylee and Olivia about it. They were always looking for new activities to offer.

The skinny Lab whined again and sat down, looking first

at Jamie, then down over the edge of the pool. She barked, twice. Nash, still unsettled, swivelled his ears and snorted.

And then Jamie heard it. A second voice, yipping and crying.

A second dog.

A *puppy*.

Chapter Two

*Success is still an option if you use Saturn's gifts of
patience and persistence.*

—Jamie's horoscope

The back of Jamie's neck tingled. Oh, God. Timmy wasn't
in the well. He was in the pool.

And Timmy was a dog, not a kid, which rendered the
metaphor useless. Like her, when she was nervous. And possibly hearing things.

She leaped off Nash's back, raced to the edge, and peered
over. The movement startled the skinny dog, who backed
away to the far side of the pool.

"Is someone there?"

She waited, her heart thudding.

Nothing. It was hard to see. The dark rocky sides were
veiled by moss and lichen, full of shadows, the water still
and black.

Her heart thudded.

"Hello?" Jamie called again. The old dog whined again
and pawed the soft dirt in front of her.

Nothing. She sat back on her haunches, observing the Labrador.

"What are you trying to tell me, girl? Did I hear a puppy, or has my brain finally scrambled?"

She stood up, rummaging in her pockets. Yes, she had dog treats with her, though they were a little crumbly. She took a step closer, but the dog shrank back immediately.

Jamie could clearly see a darkened, matted area on her back leg. Dirt? Or blood?

Something was definitely wrong here.

"I'm a friend, old girl. You can trust me. I've got a treat for you. You want a treat?"

The dog's ears perked up at the word.

"You've got to come closer."

She wanted to get a better look at that wound. She glanced at Nash, still nodding his head anxiously. No way could she carry the dog. Maybe she could convince her to follow them back to the ranch. She needed help.

Her skin twitched and Jamie scanned the greenery again. "Hello? My friends are right behind me. And my big dog, too. His name is Hannibal. Like Hannibal the Cannibal."

Just in case some psycho was on the loose and stalking her.

Great. That's exactly what she should be thinking about right now, alone, in the depths of the forest. Psycho stalkers.

This was what happened when she let her emotions and her imagination run away with her.

The dog huddled against a spray of ferns, watching but not coming near.

Jamie took a deep breath and then listened once more.

The muffled silence was broken only by the rustle of small creatures and the soft sounds of water. Had she imagined that sweet, puppyish yip?

The Lab wiggled and lifted her head in a melodic *bow-roo-roo*.

Nothing.

Then, another *yip-yip!*

"Damn, I knew it!"

Jamie dropped to her belly and pulled herself closer to the slippery, sloping edge, keeping one hand on a thick tree root, peering into the shadowy depths until . . . there it was. Two bright, shining eyes blinking at her from the heavy undergrowth. In the water? No. Beside it. On a ledge or something. Trapped, by the look of it.

"Hey, you," she said on a breath.

Another Labrador. Yellow, not chocolate. Around three or four months old. The most annoying stage of puppyhood but completely and utterly irresistible.

"Hey, cutie-pie." She snapped her fingers at him. "You okay?"

With a flash of soft-skinned belly, the puppy—male—leaped to enormous feet, scrambling on the rough, narrow surface of the rock, a whirlwind of paws and teeth and limbs and the inability to recognize danger characteristic of adolescent males of any species.

"Whoa, you knucklehead," Jamie yelled. "Sit!"

If he didn't quit flailing around, he'd be in the water for sure, and while Labs were born swimmers, this looked like a fish-in-a-barrel situation. If there was a way out of the steep-edged pool, she couldn't see it.

To her relief, the pup promptly plunked his haunches onto the rock. He cocked his head and looked at her, no doubt awaiting a reward. Someone cared then, if not enough to keep him supervised, then at least enough for basic obedience.

The older dog lowered her front legs and barked, then looked expectantly at Jamie.

"You think this is a game, huh?" Jamie held her hand up in a stop-sign motion. "Stay. Both of you. I need to think. I can do that. I can."

Fractured memories of scoldings from her little-mourned grandmother returned at the damnedest times. *Slow down! Think before talking! Just once, would you consider the consequences before going off on another wild hare.*

That saying had never made sense to her. If it was hare like rabbit, then shouldn't it be *after* another wild hare? But if it was hair like . . . hair . . . well, what the heck did that mean?

Her mind was like a wild hare.

She sucked in a deep breath, looked around again, and saw no one. "You're too little to be out here on your own, baby doll. But what to do?"

She never had been able to resist a stray. Even when she'd been one herself, she'd smuggled them in: injured birds; cat-caught bunnies that always died, no matter what she did; a cocker spaniel that had turned out to belong to the old lady across the street; and finally a kitten, half-dead thanks to the sociopath son of her last foster mother.

The kitten had gone to the pound. The son had gone to the ER. Jamie had gone to a group home with yet another flag on her file, and no regrets.

"Looks like it's your lucky day, pup," she said. "Our meeting in the middle of a freaking forest was meant to be. Hang tight and I'll save you."

But how? She hadn't brought rope. What else might she be able to use to pull the pup up off the ledge? She had her belt. Maybe, if she took off her jeans, she could make a kind of sling.

Ignoring the sensation of being watched, she tossed her denim jacket over a limb, yanked off her boots, then pulled one leg out of her jeans. She recognized the misstep a split second too late, felt the moldy edge give way beneath her foot, adjusted her balance, overcompensated, and then that was it, she was flying.

Gideon Low nudged his heels against the barrel belly of the roan mare. She grunted into a halting run, and he made a mental note to take her out with tomorrow's group. She needed more exercise.

And perhaps a ride would clear his head, though searching for Jamie wouldn't help in that regard. He should have sent someone else after her. But she'd looked so forlorn, so discouraged, so lost, so unlike herself when she'd left, that he had to see for himself that she was okay.

Now she'd been gone too long. Daphne was worried, and there'd been rumors of a bear in the area.

He reached out to hold a spiky branch away from his head as they rode under it and got sprinkled with tiny dry needles that smelled sharp and astringent.

Jamie shouldn't be on his mind at all, but things had changed between them lately. What had been a fine, workable friendship had turned into a wretched awareness that dogged him every second of every day, an attraction he hadn't asked for but couldn't ignore.

"Good girl, Rosie," he murmured, as the mare stepped over a fallen log. He could see fresh hoofprints in the soil that must belong to Nash.

It wasn't just about him now, either. Or even Jamie. There was someone else, someone more important than either of them to consider.

He'd sent the letter last week, by registered mail, so he knew Lana had received it. Anytime now, he'd have her response, and no matter what, everything would change.

He'd had plenty of time to prepare himself, but he was teetering on a knife's edge, headed for a fall either way, with no easy landing in sight.

He wished he could talk it over with someone.

He wished he could talk it over with Jamie, but he dreaded how this secret would change her opinion of him, how learning of his failure and cowardice would strip the stars from her eyes.

"Selfish bastard," he muttered.

So, he put it out of his mind and focused on the breath that went in and out of his lungs. All he had, he reminded himself, was this moment.

That was all anyone had. The trick was to accept it.

The green woods and the damp trail soothed him, despite everything. He wasn't an expert tracker, but he did okay. Jamie hadn't made it difficult. She'd crashed through the woods like a bear after honey, headstrong, heedless, thoughtless. He hoped the actual bear, if there was one, was far away by now.

The afternoon light pierced the temperate rainforest canopy unevenly, a golden ray slanting here, grey mist brightening there, the same evergreen boughs by turn yellow, jade, and black. Birds called overhead and the dull *rat-tat-tat* of a woodpecker sounded in the hollow of a stag.

"Jamie," he called. She'd left her cell phone behind, no surprise. Up here in the woods, service was unreliable, even if she had remembered to bring it. Sanctuary Ranch attempted to be self-sustaining, collecting cell phones from guests at the start of each visit, encouraging them to stay off-grid and off-line as much as possible.

As staff, of course, they needed to be able to communicate, for safety's sake. They'd all been on Jamie to carry her phone with her, but half the time she still went off on her own without it.

He and Jamie had traversed these woods on horseback together many times, but he still knew the trails better than she did. He knew where she liked to go when she was brooding.

And she was definitely brooding about Haylee closing down the training center rather than letting Jamie take over. But that was Jamie, always reaching for more, always pushing the envelope, never satisfied with the status quo.

That was the real reason this crush of hers had to be stopped before she learned the truth about him. She'd accept him, baggage and all, and that weight, which he'd grown used to, would wear too heavily on her. Seeing someone as bright and full of life as Jamie stagger because of him would be the straw that broke him.

Better to hurt her a little now than to destroy her later.

The crash of hooves ahead gave him just enough warning to knee Rosie off the trail before Nash came belting toward them, riderless, his eyes rolling white.

Rosie skittered sideways, neighing loudly to her pal, catching his contagious fright immediately. His heart in his throat, Gideon managed to snag the flying reins, nearly getting yanked from the mare's back in the process.

"Whoa, Nash, buddy, easy." He slid off Rosie and collected the panicked horse.

What had happened? Where was Jamie?

The horse reared and stomped, but finally calmed. Gideon climbed back into the saddle and, Nash's reins firmly in one fist, Rosie's in the other, started back along the path, trying not to picture Jamie lying somewhere deep in the forest, broken, bleeding.

Alone.

He could barely breathe for dread.

Oh God, let her be okay. Please, let her be okay.

Definitely not a hot spring.

Jamie kicked to the surface, gasping to draw breath into a chest locked down by muscles refusing to cooperate. She shook the frigid water from her eyes and kicked in a circle. She couldn't catch her breath. Her brain was frozen.

She could hear the horse, whinnying wildly, as he ran down the path away from her. Something or someone was out there and whatever or whoever it was, the horse didn't like it. Nor did the Labrador. She was barking like a maniac somewhere above her, beyond the pool, the sounds growing fainter as she moved farther away.

"Puh-puh-puppy? Where are thou, buh-buh-brat?" She spun around, treading water, her teeth chattering, and looked up. The pup was on the ledge again, blinking at her through the mossy curtain, his pinky-brown nose twitching with pleasure. She now saw that what had appeared from above to be a ledge with no way off was, in fact, easily accessible by land and water via a hidden sloped area.

"You . . . dirty . . . liar . . ." she gasped.

The pup wiggled in delight, then whined and scratched at something on the ground.

Jamie swam over, lifted herself onto the glistening surface and immediately saw the problem.

She reached into a crevice between the rocks, pulled out a muddy, well-loved, vaguely phallic rubber toy. She examined it. "This, my friend, is nuh-not PG rated."

The older dog reappeared, suddenly, her muzzle flecked with froth, panting hard. She bent to the pool and drank noisily. The pup howled in excitement, caught between the thrill of his friend's return and the anticipation of regaining his toy.

"Yeah?" Jamie held it out. "This is what's got you all frazzled?"

He nearly fell into the water again in his hurry to snatch it from her hand. The older dog, her thirst quenched, barked sharply. The wet pup scrambled into the underbrush, then reappeared moments later beside the larger dog, covered in leaf litter and debris but whole, happy, and extremely pleased with himself.

Chapter Three

Choose your best underwear today.

—Jamie's horoscope

Crashing and yelling came at her from all sides, it seemed, the sound being bounced and swallowed at once by the forest. Jamie shrieked and threw herself at the bank but was unable to get purchase on the slippery edge.

"I've got a gun, and I'm not afraid to use it," she yelled.

The Labrador barked and the pup joined in, yipping and bouncing. Sunlight pierced the towering overhead limbs. Shadows flickered, and massive, claw-like branches grasped from the depths, but still, she saw no one.

Then the voice came again, more clearly.

"Jamie! Where are you?"

She stopped struggling and clung to a mossy branch. "Gideon?"

He appeared beneath a needle-laden limb, on Rosie, with Nash behind, holding tight to the agitated horse's reins.

"What are you doing here?"

"Following you." He pulled Rosie up sharply when he saw her in the water, his eyes stark against the white of his face, his temples tight, his lips a thin slash above his chin. "Are you swimming?"

Incredulity sharpened his voice.

"Why, of course I am, Gideon. Ice water is so refreshing. Being half-dressed makes it special. You should try it." She flung herself up again and lay there like a drunken sea lion, horribly aware that her laundry-day underwear was creeping into forbidden territory.

"Would you like a hand?" He dismounted and came closer, extending his arm.

"Oh, I'm fine." She'd told him she wanted to be alone, and here he was, making her not alone. Maybe she'd haul him in. A dunking would cool him off.

Though a tiny part of her was humming. He'd come after her.

He gripped her by her upper arms and easily pulled her from the water.

She half-crouched, pulling the empty pant leg against her naked thigh, then took a step backward and nearly fell back in again. "What are you doing out here anyway?" Her voice was shaking with cold.

"Rangers called about a nuisance bear in the area. Wasn't sure you'd heard. Daphne sent me out. She was worried."

The humming stopped. The flood of adrenaline, not to mention the icy pool, made her limbs wobbly. "Thanks-no-thanks for the knight-in-shining-armor scenario. We were making plenty of noise. I'm sure he's long gone by now."

He cocked an eyebrow. "Sorry-not-sorry for caring that you're an hour overdue."

"An hour?" With much yanking and pulling, the wet denim skidded up over her butt.

"Yes. Come on. Let's go."

"Sorry, I'm actually handling a rescue myself."

The corner of his mouth twitched. "Really. How's that going?"

She tipped her chin at the dogs, the older dog hovering

watchfully at the periphery, the pup romping with his toy, oblivious to Gideon's arrival.

"The old dog led me here, where the pup was trapped. Or so I thought. The little one's fine. But something's wrong with the old one. Look at her leg. And she's way too thin. I need to get them back to the ranch. You can help, since you're here."

Gideon's eyes widened. "Get them back? Jamie, someone's probably looking for them right now. There's a bear wandering the area and Daphne's waiting for you. Forget about the dogs. They'll find their way home."

Suddenly, like before, the chocolate Labrador whipped her head up. Without barking, she bolted as fast as her damaged leg could take her back into the underbrush, past her, past Gideon and the horses, and was swallowed up by the forest.

"See?" Gideon held Nash's reins out toward her. "Come on. Let's go."

"Wait." Wet skin and tight jeans were not a great combination.

The puppy had started after the old dog, but his shorter legs couldn't find purchase on the sloped path. He sat back hard on his rump, whining.

Jamie pulled her jacket on and crossed her arms over her chest. "I'm not leaving the puppy out here alone."

"Fine. There's a place up the ridge. That's probably where they belong. Follow me."

"I can find it myself, Gideon. I don't need an escort."

He was trying to be nice. But having him swoop in to fix her mistakes wasn't the way to reset their relationship.

"Come on, James. Don't be difficult."

"Don't call me James!"

"Sorry." Gideon paused, and for the first time, she saw the tightness around his mouth. "When I found your horse,

I thought . . . I thought . . . damn, girl." Gideon swallowed hard, his Adam's apple bobbing his throat.

He looked away. Why was he being so stupid-ass stubborn about insisting that they were just friends, that it couldn't be anything more, when she knew he cared about her?

She glanced down at herself. Through the opening in her denim jacket, the thin fabric of her white T-shirt stuck to her torso, her nipples clearly visible through her sports bra, her navel winking above the low rider waistband of her jeans.

When she lifted her eyes, his head was still turned, but the color in his cheeks told her he'd seen the same thing she'd seen. Overhead, a woodpecker drilled for insects, the rapid-fire sound filling the tense silence between them.

"We should go."

She put her hands on her hips and cocked her head. "Oh yeah? Should we?"

"Jamie." A pained look came over his face. "Enough. You're cold and wet. You need to get back."

She took a step toward him, came close enough that she could feel the heat coming off his body. "Cold and wet sucks. But warm and wet . . ."

He looked back at her, his eyes wider by a sliver, his lips parted so that she could see the edge of his teeth, the tip of his tongue. Then his nostrils flared slightly and he averted his gaze again. "Jamie. Knock it off."

Stung, she plunked herself down on a moss-covered log and began hauling her boots on, hoping he couldn't see the heat she felt in her cheeks. "Come on. I'm kidding. Geez, where's your sense of humor?"

Gideon squatted beside her. "Let me help."

"How?" She stomped her foot on the ground, which didn't get her further into the boot, and almost turned her ankle. "Can you make my feet smaller?"

She didn't want his help. She wanted something . . . else.

She wanted him to put his arms around her and pull her tight to his body. She wanted to feel his hand on her bare skin and run her palm over the wide muscles of his back.

Instead, he knelt before her and grabbed either side of the boot. "Stand up, hold my shoulders, and push in while I hold."

He kept his head down, his face averted, like a gentleman.

She wanted to break that smooth facade, make him feel something. For her.

She pushed, bracing herself on his broad shoulders until with a squeak of damp leather, her foot popped in.

"Good. Again." Without lifting his head, Gideon positioned the other boot. But this one proved more stubborn.

"Push harder," he said.

"I am." His shoulders were warm and solid beneath her fingers and she allowed herself to squeeze them, just a little. Oh. A woman could count on shoulders like that.

"Quit groping me, James. We're losing light."

She softened her grip. "Grope your tough old hide? Don't flatter yourself."

He laughed at that, and the awkwardness lifted. "If you say so."

She bent her knees to jam her foot harder, and that brought her face near the top of his head. She inhaled. *Oh to the max*. He smelled of fresh air and woodsy-scented shampoo, something that made her think of dark nights on the beach.

She could kiss him. She could kiss him right now, force him to see what was standing right in front of him, literally.

Should she?

Through a break in the trees, she caught a glimpse of a pale moon rising against the blue sky. A sign?

She lowered her head a bit more and breathed him in. She wanted to kiss him. But that didn't mean it was the right thing to do. She was trying to be more responsible, more mature. To think before acting.

She imagined brushing her knuckle against his cheek, feeling the exciting roughness of his stubble as she trailed her way to his ear.

She imagined him grabbing her arms, yanking her to his chest, and pressing his lips against hers, kissing her, hard and deep and hot, stealing her breath, stealing her thoughts, drowning her in the taste of those full, mobile lips—

"Jamie," Gideon said. "Push."

He gave a firm tug on the boot, and her foot slipped in with a thump that knocked her off balance and sent her tumbling forward.

"Whoa there," Gideon said, straightening.

The top of his head connected with her nose, ending her fantasy in a blinding explosion of pain.

"Holy shit fuck!"

Jamie fell back, landing on her butt hard enough that Gideon could hear her teeth clack together.

"God, Jamie, I'm so sorry. Are you okay?"

Bloody tears seeped around the fingers she held clamped to her lower face. He yanked a handkerchief from his pocket and pressed it to her mouth, cupping the back of her head with his palm.

The skin at her neck was like silk. He'd heard her breathing above him a moment ago, and now it was his turn. She had a hand on his leg and her touch sent electricity singing deep inside him.

This was bad. He should step away. He wasn't being fair to her.

"Mmmmph!" She pushed him away. "You're smothering me!"

"Jamie. You're crying." He held his hands out, helpless, frozen and horrified.

She did not cry.

"These aren't real tears," she snapped. "Just, you know. Nose tears."

"Nose tears."

The puppy leaped up between them.

"Ow!" Jamie yelled as his small claw left marks on her belly.

That smooth stretch of tanned midriff had been nearly pressed against his cheek a moment ago. Warm and wet . . .

He took hold of the dog's scruff and gave him a light shake.

"Settle down pup," he said. "You've done enough damage for one day."

"Easy," Jamie protested. "He's just a baby."

"A baby with no manners." The pup whined, then licked his arm. He wore a good leather collar with a single tag that had the word CHAOS inscribed on it. Not a rabies tag. Not a municipal license.

"Chaos, huh?" he said to the dog. "Sounds about right."

"Un-fricking-believable." Jamie lifted the fabric away from her nose and examined it. "Wow. You really got me."

"I said I'm sorry."

"I know." She started to giggle, a slightly panicked sound that said it could go back to tears at any moment. "But some days, you just have to laugh." A bloody snot bubble popped from her left nostril and the giggle turned to a guffaw. She pinched the bridge of her nose between thumb and forefinger, unable to stop laughing. "I go out to the woods," she said, gasping for air, "looking for serenity. What do I find? Chaos. Literally."

She tipped her head back, wheezing, the laughter finally wearing down. To his relief, the tears were also gone.

"I've taken worse. I'm fine, Gideon. You can go. Tell Daphne I'll do all the cleanup when I get in."

But something about her was still off. "You sure you're okay?"

Something in his voice made her turn her head. "What?"

He cleared his throat, uncomfortable. "It's just . . . you know . . . I don't want things to be awkward. Between us."

She jerked her head in a stuttering gesture that was likely meant to mock the very idea, but instead screamed of vulnerability. "Pfft. You seem to think pretty highly of yourself."

He touched her shoulder. "James."

He saw the breath catch in her throat, saw the words get trapped inside, saw them struggle fruitlessly to escape.

"It's not that I don't care about you," he said, regretting the sentence the moment it left his lips.

She lurched to her feet, waving her hands in front of her ears, as if she could stop herself from hearing them.

But he had to say something. He had to address it. He owed her that much. So he pressed on, deeply miserable but determined.

"It's just that . . ." He exhaled, then tried again. "It wouldn't work between us, Jamie. There's the age difference, and my past. . . ."

She whirled around then. "You think I care about any of that? So you've got a few years on me—"

"Eight years."

"Who cares? And I know you're an ex-con. So what? We all have skeletons in the closet. It doesn't matter!"

"Maybe it should."

"Why? Did you kill someone?"

"No!" He pulled back, shocked.

"Of course not. You wouldn't be here if you had. So, what were you in for, then?"

The old shame flooded over him. He didn't like to talk about it and had successfully avoided it for a long time. People at the ranch respected each other's boundaries. If you asked about someone's story, you had to be ready to tell your own. So they didn't ask.

Until now.

"It was," he began, scratching the back of his neck, "a mistake. A horrible mistake."

She stood in front of him, her eyebrows raised, waiting.

He swallowed; it was never easy saying the words. "They called it," he said, finally, "vehicular assault. Someone was hurt. It was . . . horrible."

The prosecution, seeing a wealthy young man with a hot car, had decided to make an example of him, and Gideon hadn't fought it. He'd deserved every minute of his sentence, no question.

He was still walking, after all. Unlike the woman he'd hit.

"I'm so sorry, Gideon." Jamie reached for his hand, tugged him closer. "But that doesn't change the way I feel about you. We clicked, from the moment we met, but something's different now. We could be more, don't you feel it? I know I'm no Kardashian, but I've seen you checking me out. We could have something together. Don't you want that?"

Everything inside him ached to say yes. Because he did. But it was partly because of his feelings for her that he had to say no.

"It doesn't matter." He shook his head. "I'm not good for you, Jamie. Trust me. I'm just . . . not."

For a moment, the word hung in the air, like an echo. Then Jamie stepped back, dabbing gently at her nose.

"Okay," she said. "Whatever you say. Where's that puppy?"

Chaos, deciding it was time to play, darted away. She faked him out, pounced, and scooped him into her arms, toy and all. "Got you, you little rotter."

She was skilled at putting on a tough face. He'd seen it before, and he recognized it now. He hated that he'd been the one to make her pull it out. Would they be able to go back to their usual easy friendship, or would there always be an awkward undercurrent now?

Gideon sighed. "Put him down, Jamie. Let's go. I've got chores waiting."

"Then go." All business, no sign of awkwardness, but definitely an edge to her voice. "I don't need your help. I'll ride up to that place on the ridge. If that's where this little guy belongs, I'll give them a little lesson on puppy safety and say good-bye. If he's not theirs, I'll bring him back to the ranch and figure it out in the morning."

"Fine. But if you're not back in an hour—"

"I know, I know, you'll track me down and hog-tie me to the back of your horse. Spare me the lecture."

Perhaps anger was the best he could hope for. "You'll be okay carrying him on Nash?"

"Yes, Gideon. I'll be okay carrying him on Nash."

Pulling her jacket tight around the dog's torso, she gathered Nash's reins and swung up into the saddle. The pup, likely tired from his adventure, relaxed against her comfortably, his toy tucked in beside him.

Nash danced and skittered, quivering at the smell of blood. She tightened the reins to let him know she was in charge, then nudged him with her heel and started up the path, leaving Gideon watching the softly muscled curves of her derriere shifting in the saddle.

A beam of dappled sunlight broke through the canopy just then, making her eyes sparkle and her skin glow like a ripe peach, even with the smear of blood on her cheek.

He swallowed. She had a natural beauty about her that was all the more striking for being unadorned. She was impulsive and stubborn and . . . fresh and full of joy and hope and . . . young.

So young.

She turned in the saddle, glanced over her shoulder and caught him watching her.

"Take a picture, cowboy," she called with a grin. "It'll last longer."

A month ago, he'd have laughed it off. Now, it was like she was issuing a challenge.

Chapter Four

Romance begun during a decreasing moon tends to transform the participants.

—Jamie's horoscope

A screen of sword fern growing from the ancient Sitka spruce hid Roman Byers as he watched the girl take his pup away. Woman, he supposed, not girl, but at his age, they were all kids.

A fresh spasm slid a stiletto of pain through his hip. He pressed back against the great tree supporting him, gritted his teeth, and turned his gaze upward, willing the pain away. The great horned owl he'd been observing for months also watched, but from much higher up, blinking saucer-like eyes in irritation. He empathized with the owl. The girl and the cowboy and the horses were noisy intruders, and while she undoubtedly believed she'd run across a crisis in need of a Good Samaritan, the only reason Chaos hadn't scrambled out of the pool on his own was that he hadn't yet retrieved the damn toy he'd dropped into a crevice in the ledge. Damn Squeaky Worm.

The pup would have gotten out in his own good time. He'd have been tired and hungry, and he'd have learned a valuable lesson.

Well, he'd be tired and hungry.

Roman blew the whistle again, the high-pitched hiss inaudible to human ears, but a clarion call to Sadie. He hoped she could help him to his feet before the damp earth set a bone-deep chill aching all the way to his toes.

Or that girl happened onto him. He didn't require rescuing any more than either of the dogs did, but there was always a bleeding heart somewhere ready to butt in with well-meant but unwelcome advice.

He hissed out a breath as lancing heat drilled down to his knee. It always amazed him how the pain continued, even all these years later. He tried not to fight it, tried to let it flow over and through him, let it take its course and burn out. There was no winning that battle, and fighting only made it worse, so as long as he could still hobble into the woods, grow a few vegetables in the summer, and put up enough cordwood for the winter, he accepted that his days would always flow good and bad, in and out. Like the tide.

Everything had been going fine until Jonathan had foisted the pup on him. Roman needed another dog like he needed a hole in his head. Sadie wasn't done yet. So she was a little thin—old age did things to a body. So her sight and hearing weren't what they once were; neither were his. They made a good pair.

The pup was cute, no argument there. But Roman was too old to be dealing with piss and shit in the house again, not to mention the chewed-up socks and remote controls.

And that goddamn Squeaky Worm.

"Dad," Jonathan had argued, "you can't live out here in the boonies all alone. Not at your age. Maybe you won't get him trained to the capacity of Sadie, but at least he'll be company for you. Maybe he'll even make you laugh now and then. You spend too much time alone."

That *had* made Roman laugh. The whole reason he'd built

this place was for privacy, to escape. To be alone. One more interview and he'd lose what was left of his mind.

Roman wasn't crazy. He wasn't infirm. He just wanted to live out his days in peace.

And now, thanks to Jonathan, he spent half his days chasing a stupid pup all over hell's half acre. Jon worked with him when he could, but so far, there'd been no visible improvement in the pup's recall. At least, he didn't come back to Roman. Or rather, he'd return, grab the piece of hot dog, and disappear again.

Worse, on the days when Roman wasn't up for a hike, he still ended up limping over the mountain, waving hot dogs and yelling his fool head off. No matter how many boards he nailed to the low areas of the fence, Chaos still managed to wiggle past them.

Chaos. At least Jon had named the mutt properly.

A jolt ran down his sciatic nerve, sending another bolt of lightning into his knee. Roman squeezed his eyes shut, forced himself to inhale slowly, and pushed harder against the wide tree trunk, waiting for it to pass. Sweat prickled between his shoulder blades. He had to get home. He could see the back gate. Only a few steps to his couch and his pills, but it might as well have been a mile.

When he opened his eyes, Sadie was peering up at him, her grizzled forehead wrinkled with concern.

Relief washed over him. He reached out to stroke her ear, but the movement sent another spasm through his hip and he pressed his back against the tree.

"Ah, my poor girl," he said, seeing the blood. She followed that damn pup through anything, and today, it looked like they may have tangled with some barbed wire. In her condition, she ought to be lying next to him on the deck, enjoying the last of the season's warmth before the rain set in. Taking care of him and the puppy was too much for her.

Then he heard a voice. From somewhere on his property.

"Oh, hell," he muttered. It was the girl.

"Hello?" she called. "Is anyone there?"

"Stay," whispered Roman.

But it was too late. Sadie bounded off, ready to meet her new friend.

The fence had once been painted white but was now streaked with years of rust. Nailed to one of the posts was a wooden sign with no name, just a number stencilled onto it. A sagging three-string barbed-wire fence bisected the property from the ditch, connecting to the posts that stood sentry over the entrance.

On the left, about ten meters down, a second wooden sign was nailed to a post: PRIVATE PROPERTY. Ten meters to the right was a third: BEWARE OF DOG.

Jamie slipped out of the saddle, set the pup on the ground, and tied Nash to the post. This had to be the place.

Farther to the left, blackberry reached thorny arms into a dip that likely led to the creek. On the other side stood pockets of alder, oak, and vine maple, the pasture between densely underscored by salmonberry and wild grasses.

Private, yes. Fort Knox, no. And if the man was rich, you certainly couldn't tell from here.

She kicked the gate lightly with her boot. It creaked loudly and swung open about six inches before catching on a padlocked chain.

Jamie cupped her hands around her mouth and yelled, "Hello? Is anyone there?"

A bird scolded her from high up in the trees and wind soughed through the grass, but there was no other response. She climbed over the gate and beckoned to the pup to follow, which he did. She was certain this was where the old dog had gone, but as she walked down the narrow driveway, scraggly weeds and scrub brush caught at her pants as if to warn her off.

"Hello?" she called again. "Anyone home?"

Nothing but the scolding chatter of a couple of starlings in the pine tree above her.

The narrow driveway opened onto a weedy yard. The cabin of weathered shingle and cedar shakes looked tidy enough, but had an air of desertion and neglect about it.

"Is this your place?" she asked the puppy. He scrambled up the porch, pawed at the door, and whined.

"Yeah. That's what I thought. Let's see if anyone's home."

She knocked, three quick raps.

A clatter of nails on wood sounded from inside. The pup jumped up, barking excitedly.

Jamie lifted onto her tiptoes and peered inside the dusty half-circle of smoked glass at the top of the door. A muffled woof sounded inside, and a brown, dog-shaped mass shifted into view.

"Hey, girl." Jamie knocked again. "Is that you? Where's your person?"

The dog barked. Outside, the puppy howled in reply, then scratched and scrabbled at the door.

She thought about that wound on the old dog's leg and how thin she was.

Then she stepped off the porch and went around the side of the cabin. "Hello? Is someone there? Don't shoot me. I think I found your dog."

She reached another tall fence, but the gate leading to the back had a simple hook closure. Whoever lived here wasn't likely to welcome her intrusion. But then again, it wasn't razor wire. A gate like this was more of a . . . suggestion.

As soon as she went through, she was met by the brown dog, limping badly but still wagging her tail.

"Hey, whoa!" Jamie bent to pat the friendly animal. "I guess you have a doggie door, huh? Want to show me?"

The brown dog led her to an expansive back deck that faced west and would have a wonderful view of the sunsets, then stepped through the flap in the wall and disappeared inside.

"Okay, clearly I've found the place." She gave Chaos a nudge. "I guess this is good-bye."

The puppy balked.

"Go on," she urged him.

He sat down and whined, batting beautiful chocolate-brown eyes up at her.

"God, you are trouble in a fur coat, aren't you?"

She went to the back door, knocked again, and peered through the window. "Hello? Is anyone there?"

Nothing but the chocolate Lab, pawing awkwardly at the door.

Jamie turned the knob, just in case.

Locked.

She peered inside again. "Hello?"

She glanced around the yard. No one was around. The dog inside was definitely the same one she'd met at the creek. The puppy almost certainly lived here. But if she left him here, with no one around, what's to say he wouldn't just take off into the woods again? Did the dogs have food? Water?

Then another thought struck her. Was someone inside hurt or injured?

She banged on the door, hard. "Hello! Do you need help?"

She looked at the knob again. It was a simple pin tumbler lock. Jamie had learned to scrub these babies when she was twelve, hungry, and pissed off about the chain on her foster mother's refrigerator.

Discovering how easily a few simple tools and even simpler knowledge could breach all but the toughest locks had terrified her at the time. But it had spurred her to become the one with those tools and that knowledge, rather than remain at their mercy.

She pulled a slender leather case off her belt, took out her beloved Bogota rake, and inserted it in the lock, feeling her way gently and carefully.

"I'm not a bad person," she told the pup as she worked. "I have reason to believe that someone may be in danger."

With a soft click, the tumblers fell into place. It was a fast and dirty trick that always gave her a rush of power. The fact that more people weren't burgled every day was actually rather heartwarming, when you considered how simple it was.

She pushed open the door and greeted the older dog, then stood up and looked around.

"Houston," she said. "We have a problem."

Chapter Five

*Venus, the goddess of love and marriage, is giving
you a big thumbs-up today.*

—Jamie's horoscope

Jamie trotted up to the gate welcoming newcomers to Sanctuary Ranch, leaned over the still-sleeping puppy, and pulled up the latch. Nash, eager to get back to his pals, pushed through before it was fully open, and Jamie had to lift her knee to prevent it from being smashed against the fence post.

Daphne emerged from the shadows, and even from Nash's back, Jamie could feel the murky energy pouring off her.

"Where've you been?" the cook demanded, her hands on her hips. "I said you could take a break, not a two-week vacation." Then she saw Chaos. "Is that a puppy? I swear, if you landed on the moon, you'd find a stray alien to bring home with you. Bad enough to miss your prep shift, you had to come back with another mouth to feed."

Like that had ever been a problem for Daphne.

"Maybe the universe sent me an early birthday present, huh?" She nuzzled the puppy. He smelled like freshwater and greenery, clean soil and new, perfect dog. When she was in grade one, a classmate of hers had gotten a puppy for

her birthday. Jamie had run home and told Grandma Ellen
about it, so excited she could hardly get the words out fast
enough. It was her dearest wish, to get a puppy of her own.

She'd gotten new underwear and a Bible.

"No need to hint," Daphne said. "I think everyone this
side of the Pacific knows your birthday is coming."

"Harsh, Daff. Harsh. Don't worry, Chaos is temporary."
Probably.

But the cabin she'd found, if that was his home, was no
place for a puppy. Choking and chewing hazards all around,
that unsecured doggy door, an empty water bowl that she'd
filled for the brown dog, and no sign of a human.

She'd go back tomorrow to check it out, see if she could
find the owner. Until then, Chaos stayed with her. Where he
was safe.

"Chaos is never temporary in your world," Daphne said.

Jamie smiled. "That's his name. Cute, huh?"

"It's a warning. Wait." She peered more closely, frowning.
"What happened to your face?"

A rush of heat rose to Jamie's cheeks. "Nothing. Bumped
my nose. No big deal."

"Fine. Don't tell me." The lines in her forehead deepened.
"And why are you all wet? Jamie?"

She could almost feel Gideon's arms around her again,
smell the scent of him, hear the heavy thud of his heart in his
chest next to hers.

"I found the pup stuck in the creek."

"Uh-huh." Daphne stared at her. Then she sighed. "The
slavering horde left us a mass of dishes, and I'm an old
woman. I had to peel the potatoes myself, and you know what
that does to my arthritis. You were supposed to come back
with Gideon. Did he tell you there's a bear out there? That's
right. Can't spare a thought for my feelings, can you? Just
go gallivanting to your heart's content, no matter that I'm

stuck back here worrying myself into an ulcer. I'm too old and frail to handle everything on my own."

Daphne had neither arthritis nor an ulcer and, with her kickboxing routine and various martial arts belts, was anything but frail.

"Sorry I scared you, Daff. And I'm sorry I'm late." Jamie flipped her leg over the saddle horn and jumped down, trying not to jostle the pup sleeping inside her jacket. Her damp denim squeaked as it slid over the leather.

With one hand, she clipped Nash's halter to a mounting station, undid his bridle, and loosened the girth of the saddle.

Daphne came closer, pursed her lips, and shook her head. "That's no flea-market pup. Someone'll be looking for him."

"So maybe I'll get a reward."

First Gideon, now Daphne. Aside from trespassing and that bit of light breaking and entering, she'd done a good deed. So why was everyone jumping down her throat about it?

"You'd best get him out of sight." The cook leaned in to pat the pup. "He's darn cute. But Haylee was very clear: no more rescue dogs until after the baby."

"Haylee won't even know he's here," she said. "I bow to the wisdom of Daphne. I'll see you in ten minutes."

"Five."

Inside her little studio cabin, Jamie used a folding exercise pen to wall off the kitchen area, spread out a sheet of newspapers, then made him a bed in an unused crate. She quickly cleaned the small cut on the pad of his sweet, soft, unblemished puppy foot, set him into his temporary home, and closed the metal door of the pen. She'd about stretched the limits of Daphne's patience. Plus, she was hungry.

"See you in a bit, Bear Bait," she whispered.

The puppy sat down on his little behind, lifted his muzzle, and howled.

* * *

When Gideon had gotten back last night, he'd had barely enough time to check on the livestock and devour the plate of stew and dumplings Daphne had left in the warming oven for him, while Jamie worked through a mountain of pots and pans.

They needed to talk, he thought, drawing crisp morning air deep into his lungs. He owed her the truth. But how much, and when, he wasn't yet sure.

He found her in the barn, shovelling manure. A faded brown bandana held back her shaggy hair, and a snug, sleeveless tank top showed off her toned, muscular arms. He remembered how she'd looked the day before, how he'd come upon her rising from the water like a seal, her slender legs dripping, the curves of hips and thighs gleaming white and wet, and him frantic enough to bargain his soul for her safety, not knowing whether to weep with relief or throw her to the ground and punish her with kisses.

So he'd done neither. Brilliant.

"What's up, Gideon?" She tossed a large forkful of soiled straw into the wheelbarrow. She paused, leaned on the pitchfork, and swiped sweat off her face with the back of her hand. Since when had biceps on a woman been so sexy? He could still feel the grip of her hands on his shoulders, smell the warm, earthy scent of her wet skin, so close to his face.

"You get the pup home safe and sound last night?"

"Yeah." She took a swig of water from the bottle on the straw bale beside her.

"And?"

She lifted another load of straw. "And what?"

"Was he glad to get them back? Why were they out?"

She shrugged, avoiding his eyes. "I don't really know."

"What do you mean?" He crossed his arms. "Jamie?"

She looked embarrassed. Was she hiding something?

That didn't seem like her.

"I found the place, okay?" she snapped. "But nobody was home. There was a doggie door and the big one seemed at home, but the pup didn't want to stay."

"So?" He saw color rise in her cheeks. "Aw, James. He's in your cabin right now, isn't he?"

She propped the pitchfork against the wheelbarrow and faced him. "You should have seen the place, Gideon. You'd have done the same thing. Someone lives there, but it's a sty. Worse. A hazard! Dirty dishes all over the place, broken glass on the floor. There was a water bowl, but it was bone dry. I couldn't leave him there, could I?"

He crossed his arms. "That's a lot to see from the window."

She closed her mouth. Her jaw slid sideways. She turned back to her wheelbarrow.

"Jamie?" His heart sank. "James. You didn't."

"Do not call me that!" She tugged her sleeve down over the tattoo on her wrist, then glanced around and came closer, her voice low and urgent. "I had to, Gideon."

Her hair was tucked behind the delicate shell of her ear. He could smell the light floral freshness of her shampoo, and it made him angry. She wasn't as tough as she wanted people to think. "You just got off probation. What if someone saw?"

"Nobody saw. Besides, why do you care? It's not your problem."

He shook his head. "You're going to earn yourself an ankle bracelet if you're not careful."

Or worse. Juvie was one thing; he couldn't bear the thought of his sweet Jamie behind bars.

Not his, he reminded himself. Never his.

"I covered my tracks." She gazed at him, those blue-grey eyes clear and steady. "You're not going to turn me in, are you?"

He looked away. This was the sort of thing that drove him

crazy about her. She didn't seem to understand how little it could take to make her life fall into pieces around her.

"I'm serious, Jamie. You have to take him back. He doesn't belong to you."

"I know. I will." She shoved her hands in her pockets. "I'll go after my rec class today."

Jamie worked occasionally for the local parks and recreation board, teaching kids about tide pools and ocean safety.

"I'll drive you," he said. "That way you don't have to worry about him jumping around in the car."

And he'd be certain the pup got back to his rightful owner.

Jamie gave him a slow blink that told him clearly what she thought of the ruse. "A crate also works, Gideon. Anyway, I'm catching a ride in with Huck so I'll have to do it after I get home. Don't worry. I'll do it."

He didn't reply.

"I will. And I don't need your help." A muscle in her jaw twitched. "Now, if you don't mind, this shit won't shovel itself."

"Right."

He strode around the corner too fast, head down, and nearly ran into Tyler.

"What the hell, man?" snapped the boy. "Watch where you're going." When he realized whom he was speaking to, Tyler's face whitened. "Ah shit, sorry, man, I didn't mean—"

"Stop." He gestured to a partially dismantled stack of alfalfa hay that had been carefully piled against the north wall. "Who told you to move these bales?"

Gideon supervised Tyler's duties in the stables and expected the boy to be preparing for the sunset trail ride. They had eight riders coming, and he liked to have the horses groomed and waiting in the front corral when they arrived.

Tyler flipped a shock of dirty blond hair off his sunburned forehead. "No one, but I heard something back there.

Squeaking or something. Those bales are fuh-freaking heavy, man."

His language had improved significantly in the months since he'd been plucked off the streets of Eugene, a wary-eyed, foul-mouthed package of elbows and knees, and given the choice of detention or ranch work. Olivia had seen past all that and welcomed him as the latest in her long line of foster kids. He'd added a good ten pounds to his lanky frame since his arrival, his appetite for Daphne's cooking as insatiable as his need for structure and guidance.

"Mice." Gideon entered Rosie's stall, clipped a lead rope to her halter, and led her into the breezeway. She'd be one of the eight today. "Good girl, Rosie," he murmured, patting her wide neck. The rich smell of horseflesh rose up, filling him with a sense of well-being and satisfaction. She nudged him in the shoulder, wanting a treat.

Not to be ignored, Nash nickered from his stall, tossing his dark head and scuffing a hoof against the concrete floor. Images of Jamie's slender hips swaying in the saddle on Nash's back leaped into his mind.

"Could be kittens." Tyler cut his eyes toward the opening in the bales, his confidence returning now that he knew Gideon wasn't angry. "Haylee said rats will go after a litter of kittens if they can."

"We don't have rats in this barn," Gideon said.

"Haylee said all barns have rats."

"Who are you supposed to listen to, Haylee or me?"

"Sir, yes, sir." Tyler snapped his skinny body upright, clacked the heels of his boots together, and gave a borderline-obscene salute. "I've no opinion on rats, sir."

Gideon looked upward, trying not to smile. A little attitude was vastly preferable to the flat-eyed mistrust that was all he'd shown them at first. Bruised in body and spirit, this kid, with his freckled nose and hazel eyes, triggered a sense of protectiveness in Gideon.

He tossed a curry comb to the kid. "Help me finish with the horses and we'll look together."

Tyler responded with relative ease to Gideon's questions as they moved the horses two by two into the corral nearest the tack room. His online algebra teacher was a total dork. He'd rather do an extra night of pots and pans for Daphne than figure out x, and since he wasn't going to college, who cared anyway?

"You never know," Gideon said. "Keep your options open."

The horses ready and waiting, they went back to the hay stack. He could hear faint sounds coming from the bales now too.

"It was louder before." Tyler tugged another bale off the pile and tossed it to the side with a grunt.

Gideon stuck a hand between a couple of bales, feeling for warmth, hoping he wasn't about to be clawed by an angry mama cat.

"Anything?" Tyler's face was tight with a mixture of hope and dread.

"Not yet."

So many things to grab the heartstrings, Gideon thought. Stray pups, endangered felines, damaged sons discarded by their fathers.

Not your son, he reminded himself.

A bright-eyed woman with choppy hair and the sweet smell of rainwater on her skin.

Not your woman.

"Anyway, who cares if I go to college?" Tyler asked, lifting another bale with Gideon. "I don't even need to graduate stupid high school. It's a hoop, especially this online crap. I'd rather learn to—"

"You're going to graduate stupid high school," Gideon said, slipping on a pair of leather gloves, "and you're going to get that algebra credit. You'll give yourself the option of

college, for one day when you're something more than a
boneheaded punk. And for the record, I did go to college."
He tossed another pair of gloves at the kid's head. "In case
mama's in there and she's not happy."

Tyler caught them out of the air before they made contact.
"You did? What are you doing here, then?"

"Good question. Be careful. We don't want to crush
them."

"Hey, what's happening?" Jamie rolled her empty wheelbarrow into the storage area and walked up next to Gideon,
as if there were no new awkwardness between them. She
half-squatted, her hands on her slender thighs, and peered
into the opening. "What did you find? Kittens?"

"Or mice." He tore his eyes away from the graceful line
between waist, hip, and thigh, wishing he'd never seen her
bare leg, all slick and shining, or her nipples puckered
hard from the chill. Or heard that little sound in the back
of her throat, the one that made him imagine her writhing
beneath him.

Stop!

"Kittens." Tyler gingerly lifted away another bale. He
didn't allow himself a smile, but there was an urgency to his
movements that betrayed his excitement.

"Oh!" Jamie fell to her knees. There, in the corner nearest the outer wall of the barn, surrounded by grey fluff, was
a litter of five kittens.

"Told you," Tyler said. The street-hardened teen exhaled
audibly and hunkered down on his knees beside her. He
poked gently at one tiny creature, which opened its pale pink
mouth in a silent cry. "They're not moving much."

"They're cold. And weak." Jamie looked up at Gideon
with anguished eyes and beckoned for him to come closer.
No grudge, no agenda, no hurt feelings. Just them, right
here, right now. "I heard a scream late last night," she said,
"and when I came in this morning, there was a bunch of grey

fur in front of the barn. I thought it was a rabbit, but it must have been the mama cat."

Killed by a coyote, most likely.

Tyler's movements slowed. He leaned away from the kittens, then straightened up, his face swept blank with indifference. "I should get back to work."

Gideon knew that the boy's own mother, who'd provided a marginal existence for herself and her son with a variety of illegal activities, had died when Tyler was nine and that the kid had bounced in and out of foster homes since then.

"Hang on." He hesitated, then put a careful hand on Tyler's shoulder. The boy didn't shrink away, which was the equivalent, in a less guarded child, of a full-body hug. "Jamie?"

Her clear blue gaze met his, and understanding passed between them, just like it always had. From the beginning, they'd had a connection, started by a shared love of horses and the outdoors, and fostered by good-humored ribbing and her unyielding expectation of reciprocity. She'd wiggled her way under his cautious skin and gotten comfortable, and that was his fault.

If only he'd noticed earlier that she'd developed a crush on him, he could have nipped it in the bud, prevented all this miserable . . . awareness from starting.

"We can save them, but it's going to take a lot of work." Jamie reached for an old shirt that hung on a nail beside the stall and spread it open to form a sling. "Gideon, can you spare Tyler for a little while?"

He glanced at Tyler. The boy's initial interest had been an encouraging sign of emotional development, but he was still so guarded, with a deep mistrust of what others thought best for him.

"Depends." Gideon kept his face and voice stern. "I can't let you help Jamie if it means your chores will suffer."

"I can do both." Tyler swallowed, a wary hope in his eyes. "You . . . you really think you can save them?"

"I'm sure as hell gonna try," Jamie said. "Poor little dumplings."

Still, Tyler hung back.

Gideon punched him lightly on the arm. "Go ahead, this is your win. Good job, kid."

The boy reached into the nest and pulled out a mewling ginger-colored creature that curled into a comma in the palm of his hand. "Do you think Olivia will let us keep them? We could use more mousers in the barn, right Gideon?"

"That's up to Olivia."

"We'll look after your family," Jamie crooned, as if the ghost of the cat were hovering nearby. "Way to go, Tyler, for finding them. You're a hero."

Tyler flushed red beneath his freckles, and Gideon could have hugged her.

This was what he loved about her, what made her such a good friend: her heart. She always wanted to save everything and everyone and believed she could. And because she believed, she often made it so, refusing to consider that, sometimes, things could not be fixed.

But it was the curse of memory to dwell on possibility, to consider not only what was, and what wasn't, but what might have been.

"Gideon?" Jamie touched his leg, sending a flash of heat into his groin. "You okay?"

"Fine." He pulled away, took off his gloves, and slapped the dust off them against his leg. Some things were not meant to be. No point bemoaning the fact. "Tyler, make sure your chores don't suffer. And start letting people know we have kittens to give away."

He left the two of them and strode to his cabin, where he found, taped to the door, an envelope, postmarked Gold Beach, Oregon. Less than an hour away, and the whole reason he'd made his way here to Sanctuary Ranch in the first place.

He stood stock-still, the letters making up the return address blurring in front of him.

It was time to quit wishing for things to be different, time to face what was.

Time to deal with what he'd been waiting for, anticipating, with both excitement and dread, words that might finally allow him to undo years of mistakes.

A letter from his past.

A letter about his son.

Chapter Six

Take care around water today. The ocean can be a sneaky bitch.

—Jamie's horoscope

Jamie tiptoed over the black, mussel-encrusted coastline south of Sunset Bay, waiting for the salt air to refresh her energy. She enjoyed her teaching stints for the park board, but the relentless interruptions of helicopter parents left her jittery and craving solitude. She had about fifteen minutes before Huck came to pick her up. That should be enough.

Today's group of parents had been particularly challenging, continually comparing notes about their amazing offspring, as if raising children were a competitive event, and the endeavor only worthwhile if it produced prodigies.

Alyssum wrote her first libretto at age four. Oh, but five-year-old Danyel—spelled with a y, just to be different—was already getting paid to test video games.

Jamie didn't care if little Juniper had learned to tie her shoelaces in utero or if the siblings her mother was currently cooking under that massive tent-like garment would come out with doctoral theses in their slimy hands. The hour on the beach with her was about jellyfish and barnacles and crabs.

No wonder people said Oregon was weird. They bred them that way.

She waved to a group cavorting on the sand while their parents gathered beach toys and jackets. They just wanted to wear sea stars on their heads and taste bull kelp.

She couldn't wait to get back to Chaos, to smell his sweet puppy breath and feel his soft fur against her cheek. And then there were the kittens. She sighed with anticipation.

She could have watched Gideon lift those heavy alfalfa bales for hours. Seeing those big hands cradling a tiny, squirming kitten had melted her heart. And the way he talked to Tyler showed that he cared for the boy. She wondered if he wanted to have kids one day. He'd make a hell of a dad.

Why was she even thinking about that?

She turned her gaze to the incoming tide that isolated the rocks from the headlands and the sandy shores where the kids now chased the water, running back screaming with delight as the mighty Pacific Ocean snatched and clawed at their feet.

Jamie waved again and climbed higher onto a rocky outcrop, where the view was breathtaking. She lifted her head to the wind, pulling the sharp salt air deep into her lungs.

Did she want kids? Maybe. She'd never expected to have a home or a job, and she'd gotten those things. She'd certainly never expected to enjoy teaching the little ones, or leading trail rides for teens, for that matter. She wanted to train dogs, but until Haylee gave the okay, there were plenty of rewarding tasks to keep her busy. She'd be fine.

She'd listen to Gideon's nagging and bring the puppy back to his rightful home, too. She'd probably built the mess up in her mind to be much worse than it actually was.

A shriek of laughter caught her attention, and she jerked her head up, looking to where the families were playing. The adults, their educational duties to their offspring fulfilled for the moment, looked more relaxed now, shaking out handmade blankets they'd bought from vendors in town for outrageous prices, wealthy enough that they didn't worry about sand and debris. They were beach blankets, after all.

Jamie exhaled, relief giving way to annoyance. Gideon hadn't seen the place. Maybe Chaos shouldn't be there, at all. Maybe it was irresponsible to return him. Cruel, even.

She shuddered. Maybe she should keep him a bit longer, gather some more intel before she decided.

She ought to tell Haylee, in that case. Haylee would understand. Plus, if she saw how well the pup was doing with her, maybe she'd consider letting Jamie take on a training project.

She walked out farther, stepping carefully on the rough surface, using one hand to balance herself. Water sparkled in the dips and crevices like diamonds against black velvet. The beauty soothed her. The calls of gulls wheeling overhead and the rich, ripe smell of life and death always made her feel better.

She lifted her arms and tipped her head back, drawing breath deep into her lungs, imagining it flowing throughout her body, filling that soft, empty place in her heart that, despite all she had, still yearned for more.

Still yearned for love.

Gideon never went looking for trouble, did his best, in fact, to avoid it. But when trouble found him, he didn't back down. And he didn't lose.

But as he stood on the rocky precipice, watching small stones skitter down the path toward the ocean, he knew he was headed for a battle he might have to lose. Winning this one could cost him the very thing he sought.

He crushed the letter in his palm. All the preparation in the world wouldn't have been enough for this response.

One light nudge of his hiking boot and a bit of basalt that

had clung for years, eons maybe, on the windswept ledge, went spinning and bouncing to land who knew where. If he opened his fist, Lana's words would go even farther, the pastel sheet—as if the gentle color could ease the message— sailing on the wind, whipped past the trees, far out to the bitter sea.

A gull called high above him, cocking its grey head, eyeing the piece of paper in his hand, probably hoping it held a sandwich. He decided against throwing the letter.

"Don't waste your time," he muttered.

Gideon turned his mind to another battle, equally trouble- some and just as unlikely to end favorably. From his vantage point on Sanctuary Ranch land, he could just make out the south-most beach of Sunset Bay, where Jamie taught her classes.

She hadn't returned the pup yet. Someone was going to come looking for it. And when they found it, she was going to be in trouble.

She didn't back down easily either.

He searched the long expanse of sandy beach and the jutting rocks that bracketed the bay loosely on either side. From this height and distance, he could see the shapes and colors of the beachgoers below, young people dashing after Frisbees, dogs with waving tails following, parents and chil- dren exploring tide pools.

There she was, her lime-green windbreaker bright against the sand, introducing young minds to the wonders and the power of the sea. Miss Vaughn to them, he supposed, smil- ing at how Jamie would react to that.

Jamie had a way with most people, once she deemed them worthy, and the same energy she displayed with Haylee's dogs made her good with kids, good at teaching, even casu- ally like this.

In between talking about sea stars and crabs, she gave them information that could save their lives. She taught them how even a quick walk on a piece of driftwood could be deadly. How the ocean was strong enough to pick up a huge log and plop it down on top of you before you knew what was happening. How even the smallest logs could weigh tons when sodden with seawater. How it only took five inches of water to lift four tons of driftwood.

Yet he could tell she did it without making them fearful, with sparkling, contagious energy, her movements quick and sure. Every now and then, the wind tossed a small, high voice upward, a shriek of laughter or a yell of delight.

Or maybe he was hearing crying.

Gideon didn't know much about kids.

He knew almost nothing about his own child.

As Lana had pointed out.

He's happy. We're a happy family. Seeing you now would only upset and confuse him.

Since the day he'd gone to prison, he'd been waiting for Lana to relent and let him see their son. He hadn't wanted to push, knew how difficult she could make it, knew he could turn Blake against him if he felt threatened. So, he'd waited. Patiently.

Idiotically.

Now, not only had Lana denied Gideon's request for access to their son, but she'd countered with a plea for him to relinquish all parental rights.

I'm getting married. Elliot wants to adopt Blake. He's the only father our son has ever known. He's a good man. If you love Blake, let him go.

She wanted him to abandon their son.

His *son.*

How could he do that? But did Lana have a point?

Six months ago, he could have asked Jamie. But not now. Not anymore. That prickly exterior hid a soft heart, big as the Oregon sky, though she didn't let a lot of people see it.

She'd let him see it. And he'd thrown it back in her face.

He turned back to the path, stuffed the letter into his pocket, and walked up the rocky slope to Sanctuary Ranch. He had chores to do before dinner. He couldn't talk to Jamie about this, not now.

He aimed for the main house, positioned on a rise over-looking the western horizon. The views spanned a hundred and eighty degrees, yet it was sheltered from winter storms by stands of pine, cedar, and cypress to the northeast.

A solid place. More than a home for most of them. A refuge.

Perhaps it would be best for Jamie if he left.

He groaned. How had things gotten so complicated? The incident under the mistletoe last winter had been his first clue, and he felt like a moron for not realizing sooner that she wanted more than friendship from him.

It was a crush. That's all it was, all it could ever be, and if in the privacy of his mind he'd ever toyed with the possibility of more, Lana's words had destroyed that. Besides, Jamie de-served someone far better than himself, and if she couldn't figure that out herself, well, he'd have to be the responsi-ble one.

Olivia, the ranch owner and his boss, met him at the gate to the yard. She was wiry thin with a wispy, white braid at the back of her neck. The braid had once been blond, long, and thick, and Liv still tossed her head occasionally, as if wondering where the weight had gone.

"Huck blew a tire on the way back from the feed store. Can you go down and get Jamie? She drove in with him."

At the sound of her name, Gideon's pulse jumped. "Is Huck okay?"

"He's fine. Drove over a nail. He's getting the tire fixed now. But Daphne needs Jamie now. Do you mind?"

"Of course not. If you need me to." He heard the reluc-tance in his voice and scrambled for an explanation. "It's just, I've got to feed the horses and without Huck, it'll take me even longer."

In fact, his equilibrium hadn't quite returned where she was concerned. He wasn't sure he'd be able to act normally with her, especially preoccupied now with Lana and Blake. If she had an inkling something was wrong, she'd keep picking until he was laid bare, and the thing was, a part of him wanted that.

The selfish part.

Olivia cocked her head and frowned. "I'd go, but I'm waiting for a call on the office line. I saw Tyler wasting time in the garden with Quinn. He can get the feed going while you're gone. I'll tell him now."

He swallowed. "Great. Thanks."

"Good." Olivia narrowed her eyes. "You okay?"

Gideon returned her gaze evenly. "Sure."

He respected Olivia Hansen for what she'd created here. She knew things about all of them that they didn't share easily, and she protected that knowledge, having measured it carefully before taking them on.

She crossed her arms. "Do I need to be concerned?"

"Nope." He stepped around her and pulled the gate shut behind him.

"Let me be more specific," she continued, following him to his truck. "Do I need to be concerned about you doing a runner again? We've got a full schedule and I need you here."

He inhaled slowly. "I've never once left without informing someone, Olivia."

He climbed into the vehicle, then turned in the seat and looked at her through the open door. He owed her more, but couldn't bring himself to get specific, not yet. "Something's come up, family stuff. I'm handling it. I won't let it affect my work."

"Family stuff." She surveyed him for a long minute, then

exhaled. "Okay then. Remember, Gideon, I'm here if you need me."

He nodded once, then looked out the windshield. "Appreciate that, Honch."

She slapped the hood. "Go pick up Jamie before Daphne starts recruiting the rest of us."

He smiled. "See you in a half hour."

He pulled off the yard and onto the gravel road leading to the highway connecting them to Sunset Bay, wondering which of his many wrong turns had led him to this place. He was done with gambling; he hadn't touched a drop of alcohol in years, hadn't touched a woman since Lana.

He barely knew his son, and if Lana had her way, the narrow window of opportunity for him to develop a relationship with Blake was about to be slammed, bolted, and painted over.

And now he had to pretend nothing was wrong to the one person who, after years of going through the motions, had made him feel alive again.

Jamie hunched down to explore the vibrant tide-pool life that had been lost on the adult portion of her audience. With the water just beginning its return, she could easily see the jewel-toned sea stars that clung to the wet rock, and the rough grey and brown barnacles, their dead shells protecting delicate tendrils deep inside the return of the water. Emerald-green moss and algae, tiny, shimmering minnows, swimming in their tight little groups.

It all amazed her. Twice daily, these pools were deprived of the water that carried their oxygen and nutrients, that kept them at the right temperature and salinity, that covered them against marauding birds. Then the tide would turn, first lapping, then leaping, then crashing over and over with deadly, relentless force.

Life. So fragile, yet it went on.

She stepped carefully to avoid inadvertently crushing any of the delicate creatures. On one faraway rock, she made out the image of a harbor seal pup resting as its mother fed off shore. Seabirds cried overhead while, at the shore, small, long-legged birds ran in drift of their own, like schools of land-fish, their feathers iridescent in the setting sun. She lifted a rock and a crab scuttled away from the light, shiny and salmon colored, gritty with sand. She replaced the rock gently, so as not to destroy its home.

Every living thing, no matter how small or insignificant, deserved a chance to grow and thrive. To live, reproduce itself, and die.

With a flap of wings, a gull dashed in front of her, snatched the crab in its beak, and swooped into the air.

"Oh!" she said, lifting her hand impotently.

Here, then gone. That, too, was life.

For a moment, she let herself feel the unfairness of the world. Then she pushed it away. There was no point bemoaning reality. She lifted her face to the sun and raised her arms above her head and focused on her breath.

She couldn't mourn the loss of something she'd never had. Gideon was still her friend. It wasn't his fault she wanted something more.

She'd overcome a lot more than disappointment in her life. She'd be fine.

She was a survivor, after all.

Chapter Seven

*If you're going in the wrong direction, today is full
of opportunities to get onto the right track.*

—Gideon's horoscope

Gideon drove through town, and pulled to a stop in the
public beach parking lot. He scanned the beach, looking for that shock of green.

There she was, standing on a rise of black rock, holding
a yoga position of some kind, still as a heron, graceful as a
hawk. Quietly, he opened the door and stepped out, leaning
one foot on the running board and draping his arms over the
window, watching, almost against his will, unable to tear his
eyes away.

Blake, within his rights but just out of reach.

Jamie, within reach but utterly wrong.

He walked out toward the railing separating the parking
lot from the descent to the sand, feeling as if his heart had
climbed out of his chest to perch on that thin metal rail,
dripping and warm, while he stood behind it, empty and
helpless.

It didn't matter that Jamie was adored by kids and dogs
alike, that she'd overcome more challenges in her youth than
most would see in a lifetime, that she was strong and sweet

and smart and loyal. Lana wouldn't see past the tattooed and pierced former runaway with a foul mouth and a record of petty crime and an easygoing attitude toward rules.

She hated Gideon's checkered past already; his friendship with someone like Jamie would not help his cause. Let alone that friendship being something more.

Which it wasn't.

And never would be.

"Jamie," he called, tightening his jacket over his chest.

Jamie jumped and whirled in his direction, then leaped off the rock.

"Hey, Gideon! Did you see me? It's called dancer pose," she called, jogging toward him. "I was thinking of starting a blog about yoga by the sea. You know, different poses shot against the water and clouds with my own pithy thoughts about the meaning of life. Very moody and inspirational and shit. Some people make a lot of money blogging. Of course, I'd have to get sponsors and that would probably suck the living soul right out of it and I'd become jaded and bitter, throw myself into a bottle and die a penniless alcoholic."

She came to a stop, breathless, and squinted her eyes at him.

"What's the matter with you? You look like someone stole your teddy bear."

Listening to her made him feel better, all that bubbly chatter.

He gestured to the truck. "Huck had a flat. I'm your ride. Get in. Daphne's waiting for you."

"Oh, no, you don't, bucko." She put her hands on her hips, her eyes flashing more green than blue today. The wind caught her thin jacket, pressing it against her lithe body, outlining her small breasts and flat stomach.

Then she lowered her hands. She hopped over the railing to stand right in front of him, and he felt the concern come off her in a wave.

He said nothing, but he couldn't stop an audible exhale. The letter weighed heavy in his pocket, almost as heavy as the heart beneath it.

"Gideon?" Jamie put her hand on his arm. "What is it?"

Gideon had a choice. Jamie or Blake.

He stepped away. "I've got a trail ride to lead tonight. And you've got a dog to return."

She watched Gideon turn toward the truck. Something was definitely bothering him, and it wasn't just that she'd kept the pup.

Though that didn't help.

She glanced behind her. A few parents left on the beach had gotten a little louder. She wondered if they'd brought something extra in their thermos bottles. It wasn't allowed, strictly speaking, and it certainly wasn't smart, but people did it and trying to stop them all would be like trying to turn back the tide.

"You looked good out there," Gideon said, abruptly.

She looked back in surprise. "What, the yoga?"

"With the kids. You're good with them."

His praise warmed her heart. "They're like any little animals. They need clear expectations, positive reinforcement, focused attention, and a lot of treats. Of course, it helps that I'm not around them all the time. I'm sure it's different when they're yours."

He looked away, shoving his hands deep into his pockets. "Come on. Let's go."

As she followed him across the parking lot, an area of dark, choppy water fifty yards off shore caught her eye. Topped with debris and foam, it had the look of a rip current. Jamie's pulse quickened.

"Hang on a second," she told Gideon. She searched out the children on the beach, doing a mental tally.

Were they all there? It appeared so. What about the adults?

Five people sat on their blankets, cross-legged, leaning toward each other, utterly unconcerned. Hadn't there been more in her group? One of the dads had taken a call on his cell phone just before the end. Maybe he'd left.

Jamie didn't like the look of that wave. Distance was hard to judge, but it seemed the frothy mass had moved closer already. The picnickers were about twenty yards above the high-water mark, far up enough to be safe.

Probably.

Then, down the beach a ways, on a secluded pocket beach where the creek trickled into the ocean, she spied another family. Two kids chased the waves on chubby legs, their bottoms diaper-wide, their movements new and clumsy. The woman stood with her hands on her hips, her yoga-pants-clad legs planted firmly in the sand, her shoulders slouched a little, as if tired but determined to have fun on this family outing.

"Be right back," she told Gideon. "I don't like the look of that wave."

She jogged in their direction, keeping one eye on the rough water. She was probably overreacting, but since she was already late, she might as well give them the same speech she'd just given the other parents.

The man was farther from the water, holding his cell phone out, then bringing it in and examining it. He said something to the woman, who turned, then strode toward him, gesturing.

No, thought Jamie, picking up her pace. *Never turn your back on the sea.*

The dark, rolling mass continued to churn off shore, not coming closer, not dissipating, simply hovering at the edges, like a wolf padding around a flock of sheep, waiting for an opening, watching for the shepherd to look away.

One of the children plopped onto the sand and set up a

wail that could be heard above the surf. The other one paused, looked back, then bent, picked up a handful of sand and flung it at the smaller one.

The mother paused from her conversation, waved impatiently at the kids over her shoulder, then turned back to continue arguing with her husband.

The wolf saw its opportunity.

Jamie saw it too.

"Hey!" she yelled, racing toward them. "Get your kids!"

Somewhere behind her, she heard Gideon calling, but she ignored him.

"Get back, get back!" She waved her hands. With the growing force offshore, the surf receded, a shiny tongue slipping back into the maw of the beast. The smallest child got up, pointing her bottom into the air and then joined her brother, chasing the disappearing water across the glistening sand.

The parents looked up at her, unconcerned, then went back to their discussion. On a perfect sunshiny day like this, on a calm beach, there couldn't be any danger, could there?

"Get your kids," she yelled again. This time, they looked at her in annoyance.

It started slow, barely perceptible from land, a wall of dark water, flecked with white foam, streaked with detritus and weeds from the ocean floor, building moment by moment, inch by inch, as the gleaming expanse of sand grew, and the sound of the surf waned, beckoning the tiny humans into the grinning jaws.

It happened so quickly, yet to Jamie, time slowed to a deadly crawl. She watched, frame by frame, as the parents' body language went from distracted to irritated to confused.

In that endless moment when the water was at its farthest, and the ocean paused for breath, Jamie yelled again. "Get back! It's coming in hard!"

The mother took a step, called to the children. The dad walked away, once more concerned with catching proof of their quality time on camera. The kids stopped, turned to look at their mother, and that's when the water turned.

She was almost there. She dug her toes into the sand and sprinted, racing the wall of water heading for those small bodies. It came at them like a freight train, the bellow growing like a yell down a tunnel. The mother wasn't running fast enough. The father, looked up, still unaware of the danger, the phone still in position.

Building, building, building, the water went from nothing to a one-foot, two-foot, three-foot wall ready to slam those little bodies to the sand and tumble them end over end.

Jamie reached the scene just before the wave broke, bracing herself as it crashed against her back, grabbing the smallest child by one arm, lifting her high, anchoring her as the ocean tried desperately to pull her free, to carry her away.

She saw the other child get thrown to the sand and in two steps, she was behind him, her fingers just catching the back of his jacket. Frigid salt water boiled and foamed around them, screaming and crashing filled her ears as they were pummelled, pushed and pulled, but somehow, she managed to stay on her feet, her hands clamped like vices.

Then the wave turned to rush back out, and she braced herself again, bending her knees and leaning forward. She felt the tide suck the little bodies backwards and held on for all she was worth.

And then it was gone.

The water let go. She fell to her knees, drenched from head to foot, but immediately struggled to her feet. A second wave would catch them while they were down if she didn't hurry. She stumbled up the beach, dragging the children with her, and dropped them, like a triumphant retriever, at the father's feet.

Both kids were screaming bloody murder.

"What did you do to her?" yelled the mother, picking up her daughter. She peeled the little jacket away. Red marks were already forming on the girl's tiny wrists. "Look at this."

"Ow, ow, ow! Mommy, it hurts!"

The kid was howling for all she was worth, holding her arm like Jamie'd broken it.

She spat bitter sand onto the beach, then patted the boy's head. "Stay safe, munchkin."

The mother yanked him to her side. "Don't touch my child."

The man looked uncomfortable. "They could have been hurt, honey."

"She is hurt, look at her."

A couple of the parents from Jamie's class ran up to them then. "Is everyone okay?" asked one of the moms. "Jamie, that was amazing. That wave came out of nowhere."

The woman scowled at her husband, then stalked away. "Get the bags, Evan," she snapped over her shoulder. "The kids are soaked. We need to go home."

"Yes, dear." Evan waited for her to get out of earshot, then turned to Jamie. "What's your name?"

She shook her head, unable to catch her breath. Suddenly Gideon was at her side, wrapping his jacket over her, his strong arm holding her up.

"Why?" His voice was deadly calm. "So you can tell your lawyer?"

His solid warmth bled into her cold limbs. Now that the crisis was averted, Jamie felt like her legs might give out beneath her. A phalanx of people gathered around, bristling. "Jamie's a hero," one woman snapped.

"You're lucky she was there," another added.

"Never, ever take your eyes off toddlers at the beach," said a third. "What were you thinking?"

Evan put his hands out. "I know. I'm grateful. I saw what you did. Jamie, is it?"

She nodded warily, her teeth chattering.

Evan's wife called to him from the parking lot, her words indistinct but her message crystal clear.

"I've got to go," Evan said. "Thank you, Jamie. Don't listen to her. She gets upset and . . ."

He shrugged, then shook her hands and jogged up the beach to find his family.

Gideon led her across the beach as the crowd clustered around her.

"Are you okay?" he asked.

She nodded, soaked and shaken. "Just another day in paradise. The kids are okay, that's the main thing. Let's go home, okay?"

He tightened his grip around her. "You got it."

Jamie hugged herself and clenched her wet legs together, waiting for the heater to start working. This business of getting soaked while fully dressed was getting old.

Gideon drove with his right hand draped over the steering wheel, his fingers moving in time with the music, his left elbow out the window. But the skin at his temples looked thin and tight and a muscle twitched in his jaw.

"I'm fine, Gideon."

"I know."

She turned in her seat, so she could examine him more closely.

"What?" He spoke casually, as if nothing were bothering him in the world.

But she wasn't fooled. "Something's chewing at you. Is it me?"

Might as well be blunt.

He shot her a quick glance, his brow furrowed. "No, of course not. You scared me, though."

She bit back a smile. Good. He ought to be scared now and then. Maybe then he'd realize that they were already more than friends.

The heat started to penetrate her wet clothes, and she felt her limbs loosen. "You don't have to worry about me. I'm tough."

"You are, at that." He slanted another sideways look at her and, with effort, seemed to come back from wherever he'd been. His shoulders lowered and his jaw loosened. "How was your class? Before the *Baywatch* moment, I mean."

It was deliberate misdirection, a caginess that annoyed her. She wasn't that easy to fool and didn't appreciate him trying.

But she played along. "Pale kids missing their tablets. Parents talking as if they did nature walks with them all the time. A lot of hand-woven hemp. One little girl found a hermit crab she wanted to take home and name Harry. The usual. So, why are you tapping the steering wheel like you just had a caffeine IV?"

He reached out and turned up the radio. "I'm not."

She turned it down. "Yes, you are. If it's because of us—"

"It's not." He huffed out a breath. "It's nothing."

"I knew it!" She couldn't help but crow. "When people say it's nothing, it always means it's something. Usually something big. Look, you might as well tell me, because I'll get it out of you sooner or later."

He looked out the window. "Ever heard of personal boundaries?"

"Overrated. Speak."

"I appreciate you caring, James." He hesitated and in that moment, the chill returned. "But it's something I have to handle myself."

Bad, definitely. She cranked the heater to high and forced a smile. "Is that supposed to make me back off? You know my imagination is going crazy, right? What is it? You got subpoenaed to testify in a mob hit? You're a descendant of Rasputin? You won the Publisher's Clearing House lottery?"

He rubbed the back of his neck. "It's private, Jamie."

"Private like a bad credit score? Testicular cancer? I know: irritable bowel disorder. Your guts are definitely tied up in knots about something."

This at least earned a laugh. "You guessed it. You never give up, do you?"

"When it comes to you, my friend, never."

She used the word deliberately. He was spooked, she got it. Okay, so she'd made a fool of herself in the past few months, hanging on his coattails, arranging her schedule to match his.

Then that day at the creek. Smelling his hair. Squishing his shoulders under her fingers. The memory burned, and she forced herself to face him now, her expression open, bland. Friendly.

His smile faded. "Lucky me." He turned the wheel, and they began the bump up the long driveway to the ranch.

He held his shoulders tight, and whatever crack had been there a moment ago slammed shut again.

"Fine." Jamie hugged her elbows tight, unable to get warm. "Don't tell me. But now I'll be thinking the worst and it'll distract me from my work. I might lop off a finger while I'm peeling potatoes, and you know how Daphne is. She'll finish dinner and whip up a pie before I'll be allowed to go to the hospital. So, me being fingerless will be on your head. Can you live with that, huh? Can you?"

He parked the truck in his usual spot between the corrals and his own cabin and turned off the engine. It rumbled and shuddered to a stop, and then it was silent in the cab, except for the sound of their breathing.

He turned sideways then. His face was so solemn, her heart started thudding. This was serious. Whatever was worrying him, it was important.

He reached for her hand, tentatively, as if unsure if he could touch her or not.

"Gideon?" She grabbed it before he could pull back and his fingers tightened over hers, holding on as if she were a lifeline he hadn't known was there.

He met her gaze. His eyes were full of pain.

She swallowed against an ache that had suddenly set up in the back of her throat and spread to her chest. "You're scaring me. What is it?"

He turned her hand over, and covered it with his other hand, his warmth wonderful against her cold skin.

"I've got some stuff to deal with," he said. "Family stuff."

"Family stuff?" She ran her thumb over his knuckle. "You mean your brother?"

She knew he had a brother named Josiah and that they weren't close. Gideon had never mentioned anyone else.

"No." He took a deep breath and gently extracted his hand. "My ex."

The word hung there in the thick damp air of the truck, like fog on a cool autumn morning. Whatever she'd been expecting, it hadn't been that.

"Your . . . ex."

"Yes. Her name is Lana. What's the matter? You didn't bat an eye when you found out I'd been in prison, but this shocks you?"

He was a grown man, after all, with a life before she'd met him.

"So you have to go see your . . ." She forced herself to say the name. "Lana. Wait. Is that where you've been going on your mysterious weekends away? Are you . . . are you . . . getting back together?"

She wanted to fall through the floor of the truck. No wonder he wasn't interested in her.

"God, no." He shuddered.

The thought of him secretly going to meet up with a woman he'd once known intimately . . . that he'd never told anyone about this . . . that he hadn't told her . . .

Or maybe he hadn't kept it completely secret.

"Does Olivia know?" she whispered.

He nodded, the gesture like a slap.

"You told Olivia?" Her throat was tight. "Before you told me?"

"Aw, James, don't make this a big deal." He rolled his head, as if his neck was sore.

"Don't call me James."

"It's a term of endearment."

"Right." She slugged him, hard.

He rubbed his arm. The sad smile he gave her made her heart twist in her chest like a colt on a rope.

Get it together, Jamie.

He didn't owe her anything. And why would he trust her if this was how she reacted? Whatever was going on with him and this . . . Lana . . . had shaken him. He needed someone.

"I'm sorry," she said on a breath. She forced herself to say the only words she could. "Your personal life is none of my business. I had a crush on you, it made things awkward and uncomfortable. You're not into me—I get it. It's fine."

Deep lines bracketed his eyes. He reached for the door handle. "Let's forget it, okay?"

"Wait." She swallowed. "I hope you know that you can still talk to me. You can always talk to me."

He turned away, staring beyond the windshield. Green

leaves swished back and forth above the truck in the breeze, dappling the dashboard with light and shadow. His profile might have been carved from oak, for the emotion he showed on it. Yet she held her breath, sensing that, beneath the sun-bronzed skin and his glittering charcoal eyes, a battle was being waged.

Chapter Eight

*When Mercury squares Uranus, be on the lookout
for unexpected or unwelcome communications.*

—Gideon's horoscope

Gideon walked on stiff legs back to his cabin. He needed
to get a handle on this, figure out his next move. Until
then, the less anyone knew the better.

Even Jamie.

Especially Jamie.

She'd been shocked to learn about Lana; what would she
think about him being an absentee father?

Inside his cabin, he tore open the envelope again.

He scanned the single sheet quickly, only a few lines, in
Lana's barely legible scrawl.

The gist of it: she didn't want innocent, six-year-old Blake
around "negative influences."

Like his father.

He could demand access, of course, but with his past, a
judge wasn't likely to side with him. Biology was no guarantee, especially when it came to fathers. And Lana had
hedged her bets well.

No, his best chance with Blake depended on her cooperation. Lana, with her gated community, her chauffeur to

take Blake to his exclusive private school, all paid for by investments Gideon had put in Lana's name before he'd gone away.

He pulled a duffel bag out of the closet and began throwing clothing into it. If he left first thing in the morning, he'd be in Portland by noon. He could talk to Lana in person, make her see that he wasn't backing down, but that they both wanted the same thing. They both wanted what was best for Blake.

Blake was the main thing.

Surely, Lana would understand that a boy needed his father. And that, despite everything that had happened, Gideon was still a good man.

They could resolve this without a battle.

And then, once they'd come to an agreement, he'd bring his son to Sanctuary Ranch.

He'd tell Jamie everything then.

But before he left, he had work to do. It wasn't fair to leave Huck in the lurch, and he didn't want Olivia to have to pick up the slack. He tossed the bag on the bed and strode out of his cabin heading for the barn.

"Hey."

He jumped as Jamie pushed off from where she'd been leaning casually against the cedar shake facade of his cabin. She'd taken time to change into dry clothes, but that was about it. Now she was back, like a bloodhound on the trail.

"I changed my mind," she said, falling in with his rapid pace. "I was going to be all mature and let you go on with your strong, silent act, but let's face it. I gotta be me. So to hell with your privacy. I'm not a tabloid reporter and you're sure as hell not Leonardo DiCaprio. So you might as well tell me what this blast-from-the-past wants from you and why you look like you're getting ready to do something rash."

He stopped short and turned, and she nearly bumped into him from behind.

"What?"

She laughed at his expression. "Come on, it's written all over you. I'm the queen of impulsive actions. I recognize the symptoms in others. Where are you off to in such a white-hot panic?"

He pushed past her. "I'm not in a panic. I forgot some chores, that's all."

"You've never forgotten a chore in your life."

He lifted the latch to the horse barn and went inside. She followed.

"Maybe I'm getting a head start for the morning."

"Nope," Jamie said, grabbing at his sleeve. "Try again."

He stopped and faced her, reluctantly. The dim light in the barn cast shadows across her face, making her eyes even shinier than usual. There was an urgency about her that he recognized.

She was afraid, and trying not to show it.

Against his better knowledge, he lifted a knuckle to her cheek. She inhaled sharply and closed her eyes at the contact. Her lips were slightly open, plump and inviting. *One kiss*, he thought.

No.

He dropped his fist and stepped back. "It's personal, Jamie. But I promise, I'll tell you about it soon. Okay?"

She bit her lip, then nodded, her expression troubled. Her throat looked milky white and soft as one of the kittens Tyler was raising.

"Gideon?" Her voice was quiet and serious. "People like us can't afford to be overly stupid. If you won't talk to me, talk to someone. Okay?"

Her words spiked his heart. She meant so well. She was going to find out sooner or later. He should just tell her.

He hesitated. As much as he wanted to tell her about Blake, the situation didn't paint him in a good light. He knew how Jamie felt about deadbeat dads, and though he'd been more than generous in looking after Blake financially, he'd provided nothing emotionally. He wanted the custody dispute to be settled before he tried to explain.

"You don't have to worry about me," he said eventually.

As if recognizing the cop-out for what it was, she tightened her jaw. "If you say so."

He opened his mouth, then exhaled loudly, closed it again, and shook his head. "Make my apologies to Daphne."

"You're not coming in for supper, either?" she said in disbelief.

"Not hungry."

"You have to eat."

"I'll come up later for leftovers."

"There might not be any. It's lasagna night. Everyone loves Daphne's lasagna."

"I'll be fine, Jamie." He turned for the door, but she reached back and braced her arm against it, holding it closed.

"This isn't over," she said, the words coming low and hot. "You're not off the hook, yet. If you go off half-cocked and do something stupid, I'll never forgive you."

She huffed out a breath and dropped her arm to her side. She opened her mouth, then closed it, then opened it again. Under the bravado, she looked so uncertain that it made him ache.

"I'm not going to do anything stupid, Jamie." He hung his head. "I've got too many stupid mistakes I'm still trying to fix."

"Who doesn't?" she said, touching his arm again.

"I mean bad mistakes." He swallowed. "I'm not the man you think I am."

"I don't care." Tears sparkled in her eyes now.

"You should." Though he knew he shouldn't, he wiped his thumb across her cheek, where one warm droplet glistened. "You truly see the best in everyone, don't you?"

She covered his hand with hers, pressing it against her cheek, then her lips. "I see the truth," she whispered. "I'm here. Whenever you're ready."

Then she turned, scooted beneath his arm, and ran out of the barn.

Slowly, he walked back to his cabin. He looked at the jumbled clothing on his bed while his heart beat fast and hard against his eardrums.

That shouldn't have happened. He hadn't intended to tell Jamie anything, let alone touch her. But she was relentless and this secret had been festering inside him since the letter had arrived, making his chest hard and tight, like a wound that needed lancing. When she turned those sparkling eyes on him and started probing, it was all he could do not to pour the whole sordid mess out before her, bow down, and await her judgment.

But she didn't deserve that. She would give and give and give if he let her, and what kind of man would he be to do that to someone like her, when he knew how she felt about him?

His burdens were not hers, and sharing them went above and beyond their friendship. He didn't want to imply an intimacy he couldn't give her.

He sat down on the edge of the bed, feeling his breath return to normal, and looked at the half-packed duffel bag.

Jamie was right. Ambushing Lana was the worst thing he could do. She was scared. Showing up uninvited and angry would only make her more defensive.

She'd provided her cell phone number and email address. That's what she wanted, so that's what he'd do.

* * *

The soft sounds of evening drifted in on the breeze as Jamie lay curled in a ball on the love seat facing the fireplace, where Daphne had sent her after she'd broken one of her favorite patterned china plates on the edge of the cast-iron sink.

She hadn't corrected Daphne's clucking assumption that her clumsiness was a delayed reaction to the episode on the beach.

Better to have Daphne focused on her so-called heroism than to think she was mooning after Gideon.

She wasn't mooning.

She was *hurt*.

With a touch of worry thrown in.

Ninety-nine percent hurt, one percent worried.

She forced herself to breathe slowly and deeply, then tugged the quilt off the seat back and flopped backwards. A couple of the guests were playing cribbage nearby, and she definitely didn't want to talk to them.

None of the usual calming elements of evening—the soft breeze, the occasional nicker of the horses in the nearby corrals, birdsong, quiet conversations of people in the great room—were doing the trick.

Even taking Chaos for a quick romp in the apple orchard hadn't helped. He'd found and rolled in the carcass of something indescribably foul, which meant she had to hose him off, which made her late for KP, which made her rush, which led to the plate incident, which led to . . .

Here now, on the couch, mad at herself for not returning the pup earlier, like Gideon had told her.

She punched a pillow. The man was making her crazy.

She'd never seen him like this. He hid it well, and maybe no one else noticed, but his shoulders rode higher than usual lately and that line at the side of his mouth had grown deeper.

Okay, ninety percent hurt, ten percent worried. That was still a lot of hurt.

She rubbed her arm where she'd scraped it on something. Her shoulder ached, too. Those kids had been heavier than they'd looked.

But not nearly as heavy as whatever lay in the back of Gideon's eyes.

Sixty-forty.

The warmth of the quilt started creeping into her bones and she snuggled deeper into the thick upholstery. What kind of trouble was he in?

The carbs from Daphne's lasagna headed straight to her brain, doing what carbs always did.

A few minutes, she thought, already drifting. That's all she needed.

At the sound of Gideon's voice, her eyes flickered open a crack. The subtle change of the light told her she'd dozed off. She hadn't heard him come in.

He spoke low and slow as always, in the same soothing, firm tones that eased the horses and sounded, to Jamie, like the surf on a calm night. But solid, like an old-growth forest. She could listen to that voice for hours.

"You sound good, Lana."

Her head popped up, and she peered cautiously over the edge of the couch. Gideon was leaning against the post near the window, his cell phone pressed to his ear.

Lana.

His ex-wife.

Or whatever.

Already in Jamie's mind, a picture had formed of the woman who'd once owned Gideon's heart. She'd be a cute little blonde who wore high heels and false eyelashes and push-up bras and had impeccable manners and clean hands and could make polite dinner conversation with the Queen of England, if she happened to drop in.

She probably had a fancy degree from some college back east, with a gaggle of sorority sisters she went on retreats with. She'd have a career in interior design or health care or management. Something clean, something necessary. Something with benefits.

Because she was smart.

Jamie was smart, too.

But while other people had been preparing for a lifetime as a productive member of society, Jamie had been lurching from moment to moment, sleeping with one eye open, picking locks and stashing food under her bed. Future planning hadn't exactly been on the docket.

And where had this paragon been when Gideon was in prison, she wondered? What role had she played? Had she been supportive? When had they split up?

So many questions. And what if the answers weren't what she wanted?

She could ride a half-pipe in the morning, green-break a colt in the afternoon, and still exchange barbs with Daphne while slinging hash at supper, but she had no armor against women who were pretty, smart, and stylish.

Sexy, she could pull off. Sexy biker chick, no problem.

And apparently, that wasn't Gideon's type.

She hazarded another look. He was gazing at the sunset, clearly unaware of her presence.

"Yeah, I know." A pause. "Too long."

She recognized the low softness in his voice for what it was: intimacy.

Something twisted inside her, and she was suddenly eager to leave. Who Gideon talked to was no business of hers.

Then his tone changed.

"Can I talk to him? Please?" His voice cracked on the simple request.

Jamie froze. Gideon rarely asked for anything. He certainly didn't beg. But he was begging now. She needed to leave, but the optimal moment had already passed. Seeing her now would only embarrass them both. She hunkered back down and pressed a pillow over her ears.

But she couldn't block out the conversation.

"Hey, buddy," he said, his voice growing lighter, brighter. "How are you doing, son?"

Son.

The pillow fell away from her head. What the heck, if he wanted privacy he should have stayed in his cabin.

She strained to hear more. She must have misheard him.

Gideon, who kept a polite distance from chubby, drooling Sal, as if babies were a contagion, who was conveniently busy when guests with small children showed up, who'd never given the slightest indication that there was a small someone in his life, couldn't be a father.

Could he?

"You've never ridden a horse?" he was saying. "We have to change that."

He spoke differently, his voice a little softer, a little higher, a little more . . . tentative.

"Your mom and I have to figure that out," he said next. "I know it's confusing, to find out you have a dad you haven't met. I'm sorry about that."

She shoved her fist against her upper lip.

A dad you haven't met?

What?

No. Not Gideon. He wasn't the kind of man who abandoned a child. He couldn't be. Questions whirled through her head. How old was the boy? Why hadn't Gideon seen him?

Is that what he'd meant when he'd said he wasn't who she thought he was?

No shit, Sherlock. Her breath came quick and fast, as if something were on fire inside her chest. Had he abandoned his family?

Surely not. She knew how it felt to be fatherless, adrift, and unclaimed, like a piece of lost luggage with no label, nothing to explain where and to whom she belonged. Surely Gideon hadn't put that on his child intentionally.

Then a worse thought arrived.

Maybe he was going back to them, despite what he'd said. Maybe he had a white-picket-fence life in the suburbs somewhere, with a woman waiting for him to come to his senses, and a kid and no doubt a dog, too. A family.

No wonder he wasn't interested in her. He had a whole other life, somewhere else. Sanctuary Ranch was just a pit stop. He was someone else entirely.

She pulled her knees up to her chest and hugged them with her elbows, putting her hands over her ears, but it was no use.

A pause. "Oh. All right. Have fun with your friends. I'll talk to you soon, okay?"

There was an undercurrent in his voice Jamie didn't recognize. A desperate friendliness. He was talking too much, trying too hard. That was her style, not his. This mysterious child of his meant a lot to him.

"Look, Lana." The intensity was back. "All I want is a chance. I know it's been a long time. I didn't want to push you. But I should have. I want to see my son."

Anger burned through the hurt inside her and she sat up, fully. He deserved whatever he felt.

"Ahem," she said.

He jumped, nearly dropping the phone. "Jamie! What . . . no. Sorry, Lana. There's someone here. I have to go."

Jamie crossed her arms over her chest, and fixed her gaze on him. His skin was pale beneath the tan, almost grey. The tendon in his throat twitched. She could hear the voice on the other end of the line now, high and demanding, not letting him go.

He tried to talk but couldn't. Finally, the voice stopped and his hand dropped away from his ear. He looked utterly spent.

"How much did you hear?" he asked.

"Enough. No. Cancel that. Not nearly enough." Jamie

felt the words bubble up out of her and knew she should hold them back but couldn't. "You have a son, Gideon? And you never thought to mention it? Last Christmas, when you were here, with the rest of us, you had a kid celebrating somewhere else? What's his name? Why doesn't he know you? Do you have other kids you haven't told anyone about?" She got to her feet but didn't approach him. She balled her fists and glanced toward the other room. The crib players were still doing their thing, and she could still hear Daphne banging around in the kitchen.

"How could you do this? You said I didn't know the real you, but I never imagined this. Tell me, how does your wife manage? Does she have to work two jobs to support your child? Is she forced to leave him with resentful grandparents because there's no baby daddy to help out?"

She made herself stop. This wasn't about her or Grandma Ellen. Surely Lana was a responsible mother. Surely she didn't drink too much, or forget to buy groceries or drive her car into lamp posts.

Surely Gideon wouldn't have left his child with a woman like that. Gideon wouldn't have gotten involved with a woman like that in the first place.

But then again, he was the rescuer of kittens, a hero to the forsaken, the keeper of secrets, and a friend to the friendless.

And she didn't know him, after all.

For long, stretched-out moments, he stood at the window, motionless, following the sun as it continued its inexorable slide into the sea.

"His name is Blake," he said dully, without looking at her. "He was born two months after I went inside. Three months before Lana dumped me. I told you I've made a lot of mistakes. Well, I'm trying to undo one now. It might be too late. But I'm trying. And," he added, "she's my ex. But we were never legally married."

He started to walk out of the room.

Jamie leaped off the couch and stumbled after him. "Not so fast, Buster."

She lowered her voice and smiled as they walked past the guests at the games table, but as soon as they were outside, she grabbed his arm.

"That's not all," she said. "Something's changed. What is it, Gideon? You can trust me."

He looked at her for a long moment, his dark eyes fathomless, unblinking.

She waited, not wanting to break the connection. He trusted her, she knew he did. But he was being eaten up inside and she so desperately wanted to help.

"A month ago," he said finally, "I wrote to her through my lawyer, requesting visitation."

Relief flooded her. He was trying. He hadn't abandoned his child. "That's great, Gideon. When will you see him? I can't wait to meet him!"

She put an arm around his waist and side-hugged him, but he only patted her arm and pulled away.

Uh-oh. "What's wrong? She didn't turn you down, did she? She can't do that. Surely your lawyer—"

"It's not about what she can or can't do," Gideon replied quietly. "It's about what's best for Blake. Being torn between the two of us won't do him any good."

"Hold on." It took her a moment to process what he was saying. "You mean you're thinking of giving up? Of not fighting for him?"

"I don't want to." His voice was harsh. "He's my son. I want to know him, I want him to know me. But he's just a kid. Meeting me would turn his life upside down. Lana's not wrong about that. Maybe the right thing is to let him go."

"Bull, comma, shit, my friend. Let me be clear. What's best for Blake is to know the truth. You're his father, you're awesome, and he deserves to know you."

At some point, they'd clasped hands, and now, he looked down at their interlinked fingers, then lifted tortured eyes to meet hers.

"It's not just that, Jamie. Lana's finally settling down, getting her life in order. She's getting married. To a guy she's been with for the past three years. The guy who's helped raise Blake. The closest thing to a father he's ever known."

"So what? He's still your son."

Gideon exhaled, then swallowed. "She's marrying Blake's stepfather. This guy, her fiancé, wants to formally adopt Blake." He paused. His Adam's apple bounced as he struggled to regain control.

"Gideon—"

He dropped her hands and put his up, palms out, to stop her. Whatever she had to say—and even she didn't know what that was—he didn't want to hear it.

"I'm not on the birth certificate, Jamie. To Blake, I don't even exist."

Chapter Nine

Tell your dearest wish to the first star you see in
the celestial sphere tonight.

—Jamie's horoscope

The little dog howled.

"No, no, shh!" Jamie dropped to her knees. She knew just how he felt. She'd accused Gideon of going off half-cocked and then what had she done? Unloaded on him like a nervous cow.

"Until I figure out what to do with you," she told the puppy, "you need to keep a low profile."

Something he seemed incapable of.

A knock sounded on the screen door. Perfect.

"Shush now, you," she whispered. Chaos put his head down on his paws and sighed.

She opened the door slightly, using her body to block the view inside.

Abby Warren stood in front of her, a wicker basket of flowers slung over one arm and a pair of pruning shears in the other. Her chestnut-brown hair curled softly over her shoulder, where she'd tied it back in a single side ponytail.

Jamie put a hand to her own mud-colored locks, still growing out the latest jagged cut.

"Hey, Abs," she said. "I'm on my way to the main house. I'll walk with you."

Abby peered over her shoulder. "Oh, what a cute puppy! Can I see him?"

Jamie sagged, then pulled open the door and let her in. "He's supposed to be a secret."

Abby laughed, set down her items, and reached over the exercise pen to pet him. "Good luck with that."

Her voice always made Jamie think of smoky jazz bars. Not at all what you'd expect from someone so fresh and perky.

"He's a stray," Jamie said. "I found him in the forest while I was riding. He's not staying so don't bother telling Haylee."

"Like she's focused on anything but the baby right now." Abby pulled a twine-tied bouquet from the basket and handed it to Jamie. "The rudbeckia is fantastic right now, but it's running a little wild. I thought I'd share the cuttings, rather than tossing them on the compost heap. Have you got a vase?"

Jamie spread her hands out. "Do I look like the kind of person who has a vase?"

Abby cocked a beautifully arched eyebrow at her. "Everyone has a vase."

"Not me. But I might have a pasta sauce jar in the recycling. Hang on." She pushed the puppy aside and dug around in the cupboard beneath the sink. She usually ate in the main house with the rest of them, but now and then she chose to hang out on her own. Daphne could always be trusted to bring a plate of leftovers or a basket of breakfast pastries. She had a sixth sense as to when someone needed a little privacy, but refused to let anyone starve. Not on her watch.

Jamie found the jar, and Abby took it from her.

Abby rinsed out the jar, filled it with fresh water, and

arranged the flowers. She set them on the two-seater table next to the window. "There. Doesn't that look nice?"

"Very."

Abby narrowed her eyes. "Are you okay?"

"Of course. I'm great. What do you mean?"

"You're being weird. Weirder than usual, I mean. I figure it has something to do with Gideon."

Jamie felt blood rush into her cheeks. "I don't—"

"Oh, spare me." Even when scolding, Abby sounded like she was narrating a steamy romance novel. Apparently she'd once worked as a telemarketer. Jamie guessed she'd been very successful at it.

"I know you two are tight. But, lately, you've hardly been in the same room together and you seem a little spikier than usual. Is something wrong?"

"Yes," Jamie said. "I'm about to get my ass handed to me if I don't hose down the kennels for Haylee before lunch. And I'm not spiky."

"Relax. Who do you think sent me? And yeah, you're spiky. Your hair. Your voice. That thing in your eyebrow. Anyway, I'm not trying to pry—"

Jamie guffawed. "Right."

Abby's peaches-and-cream skin grew pink. She lifted her chin. "Look. Haylee's worried about you. You two are like sisters—"

Jamie sniffed. "Not lately."

Not since her reunion with Sage, and little Sal's arrival.

And Aiden.

And the new baby they were about to have together.

"I know things have changed." Abby hesitated. "That's why I thought I'd let you know that I'm here, if you need someone to talk to. About . . . Gideon. Or anything."

Since Abby and her quiet younger sister had arrived on the ranch as summer workers, they'd kept mostly to them-selves. Huck said Abby was magic in the garden and Daphne was sufficiently impressed with the way the two cleaned guest rooms that she allowed them to practice baking. Abby's pies were as good as anything Jamie had ever tasted.

But that hardly made them bosom buddies.

"I've been a big sister for a long time." Abby fussed with the flowers in the pasta jar, adjusting and rearranging the long stems. "According to Quinn, I'm pretty good at it. That's all. Okay, quit glowering at me, I'm going."

But before she left on a waft of blossom-scented air, she gave Jamie's arm a quick squeeze. "You've got lots of friends, James. If you want them."

Abby's use of Gideon's pet name for her, which should have been annoying, felt unexpectedly tender instead.

Jamie swallowed, watching the other woman step gracefully out of the cabin. Everything about Abby was soft and sweet and feminine. She couldn't possibly be as innocent as she looked—there was something about the way Quinn clung to her that suggested a rough past for the two of them—but she still radiated a sort of girl-next-door freshness that Jamie would never have.

Is that what Lana was like? She pictured Gideon, tall and dark, standing next to a pretty woman with big eyes and a shiny ponytail and a little boy with a shy smile. They'd look like the photos that came with picture frames, a happy family, laughing into the sunset.

No one deserved that more than Gideon. And if there was a chance of that for his child, Jamie ought to be standing on the sidelines, cheering her head off.

"Rah-fucking-rah." She gritted her teeth. "Geez, James. Pull your head out. You never had a chance with him anyway."

She was too broken for someone like him. She was a person made up of mismatched pieces, like God had thrown all his spare parts into a box, shaken it up, and then done the best he could with them.

Chaos cocked his head comically at her and whined.

She took a deep, centering breath. "You," she said, once she was steady again, "be quiet."

She was making a second visit to the house on the ridge this afternoon. She hoped she wouldn't need to use her tools again.

After that, if all went well, she was sending the dog back to his proper home.

She'd do the right thing. And she'd be happy for Gideon. She could do that.

Jamie got into her ten-year-old Toyota 4Runner and fired it up, revving the engine with relish. She felt irrationally loyal to the battered, gas-guzzling monster. Up high, surrounded by metal, she felt safe, and the beast had been a means of escape more than once. Plus, she owned it outright. It was probably as close to owning a home as she'd ever get.

Chaos was safe on the ranch with Abby and Quinn right now, since they knew about him anyway, and she was on her way to find out if that's where he'd be staying.

She hadn't seen Gideon all day. For all she knew, he might never speak to her again. That was fine with her. They each had wounds to lick. Maybe, in time, they'd be able to talk about it. Maybe not.

She had to accept that.

She plugged a Keith Urban disc into the CD player and opened the windows, letting the fresh air whip through her hair, filling her with courage. Green grass, blue sky, the clean smell of rain-washed earth.

This was paradise, she reminded herself. And she was doing a good thing, in making sure the puppy was safe. Every living thing deserved a safe and happy home.

The owner of the house on the ridge had done his best to remain anonymous. But for people like Huck, who knew more about bypassing locked walls than Jamie ever would, there was no such thing as personal information. He could find out the brand of deodorant your first-grade teacher used, if he wanted to.

Huck's special skills were a closely guarded secret, and he used them judiciously. Sometimes, when justice and the law didn't line up, and animals couldn't be protected, Sanctuary Ranch became a stop on an underground railroad that could whisk them away. Huck helped "lose" these animals, if necessary, helped save them from a lifetime of misery and place them instead in loving homes.

It had taken him only five minutes to hack into the county records and get her everything she needed.

The owner of the house on the ridge above Driftwood Creek was a man named Roman Byers, age sixty-nine, who'd been a film agent in L.A. around the same time Jamie had lived there. He'd retired five years ago after legal issues related to a workplace accident.

Huck had offered to dig deeper but Jamie didn't care. Everyone in Hollywood had legal issues, eventually.

Byers was a big shot.

Or had been, at least.

Surprisingly for someone in the movie industry, he'd stayed off social media. Industry photos showed him to be a striking man with the robust build of an outdoor enthusiast, a full head of salt-and-pepper hair, a chiselled jaw, stubbled cheeks, and smiling eyes.

But, as the sociopath son in her last foster home had taught her, smiling eyes guaranteed nothing. What mattered to her was how Byers looked after his dogs.

If this man tweaked her meanness-radar, if she found evidence of neglect, Jamie didn't care how rich and famous he was, she wasn't giving Chaos back. Haylee would back her up. In fact, she'd help get the brown dog out of there, too.

Rounding the bend, Jamie saw the narrow driveway, fronted by the metal gate she'd climbed through before. With a crunch of gravel, she pulled the truck to the side of the road and stepped out, watching the dust settle lightly in the warm air. The gate was closed but unsecured this time, the chain and padlock hanging from a post.

One of the nails in the No Trespassing sign had loosened, she noticed. She stepped closer and, after a quick glance over each shoulder, gave it one sharp kick. With a ping, the sign disappeared into the tall grass.

"It's practically a welcome mat now," she said.

She grabbed the clipboard she kept in the side compartment of her passenger door—you never knew when you'd need to write something down—pulled her Portland SPCA baseball cap from the glove compartment, straightened her shoulders, pushed the gate open, and walked through, down the center of the narrow driveway, where a thin line of sunlight pierced the thick trees.

The house looked just as she remembered.

She strode up the porch steps, rapped on the door, and backed away.

"Hello?" she called. She cleared her throat and tried again. "Mr. Byers, we've received a complaint—"

Chapter Ten

If you wish upon a star, pick one that twinkles.

—Gideon's horoscope

"A little saddle soap goes a long way, Duke," Gideon said, lifting the jar out of the teen's hand. "And ditch the brush."

He tossed him a soft cloth instead.

"You should trash this thing and get a new one." Duke scowled at the cracked leather of the seat and then flipped the stirrups to get at the underside, nearly dislodging the saddle from the two-by-four storage rack.

"First of all, it's Olivia's. And they don't make them like this beauty anymore. It's a shame to see it in this condition, but I think we can bring it back."

Gideon didn't know how the kid saw anything with all that long hair in his face. But he didn't know how the kid walked in those pants either. The mysteries of adolescence.

"How are those kittens doing?"

Duke's scowl disappeared. "Great. Tyler and I are keeping them in our cabin. They're starting to scratch at the top of the box. Pretty soon the little buggers will be running all over the place. Honch says we can each keep one for ourselves as long as we get them fixed. I wish we didn't have to. I like having kittens around."

"The way cats appear on this ranch, I guarantee you'll see more sooner rather than later."

Gideon had quickly learned that there was no shortage of people who believed that their unwanted family pets would be welcome additions to a working ranch. It wasn't unusual for a wary new face to appear at the food bowls in the morning, the result of a surreptitious drop-off under cover of night.

He tried not to judge. Sometimes, due to circumstances beyond their control, this was the best choice they could make. Sanctuary Ranch had a reputation, after all. And Gideon knew better than most how easily one bad decision could snowball into a lifetime of regret.

But most of the time, the pet had become an inconvenience, a "throwaway" to use Haylee's term.

If he did what Lana wanted, and didn't fight for a place in Blake's life, would his son one day feel the same? Would he think he'd been an inconvenience to his birth father, a throwaway best left for someone else to raise? Or would he be grateful that the loser sperm-donor responsible for his being had stayed the hell out of his life?

"Hey, gentlemen," Olivia said, striding up to them. She ran a hand over the saddle, pursed her lips, and shook her head. "Duke, have you ever had a girlfriend?"

The boy raised his eyebrows, then tossed that hank of greasy hair and snorted. "Duh. Tons. It's a relief to be here, away from them."

A sure bet the kid was massively inexperienced, maybe even a virgin.

"Treat this old leather like you would a girl." Olivia took the soft cloth from Duke's hand and stroked it softly over the dry surface, moving with the grain of the leather, working in light easy circles until the conditioner was fully absorbed.

"Gently, see? Slowly, like you can't believe how soft her skin is. Like you're hoping your breath doesn't stink and your pit juice is still working and maybe, if you're very lucky, you'll get to second base with her." Then she returned the cloth and looked at him sternly. "Not like you're spanking the monkey. Got it?"

Gideon turned away to keep from laughing out loud as the boy's entire face and throat turned scarlet.

Olivia turned her back on the saddle and addressed Gideon. "There's an estate auction happening this afternoon, with some nice riding horses on the docket. Thought we'd check it out if you have time. It's the Altman farm. We could bring Duke too, if you can spare him," Olivia added.

Duke's head whipped up, his color still high. "I'm done with the stalls. I brought the supplements into the feed room like you asked and swept up, too. Can I go, Gideon?"

Olivia demanded a lot from her foster kids, but when she offered a chance for some one-on-one time, they always jumped at it. She had a way with them.

"Means Tyler will have to do afternoon chores on his own. You'll owe him." He didn't want to make it too easy for the kid.

"I'll make it up to him. I'll shovel his sh . . . I'll muck out his stalls tomorrow. He won't care. He knows I'd do the same for him."

Reciprocity. Teamwork. The kid was making progress.

Gideon pretended to think about it. "I guess that's okay."

"Good." Olivia slapped a piece of straw off her jeans. "We'll leave in two hours."

As they drove out to the Altman farm, she explained to Duke why this sale was of particular interest to her.

"Usually when people have horses to sell, they send them to a broker. They get a fair price, but they don't have any control over who buys their animals and, unfortunately, a lot of horses end up going to the slaughterhouses."

Duke's jaw dropped, though he picked it up quickly. "People eat horses? Gross."

"There aren't any horse slaughterhouses in the U.S. It's not illegal, but every time a company tries to open horse-meat packing plants, public outcry shuts them down before they can get started."

"Good." Duke looked out the window. "Horses aren't meat."

"They are to some people," Olivia said. "And at livestock auctions, they often end up being sold to foreign markets looking for horsemeat. Wild horse culls especially."

Duke snorted. "It's disgusting. People who sell horses for meat should be shot."

Olivia gave a one-shoulder shrug and tipped her head side-to-side. "Horses are expensive to look after, and they live twenty-five or thirty years. Sometimes people buy them without realizing the commitment required. Or, like Mrs. Altman, their circumstances change. Her husband had a stroke last year and is in a nursing home now. She can't manage the farm on her own and it'll take time to sell. Meanwhile, she's got some nice saddle horses she desperately wants to keep out of the slaughterhouses. So, she's holding a local sale, hoping to find new homes for them, places where she knows they'll be looked after and loved."

Gideon understood Duke's disgust, but Olivia was right about the practicalities. He was grateful these horses at least had someone willing to take the time to resettle them.

He'd delivered feed to their place once, when the husband had first become ill, and he knew they raised American quarter horses, smart, sure-footed animals that had been the working breed of choice on cattle ranches in the Old West and were still valued in Oregon's ranch country. They also made excellent family horses for trail and pleasure riding.

Sanctuary Ranch maintained a full stable year-round, but Olivia always kept her eyes open for that gem of an animal that would be perfect for one reason or another. He'd like another horse like Nash, smart and strong. Perhaps a sweet-natured pony, too. One suitable, say, for a six-year-old boy.

They pulled into the driveway and parked next to a row of pickup trucks that all looked pretty much the same. Gideon climbed out of the passenger seat. Duke unfolded his skinny limbs from the backseat and followed him.

The auctioneer had set up his stand and mic just outside the nearest corral, and people lined up on three sides of the fence, some perched on the top rungs, some hanging their arms over, their booted feet resting on the lower rungs. Olivia nodded to various acquaintances as they walked by. Everyone in the horse community tended to know each other to some degree. Sanctuary Ranch had an excellent reputation, and her compatriots in horse rescue respected her work on behalf of the animals they all loved.

Gideon noted several families with school-aged children with them, likely looking for a sweet-tempered, sturdy riding horse for someone's dearest dream.

The sale hadn't begun yet, and many people were walking through the stalls, observing the horses, taking notes on the ones that caught their eyes. There were a couple with Arab blood, from the curve of their elegant heads. A large, docile-looking draft horse with gorgeous white feathered hair on his lower legs that made him look like he was wearing bell-bottom pants. And one rough-looking mustang that watched the crowd suspiciously.

Duke pointed to a perfectly marked paint. "Ooh, look at that one," Duke said.

"A beauty," Gideon agreed.

They were all gorgeous: roans, palominos, a striking buckskin mare, and that watchful grulla. The Arabs were both soft dappled grey; the draft horse was mostly black with a perfect blaze down his big muzzle.

Olivia pointed to the grulla, pacing in her stall. "A true throwback to the original wild horses. See the shoulder stripes and black barring on the lower legs? Classic. Looks similar to roan coloration, but where roan is made of a mixture of dark and light hairs, in this case each individual hair is mouse-colored."

"She's kind of homely." Duke leaned against the boards, watching the mare, who watched him back, flicking her ears when he spoke.

"She's a Kiger," Olivia said. "You can bet she's smart as a whip, that one."

"If she's so smart, how come she's not still running wild?"

The kid laughed at his own lame joke. Gideon did not. Wild horse management was a controversial issue not likely to be solved anytime soon. Freedom sounded romantic, but the truth was more often a short life and a rough end.

"The Bureau of Land Management rounds up the horses every three or four years," Gideon said. "They choose the horses that most closely exhibit the build and coloration of the original wild mustangs and return as many to public land as the range will support, often transferring horses between herds to maintain genetic diversity."

"What do they do with the rest?" Duke asked.

"They usually get auctioned to the public," Olivia said, "which is how this girl got here."

Wrong place, wrong time. Who didn't understand about that? Gideon crossed his arms on the stall rail and tapped his fingers.

The auctioneer's voice sounded over the speakers, inviting prospective purchasers to the corral where they'd set up the bidding station. Olivia and Duke chose to stand near the front. Gideon moved to the back, ostensibly because of his height but mostly because he didn't like to have a crowd behind him.

The first six horses sold quickly, the bidding enthusiastic and competitive. He saw one preteen girl who would be going home in tears of joy at having her dearest wish fulfilled in the form of the gentle but spirited Arab mare.

The horses had followed the trainer into the corral and stood quietly during the bidding, calmly enjoying a carrot or two until the auctioneer hollered, "Sold!"

But the grulla wasn't so cooperative. The trainer rode in on a second horse, leading the mustang by a short rope attached to her halter. But as soon as she saw the people, she shook her head, the whites of her eyes showing, and began dancing at the end of the rope.

"This is Hacer el Jaimito," the auctioneer read off the paper. He lifted his head and put a hand behind his ear. "Which means to horse around. I'm guessing she's got plenty of spirit. She's registered with the Kiger Mesteño Association and comes from a band in the Steens Mountain area. Her owner called her Bonita, which means beautiful in Spanish."

A ripple of laughter went over the crowd.

"Chica Loca would be a better name," called someone. "She looks like a crazy girl for sure."

More laughter. The loud speakers and the crowd of unfamiliar people weren't doing the mustang's nerves any good. Gideon moved around the side of the crowd to get a better look.

"Kiger Mustangs are descendants of the Spanish horses brought to North America in the 17th century," the man continued, speaking over the mare's frantic whinnies. "Let's start the bidding at one hundred dollars. One hundred dollars, do I have a bid? Bidder, bidder, bidder. One hundred dollars for a proud piece of American history."

A teenage girl elbowed the man standing next to her. "Dad! What about her? She's a real mustang."

"Forget it, Mandy. She won't even walk into the ring. Your mother would kill me if I brought home an animal like that."

"But Dad, I'll work with her. I can tame her, I know I can. And she's only a hundred dollars! Please!"

"Excuse me, bidders, we're going to switch Bonita to the end of the program. Instead, next we've got handsome Hank, who looks like he'd be great for riding or pulling your sled in winter."

The auctioneer went on to list the attributes of the big horse while the trainer led, or rather, herded Bonita away from the corral. A thump sounded as the mustang landed a kick on the gate as she left.

"Not the best way to win over the crowd," Gideon said, coming up behind Olivia and Duke.

Olivia met his eyes, her brows raised just enough for him to know she was thinking the same thing he was.

"Let's see where they're taking her." Olivia left her spot at the rail and motioned for Duke to follow them.

Following Bonita's loud whinnying, they found her in the corral on the other side of the barn. Mrs. Altman stood at the railing, clutching her fingers so tightly her knuckles were white.

"Olivia, Gideon." The woman wiped her face and then caught them each by the hand. "Thank you for coming. That damn horse is going to get herself killed. She misses Jack so much. I think her heart is broken. It took him a long, slow year to earn her trust and now she's practically feral again. I promised him I'd keep her if I couldn't find a home where someone would work with her again, but I can't manage her without him."

Gideon looked at the sale sheet. *Hacer el Jaimito.*
Jaimito.

The idea came to him in a flash. He looked up and met Olivia's smiling gaze again. Had she dragged him here with this in mind?

He didn't care.

"I know the perfect person for Bonita," he said.

"Really?" the woman glanced between them, as if afraid to hope. "She's not an easy horse."

"Trust us," Olivia said. She squeezed the woman's hands. "Jack's horse will get exactly the kind of love she needs. Tough but one hundred percent reliable. This person won't give up on her, I guarantee it."

"Are you buying her for Jamie?" Duke asked, his eyes wide.

"It's a surprise. For her birthday." Gideon leveled an even look at him. "Don't mess it up, understand?"

Duke nodded, his eyes impressed. "Wow, man. This'll get her back for sure."

Gideon gritted his teeth. "She's my friend. She's always wanted a horse of her own. I'm giving her one."

"Whatever you say, dude." Duke waggled his eyebrows, then ducked away from Gideon's elbow.

"Jack used a hackamore with her. You can have that too, plus an extra halter, lead ropes. Oh, I've got a blanket too, but I'm keeping his saddle." Her eyes filled again. "He tooled it himself. I'm sorry, but I can't give it up."

"That's fine," Olivia said, with another smile. "We've got a saddle that'll fit her."

"We can't take her for a couple of weeks though," added Gideon. "Is that okay?"

"Absolutely!" She smiled through her tears. "Thank you. I can't wait to tell Jack. He'll be so happy!"

Roman Byers dreamed he was riding his ATV over the dunes. Wind-whipped sand stung his cheeks, and his quads and glutes burned from holding his weight over the ridges. He gunned the throttle over a rise, catching air, sending his stomach plummeting, then lurching into his throat as he clung to the vehicle and flew, free as a gull.

He awoke suddenly, his cry of exhilaration in fact the half-choked snort of an old man with sleep apnea. He pulled himself upright, wincing as pain shot from his sacrum down to his knee and up to his flank. He paused, breathing hard. Was he passing a goddamn kidney stone again?

No. Just the usual.

Outside, Sadie barked. He had to remember to close the doggy door when he napped. She was getting too adventurous for her own good, especially since the bird-watching escapade and the whole Chaos debacle. At least he didn't have to worry about the pup. That girl looked like she'd take good care of him. Jon wouldn't like it, but that was his problem.

He shuffled to the screen door. "Sadie," he yelled. "Get in here. You do me no good outside."

She peered at him briefly, then took another step down the driveway. That's what he got for letting up on the training. Dogs needed a firm hand, clear direction. They'd fallen into a rut. The puppy had disrupted everything. Served Jon right that he'd run off and found a new home. Roman didn't want to deal with a puppy all over again. He and Sadie were fine.

But now, Sadie kept straying away, looking for the little

mutt, disobeying Roman and sending his blood pressure up. It was intolerable.

He glanced at the computer screen Jon had set up on the desk, the one attached to the security cameras that he'd hidden in the trees.

Damn it. A figure walked down the driveway, the image grey and pixelated, the movements jerky. How? The gate was closed. It was always closed. Now he'd have to check it.

He stood up straighter, ignoring the fresh pain. Immobility was his enemy. That's what he got for sleeping during the day. He'd have plenty of time to sleep when he was dead, which would probably come far too soon anyway.

The brown dog trotted stiffly around the corner, wagging her tail.

"Hey, old girl," Jamie said. She held out her hand, watching for someone to join the dog.

Instead, the porch door crashed open, revealing an elderly man holding a shotgun across his chest.

"Sadie!" He gestured to the brown dog and she promptly climbed the steps, circled behind him, and sat at his left side. He looked at Jamie and drummed his fingers on the stock of the gun. "Whatever you're selling, I'm not buying."

"Roman Byers?"

He looked nothing like the photo she'd seen on the Internet. His face appeared sunken and drawn. His head was shaved, his shoulders were stooped, and his clothing hung loosely. No smile in those deep-set, hooded eyes.

No smile, period.

Her conviction wavered. But she'd come this far, might as well go for it. He looked like he was from a generation that believed in delicate female sensibilities, so she swallowed her inner revulsion and let her hands flutter to her throat.

"Oh, dear." She glanced over her shoulder with not entirely false apprehension. "The gate was open, and this is the address I was told to go to. I'm very sorry for disturbing you, Mr. Byers. That is your name, isn't it?"

His nostrils flared. "The gate was closed. Someone told you wrong."

"I'm from the SPCA," she continued, offering an obsequious smile. "It's about a dog that someone believes to be in need of medical attention. We're required to check on all such reports. You understand."

"Sadie here is just fine, as you can see." He took a step closer. "I'll see you out. Check on that gate, while I'm at it."

Reflexively, she backed away. Her radar wasn't pinging. But he wasn't friendly, and he certainly wasn't offering information.

"Then I apologize for the intrusion." She gave him her best, wide-eyed smile. "If you could just confirm your name for my report? And perhaps I could take a closer look at— Sadie, is it? Since I'm here anyway."

That earned her a brief, unamused smile. "I don't know what you want, but you're not from the SPCA. My dog is none of your business. So get the hell," he said calmly, "off my land."

He came closer and she put up her hands.

"All right, all right, no need to get huffy," she snapped. "I don't like to see animals in distress, that's all."

He stalked past her, his gait uneven, as if there was no question of her following him. "Why don't you tell me why you're really here?"

She stopped. "What do you mean?" She aimed for bravado, but her voice quivered.

"I saw you."

"What . . . what are you talking about?" She really hadn't thought this through. Gideon was going to kill her.

The man stumbled, grabbed for the fence post, missed. "Bloody hell," he said, going down on one knee.

Jamie took a few steps closer. "Are you all right?"

He lifted a hand to keep her from coming nearer. "I'm fine. I know you took Chaos. Keep him. I don't care. Just . . . get the hell . . . off my property."

"But . . ."

He knew? How? Why hadn't he said something? She wanted to run back to the truck and take off, but she could hardly leave him now, could she?

He lowered himself to the ground, clutching his thigh, pressing his back to the fence post. His face had a strange grey pallor to it. He wasn't okay at all.

Before she could think of further action, the skinny chocolate Labrador went to his side, nuzzling, circling, and whining.

"This might be a really stupid suggestion," she said, hoping she wouldn't regret it, "but can I help you?"

He groaned and uttered a string of profanities, interspersed with gasps. The dog leaned against the man, pushing against him.

"Good girl, Sadie," he rasped. He took hold of the dog's collar. Sadie leaned backward, digging her toes into the ground, and with her help, Roman Byers levered himself upright.

Leaning against the fence post again, he wiped the sleeve of his jacket over his face. "What's your name, girl?"

"Jamie."

"For fuck's sake, Jamie," he managed, without meeting her eyes. "This is your fault. Give me your goddamn hand and help me back to the house. And bring my gun, will you?"

He leaned heavily on the girl's arm, cursing himself for a weak old fool. He should have ignored her. Kept Sadie inside, waited for her to go away. But no, he had to go out, stand his ground, scare her away so she wouldn't return.

And she hadn't even brought the blasted pup. Least she could have done.

Though he didn't want the beast, he reminded himself. But there was Jonathan to consider.

"In there." He waved her toward the front door, and she walked him through and helped lower him onto the nearest kitchen chair. He stretched out his leg. The damn thing was on fire.

"Can I call someone for you?" asked the girl, fisting and flexing her hands. She could've been pretty, but she had tattoos on her forearms and several piercings in each ear, as well as one in her nose. What was wrong with a little good, old-fashioned femininity? Why were women so determined to look rough and tough?

Sadie, having completed her mission to get him into the house, now shamelessly rubbed up against the girl's legs, groaning with pleasure.

"No. I'm fine. I'll be fine."

The girl narrowed her eyes and crossed her arms.

"You don't look fine. You look like shit, actually. How about a glass of water?"

"How about you give me back my dog."

"I thought you didn't want him."

"I don't." He shifted position. The pain intensified. He should have had her take him to his armchair.

"Well, then." She walked past him into the room. "I guess I'm done here."

And damn it, he saw when she noticed his wall. The clippings of him with various celebrities, some of them holding golden statues, the framed movie posters, the awards.

"So you are Roman Byers, then." She moved from one to the next, making herself right at home. "Cool."

Sadie, the useless guard dog, wagged her tail, ready to lead the girl to the silver and help her carry it out the door.

"How did you know my name?" he asked. He watched for her face to change, for recognition to set in, for memories to return, for pity and disgust to send her back to the door.

But it didn't happen.

"I'm from Sanctuary Ranch." She gestured vaguely out the window. "Someone there knew about you."

So much for privacy. "Where's your boyfriend?"

She started. Color rose in her cheeks. "My what?"

Despite himself, he was amused. "The cowboy."

She scowled. "We're friends."

"Looked like more than that the day you stole my dog."

Her jaw dropped. "You saw me?" Incredulity lifted her voice. "Then you'll know I didn't steal him. I rescued him. He was lost. He could have drowned. Or been eaten by a bear. Lucky for you I was there. Besides, I thought you didn't want him. You haven't exactly beaten the bushes looking for him, have you?"

"Friends, sure." Her bluster amused him. He'd spent a lot of years observing human nature, judging which actor was right for a part, waiting to see the right gesture to portray the emotion of a scene. This girl was protesting an awful lot.

She hesitated, then seemed to come to a decision. "I didn't know if I should bring Chaos back or not. That's why I'm here. To see if this is a good home."

"You've got a lot of nerve, don't you?" He rubbed his leg. The spasm had eased, but he knew from long experience that once triggered, it was likely to recur.

"It's been suggested. So, is this? A good home?"

He tried to see his place the way she might. Dirty dishes piled in the sink. Boots kicked off at the door, the floor gritty and stained, the windows streaked with grime. No one for company but a cranky old man who yelled at the TV and couldn't give them enough exercise or stimulation.

"I don't have to justify myself to you."

"True." She smiled, leaned against the wall, crossed her arms, and nodded toward Sadie. "What about her?"

He sighed. Sunset was an hour away. He was hungry and he needed his pills. It was almost time for Sadie's meds, too. "What about her? She's falling apart like an old Ford, just like me."

"Has she seen a vet? She's too skinny for a Lab. And that leg looks bad."

Her self-righteousness pissed him off. As did the reminder. Roman swallowed. The pain was ratcheting up fast, and the rate this girl was going on, he wouldn't be able to get ahead of it. He needed to eat before nausea set in, but that meant heating up one of the casseroles Jon had left for him in the fridge. Which meant getting up.

Pain, pills, food, movement, rest. He had to keep everything in balance, and this Jamie girl was throwing him off.

"Aw, hell," he muttered. "She's got cancer. It's in the bone."

"Oh." Jamie blinked. "Well, that sucks."

"Yes, it does. She's a good dog. Doesn't deserve this." He looked away, wishing he'd kept his mouth shut. He didn't want her goddamn pity.

"No one deserves that." She chewed on the corner of her cheek. "Nothing they can do?"

She wasn't offering pity, he realized, only concern. Chin high, arms crossed, she was ready to go to bat for an old dog she didn't even know.

"It's in the femur." It was a relief to talk about it. Jon didn't understand. He thought he could slide another dog into her place and that would solve the problem. "Amputation would buy her time, but she's already twelve. I won't do that to her."

His throat thickened and he looked away. It had been a long time since he'd spoken to anyone besides Sadie's vet about it, and it was weighing on him. But this girl was still butting in where she had no business. And she had Chaos.

"You've given up then?" Jamie asked.

"On her?"

She raised her eyebrows. "Who else?"

Pain was making him stupid. He couldn't think when the throbbing in his hip began shrieking down his leg. And it was setting up a true howl.

"Look, girlie, I've got stuff to do." He could feel perspiration breaking out on his forehead. "Me and my dog are no business of yours."

Her nostrils flared. "So you're just letting her suffer?"

"Good God, is that what you think? You see those pills on top of the refrigerator? Steroids, pain relievers, anti-inflammatories, anti-nausea, you name it, she's on it. Nothing will change the end, but she's getting everything she can to ease the journey. She's still happy. Mostly."

Jamie walked to the refrigerator, took down one of the pill bottles, then another. "Some of these are for you. What's your problem?"

"Get out." He shook his head and rubbed his thigh. "I've got no time for this."

"Fine." She replaced the pill bottle, went to Sadie, and stroked her ears. "Sorry you're not feeling well, girl. I wish I could help."

"You owe me an apology." He poked his index finger at her. "I don't mistreat my animals. Never have. Never will. You understand?"

She shrugged. "If you say so. Remind me, why were they running loose in the woods, without you?"

"Look at me!" He gritted his teeth and lowered his voice. "You don't think I'm trying? The pup's a freaking escape artist. He gets out, Sadie goes after him, and I follow. You got there ahead of me, that's all. I saw it and thought good riddance. I can't handle the bugger. He needs more than I can give him. So get off your high horse. You got anything else against me, I don't want to hear it. You can show yourself out."

She went to the kitchen, found a glass, and filled it with water. Then she took several pill vials off the top of the refrigerator and brought them to him.

"Where's Sadie's food?"

He shook his head. He couldn't think. He reached out, loathing himself for needing her. "Help me to the couch."

She was stronger than she looked. And gentler, too.

"Better?" she asked, after he tossed back his dose.

"Not yet." He pointed to the cupboard. "Kibble's in there. There's canned food in the fridge. Put her pills in that."

He lay back while she got Sadie's meal ready, waiting for the pain to ease. He didn't know this girl from Eve. Where she came from. Why she cared. If she had some other motive. But right now, he didn't care.

Jon wouldn't be happy that a stranger had been inside. Or maybe he would be. He was always pestering Roman to make friends with the neighbors.

The microwave dinged and suddenly Roman smelled food.

"Here," Jamie said, setting a bowl on the coffee table. "Found this in the fridge. Didn't see any mold so hopefully it won't kill you."

His stomach growled. "You're kind of a busybody, aren't you?"

"You're welcome." She walked to the door. "I'll be back in the morning with your pup."

"Keep him."

"I saw all the toys and treats in the cupboard. That's a heavy investment in a pup you don't want." Beneath the attitude, ink, and hardware, she had a pretty smile.

"Aw, hell in a handbasket. My son bought me the mutt so I guess I'll have to learn to live with him." The task of training Chaos to take over for Sadie felt like asking a small engine to haul a long train up a steep mountain. He didn't have the steam to do it again. But he had to do something with the mutt, didn't he?

Jamie pursed her lips, bit at the corner. "I could help you train him. If you wanted, I mean. I'm, uh, pretty good with dogs."

Roman hesitated. He was probably going to kick himself later for this. But there was something waifish about her that made him long to see her smile again. She didn't back down, and he liked that. And she cared enough about Sadie and the pup to come in despite his security measures.

He cleared his throat. "How about you keep him a few more days, knock some sense into him for me."

There it was again: joy, washing over her elfin features like a time-lapse sunrise. Something broke through his pain-hardened heart, like a bud unfurling through rough bark after a long, cold winter.

"Really?" she said.

"Don't mess him up," he said, waving her out the door. "And don't get attached. He's a little asshole, but he's still mine."

Chapter Eleven

*Venus–Jupiter and Venus–Neptune are openhearted
and loving but they both have trouble with
boundaries.*

—Jamie's horoscope

Jamie was in the garden with Abby, pulling baby carrots for
Daphne's stew, when a strange vehicle pulled up on the
yard, and she was too busy feeling inadequate to notice
immediately. The pup was more of a challenge than she'd expected, and she wished she'd been upfront with Haylee
about it from the beginning. She could use the help. Plus, the
subterfuge was eating at her. She had a sneaking suspicion
Haylee knew about the pup but was waiting for Jamie to
come to her about it.

She didn't normally play into open secrets. She was the
one people counted on to blurt it, spill it, spit it on the wall
so they could read it. Now look at her.

Abby straightened and pushed the chestnut braid over
her shoulder, letting it swing onto her back, making Jamie
painfully aware of her unruly hair. Now that she was letting
the bootblack color grow out, it looked worse than ever.

"Are we expecting anyone?" Abby said with a frown.

A light sheen of perspiration brightened her brow. Small freckles dotted her arms and nose.

"How can you spend all morning digging in the dirt and end up cuter than when you started?" Jamie swiped a dirty hand over her cheek. "You look like Perky Cheerleader Barbie. Which makes me Street Rat Barbie, I guess. Which is kind of my vibe, so never mind."

"Jamie. Do you recognize that car?"

The anxiety in her tone caught Jamie's attention. She looked up to see a fully loaded import SUV, dark maroon with tinted windows, sparkling clean.

"Nope. Why? You expecting someone?"

"Here." Abby pushed the basket into Jamie's arms and slipped to the shade of the apple trees lining the garden. "I need to find Quinn."

"What's the matter?"

"Nothing." Abby tugged a wide-brimmed sunhat low on her head. "I just remembered I have to tell her something."

She disappeared through the back gate, to the little path that led to the cabins where Quinn was likely changing sheets and scrubbing toilets.

The driver of the SUV opened the door and stepped out. A man, well-dressed, a hair under six feet, Jamie guessed. He took off designer sunglasses, glanced around the deserted yard, spied her in the garden, and waved.

"Good morning," he called. He looked like Timothy Olyphant, lean and lanky, all smiles and aw-shucks swagger that immediately put Jamie on alert.

"Morning." She slung the basket of vegetables higher onto her arm and approached him, wiping her hands on her jeans. "Welcome to Sanctuary Ranch. What can I do for you?"

"My name is Elliot Hudson." He stuck out his hand. "I'm looking for Gideon Low. I understand he works here."

"He does. I'm Jamie. Is he expecting you?" He had a

good, firm grip, but something about the way he glanced around the yard made her nervous.

He hesitated. "Um. Not really."

She gestured for him to follow her to the main house. "You can have a seat here while I find him for you."

Jamie led him up the porch steps to the small front office. He politely took his boots off at the door and followed her inside.

"Smells good in here," Hudson said, peering toward the kitchen.

She steered him into the room and pointed at the love seat across from the desk.

"Always does. Would you like some coffee while you wait?"

"That'd be great." His smile was one you'd give a doctor who was bringing bad news.

"You got it." She pulled the door shut. She hated this part of the job, the sales and service part that made her feel like a waitress. She didn't work for tips. She didn't make a commission on bringing in guests. In fact, she'd prefer that they didn't take guests at all.

"Who's the rock star?" Daphne wiped her hands on a dishtowel, nodding toward the office. She took the basket from Jamie's hand, nodding in approval.

According to the smell, her stew was already well under way, tender home-grown beef simmering in her own concoction of stout and deep, rich broth she made in huge vats and jarred for the pantry. The freshly dug baby potatoes and carrots, plus the tiny sweet green peas she'd add at the end, would turn it into a masterpiece. Like all Daphne's meals.

Jamie rolled her eyes. "Drove up in a sixty-thousand-dollar vehicle, has no idea what we do here, or what he wants. Something's fishy."

"You were born suspicious, Jamie-girl." Daphne set a cup of coffee on a tray with creamer and sugar.

Then she peered more closely into the basket. "There's no rosemary or curly parsley in here. Where's Abby?"

"She was in the garden but left when he arrived. Said something about needing to find Quinn."

Daphne looked up sharply, her eyes cutting toward the office. "She did, did she?"

"Yeah. Why?"

The cook exhaled and rubbed her forehead with the back of her hand. "Those two spook like wild horses. Never mind. You go find Gideon. I'll keep our guest company while you do. Go."

"Who?" Gideon's head snapped up so fast he almost lost his hat.

She'd found him in the back of the tack room, where he was bent over something that looked like an old saddle. He'd pulled a tarp over it when she came in as if embarrassed at his workmanship.

"He said his name was Elliot Hudson. Seemed a little nervous."

"I'll bet he did." Gideon yanked his gloves off and threw them down on the workbench. "Where is he?"

He strode out of the tack room on long legs, and Jamie had to jog to catch up.

"Probably in the kitchen, eating his weight in carbs, if Daphne has her way. Why? What's wrong, Gideon?"

He was muttering under his breath, and suddenly Jamie became alarmed.

"Gideon!" She yanked at the back of his shirt. "What the hell?"

He stopped short, then slowly turned to face her, his expression like an off-shore storm.

"I'm going to the music room. Alone. Tell him to meet me there."

He turned back and continued his path, but now his movements were controlled, his steps even. Whatever was going on, he wouldn't lose his shit.

She hoped.

He disappeared around the side of the main house, choosing to enter via the lower-level door. He really didn't want witnesses.

She hurried into the house and found Elliot Hudson popping the last of a cinnamon bun into his mouth. He got to his feet, dropping the conversation with Daphne mid-word.

"Did you find him?" he asked.

"He's in the music room. I'll take you," Jamie said, beckoning.

It was merely a wide-windowed room on the lower walkout level of the sprawling ranch house, containing an ancient upright piano and a couple of guitars. Daphne and Huck both played a little, though it was mostly used by guests.

Its main feature was that it allowed privacy from the great rooms above, which was undoubtedly why Gideon had chosen it.

"How do you know Gideon, Mr. Hudson?" she asked as they walked down the spiral staircase. Her curiosity was almost unbearable.

The man gave her a quick look. "He and my fiancée used to be together, years ago."

Oh. The first thing she felt was relief. The lovely Lana was no longer available then. Gideon had no reason to feel obligated toward her, and she had no need to try and get him back.

"That's great. Well, here you go." She pushed open the door and ushered Elliot inside.

Gideon stood at the piano, leaning one elbow on the top, like a squire just waiting for a cigar. But she could tell his casual confidence was an act, his posture too perfect and at odds with the tight set of his jaw.

"Have a good visit," she added, inanely. "If you need anything—"

Gideon strode toward her, took the doorknob, and gently pushed her out. "Thank you, Jamie."

She waited on the other side for a moment, then remembered she was an adult and ran up the stairs back to the kitchen.

"It's Gideon's ex's next," she explained breathlessly to Daphne, who stood in the doorway, flexing her fingers. "What do you think it's about?"

The cook's face darkened. "Nothing good. I'm hoping it doesn't come to blows because there'll only be one left standing and I guaran-damn-tee you it won't be either of them."

Daphne didn't tolerate violence. Unless she was doling it out herself.

Olivia slipped into a chair by the island. "We've all had our share of incidents. It's Gideon's turn, I guess."

Jamie shot her a glance. "You know about . . . ?"

Olivia just smiled. "I know everything, Jamie."

She had no right to feel annoyed. It was Olivia's ranch. Of course she knew everything. She couldn't run the place otherwise.

But she wanted to be the one who knew everything about Gideon.

And it seemed there was much he'd kept hidden.

Suddenly they heard a door open below. As one, the women rushed to the window, where they saw the two men walking up the path to the parking lot.

Gideon held the man by the elbow, and for someone known for the tight rein he kept on his temper, he sure looked like his rivets were loosening.

Jamie ran out the door and caught up with them by the hedges. Olivia and Daphne followed, but at a reasonable pace.

"What's up, bros?" Jamie asked, bouncing to a halt.

"Mr. Hudson is leaving." Gideon's expression brooked no argument.

"Thank you for the coffee, Jamie." Hudson nodded at Daphne. "Ma'am. I'll be in touch," he said to Gideon.

"No, you won't," Gideon said, slamming the car door.

Hudson gunned the engine and drove off in a flurry of gravel.

"That was interesting," Jamie said, after the reverberation stopped and the dust settled, leaving them in silence. Gideon stood with his back to them, as if he were made of granite.

They quietly walked away from him, back to the kitchen, where they found Abby peeking out from around the corner.

"I already brought in the veggies," Jamie told her. "You owe me a foot rub."

"Sure," she said. "Who was that guy?"

"Some guy named Elliot Hudson." Daphne's face was like a thundercloud. "Gideon knows him. It's not a friendly situation. Why?"

Abby gave a short little laugh. "No reason. Just curious. What did he want?"

Jamie snorted. "That's the million-dollar question, isn't it?"

"Slick as snot on a glass doorknob." Daphne used a deep Texas drawl as she picked up the spoon to stir her stew. Accents came and went with her, like viruses in a doctor's office.

Gideon slammed back into the house and went straight to Olivia. "I apologize about that. May I speak with you in private for a moment?"

Jamie's jaw dropped. "No way, man. Whatever's going on with you, I think the rest of us have a right to know."

Gideon's nostrils flared. A tendon in his throat twitched. He opened his mouth to speak, but Olivia stopped him.

"Not now, Jamie." Her voice was gentle. "Come, Gideon."

Chapter Twelve

Big upheavals on the horizon. Hold on tight.

—Gideon's horoscope

The goddamn nerve of the man, showing up out of the blue to do some kind of ad hoc surprise inspection.

Jamie's outrage had bolstered his conviction. He was within his rights to request time with Blake. He knew he was Blake's biological father. The only reason Lana hadn't demanded a paternity test was because she knew it would prove his case. She had no reason to doubt his fitness, or question his occupation or the safety of his home.

"Breathe, Gideon," Olivia said. "Let's talk in the stables. I've been meaning to talk to you about Apollo anyway."

Olivia walked ahead of him, her long legs even thinner than usual in her customary blue jeans. He fell in with her gait, glad to head back under cover, to the soothing company of the animals.

He'd been ready to deck Hudson, seeing red, and his veins and arteries and nerves and muscles were still singing with adrenaline, his skin barely registering the cool air laden with mist.

The sky had a heavy, sullen greyness that warned of a summer storm. He ought to be used to the Oregon weather here by now, but he still found his spirits dipping after too many days in a row without sunshine.

"Sorry about that." He bit the words off and spat them out.

"We'll discuss it in a minute." Olivia's voice was low and even, not reacting to him. "How's Apollo's appetite?"

He forced his attention to the aging stallion. She'd found him at an auction where he'd been one bid away from going to a meat-packing plant. He was a patchy rib-sprung chestnut brindle with four high socks, a wide, white face, a sway back, and a balding tail. He'd likely been used for stud—no other reason to keep him uncut—but it wouldn't have been for his genetics.

According to his teeth, he was at least twenty years old. Olivia guessed he'd spent most of his years at a PMU farm, impregnating mares so their urine could be harvested for hormone treatment for menopausal women.

She opened the stall door and walked in. Apollo lifted his head from where he'd been dozing in the corner, resting his weight on one bony hip. "Hey there, old man. How you doing?"

If she wanted to wait, there was no point in rushing her. He forced his breathing to slow, inhaling deep into his lungs the way Quinn taught them in her yoga classes. Hudson had caught him off guard. Had Lana agreed to this? The thought of being checked out like this sent his blood pressure soaring.

"He's not gaining weight the way I'd hoped," Olivia commented. "What do you think?"

Gideon took a clipboard off the hook in the wall, blinked to make the words come into focus. "Uh, let's see. Tyler's been on stable duty this week. He's feeding him the way you asked, according to this."

"Good kid, Tyler," Olivia smiled. "When he's not spending his work time playing with kittens, at least."

"I heard that," called a voice from the far end of the

breezeway. Tyler came into view, backing out of the last stall with a wheelbarrow full of soiled straw.

"Come," Olivia said, waving him over. "Take a break."

"Have you seen them? They're so cute!"

"I have," Olivia said. "You're doing a great job with them."

Tyler, like all the kids who made it past the first few weeks at Sanctuary Ranch, adored Olivia. Worshipped her. She was the queen bee they wanted to serve, the head honcho, the big cheese, the mother they'd never had but always wanted in a home they'd never known to dream of.

As much as Gideon wanted to, he couldn't hate Lana. She was Blake's mother, and despite everything that had gone between them, he never doubted her love for the boy.

Hudson, however, was another story.

"What's up with Apollo, Honch?" Tyler wiped his face with his sleeve, leaving a streak of dust on his cheekbone.

"You giving him his rations?" She patted the big horse's rump, then made her way over his back, down his legs, to his neck and head, her hands measuring body condition, the roughness of his coat, feeling for injuries, bruises, and inflammation.

"Yes, Olivia," he said. He itemized the amounts of hay, grain, and supplements, as well as the amount of time Apollo was allowed out to graze. Gideon was impressed.

"He's getting daily access to the north pasture?" Olivia asked.

"The north pasture?" Tyler frowned. "I've been exercising him in the corral."

She frowned. "I specified the north pasture. It's for grazing, not exercise. No wonder he's not putting on weight."

The boy flushed scarlet. He shifted his weight from foot to foot. "I did what Gideon told me to do."

Gideon held out the clipboard. "You're supposed to ask if you've got questions."

His jaw tilted forward. He balled his fists, his knees

loose, his stance ready. "I did what you fuh"—he shot a quick look at Olivia—"freaking told me to do."

"Ease up, man," Gideon said. "Everyone makes mistakes." He suspected that Tyler had an undiagnosed learning disability. Kids like him learned quickly to cover their weakness, to avoid situations—like school—that would spotlight it. To come out swinging in the face of criticism.

"Thank you, Tyler. You can go back to mucking the stalls," Olivia said. "You're doing a fine job."

Gideon watched the boy escape back to the refuge of the storeroom, where the kittens were. "I should have caught that."

"No big deal. I'm sure Apollo will perk up once he starts getting more fresh air." She pursed her lips, then turned on her heel and left Apollo's stall. "Walk with me."

Gideon's senses went on alert, but he followed her, closing the stall door carefully behind him. You couldn't push Olivia. She'd say her piece when she was ready.

Olivia climbed through the fence and headed toward the slope overlooking the ocean. A footpath wound through it, and in nice weather, it made a pleasant hike to Sunset Bay, taking in blue water and fresh, salty air.

Today, the water reflected the dull, metallic grey of the clouds. The air felt weighted, as if iron filings hung from the stars, tiny, sharp, unseen, but ready to draw blood at the first movement.

"Sit." She patted the ground beside her.

He hunkered down, but kept several feet between them. Olivia was his employer, and as much as this place had saved him, he strove to remember that business was business. People like Daphne liked to call them family at Sanctuary Ranch, but that simply wasn't true.

She got right to the point. "Even before Hudson arrived, you've been distracted, Gideon. You're not yourself. Haylee's noticed it too. Tyler's not the only one avoiding you.

Duke stays out of your way. Sage says there's a black cloud around you."

"I barely even see Sage." He couldn't bear to watch the happily ever after going on with Haylee and her daughter and granddaughter. Haylee hadn't even wanted a relationship with the kid she'd given up for adoption. And she'd been afraid of the baby, Gideon had seen it.

He knew what that felt like.

"Sage makes sure of that. She doesn't want negative energy around Sal."

"I don't have negative energy." But hadn't Lana said something similar?

Olivia gave a little laugh. "You're quieter than usual. You disappear after meals with hardly a word to anyone. I think Jamie's worried, too. It was a lovely thing you did, buying the mustang. She'll be thrilled." She paused. "Did you two have a fight or something?"

Or something.

"No fight." Gideon looked out over the valley, as the first few spots of mist dampened his forehead. He didn't want to talk about Jamie. Even the horse might not be enough to get back in her good books, given how he'd been treating her lately.

But he couldn't tell Olivia about how, since that afternoon at Driftwood Creek, he hadn't been able to get the scent of her silky skin out of his mind, the feel of her lean flesh, how the only way to keep the wanting under control, to stay sane, was to avoid her and that was his own damn fault for letting himself get close to her in the first place.

How he had a choice to make: Jamie or Blake. And the choice could only ever be his son.

He cleared his throat. "I'm still dealing with those . . . family issues I mentioned. That's all."

Olivia lifted her face to the clouds, a soft smile on her

face, as if she loved nothing more than sitting outside on the damp ground. "Elliot Hudson's part of that."

"Yeah."

She had her eyes closed, and Gideon took the opportunity to observe her. Serenity emanated from her weathered skin, her sun-bleached hair, her wiry limbs, her calloused hands. He'd seen her in the mornings, walking hand-in-hand with Gayle before the day began, their love steady, tender, remarkable.

Enviable.

Her serenity was hard-won. Maybe he could learn from her.

He gritted his teeth, then exhaled and leaned forward, his elbows on his knees. "Hudson's marrying the woman I used to live with. We had . . . have . . . a son. They want . . . she wants her fiancé to adopt him. Wants me out."

"And you want?"

"Not that! They're the whole reason I moved here, but it's taken me almost two years to convince her, to convince myself, that I deserve a chance to know him."

Above them, a hawk circled, crying its mournful call.

"And Jamie?" Olivia asked.

He shook his head, picturing the slender length of her throat, how it moved when she laughed, how often he'd yearned to press his mouth to the hollow at the base. "That can't happen. It can't."

She made a small noise in the back of her throat. "Interesting choice of words."

"We're friends. I care for her. She knows that." He shifted his position on the rocky hillside. They'd both have damp spots on their jeans if they stayed much longer.

"You're a terrible liar, Gideon."

He forced himself not to move. She was always so damn perceptive. He had to allay those suspicions. Turning it around on her might be the only way to do it.

"Okay," he said. "She's twenty-six, with a rough past and a desperate craving for a happy ending. I'm almost thirty-five, with a record, an ex-lover, and a kid I hardly know."

He raised his eyebrows at her questioningly.

"Long odds, no matter how you cut it." Olivia sighed. "She knows about the boy?"

"Ah, hell." He closed his eyes and rubbed his hand over his face. "She does now. I should have told her. She overheard me talking to Lana. That's why she's pissed."

"Hurt," Olivia said. "Not pissed."

Despite being only a decade or so ahead of him, she spoke with the authority of a woman much older, with strength far exceeding mere age or experience. She cared, which made her dangerous.

He looked at the clouds building above them. The arrival of Lana's letter had torn away a carefully glued piece of his life, like a piece of plywood nailed over a broken window, ripped by a tsunami, letting the waters of destruction into the simple home he'd built for himself.

"I'm sorry, Olivia." He stood up, his boots slipping slightly on the grass. "I never meant to hurt anyone. Least of all Jamie. But I don't have a choice here."

She turned then and reached out. He took her hand and helped her to her feet, and when she was standing, she did not release his hand but squeezed it lightly, as if aware of the storm crashing inside him. "We always have choices. Whatever you need regarding your son, just ask. This is your home, Gideon. Okay?"

His throat closed. "Thanks," he said, hoarsely.

"Don't shut Jamie out. That's all I'm saying." Olivia nudged him with her shoulder and they began walking back along the path to the house. A coyote howled in the distance and others joined him, their eerie cry lifting the hair on his arms.

Gideon thought of the feral cat, devoured while her kittens lay mewling in hunger beneath the bales. Of Apollo, standing year after year alone in a stall, of the bland-faced steers in the finishing pasture, fat and happy, unaware of the fate that awaited them.

He thought of Jamie and her eternal optimism, how she believed the best of everyone, even him, even when all the evidence spoke against it.

"Hey." Olivia leaned over sideways and nudged him again. Her voice was devastatingly kind. "Don't shut any of us out, okay? Me, Gayle, Haylee, Daphne, Huck. And especially Jamie. We're here for you. Maybe, if you let us, we can help."

Chapter Thirteen

*Sometimes, enough's enough. Today, nothing is
   too much.*

—Jamie's horoscope

"James, can you help me?" Haylee waved at Jamie from
the doorway of the kennel room late the next afternoon.

Jamie paused, surprised. "I'm on my way to supper prep.
What do you need?"

"You'll see."

She'd been keeping out of Haylee's way, unsure of when
and how to tell her about Chaos and what she'd learned
about Roman Byers.

And then there was the Gideon situation. By now, everyone knew he was trying to get access to his son and that
Elliot Hudson's visit had been a reconnaissance mission,
looking for dirt to use against Gideon.

There had been a general upswell of support. In fact,
Daphne had offered to pay a return visit to Hudson, along
with her rolling pin. Everyone had laughed. Jamie had volunteered to join her.

She ached for Gideon as day after day went by and his

face remained closed and tight. Lana must be putting him through the wringer.

She followed Haylee inside, hoping her friend wouldn't bring up the subject. Jamie wasn't exactly an armored vehicle, when it came to her feelings, and if Haylee caught a whiff, she'd poke until it all came out. Jamie wasn't ready for that.

"Oy vey," she said, looking at the grooming stand. "Is there a dog under there somewhere?"

On the table, hunched and shivering, stood a mass of matted, dirty-white fur. A pair of eyes blinked warily out from the head end.

"Believe it or not." Haylee tugged the waterproof apron over her baby bump.

"Poor baby." Jamie put her hand out to let the poor animal sniff it.

"I feel like Michelangelo, except my David is a standard poodle and my clay is that disgusting mess you see." Haylee wrinkled her nose. "Can you talk to her while I get this gunk off her back end? Can Daphne do without you for a few minutes?"

Jamie looked toward the main house. She was on the schedule for the evening meal, but earlier, she'd heard the cook giving instructions to Sage.

"Daphne's got plenty of help." She didn't miss peeling vegetables one bit. But it rankled that she'd been so handily replaced. "What happened to your ban on rescues?"

"I know, I know." Haylee rolled her eyes and picked up her clippers. "But Aiden brought me this one. She was found by paramedics in the house of an elderly deceased woman. A bad situation, the woman was a hoarder, a recluse, no family, no friends. This wasn't the only dog. She may have been part of a puppy mill."

"Oh, you poor soul." Jamie found a spot on the dog's

muzzle that wasn't matted solid and gave it a rub. "How bad was it?"

A few years ago, she'd volunteered at a Seattle shelter that had been part of a puppy mill bust. Wire crates stacked on top of each other, the dogs on top suffering sore feet from the wire bottoms, the dogs in the lowest crates having excrement rained onto them.

"Besides this one," Haylee said, "they found a male chained to a tire in a shed outside, an older bitch who looked like she'd just weaned a litter and two dams with nursing puppies. Those are all staying with Janice while they recover."

Jamie put her face closer to the dog. "She's a sweetheart." The dog blinked and lowered her head, her ears flat in submission. "Can you do her face first, so she can see properly?"

"Good thinking."

A few swipes later, the crusted mats lay on the floor and they got their first good look at the creature's soft, friendly face.

"You're beautiful," Jamie said as the dog licked her hand with the delicacy of a princess. "At least, you will be."

She had lovely bone structure, a good strong muzzle, not harsh but not snipey either. Bright eyes showing intelligence and, amazingly, trust. She put her head against the dog's freshly shaven muzzle and made baby-talk noises to her. The dog wagged her clotted tail, her body lighting up at the affection.

"You do have a way of bringing out the best in them." Haylee picked up the dog's feet one after the other, watching for a reaction. The dog didn't resist, which was a good sign. She held her muzzle and examined her face. The skin beneath her eyes was red and angry looking. When she lifted the left ear, the dog yelped and pulled away.

Jamie turned away from the rotten, fermented smell that wafted up. "Man, that is one nasty ear."

When she looked back at Haylee, she noticed a greenish tinge to her cheeks. "You okay?"

Haylee nodded tightly.

"Want me to look at it?"

"Would you?" Haylee pressed the knuckles of her left hand against her nose. "Baby does not like that smell one bit."

Carefully, Jamie lifted the filthy, matted hair, seeking the canal hidden beneath it, testing the leather for warmth.

"Infected?" Haylee asked.

"Almost certainly." She checked the other side. "This one's better though, lots of wax and dirt but no pus."

"Okay, let's get this done fast so I can put my feet up. I'll do a rough clip first. It'll be hell on my blades, but it's the only way. Then, if you've got time, we can bathe her. I'll do a finish clip and scissor after that."

She turned on the clippers behind her back, to muffle the sound, but the dog darted and backed away, her long claws scratching against the rubber surface. Jamie held her tight enough to keep her from hurting herself, but loosely enough so she wouldn't panic.

"It's okay, baby," she crooned, breathing through her mouth. "What are we going to call her?"

"Sweetie, baby, lovey." Haylee held the dog's back leg, stroking and patting. "Doesn't matter. Once she looks like a poodle again, and Janice gives her a clean bill of health, we'll have no trouble finding her a forever home. They'll give her a name."

As the poodle quivered, a heavy mat hanging off her flank rocked back and forth, tugging on the thin skin. Jamie couldn't wait until it was off, but dreaded what they might find under it.

Fleas, ticks, ringworm. Hot spots. Maggots.

Jamie's heart went out to the creature quaking in front of them. So much untapped potential. Such a waste. "Or," she said, "we could train her to be another therapy dog. Jewel's getting older, you know. Maybe, um, you could train me and her to do what you and Jewel do."

It was going to hurt when she brought Chaos back. She'd gotten attached, as Gideon had predicted. And then what? She had so much love to give and no one to give it to.

"Maybe in spring." Haylee grunted and bent over, massaging her belly. "I can't even think about it right now."

A spark of disappointment flared, and Jamie waited for it to fade away. She shouldn't have hoped for a different response. She hugged the poodle, feeling the warm heartbeat against her arm. The dog would find a good home somewhere. Haylee would see to that.

It was probably for the best. Things were fine as they were. She had work she enjoyed. A place to lay her head. A small but growing bank account.

So why the emptiness? She wished she could go back to how she'd felt a year ago, before Hannibal the mastiff-cross had sparked her own ambition. Before she'd messed up things with Gideon. Before he'd decided to do the right thing with his son.

Life had seemed easy then. Uncomplicated.

Sometimes, now, when Jewel lumbered up to Haylee and butted that big head against her thigh, Jamie had to look away. And when Aiden looked at Haylee across the room, his eyes so full of love, Jamie felt like crying.

Sanctuary Ranch was changing.

They would get married eventually. They'd probably get their own place. She and Haylee would be work friends. They'd drift apart.

Daphne barely had time for her anymore, taken up as she was with training Sage and playing with little Sal, who stole everyone's heart with her drooling smile and dimples and multiple chins.

Worst of all was Gideon.

Even thinking about it made her feel about an inch tall. It

wasn't about her. It was about the boy. And children should always take priority, she knew that as well as anyone. She could never begrudge a child his father.

But it meant that Gideon, too, was moving on.

Moving on. Without her.

Story of her life.

All she wanted was for someone, anyone, to want her above all else.

No. Not anyone. Him. There was no one else for her.

"Speaking of rescues," Haylee said, "what's with the puppy in your cabin?"

Her gloomy thoughts vanished. She scrambled for an appropriate response. "Uh . . . oh. You, um, know about him?"

"I'm pregnant," Haylee said, "not blind or deaf. He doesn't like being left alone."

Jamie shrugged, as if mentioning it to Haylee had simply slipped her mind. "I found him in the woods the other day, lost. I didn't know what else to do so I brought him home while I figure out where he belongs. He's a sweet little thing."

Too sweet for a cranky old man who did not appreciate him.

"And you found his home?"

"It's a place not far from here, beyond the ridge. I've contacted the owner. The pup gets out a lot, apparently. The man is tired of chasing after him, so I thought I'd keep the pup for a few days, give him a chance to rest. Hopefully," she added casually, "I can teach him a few manners while I'm at it."

She held her breath, waiting for Haylee's response.

Her friend just lifted an eyebrow and continued moving the clipper over the poodle's back and sides. Roll after roll of once-white fur fell away, revealing skin patchy with filth, half-healed sores, and the telltale reddish flecks of flea dirt.

"Why didn't you tell me? I've got room in the kennel."

The dog flinched and Jamie loosened her grip. "Really?"

Haylee stopped. A large clump of dirt-filled hair fell onto the table. The smell was nauseating. "Sure. Why not?"

Jamie leaned over the dog, keeping her voice even so as not to distress the animal, but determined to look Haylee in the eye. "Because you told me you don't want me working with the dogs without you. Because I want to train him. Because I'm not entirely sure what the owner situation is and I'm not taking him back until I am."

The poodle whined and pulled backwards against the grooming leash. "Sorry, honey-girl," Jamie murmured. "I'm not mad at you."

"Wow," Haylee said, smoothing the naked skin on the animal's back. "Let's give her a break. What's going on, Jamie?"

The dog licked Jamie's chin. Poor thing looked half-butchered, a grotesque caricature of herself.

"Sorry, Haylee," she said abruptly. "I've got a lot on my mind."

"Gideon?" Haylee guessed.

And there it was. Jamie sucked in a breath and turned her head so Haylee wouldn't see her face. She had known this would happen and was helpless to stop it, helpless in the face of the relief at sharing what had been bottled up inside of her. "He's got a kid, Haylee. A little boy. How could he have this big secret, all this time, and not tell me?"

Tears threatened. She shook her head and squeezed her eyes until they receded.

"He blew it, big time," Haylee agreed, picking a wisp of hair off her nose. "I guess this complicates things between the two of you."

"I wouldn't know." Jamie felt herself flush. She wanted to be a bigger person, but hey, what are friends for but to see you at your smallest and pettiest? "Why would I? It doesn't concern me. It's none of my business, in fact."

The bitterness in her voice embarrassed her. That's not who she was. Before Haylee could respond, Jamie continued. "Pretend I didn't say that, okay? We're kind of on the outs, and I'm a little raw about it. I thought we were closer than we are, that's all. I know he's going through a lot right now. I'm trying to give him space. But you know me."

Haylee's expression softened. "I know your heart."

Heat pressed against the inside of Jamie's eyes. She swallowed. "I also may have tap-danced over a boundary or two. Now he's avoiding me."

Haylee lifted an eyebrow. "How much tap-dancing?"

Jamie put her head in her hand. "That day in the woods. I found Chaos—that's the puppy—in a pool, drowning, or so I thought. I was taking my jeans off and I fell in, like a total dweeb. Gideon happened on the scene right then and helped pull me out. I may have made a suggestive comment. Seizing the moment, so to speak." She sighed, recalling his grip on her arms, the heat in his eyes when he'd noticed the transparency of her shirt. "I smelled his hair, Haylee. I almost kissed him. I think I moaned. He backed off like I was radioactive. In fact, we clonked heads. I got a nosebleed. Not exactly a shining romantic moment."

Haylee walked to Jamie's side of the grooming table and enveloped her in as big a hug as she could, with the baby between them. "I'm sorry."

"Oh, Haylee," Jamie wailed. "I'm in trouble here, aren't I?"

"Yes, James, I'd say you are. Thank goodness you're tough as nails. If anyone can get through his thick skull, it's you."

She held Jamie back and leveled a look at her. "But he's in a crazy place, as I know all too well. He's about to meet a boy who doesn't know him, who may or may not have preconceived ideas put there by a woman who'd rather write Gideon out of her kid's life. He's probably scared shitless that he's going to do something wrong, say something wrong, scare the kid, forget to feed him, who knows? It's not logical. But I'll tell you this much. What he does not need is space, especially not from you."

How she wanted to believe that. "I'm afraid I've destroyed our friendship," she whispered.

"You haven't," Haylee replied promptly. "He's an idiot. I've seen you two together. There's something more there, whether he's willing to admit it or not. I'd have been lost without all of you. Gideon needs that same support now from the people who care about him. And I think you head up that list, don't you?"

Jamie managed a wobbly smile. "Thanks, Haylee."

"I'm sorry I've been so preoccupied," Haylee said. "I haven't been a very good friend."

"Don't say that. You're having a baby. You should be preoccupied." Guilt twisted her gut. "But since we're having a bonding moment, I should tell you something else. About the pup."

"Jamie." Haylee's voice was a warning. "What did you do?"

"I had a bad feeling, okay? So I did a bit of light . . . trespassing."

Haylee sagged. "Tell me you didn't break into his house."

She met Haylee's eyes. "I didn't break into his house."

It was the truth. Nothing broke.

The half-shaved poodle danced sideways, looking between the two of them, anxiety in her eyes. Jamie pulled her close, like a shield.

Haylee swept her hand across the table, sending filth and matted hair into the trash can. "You represent Sanctuary Ranch, Jamie. You can't go off like a loaded gun whenever you think someone's not looking after their dog exactly the way you think they should."

"I know that." It was a struggle to keep her voice calm. "But the situation is complicated. I met the owner yesterday. His name is Roman Byers. He's an angry man. And, I think, a sick one."

"What do you mean, sick?"

She thought about how tightly he'd gripped the arm of his chair, the grey cast to his complexion. Those were big-time painkillers on the top of the fridge. The pictures on the wall that reminded her of something she couldn't put her finger on.

"I'm not sure," she went on. "But he's not strong enough to manage a puppy and he seems resentful about it. He's got an old dog who won't last the winter. Apparently his son gave him Chaos as a replacement."

Haylee sighed and picked up her clippers again. "That's why you want to train him."

It wasn't a question. Jamie's heart skittered. "With your guidance, of course."

Haylee ran the clipper over the dog's flank, wincing when the blade caught in the chunk of debris matted into the hair. "I'm tired, James. Let's get this poor thing finished before Daphne starts yelling for you. We'll talk about this later."

Chapter Fourteen

*Although the Leo Full Moon is a good time to
examine your desires, Mars clouds your vision
with audacity.*

—Jamie's horoscope

They had twelve riders for the Sunday afternoon ride, a
mixed group of novice and intermediate skill levels,
from the twelve-year-old who rode regularly at home, to
her sixty-five-year-old grandfather who hadn't ridden in
decades.

Haylee had instructed Jamie to take the lead today, with
Gideon in the middle and herself bringing up the rear. Gideon
had tried to get Huck to fill in for him, but Haylee had put
the kibosh on that. She wiggled her eyebrows and gestured
for Jamie to address the group.

"Hey, Gideon." Jamie walked past him, took her place in
the center of the group, and clapped her hands to get their
attention, hoping she looked authoritative and leader-like.
Try and avoid me now, she thought.

"We've got a great ride planned for you today." She made
the necessary introductions and said a few words about
Sanctuary Ranch.

Haylee stood beside her, her baby bump visible beneath her yoga pants and stretchy tank top. Instead of her usual Stetson, she wore a baseball cap, with her curly blond ponytail stuck through the back opening, but an oversize button-down shirt and worn cowboy boots added the western flair.

"Aren't you too pregnant to ride?" one of the women asked, her eyes on Haylee's midsection.

Haylee gave her practiced reply. "In a normal, healthy pregnancy, it's no riskier than any other exercise. I have a bomb-proof horse, and I never ride alone."

The woman hesitated. "I guess we'll just be walking, then?"

"I'll just be walking," Haylee assured her. "Jamie and Gideon will have the rest of you trotting and galloping until you beg for mercy."

The woman smiled, relieved.

Jamie and Gideon.

She sighed. Their names went so well together.

What a lovesick calf.

She shook herself. Better get started before the drooling set in. Or Gideon found a way to beg off.

"Now," she addressed the group, launching into her usual spiel, "we're going to do a beautiful loop today. The first hour will take us first deep into the famous Oregon forest. Then we'll circle down to our beach access. The sand is packed hard there, so those of you who want to run will have your chance. After that, we head up through the fields that parallel the road and will be back at the ranch in time for Daphne's beef roast, garlic mashed potatoes, and Yorkshire pudding. How does that sound?"

A cheer rose up from the group.

"Right on." Jamie put her fist in the air. "Remember,

there are no washrooms on the trail, so go now or forever hold your pee."

The old joke tickled new ears as if she'd just come up with it. A couple of women made for the stable bathrooms, and Jamie led the rest into the corral where their horses were waiting, their lead ropes tied loosely to the top rails, tacked up and ready to go.

While Gideon helped the older gentleman adjust his stirrups, Jamie went to the tack room to replace an extra lead rope and get her nerves under control. This would be the most time she'd spent around him since she'd learned about his ex-wife and son.

Ex-not-legally-married, she reminded herself.

Whatever her status, she'd had a child with Gideon. She had far greater claim on him than Jamie could ever hope for.

"Hey."

She jumped as Gideon came up behind her, and felt her face heat up. "Sheesh, buddy, you might want to give a girl warning. Good thing it's me and not Haylee. She'd have wet herself." She tossed the lead rope over the hook, then adjusted the lengths so that they were hanging exactly even on both sides.

"Everything okay?"

He stood in the doorway and, backlit by sunshine, she couldn't see his expression, just the solid bulk of him.

"Of course, why wouldn't it be? It's just a trail ride. I haven't led before, but come on, how hard is it? Nash knows where he's going, and the rest of the horses will follow him. All I have to do is talk, and that's not generally a problem for me, so I'm good to go."

She held on to both ends of the lead rope with shaking hands, trying to hold back the words knocking against her teeth. Until this very second, she hadn't realized that she was, in fact, angry at Gideon.

"I meant . . ." Gideon glanced around to make sure no one was in earshot. "I noticed the puppy's still here. What happened to you taking him back?"

She tightened her grip on the braided leather. "What business is it of yours?"

"I thought—" He stopped. "Never mind. You're right. I'm sure you've thought it through."

"I have, actually. I met the owner. He's a total crab-ass, but he's more than happy to let me teach his puppy a few manners. Haylee knows, in case you're thinking it's still a big secret. Not everyone hides things."

"Gotcha." He pressed his lips together and turned to leave. "Just wanted to check in. Haven't seen you much lately."

She dropped the rope and whirled on him. "Whose fault is that? I've been here. You're like a ghost. And since you ask, I'm pissed off about that. You're dealing with this whole huge part of your life I never knew about, and I have no idea if you're okay or if you're planning to disappear or what." She clenched her fists, but the words kept coming. "I'm worried about you, Gideon! But it's none of my business. So, that's me. How are you?"

He took off his hat and scrubbed at his forehead, his wide shoulder brushing against the rough door frame. Shadows danced across the planes of his face, deepening the lines around his face and darkening the skin beneath his eyes. He looked tired, she realized. Tired and alone and discouraged.

"I'm sorry." She screwed up her face. "I shouldn't have gone off on you."

"No, I'm sorry," he said. "I deserved that."

His voice was hollow, like an echo bouncing off an empty canyon. She couldn't help herself. She walked forward and put her arms around him, pressing her ear against the plaid shoulder. "I just want to help. That's all. No pressure."

They'd hugged before. It shouldn't be weird. But instantly, the room and the horses and the people outside disappeared. The feel of him against her was like a hot bath on a cold day, like something you could sink into and stay in for hours. She pressed her face against his shoulder, breathing in the faintest whiff of seaweed and driftwood. He should stink of sweat or horseflesh or manure, but no. He had to smell awesome.

"Mmm."

She froze. *Oh, no, not again.*

His arms stiffened. Carefully, he placed his hands on her upper arms, pushed her away, and took a step back.

"We should get back to the group."

She stumbled backwards. "Of course. Right. God, I'm an idiot."

"Jamie, don't." He leaned down, his voice low and private. "This is why I've been keeping my distance. I don't want to hurt you. I know you have . . . feelings."

"Feelings, schmeelings. We're friends. What about that? You thought you'd pretend that away? Let it die of neglect?" She tried to keep her voice down, but the hurt he hadn't meant to inflict was bubbling up like lava. "That's not like you. Or maybe it is. Apparently we're just casual acquaintances, so what do I know?"

He reached for her, then let his arm fall away. "You know better than that."

"Do I? Convince me. Because the evidence isn't leaning in your direction."

He exhaled in a short, sharp huff. "I care about you. Very much. But I don't need more complications right now."

"And that's what I am? A complication? How lovely. You should write greeting cards. 'Roses are red, violets are blue, you're a complication to me, but I care about you. Very much."

"Come on, Jamie. Quit putting words in my mouth."

"Well, what else am I supposed to think? Since you went into lock-down mode."

"This isn't the time, Jamie." He glanced around them again, his lips tight.

"Right. It's never the time. I get it."

She pushed past him, to go back to the corral, but he captured her arm.

"I have a lot on my mind. It's not about you."

Stung, she shook him off. "I know that! I don't understand why you're so darn determined to deal with this on your own. So you have a gnarly ex situation. I don't care. Are you going to live out your life in an emotional cave, wearing a hair shirt and whip marks? Give it a rest, Gideon."

She was breathing hard and wanted to smack him. For a long moment, he watched her, a small frown creasing his forehead, as if she was uncharted territory he had to navigate whether he wanted to or not. Then he shook his head, touched her cheek with his knuckle, and smiled at her.

"Ah, James," he said softly. "Whatever would I do without you? Come on. They're waiting for us."

Her anger evaporated, and in its place came a raw sadness that made her want to put heels to Nash's sides and run into the wind until they were both hot and heaving.

Gideon wanted boundaries, damn him. Well, fine. She could do boundaries. She didn't want to, but she could.

If boundaries were what it took to keep him in her life, she'd fucking live on the fence between them. She'd talk over it, yell over it, eat, drink, sleep on it, if necessary.

Because it was killing her to see him so alone.

She stormed out of the tack room, leaped onto Nash's back, and circled around to the group. "Everyone ready? Watch your knees at the gate."

Haylee, who was using the mounting block to swing herself into the saddle, gestured for Jamie to head out.

Jamie turned her attention to the group and, for the next hour, was successfully distracted by their enthusiasm. There was plenty of conversation and questions to answer as she pointed out the natural beauty of the conifers and deciduous trees populating the hills below Roman Byers's place.

Don't think about Gideon. She was aware of him, caught sight of him occasionally in her peripheral vision, riding three or four horses behind her. But she wasn't thinking about him.

Right. Like that was possible.

But she did her best.

She led the group on her favorite trail and suddenly she realized they were almost at the creek and the pool where she'd met Sadie and Chaos.

The pool, where she'd almost kissed Gideon.

She shuddered. "Let's keep moving," she called to the group, pointing ahead of her. "Lots to see, still."

"But it's so pretty here," one of the riders responded. "Can we stop for pictures?"

Jamie turned in the saddle to look at Haylee, shaking her head, hoping she'd understand the silent but not-so-subtle message.

Nope.

"Why not?" Haylee called back. "The horses could use a drink. And I could sure use a stretch."

Without looking at Gideon, Jamie nudged Nash to the far side of the clearing and waited, without leaving the saddle. Poised for a quick getaway, she thought.

Several riders dismounted, their cell phones out for pictures.

"It's so romantic," said the silver-haired woman, who rode as part of a challenge following a hip replacement. "Does anyone ever swim here?"

"I don't know." Haylee looked at Jamie with wide, inno-cent eyes. "Jamie? Have you gone swimming here?"

She glanced at Gideon, who wasn't doing a very good job of hiding his smile. "Not by choice. It's a glacier-fed stream. I recommend enjoying it from land."

"You fell in?" The twelve-year-old laughed. "That's awesome!"

Jamie felt all the eyes of the group on her. She was used to being embarrassed, but today, as the trail leader, she ought to have their respect.

"Not at all," Gideon said. "She was rescuing someone."

Now all eyes swiveled to him. He sat tall but relaxed in the saddle, as if he had been born to ride. One arm rested along his lean thigh and his gaze met hers, as if no one else was around.

She shook her head slightly, and casually drew a finger across her throat, hoping he'd get the message.

"Rescuing who?" asked the girl.

"What happened?"

"Tell us the story!"

Jamie held up her hand. "There was no rescue. I slipped—"

"She was rescuing a puppy," Gideon interrupted.

A collective gasp went up. Haylee turned to look at Jamie, her eyebrows raised in amused understanding.

"A puppy!" the young girl said. "You're a hero!"

"Hardly," Jamie replied. "He faked me out, the little rotter. He was fine."

"Then Gideon rescued you?" said the girl's grandfather.

"There was no rescue!" Jamie looked to Gideon for backup, but he just smiled.

"She was fine. I helped her out, that's all." He appeared to be enjoying the story as much as anyone. "Though there was a bear in the area at the time."

"So romantic!" said the silver-haired rider, ignoring

Jamie's contribution to the conversation. "What happened then?"

"My lips are sealed." Gideon looked skyward. "I'm a gentleman."

"Did you kiss her? Did she kiss you? What a perfect meet-cute." The woman put one palm over her heart and sighed with delight.

"There was no rescue, no kiss, no meet-cute, and definitely no gentleman." Jamie's face felt like it was on fire.

Damn that Gideon. What a time for his sense of humor to finally surface. She hoped he didn't continue on to the nose-bleed part of the tale.

But it appeared he was ready to take pity on her. "Folks," Gideon said, "Jamie's got a lot more to show you while you ponder the romance of Driftwood Creek, and what may, or may not, have taken place here. Jamie?"

He winked, then laid his reins across Rosie's neck and made way for her to lead the group out.

"I'll get you for this," she muttered as she passed by him.

He guffawed, and her annoyance melted. It was so good to hear him laugh.

Chapter Fifteen

A mixed bag of aspects. Stay on your toes.

—Gideon's horoscope

At three o'clock in the afternoon, Gideon leaned over the small mirror and ran his electric razor over his cheeks and jaw. Aside from the rooms in the main house, accommodations at Sanctuary Ranch ranged from studio units with Murphy beds to two-story cabins with three bedrooms and full kitchens. Gideon's was a small one-bedroom with a hot plate, fridge, and microwave. It was all he needed, and the austerity pleased him.

Today, it seemed cramped and inadequate.

He rubbed his jaw, noting the dark circles under his eyes. He'd already shaved that morning, but Lana had always complained about how quickly his whiskers returned. He didn't care about impressing her for his own sake; but he'd do anything to predispose her to let him see Blake.

He knew already that the life he led now was not going to work in his favor.

Before he'd gone to prison, he'd set her up for life, caring only that she was secure and that his mistake wouldn't jeopardize her future or that of their unborn child. He couldn't see past the four bleak years yawning ahead of him and trusted her to look after everything so that, when he got out, he'd be able to fold time over itself and step back into his life as if nothing had changed.

Then, before the echo of locked steel doors had stopped ringing in his ears, she'd ended it with him.

He'd gotten over losing Lana. He couldn't care less about the money. But his son mattered.

Now, as Gideon looked around his sparsely furnished cabin, he regretted his lack of material possessions. The boy would need a bedroom, a bathtub, a place to keep his toys, his clothes.

He put on a fresh shirt, then looked around his place, trying to see it as she would. Generic sofa and coffee table. Light-toned wood dining table and two straight-backed chairs. Framed acrylic prints of ocean scenes on the walls.

He rinsed his coffee mug in the sink, dried it, and put it in the small cupboard beside the window. Picked up a throw cushion, moved it to the other side of the couch. Moved it back.

"Stop it," he muttered to himself. She'd be here in ten minutes. He might as well head up to the main house and wait on the porch, where at least the background sounds of Daphne and Sage in the kitchen and Olivia in the office could lend some normalcy to the occasion.

Maybe he should have scheduled their first meeting on neutral ground, a coffee shop in town perhaps.

But he'd wanted home advantage, still angry that she'd sent Elliot Hudson to suss him out. He couldn't believe she'd grown so distrusting, so petty. Was that Hudson's doing?

Gideon had made it clear to Lana that he would deal with her alone.

He hoped that Lana would be impressed by the fresh wide-open space, the wholesomeness of the ranch environment, and how friendly and nurturing the people here were. Also, it was Jamie's afternoon working in town.

Five minutes passed. Ten. Fifteen.

Little Sal wailed from a back corner of the house. Daphne yelled something at Sage, who yelled something distinctly unwholesome back. Footsteps sounded, followed by the slamming of pots and pans.

When twenty minutes had passed after the agreed-upon time of their meeting and there was still no sign of her, he got up and strode to the stables. He was going to lose his mind.

As distracted as he was, he wasn't watching where he was going and almost crashed into Jamie, coming around the side of the kennel house with an enormous bag of dog food slung over her shoulder.

"What are you doing here?" The smell of coconut and wet dog told him she'd been working in the grooming room.

"Whoa!" She sidestepped him, neatly shifting the bag to her other shoulder. "Nice to see you, too."

"I mean," he backpedalled, "isn't this your day teaching for the parks board?"

"Class got cancelled." She plopped the bag at her feet and narrowed her eyes. "What's wrong?"

He glanced toward the driveway. "Nothing." Just as well Lana was late. He did not want to deal with her with Jamie around.

"Don't bullshit a bullshitter. Hey. What's with the baby face?" Jamie reached out and stroked his chin with her thumb. "Did you shave for a second time today? Wait. Do you have a *date*?"

He jerked away. Her casual touch suggested a closeness he couldn't allow, and the visceral reaction to the warmth of her fingers on his face made him snap, "Don't be ridiculous."

The dogs in the kennel started barking, followed by the

low growl of an engine. Moments later, a sleek, black Audi appeared on the driveway.

Gideon's stomach tightened. He shaded his eyes. Definitely her.

Jamie turned to follow his gaze. "Who's that?"

"Nobody. Don't worry about it."

"Really?" Jamie trotted behind him. "Let me see. You're all in a snit about something. A woman in a hot car shows up and you run over to her like she's . . . oh."

The first thing Gideon saw of the woman he'd almost married were her shoes as she stepped out of the vehicle. Narrow-strapped, open-toed heels, three inches at least. Nylon-clad legs appeared, followed by a skinny grey skirt that hiked up to reveal her shapely knees. White blouse, a multicolored scarf. Painted nails.

So much for a tour of the ranch. He was painfully aware of Jamie behind him, watching closely, no doubt evaluating his former lover and creating a narrative in her head about the two of them that had little to do with reality.

He strode up to Lana, his mouth dry. She'd visited him exactly three times in prison. She hadn't accepted his calls or responded to his letters. When he had finally heard from her, it had been through her lawyer.

"Lana," he said, holding out his hand. His voice was full of gravel.

She glanced down at it, as if surprised that he'd offer the greeting, then took it and shook, once.

"Gideon."

A diamond engagement ring sparkled on her left hand. She stepped back and gave her head a little shake, making her hair shift and settle softly around her face. It was shorter now than when they'd been together. He used to like her hair.

Now, it was someone else's hair, like something from a salon magazine.

An awkward silence settled over them. She tugged her big bag against her side, like a shield.

"So. Elliot said you were a cowboy now." Lana glanced around, her expression carefully neutral. "I never would have guessed you'd end up on a farm again."

Sanctuary Ranch was nothing at all like the gardening business his parents had run.

Gideon struggled to find something to say that wouldn't be inflammatory. He could hardly reconcile the brittle woman in front of him with the carefree girl he'd once thought he loved. She'd gotten the wealth she'd always sought, but single motherhood had been the price. He guessed that there was no amount of money that would ease the task of raising a child alone.

Guilt chewed at his stomach lining. He'd done that to her. She'd once shone with a bright, fun-loving energy, not unlike Jamie, he realized, with a start.

Boots clattered over the stones in the yard. "Welcome to Sanctuary Ranch." Jamie walked up to Lana and stuck out her hand. "Jamie Vaughn. I'm a friend of Gideon's. I'm guessing you're Lana. The ex."

Lana looked down at Jamie's hand. "Yes," she said.

Jamie's choppy bangs flopped around her eyes as she pumped Lana's arm. He'd seen her in her cottage with a pair of dog-grooming scissors once, snipping the spiky strands until they stood up when she ran her hands through them, setting off her flashing eyes and delicate features.

Jamie stepped back alongside Gideon and shoved both hands into the back pockets of her jeans.

He hadn't wanted her there, but now her presence buoyed him. "I'd like to start by showing you what Blake will be exposed to," he told Lana. "We've got dogs, cats, horses, cows, chickens. Or we can go to the main house first and I'll introduce you to the group."

"Don't forget the new kittens," Jamie added. "You should see Gideon bottle-feed them. It's adorable."

"I'm sure." Lana cut her eyes sideways at Jamie, then took a step closer to Gideon. "Is there somewhere private we can talk?"

Her tone of voice didn't bode well for the conversation.

"Let's go to the stables. It's pretty private there." Jamie crossed her arms and widened her stance. "Oh, don't worry about me. I'm the soul of discretion. If you want to talk about ancient history, your relationship, your breakup, his time in prison, how you're keeping him from seeing his son, pretend I'm not here." She made a lock-and-key motion at her lips. "I'm completely trustworthy. Also, he doesn't like to admit it, says it makes him feel like a rock star, but I'm Gideon's bodyguard. So, you're stuck with me."

She stuck her hips forward and swayed back and forth, as if she were a mean three-hundred-pound bouncer and not a willow-thin dog trainer who didn't know what she was getting into.

"Jamie." Her loyalty touched him deeply, but it wasn't helping.

"Okay, fine." She huffed, put her hands up, palms out. "I'll be around. You need me, just holler. Nice to meet you, Laura."

Lana's nostrils flared. "Lana. Yeah. You, too."

Jamie strode toward the stables, watching them out of the corner of her eye until she rounded the corner.

He turned to this woman he barely recognized now, his chest hot. "We've been over this. You can't change your mind now."

"When it comes to my son's well-being, I have to be one-hundred-percent certain before I agree." She glanced at Jamie's retreating figure. "And I'm not."

He shook his head, balling his fists at his side. She

couldn't do this. She couldn't go back on her word, set out new conditions after they'd already agreed.

But if the tables were reversed, wouldn't he do the same? Lana didn't know him anymore. She was simply looking out for Blake.

He inhaled slowly, quietly, willing himself to stay calm, rather than say anything that would further her distrust.

"Of course." He turned toward his cabin. "We can talk in my quarters."

He walked ahead, just fast enough to stay ahead of her, not so fast as to appear rude. A scuffling sound made him turn around.

"Damn it," Lana muttered, picking her way over the rugged surface. "These shoes were expensive."

Gideon offered his arm. "Need help?"

She straightened and lifted her head. "I'm fine. Let's get this over with."

He opened the door to his cabin and gestured for her to enter first. She ducked her head, though the doorway was plenty tall.

"Relax, Lana. Have a seat. You're in luck, I just fumigated. You want coffee?"

"No. Thank you."

"Well, I'm making a pot, if you change your mind."

He busied himself in the tiny galley kitchen, regretting his decision now to meet on his turf. This meeting, which should have been merely pro forma, had a bad feeling about it.

"I won't be here long." She looked at the couch as if uncertain whether he'd been joking or not, then lowered herself to perch on the front edge of the cushions. "This is very . . . rustic. But I suppose it's palatial compared to prison."

Gideon poured water into the top of his coffeemaker, cursing as some splashed over the edge and dripped to the floor.

"It wasn't super-max, Lana. I saw no cage matches, became no one's bitch, joined no gangs."

He'd paid his debt to society with a few years of his life, and now, yes, the freedom to come and go as he pleased was indeed a luxury he would never again take for granted.

"Blake is very innocent." Lana spoke abruptly, without looking at him. "I don't want him exposed to anything . . . disturbing."

The coffeemaker gurgled and spat behind him. "Meaning what? You think I'll be a scarring influence on him?"

She turned her head toward the window, angling her body away from him, tugging the tote to her hip again.

He followed her gaze. Jamie and Tyler were walking across the yard toward the stables, kicking stones back and forth to each other.

"Having an ex-con for a father is one thing. Being out here with all these . . . other people."

"This is a good place, Lana. These are good people."

She swiveled back and met his gaze. "No, Gideon. They're not. Elliot did background checks. Do you really know the people you're working with here? How can I allow my son to visit a place that employs people like . . ."

Steam sizzled beneath the pot. "People like me, Lana? Is that what you mean?"

She stood up. "Yes, Gideon. You're not the only ex-con here, did you know that? You probably thought you were special—well, you're not. This place is crawling with felons, people with mental illnesses, street kids picked up for drugs, homelessness—"

"Careful, Lana. These are my friends you're talking about."

He pulled the coffeepot off before it was quite finished, the last few drips hissing on the hot plate. He poured two cups, added the dash of milk he guessed she still took, and set it in front of her, willing his hands not to shake, willing himself to stay calm, to not let her bait him into saying something he'd regret.

She was looking for a fight.

She wasn't going to get one.

"We cared about each other once, Lana. Now we care about Blake. I don't want this to get ugly. But make no mistake, I will be seeing my son here, at my home." He sat down across from her. "When shall we begin?"

Chapter Sixteen

*Mars–Uranus squares go hand-in-hand with
mishaps, so take extra precautions today.*

—Jamie's horoscope

Jamie was hosing down the large dog runs when she saw
Haylee and Olivia heading her way. She lifted her head
and turned off the hose.

"Hey, guys, come on in, the water's freezing and smells
like shit." Then she saw their expression. "Whoa, what's
wrong? Is it Gideon?"

Ever since his ex had pulled up in her fancy car, Jamie
had been on edge. He'd taken her to his cabin, to hash out
the details of Blake's first visit, and they'd been there a long
time. Cleaning the runs at least gave her something to do.

She hung the hose up next to the tap and wiped her hands
on a towel. Then she took off her hat, ruffled her hand through
her hair a few times, and replaced it. She probably looked
like a drowned rat from the humidity in the enclosed area.

"It's not Gideon," Olivia said.

"You know that incident on the beach a few weeks ago?"
Haylee asked, rubbing her belly.

"Yeah? What about it?" Jamie took off her hat again and
smacked it against her jeans, then grabbed a bottle of water

from where it lay with her jacket and took a swig. She wiped her mouth with the back of her hand. "Is someone giving me a medal?"

She liked that Gideon had been there to witness her haul those kids out of the way of the wave. She didn't need his approval or his validation, but his support had been most welcome, especially after getting yelled at by that crazy mother.

"I'm afraid not," Olivia said.

There was a sympathetic tone in her voice that Jamie didn't like. "What?" She looked between them. "Oh, God. It's the crazy mother, isn't it? She was mad because she didn't realize the danger. She thought I was manhandling her kids for no reason. But there were witnesses. You can talk to the other parents who were on the beach—I've got the sign-in sheet. Some of them saw what happened, and they know those kids would have been hurt if I hadn't grabbed them. That mother was spouting off, but I thought she was just scared. And embarrassed, because she wasn't watching her kids properly and I made her look bad. You should talk to her husband. He seemed to appreciate the situation."

Olivia nodded. "Jamie, you have good instincts, and I've no doubt you did what you needed to do. Just tell me again what happened? Okay?"

Jamie took a deep breath. "I was about to leave with Gideon, after my 'Exploring Tide Pools' talk for the nature conservancy. There was a family out there, not part of my group, though they should have been because they knew dick-all about ocean safety. Mom's oblivious, Dad's fiddling with his cell phone video, neither of them watching the kids." She got angry all over again thinking about the danger they'd unwittingly put their children in.

She forced herself to stay calm. Olivia wanted the facts, not her opinion. "Two little ones, preschoolers, I guess. I saw a nasty rip heading in, the kind that would have taken the kids for quite the tumble, so I ran down and grabbed them before it could. Mom pitched a fit, but Dad seemed to realize that the kids could have been hurt."

Haylee nodded. "Unfortunately, the mother says the little girl's arm was dislocated when you lifted her up."

Jamie snapped her head up so fast she tweaked her neck. "What?"

"I just took the call now," Olivia said. "We're going to get Aiden to check into the hospital records, but we wanted to get your side of the story, first."

Her soft, smooth voice usually calmed Jamie's spiky nerves, but this time, it wasn't enough to counteract the message.

She rubbed her neck, then took a step backward, feeling behind her for the barn wall, feeling the ground tilt beneath her feet. "I dislocated her arm?" Her hip hit the rough wood with a thud. "Oh my God. I had no idea. Is she okay?"

This was horrible. The poor little girl. Jamie clutched one arm across her stomach and put the opposite hand against her mouth. "I have to go see her, to apologize. Is she still in the hospital?" She walked a few steps to the left, then a few more to the right. Should she bring her something? A toy? A stuffed animal? They sold stuff like that at the hospital, didn't they?

Haylee took hold of her sleeve. "Jamie, stop. It's no big deal and certainly better than drowning. We just needed to know if what the mother claims jives with what you remember?"

Jamie squeezed her eyes shut for a moment. Cold salt water pounding on her back, the feeling of those little bones in one hand, the boy's jacket in the other, hauling them up onto higher ground and dumping them at their parents' feet like a couple of sacks of feed. The bitter taste of adrenaline and seawater. Yelling, screaming, crying.

"Yeah." She swallowed. "The kid was howling when I

left, but I thought it was because she was scared. The mom was yelling at me, the kid was wailing. The dad and the little boy were fine, so I just thought . . . Oh God, this is awful."

Olivia took hold of Jamie's upper arms and gave her a light shake. "Jamie. Look at me. You did the right thing. Those kids would have been hurt far worse without you. Okay?"

She sucked in a shuddering breath. She didn't know that children's arms could be yanked out of joint that easily. She thought of how badly Gideon wanted to meet Blake at Sanctuary Ranch.

How much she wanted to be part of that.

And how little it would take for Lana to deny him.

Gideon heard the yelling and ran out of the stables to see Jamie chasing after Chaos. The little escape artist had gotten out of the training yard.

He ran at an angle, hoping to cut off the dog before he slipped under the main fence into the pasture. Olivia had a new rescue horse in there, fresh from a PMU farm, and a wild puppy would certainly spook her.

The laughter he'd heard from Jamie a moment ago stopped abruptly. The look on her face told him she recognized her mistake.

She muttered a curse, then yelled over her shoulder.

"Sorry, Haylee. I've got him. I'll get him. Chaos!"

Gideon ran faster. The horses had stopped grazing to look. The new mare, a white-faced bay, was already twitching, waiting for the herd to react.

"Wrong way, pup," he called, making his way between the dog and the horses. "Back off, go home!"

Rosie, usually a calm presence and comfortable with dogs, tossed her head and pranced backward. That was all the new mare needed. She wheeled around, and in a flash of hooves and dust, was off, sending the herd into a panic.

The thunderous noise got through to the puppy as the yelling hadn't, and he slowed his pace long enough for Jamie to head him off. He still evaded her grasp, but at least he moved away from the corral.

Poor Jamie. She was trying so hard to impress Haylee.

The horses whinnied and pounded the earth, moving like a flock of seabirds over the brown grass, a froth of flickering manes and tails.

He kept running until he was in the center of the corral, then stopped. If he was lucky, Rosie would see him and realize there was no danger. Once she settled, the rest would follow suit, though they would be nervous and restless for hours and the new mare might be sensitized to dogs in the future.

A clear, high-pitched sound split the air. All heads whipped toward Haylee, who held a whistle in her mouth. The second Chaos looked at her, she clicked the training device.

"Come, Chaos," she called, her voice calm and authoritative.

The pup slowed, changed direction, then went pelting back to the training yard and Haylee—and the treat he knew would be waiting.

Jamie jogged to a halt and as she watched Haylee with the pup, the smile faded from her face. She looked toward Gideon and her shoulders fell. Then she bent to pick up the leash the pup had dropped, and walked back to the kennel house.

"Sorry, Haylee," he heard her say.

The horses had slowed their mad dash. Rosie trotted up to him and nuzzled his pocket for an alfalfa pellet.

"Here you go, girl," he said.

She was breathing hard but not overly excited. Nash and a couple of others came up to nudge him for their own treats. The white-faced mare stayed back, her eyes rolling, her feet dancing back and forth on the soft ground.

No real damage done, he thought.

He walked among the herd, patting necks and stroking faces, calming and reassuring them. When he walked back to the barns, Jamie was nowhere to be seen.

But Haylee and Aiden were closing up the training yard.

"It was a mistake, Haylee," Gideon said.

"He could have been trampled." Haylee pulled the gate shut with a snap.

"It could have happened to anyone."

"He's a valuable dog that doesn't belong to us." She secured the lock and turned toward her cabin.

Aiden sighed, caught Haylee's hand, and pulled her back. "Haylee, it's okay. Don't be too hard on her."

She looked at Gideon. "What do you think?"

He understood her anger. This was classic Jamie, rushing headlong into things without considering the consequences. And those consequences, he thought now, could reach farther than she realized.

Lana was already nervous about letting Blake come to the ranch. What if Jamie did something like this while he was around and accidentally put him at risk? Lana and Elliot would take any opportunity to discredit Gideon's judgment and use it to limit his access to Blake, or deny it entirely.

"It was a mistake," he said again. "She didn't mean for it to happen."

Haylee looked out toward the pasture, where the horses had finally gone back to grazing. "I know," she said. "But that's not good enough."

Chapter Seventeen

Lots of masculine fire energy this week. Stay alert.

—Jamie's horoscope

Jamie knocked on Roman's door. "Hello? You home? I've got your pup."

A low, rough bark of welcome sounded from within and set Chaos barking and squirming to be let down.

"Ouch! Wait. You little monster." The puppy's sharp claws dug into the soft flesh of her upper arm as he wiggled and whined.

Then Roman's grumbling voice. "Hold your horses."

Chaos barked again and Sadie yelped eagerly.

The door opened, and Sadie rushed out first, weaving herself around Jamie's legs, sniffing and whining. She set Chaos down. "Don't run away, you little brat."

The older dog licked and nuzzled the puppy, while Chaos leaped all over her, slipping and falling in his excitement. Jamie winced as his hard head cracked on the cedar deck, but the pup seemed to barely notice.

"You've brought Chaos." Roman sighed. "My son will be glad."

"Not you? I'll keep him, just say the word. He's adorable and deserves to be with someone who appreciates him."

Someone without livestock. He'd had way too much fun chasing the horses. Jamie had hoped to keep Chaos for a few more days, but knew better than to push her luck. Haylee had been pissed.

"I suppose you'll want to come in and check on Sadie." He sounded genuinely put out, but he held the door open.

"Pardon me if I offended you earlier. When it comes to animals, I subscribe to the guilty-until-proven-innocent philosophy. You didn't seem much like a dog enthusiast."

He was moving better today than he'd been the day she'd helped him to his house, and his face had better color in it.

"I only had him a month before you kidnapped him."

"Rescued him."

He walked ahead of her into the kitchen. "Whatever. I'm making tea."

"Is that an invitation?"

"It's information. Do with it what you will."

The puppy gambolled behind Sadie. The wound on her bad leg had scabbed over, but the entire leg was visibly more swollen today. Cancer sucked.

The pup raced to Sadie's bowl, then dropped his butt end down and looked up at Roman eagerly.

"You'll get your supper when it's suppertime," Roman said.

The puppy stomped his front paws and barked, but held the sit position.

"He's really smart, you know."

"Too smart. As evidenced by his ability to get through the fence."

"He's growing fast. Soon he won't fit." Jamie smiled as Roman gave the pup a treat and a pat. "Sorry I couldn't work with him longer, but he should be bonding with you, anyway."

The old man harrumphed. "Maybe I don't want to bond with him."

"What? Why not? Why did you get him in the first place, then?" Jamie lifted her hands and let them flop down at her sides. "I'm serious. If you don't want him, I'll take him. But make up your mind."

"I don't want him. I need him," Roman snapped. "We're stuck with each other."

He wasn't making sense. She shook her head, waiting for him to go on.

He levelled a tired glance at her, then snapped his fingers at Sadie. "Get me my cane, girl."

The dog limped to the living room, took the wooden walking stick in her mouth, and brought it back.

Roman rubbed her wide head, and suddenly, Jamie saw what was standing smack in front of her, what should have been obvious from the beginning.

The way she watched him, how she'd helped him to his feet when he'd fallen outside, his anger at her impending death, it all made sense now.

Sadie was a service dog.

"Chaos is meant to be her replacement," she said softly. "Why didn't you tell me? You're definitely going to need help training him to take over. When Sadie retires, I mean."

No wonder he resented the puppy. He was grieving.

"Not interested in going through all that work again. Travelling to the training center. Strangers in my house, telling me what to do." Roman busied himself at the counter, keeping his back to her. "Besides, nobody will ever take Sadie's place."

"Of course not. But you're used to her help. And you're in luck! We train dogs like this, on the ranch. Among other things."

He snorted. "I'm even less interested in neighborhood do-gooders."

She needed to change tactics. He hated helplessness and he didn't want pity. She'd have to appeal to his anger. "No problem. It's a big commitment, and I doubt you'd meet our requirements. Plus, you probably can't afford us."

Roman's head popped up, and he paused in the act of pouring steaming water from a kettle to a teapot. His eyes narrowed and Jamie could see him calculating his response.

She jumped in before he could make another attempt to cover himself.

"What's wrong with you, anyway? Mobility issues, chronic pain, what else?"

He blustered. "None of your goddamn business."

"Don't get your shorts in a twist. We can't train dogs unless we know what their owner needs."

"I don't want you to train my dog! I was doing just fine before you showed up and I'll be fine once you leave." He slammed a ceramic bowl on the table. "There's sugar. I've got no milk so you're out of luck if you want it."

Jamie grinned. "I don't take milk and I'm sweet enough already as I'm sure you've noticed."

She slid one chair out in front of the place mat where Roman's glasses and crossword puzzle lay. She pulled another out for herself and got comfortable.

Roman plunked the teapot and two cups onto the table.

"So. What kind of trouble did he give you?"

Jamie lifted her cup in a toast. "Destroyed two socks and one chair leg and nearly caused a stampede. You've got your work cut out for you."

"We'll manage."

She took a sip. The bitter brew nearly puckered her mouth. "Are you always such a conversational whiz? Or is it just me?"

"You're annoying, you know that?"

"That's just hurtful." She stirred a generous spoonful of sugar into her cup. "And untrue. I'm delightful, as a matter of fact. But back to Chaos."

"I think I just found the title for my biopic," Roman grumbled.

Then he winced, angling his body as if a sudden spasm had run up his side.

"You okay?"

"Yeah, I'm frickin' fantastic. How does it look?"

His face had gone grey again, and his eyes were screwed up tightly.

Jamie glanced over at the counter, where several vials of prescription medication sat. "You want something from your pill collection?"

"My pills are . . . none of your business."

"Okay, then." She sat back and waited. "I believe there's a saying, something about pride goeth-ing before a fall. I'd suggest you remain seated until the ride you're on comes to a complete halt. With your pride, I don't like your chances of remaining off the floor."

He hissed. "Do you always talk so much?"

"Only when I'm nervous. You could try being nicer to me."

"I gave you tea."

"That's true." She let the silence grow between them for a moment. "See? It's working already."

"If I give you a loaf of bread, will you shut up?"

The toughness was all an act, that was obvious. He needed help, maybe with more than the dog. She made a mental note to ask Gayle how to arrange for a visit from social services.

Then remembered the gun and erased the note.

She couldn't keep Chaos at the ranch, but that didn't mean she couldn't pop out to help Roman train him here. If he'd let her. With no classes for the parks board at the moment, she could easily fit it into her schedule.

Roman groaned. A sheen of perspiration glistened on his forehead. Jamie got to her feet, gathered the yellow plastic containers in both her hands, and dumped them on the table in front of him.

"Here, you old goat. Take your drugs. You're making me uncomfortable."

"Can't have that, can we?" Roman muttered. Bracing himself on the table with one hand, he reached out with the other, only to grab the seat of his chair before he made it.

"You look trapped, good sir," Jamie said, giving him a big smile. "I'd offer to help, but . . ."

Curses spilled out past gritted teeth. "That one. Two."

She examined the vial, then whistled. "Oxy. Nice. Hillbilly heroine. How often do you take these?"

"Not often enough. Come on. Hand 'em over."

Jamie took the vial with her to the sink, where she filled up a glass of water. "It says one to two pills, as needed for pain. Shouldn't you start with one?"

"Are you my doctor? This isn't funny."

"No, it's not." She went to his side and eased her arm across his back. "Come on, old man. Let's get you to the couch, first. Sitting at the table isn't doing you any favors."

He leaned heavily on her, his breath wheezing in and out with the effort, but he didn't argue. She got him settled, lifting his bad leg onto the pillow he indicated.

"How's that?" she asked.

"My pills."

She shook one of the painkillers into her hand and passed it over with the glass. "Start with this."

"Fuck," Roman said in one long, slow breath. But he swallowed it and lay back against the cushions. "You can go now."

She snorted. "And who's going to let your doggies outside? You see, this is what I'm talking about. You need help, my friend."

"In twenty minutes," he said, "I'll be leaping tall buildings in a single bound. He can pee then."

"Forget it." She clapped her hands. "Come on, Sadie. Come on, Chaos. Let's go outside!"

Chaos ran to the glass door leading onto the porch, slipped on the hardwood and crashed into it. He got to his feet, shook his head, then jumped up against it, whining in excitement.

Sadie limped over, wagging her tail, a big Lab grin on her wide face.

"Good doggies," she said, opening the door. "I'll be back in twenty minutes."

Within minutes, Roman began to feel the effects.

The tightness in his lower back eased, which let him relax the chokehold he had on his reclined posture. He pictured his skeleton, the spicules of bone and cartilage that battled each other like children playing war with sticks. Then he imagined molecules of warmth bubbling through his veins, settling into those shrieking war zones, attaching to throbbing nerve endings like tiny balls of cotton batting, or balloons, or jellyfish, bobbing in the plasma sea.

Bob, bounce, flutter, drift.

The red, angry shards of pain faded to pink, the way the scar on his palm had formed when he'd sliced it with the bread knife. He exhaled in gratitude.

If only the bones of his hip could form a scar. Instead, every day, the weapons grew sharper, more brittle, with no way to dull the blades but to wrap his brain in drugs and distract himself.

He hated that the girl had seen him like this.

The porch door crashed open and what sounded like

hundreds of paws scrambled and clattered over the scratched hardwood.

"Treats are in here, Chaos! Sadie knows. Come on, you two." She led them to the pantry, where she'd found the bin of freeze-dried liver bits.

He couldn't see them without turning his head, so he just listened.

"Sit," she commanded. Then: "Good girl, Sadie! Chaos, sit."

He smiled to himself. Chaos didn't have that much self-control yet.

But then, they surprised him.

"Good boy, good boy, what a smart boy you are!"

More whining and claws, and then the sound of crunching and smacking. He felt the couch move and he opened his eyes.

Jamie was perched on the upholstered arm, carefully avoiding his legs. "You look a little less hostile. Feeling better?"

He thought for a minute. Having the pain lift was like watching sunshine break through the clouds after a storm. "Half as good as I want. Ten times better than I was."

"Not ready to polka," Jamie said, "but a big improvement. So, tell me, what's the deal with you?"

A noise sounded at the front door.

Chaos growled, then leaped to his feet. Sadie followed him, her tail wagging.

"You expecting someone?" the girl asked.

"No," Roman said. But he knew who it was.

The lock clicked over, the door opened, and Jonathan walked in.

"Dad?"

* * *

So, the cranky man had a son. A handsome son who cared about him enough to be concerned about the presence of a stranger.

"Excuse me?" he said. "I didn't realize my dad had friends."

Jamie went forward, her hand extended. "Pretty sure he doesn't. I'm Jamie Vaughn. From the ranch on the other side of the ridge."

"Jonathan Byers." He had a cool, firm grip. He went to the couch and knelt at Roman's side. "Dad, are you okay?"

"Fine, fine," Roman said, somewhat indistinctly. "Just my fucking leg."

"Nice, Dad." He shot an apologetic look at Jamie.

She laughed. "I've heard worse, trust me."

Jonathan nudged Roman's shoulder. "What pills have you taken?"

The man snorted.

"He took one of these." She tossed Jonathan the pill vial and tipped her head at Roman. "What's wrong with him? He's playing tough guy, but he's in rough shape."

"Football injury," Roman said with a growl. His eyes closed.

Glancing at the wall of photographs she'd noticed earlier, Jonathan beckoned her out of his father's earshot.

She followed, looking again at the dusty framed photos. The one actor, the girl, she'd died, hadn't she?

Then it clicked. Memories trickled in, pushing aside the sympathy she'd begun to feel.

"The Vasquez Rocks accident."

"He was an executive producer." Jonathan exhaled, then scratched his chin. "He doesn't like people to know."

"No shit." A film crew working on a project near Agua Dulce had been involved in a catastrophic accident. A chunk of sandstone had collapsed beneath the set, resulting in numerous injuries, including the death of a girl working her first job as an extra.

Jamie'd been waiting tables in L.A. along with several aspiring actors when it had happened, and rumors had run wild. Media had speculated that budgetary issues had led to corners cut, rules bent, and safety measures being bypassed. She didn't recall any reports of any producers or directors being injured. Only of their negligence.

Jonathan's lip quirked up in a sad half-smile. "They didn't think he'd ever walk again. It's a miracle he's as mobile as he is."

Most of her friends had been desperate enough to take any acting job that might lead to a break. Unsafe working conditions, sexual harassment, demeaning roles, it didn't matter if it brought them exposure.

And there was always someone willing to exploit that desperation. She slanted a look at the now dozing man.

"Too bad everyone wasn't so lucky."

"He wasn't at fault."

"Okay."

"He wasn't." Jonathan spat the words out as if they tasted of ash. "His colleagues threw him under the bus. The media needed a scapegoat, and by the time he was able to defend himself, it was too late. His so-called friends disappeared. My mother left him. It wasn't his fault, but that woman's death nearly destroyed him."

Dead was dead. Was she supposed to feel bad for him because he survived? "Yeah, I'm sure it was rough," she said finally.

Jonathan looked toward his father, his expression unreadable. He was quiet for a long minute before continuing. "He had a broken arm, three broken ribs, and a crushed pelvis, but the paramedics had to drag him off her body. He was trying to do CPR on her."

She winced. She didn't want to hear his sob story. Everyone had one, after all. He could have stayed and fought. Or he could have remade himself, started over. No one had forced him to become a foulmouthed, bad-tempered recluse.

"I hoped this place would give him a fresh start," Jonathan said, echoing her own thoughts. "He got away from the movie industry, but I guess it wasn't enough."

Jamie moved toward the door, took the knob in her hand, then stopped, looked at the bluegrass and vine maple and brambles beyond the window. "He can't handle the pup on his own," she said. "I'll help, but he has to ask. My card's on the table."

Haylee was going to freak.

But she had to offer. For the puppy.

Chapter Eighteen

Mercury's in Virgo. Time to sweat the small stuff.

—Jamie's horoscope

Jamie was playing with a couple of golden retrievers who were boarding while their owners were in Hawaii when the door to the kennel office opened.

"Looking good, Jamie." Haylee leaned against the frame and took a sip from her water bottle, observing them.

"Thanks." Max dropped a ball at Jamie's feet. She bent down, picked it up, and threw it to the far end of the yard, feeling self-conscious. Maisie joined her pal, both of them romping past in a blur of shining fur and joy. Being around the big, friendly dogs soothed her ruffled spirit, but she missed Chaos and worried about how he was doing.

She was struggling with a kind of emotional whiplash about Roman Byers, too. Until she'd realized who he was, she'd had a kind of bemused sympathy for the crotchety recluse. The powerful industry mogul who'd run roughshod over the needs of his workers, however, had inspired disgust.

She'd gotten Huck to dig for more information about the accident and he confirmed that Jonathan had been telling the truth. Now, she was ashamed that she'd so quickly swallowed the media misrepresentation. Roman wasn't a fun guy.

But he wasn't the villain they'd made him out to be, either. He had reason to be bitter.

She rubbed her hand against her jeans to get the dog drool off. "Did you need something?"

She doubted Haylee wanted her on anything but scut work, and couldn't blame her for that. If she hadn't been showing off for everyone, Chaos never would have gotten away on her and gone after the livestock. So much for her brilliant plan to impress Haylee with her training skills.

Naturally, Gideon had been there to witness the Jamie-fail, too. Maximum embarrassment, that seemed to be her path in life.

Thank God he'd stepped in, of course. She shuddered to think of Chaos beneath those sharp hooves, or the horses themselves being injured in their panicked flight.

He'd saved her bacon, no doubt.

But why couldn't he have been there when the puppy was behaving himself? See how well he was learning his basic obedience? She was doing a good job, she knew it.

But no one saw that.

"How much longer will you be here?" Haylee asked.

Jamie glanced at her watch. "A few minutes. I've got cleanup to do after that though. Why? What's up?"

"Olivia and Gayle are in the stables. They want us to join them for a quick meeting."

"Oh. Okay. I'll leave these two in the yard and do the cleaning after. Do you know what it's about?" A frisson of unease tightened her spine. Something was clearly up. "This isn't pink slip time, is it?"

The laugh she tagged onto her question sounded as fake as it felt. Olivia and Haylee were her bosses, after all. And Gayle was head of human resources at the hospital.

But Haylee's smile reassured her. "Something about Apollo. They want our input."

Relief sent a breath whooshing through her. "God, don't scare me like that. Wait. Both of us? They want my input, too?" Her spirits lightened even more at the inclusion.

"I'll let them explain."

They left the kennel yard and made their way to the stables. Haylee had her hand on her back again and her gait had taken on a slight side-to-side motion in the past week or so.

Gayle was waiting for them at the stable entrance.

"What's up, Gayle?" Jamie said. She'd always found the quiet Asian woman a tad unnerving, probably because of her background in psychology. Jamie'd known her share of psychologists, counselors, therapists, and social workers over the years and had learned to be cautious around them lest they perceive more than she wanted to reveal of herself.

A person who could write life-altering recommendations based on a ten-minute interaction was a person to be feared.

But she wasn't a bratty foster kid anymore, Jamie reminded herself. Gayle worked primarily in administration now, and she wasn't talking about her anyway.

Still, if only she'd have the courtesy to grow a zit on her nose or swear when she stubbed a toe or come out of the bathroom with toilet tissue on her shoe, it would help Jamie's comfort level with her a lot.

Gayle cleared her throat. "I recently had a conversation with a community health nurse regarding the hospital's outpatient mental health program. I think the ranch has something to offer."

"Sounds great," Jamie said, waiting for more.

Gayle's almond-shaped eyes got brighter as she explained. Apparently the program coordinator was concerned about one of her patients, a man suffering a major depressive episode. She wondered if spending time on the ranch, with the animals, might speed his progress.

Gayle led them to Apollo's stall, where they found Olivia.

"Hey, old boy." Gayle fished a treat out of her pocket.

Apollo walked slowly from the back of the stall to greet them, his steps lumbering and hesitant, his head low with defeat.

"Talk about major clinical depression," Jamie said.

"Gideon had Tyler switch up his feed, but he's still really struggling," Olivia said.

Jamie reached over the stall door and patted Apollo's bony head. "I'd love to help, but I'm not sure how. And speaking of Gideon, he's the one you should be talking to about this, not me. Right?"

Jamie glanced at Haylee, who was suddenly fascinated with her fingernails. Gayle's lip twitched, and Olivia bent her face toward the horse.

"Uh-oh. What am I missing here?"

"Again with the paranoia," Haylee murmured. "Listen up, my friend."

Olivia left the stall to stand next to Gayle, then reached out to smooth a strand of ebony hair off Gayle's cheek. Gayle caught her hand and smiled at her.

There was an easy, unconscious grace in their companionship. Gayle and Olivia had been together the whole time Jamie had been on the ranch, and the two were like an old married couple, kinder to each other, in fact, than most straight pairs Jamie had known.

"Gayle thinks that spending time with a horse like Apollo might help this man," Olivia said. "He can brush him, talk to him, just be with him. It would give him something to do, someone to connect to on a deeper emotional level, without fear of judgment. Horses are good that way. The increased attention might help Apollo, too."

"I get that," Jamie said. Who did she turn to but Nash when she was upset, especially about Gideon? The gentle gelding always listened, and she always came back from a ride feeling better.

Gayle offered the horse another pellet, but he only sniffed it and turned his head away. "The relationship between humans and horses has a neurological basis, a kind of reciprocal limbic resonance. Through becoming attuned to horses again, people with mental illness can gain awareness of their own emotions, and build empathy to the emotional states of others. We call it equine therapy. You guys already know what I'm talking about."

Olivia stroked Apollo's long nose with smooth, easy motions over and over, and the horse's eyes drifted to half-mast. "We've all seen it. We've all experienced it."

Haylee nodded. "Humans were meant to live with animals. We're not whole without them."

"Totally, man," Jamie said. The conversation had taken an academic, ethereal turn that made her squirm. "This is feeling a little drum-circle to me. We don't have to hold hands and talk about our vaginas now, do we?"

"And the moment is gone." Haylee punched her arm lightly. "It sounds like a good idea to me."

Olivia and Gayle exchanged glances.

"We want Gideon to supervise the patient," Gayle said.

"Makes sense," Jamie said. "But he's pretty distracted right now. I assume you know what's going on with him?"

"Of course," Olivia said. "That's partly what this is about. We've been brainstorming how best to show our support, but he's not making it easy."

"Tell me about it," Jamie said glumly. "If I hadn't accidentally overheard him talking to his kid, I'd never have known."

"Such a moron." Haylee kicked at a piece of straw. "I mean, I love the guy. And believe me, I sympathize. But I can't believe he won't talk to you about it. What's his problem?"

"He's a douche-canoe?" Jamie suggested. Tears started to prickle behind her eyes. If anyone would understand the challenges Gideon was facing, it would be Haylee.

"We all care about him, hon." Olivia touched her arm gently. "He's his own worst enemy right now. He's spending too much time alone, brooding, waiting. It's hard to watch. It's hard to see you hurting too, Jamie."

Jamie swallowed. Her feelings for Gideon weren't a secret, but she wasn't sure how to respond to their collective pity.

"For almost two years," she burst out, "we talked about everything. We were so close. I thought . . . I thought . . . well. I was wrong. Now his life is complicated and he's avoiding me. Whose life isn't complicated? I hate him!"

Olivia stroked her back, the same way she'd stroked Apollo's nose. "You love him." Her voice was soft and warm, like oil smoothed onto aching limbs.

"And he doesn't feel the same way." Jamie leaned into her. "It's ruining everything between us, but I can't help myself. I don't know what to do. I want to make it stop. I just want to go back to how things were before I noticed how good he smells and how gentle he is with the horses and how hot he looks with a tiny kitten against his chest."

Haylee gave a half-smile. "You've got it bad." She looked between her aunt and Gayle. "You want to tell her or should I?"

"Go ahead," Olivia said.

"Here's the deal, James." Haylee turned to her and spoke quickly, as if afraid Jamie was going to take off on her. "The patient is Roman Byers. I believe you're acquainted with him through his puppy."

Jamie's jaw dropped. Heat rushed into her cheeks. "What the—? Oh, that Huck. I'm gonna tear him a new one."

"No, you won't," Olivia said mildly. "Come on, Jamie. It's my ranch. Nothing happens here that I don't know about. Continue, Haylee."

"His son is worried about him. He called us requesting,

begging actually, for you to help train the puppy. Apparently they're very impressed with your abilities."

Jamie shoved her hands into her pockets. "Yeah, about that . . ."

"Geez, James." Haylee lifted her arms and then flopped them against her thighs. "You might have mentioned that Chaos needs specialized training. I would have understood."

"I didn't realize myself until yesterday," Jamie admitted.

"That bit got past all of us," Olivia said, a small frown creasing her forehead.

Haylee exhaled deeply. "Anyway, of course we'll train the pup for him. Well, I will. But you'll help."

Jamie blinked. "Really?"

Haylee took a shuddery breath. "Really. I haven't been a great friend, and I'm sorry. I should have been more supportive. And I will be, starting now."

"No," Jamie said, pulling her close. "I should have been upfront with you from the beginning. If only people said what they meant, the world would run a lot easier, wouldn't it?"

"It sure would," Gayle said. "But most people are lying to themselves as much as anyone else. Learning to be honest with yourself is the hardest lesson."

Maybe Gideon was lying to himself, too. Maybe she should be more patient with him.

And dang and holy smokes. She'd be training Chaos!

With Roman Byers.

Under Haylee, of course.

"Hold on." She pulled away to look her friend in the eye. "Roman Byers is the one you want to bring here to spend time with Apollo?"

"Yes." Olivia brushed her hands against each other, all business now. "He'll come out three afternoons a week to visit the horse. You and Gideon will supervise. Then you'll work with him and the pup, under Haylee's supervision."

Jamie lifted her hands and took a step backwards. "Whoa. You clearly haven't met the man. Mr. Byers is an extremely . . . difficult person."

"I know. His son explained everything," Olivia said. "You know me. Can't resist a challenge. Besides, he likes you."

Again, Jamie felt her mouth drop open. "What?"

Liv grinned. "Yup. According to his son, he doesn't stop talking about you."

"Only because he thinks I'm a giant pain in the ass."

Gayle spoke up. "Jonathan has been taking his father to the depression support group, but after meeting you and learning about the ranch, he believes visiting here will be helpful. My colleague at the hospital and I are inclined to agree."

"It's a win for everyone, Jamie," Haylee said.

Jamie stared at her. "Not Gideon. Trust me. This is a punishment."

"But he'll have you, James." Haylee straightened off the wall of the stall, nudging Jamie with her shoulder. "He'll need your help, won't he? And therein lies the true genius of our diabolical plan."

Inside her chest, hope fluttered like butterfly wings. She knew they would be good together, but loving Gideon was like dragging a horse to a trough and watching him die of thirst. Would he resent the intrusion? Or was it the push he needed to finally see her for the woman she was?

"I don't know whether to throw a pitchfork or say thank you," she said honestly.

"You're welcome." Gayle gave her a one-armed hug, then took Olivia's hand and walked out, followed closely by Haylee.

Jamie got a broom and swept a few stray pieces of straw out of the way. Apollo stood with his big head over the gate, watching her silently.

"Maybe," she told him, "we should be apologizing to you."

* * *

Gideon nudged the old stallion lightly with the quirt, until he was walking at the edge of the lead rope, stirring up lazy puffs of dust with every drag of his foot. How Olivia thought this animal would make an appropriate therapy horse, he had no idea.

But once Liv got her teeth into an idea, she didn't let go. And worse, she expected him to handle it. With Jamie.

The horse stumbled.

"Whoa, boy," he said.

Those hooves had been a nightmare, yellow and over-grown, more like horns curling on the bottom of his feet. The farrier had told them it would be months before he'd get them back to proper form. Apollo was moving easier now, which told them he was more comfortable, but he still wasn't happy.

Join the club. After numerous conversations that had left Gideon feeling flayed inside and out, he and Lana had finally agreed on a date for Blake's first visit. But would she follow through? What kind of supervision would she require? How was she preparing Blake? They'd managed to avoid lawyers and mediators to this point. Lana's behavior would determine whether or not that would continue.

Apollo snorted and yanked on the lead, annoyed at the unaccustomed activity.

"Sorry, boy, but you've got to keep moving."

It would be tricky to give the horse the amount of exercise he needed to regain muscle mass and fitness without over-straining the delicate tendons and ligaments in his lower legs. Years of neglect couldn't be undone overnight.

Years of neglect.

He couldn't help neglecting Blake for the first four years of his life. But these last two, that was on him. He had excuses, of course. He'd had nothing to offer the boy when he first got out. He'd needed time to put his life back together. He hadn't expected Lana's resistance, hadn't known how to handle that. Hadn't wanted to alienate her completely.

Weeks had turned into months and before he knew it, she was asking him to give up Blake entirely.

He'd done this. Now he had to undo it.

The horse slowed, and he stroked the whip softly over the cachectic hindquarters to keep him moving. "Come on, Apollo. I'm not asking for much."

Liv's request that he and Jamie work together with the man had been a curve ball, but since he was the owner of the pup she'd found—rescued, stolen, kidnapped, he wasn't sure—and she had a relationship of sorts with him already, it made sense.

He should have argued harder. He didn't want any more responsibility now, not when he was so distracted preparing to meet his son. But he missed Jamie.

It was selfish of him to crave her company, knowing how she felt about him, knowing he'd never be able to reciprocate. The hope radiating from her tore at him every time they spoke.

So he didn't.

He couldn't seem to avoid hurting her.

Was he being selfish in his desire to see Blake, too? He had no idea how to be a father. Perhaps Hudson was great with him and Gideon's sudden presence would only confuse and frighten the boy.

If you didn't know you were missing something, was it worth the upset to explore the discovery?

The animal shuffled through the thick layer of sawdust they'd put down for him that morning, his steps slow and heavy. This old horse had lived most of his life confined and alone, his days and weeks punctuated with feedings, stall cleanings and semen collection, denied even the pleasure of natural mating.

What constituted happiness in such a life? Was he aware of being miserable? Bored? Lonely? Olivia had seen something in him that told her there was life left in the beast, but Gideon couldn't see evidence of it today.

Inertia was its own comfort.

Breaking out of it required effort and brought discomfort and confusion and fear.

Would it be worth it for Apollo?

Would it be worth it with Blake?

And what about Jamie? Was she asking the same questions about him? She was dismantling a comfortable, solid friendship, and for what? The pieces didn't fit any other way, despite her hopes. Why couldn't she see that?

At Gideon's urging, the old horse put one foot in front of the other, over and over again, but his head hung low, his eyes dull and listless, as if he knew he was on a road to nowhere but had as little choice as he had when he'd stood in a windowless stall for months and years on end.

"It'll get better, buddy," Gideon murmured.

At least, he hoped so. If Olivia's predictions were right, the horse's strength would return, little by little, as muscles long atrophied returned to fullness. His coat would grow glossy again, his mane and tail would shed the brittle, broken strands, and shine with health once more. One day, he'd lift his head and consider the path before him with interest. He'd pick up his heels and step without thought into a world he'd never known.

Either that, or they'd call the vet and ease him out of this world with whatever dignity he had left.

He put a feather-light touch on Apollo's hip again. "Come on, buddy. A little more. You can do it."

Selfish or not, he wasn't going to give up on the old horse any more than he was going to give up on his son.

He had no idea what to do about Jamie.

Chapter Nineteen

*A Venus–Saturn opposition can pave the way for a
serious blow to your self-esteem. Beware.*

—Gideon's horoscope

Gideon was on his way to the stables when an older grey
sedan pulled up onto the ranch yard, a young man at the
wheel and an older man in the passenger seat.

"Jamie," he called toward the kennels. "They're here."

But there was no response. This was a preliminary meeting, an opportunity for him to get acquainted with Roman
Byers and to show him around the ranch, establish a rapport,
get a feel for his needs.

Two hours ago, he'd gotten a message from Lana. She'd
be sending Blake to see him next Saturday at 2 PM.

He hadn't been able to think straight since then. The last
thing he wanted to do now was meet Roman Byers. And
where was Jamie? She was supposed to be here to greet
them and make introductions, since she already knew them.

He scanned the yard, but she was nowhere to be seen. No
sound of her either. Given her tendency to talk to whoever
she was with, human or animal, her voice had become part
of the comforting background noise of the ranch. But today
the breeze soughed through the trees accompanied by

nothing but birdcalls and the distant surf that seemed to whisper his son's name.

He walked to the yard, dusting off his hands, forcing himself to set Blake and Jamie aside.

"Hello," he said, as the driver stepped out. "Welcome to Sanctuary Ranch. My name's Gideon."

The younger man came forward, his hand extended. "I believe you're expecting us? I'm Jonathan Byers. My father, Roman." He gestured to the older gentleman, who'd opened the passenger's door but remained inside, glowering.

They'd brought the dogs, he saw. The puppy Jamie'd become so fond of hopped out and raced to greet him.

"Hey, little guy." Gideon bent down to pat the youngster, who seemed to be built entirely of teeth, claws, and excess skin.

"Chaos," snapped a gravelly voice. "Damn it, Jon, get the leash on him."

"It's great to meet you." Jonathan made a grab for the pup and missed. "Dad's been so lonely. Jamie's company was a real lift for him. I think knowing she's involved is the only reason he agreed to any of this."

Gideon wondered if they knew that Haylee was shutting the training center down when the baby arrived.

"Gotcha!" Jonathan snagged the puppy's collar and snapped on the leash. Chaos mouthed the leather, tugging and growling good-naturedly as if it were his favorite toy.

Jonathan stood up and looked around at the freshly painted corrals and outbuildings, the landscaping that Ezra maintained so meticulously, the serene cattle grazing on the hill. "It's a beautiful place. I'm almost grateful now that Chaos has been such a pain. If he hadn't escaped that day, we'd never have met Jamie."

How much time had she spent with them? Gideon glanced at the older man in the car. From the look on his face, he did not share his son's enthusiasm.

"A lucky break."

Jonathan's smile faded. "I understand that Haylee Hansen will be working with Chaos. She's good, is she?"

Gideon glanced over at the kennels. "The best. Frankly, I'm surprised she agreed to take on another dog. She's expecting a baby in about a month and will be taking maternity leave."

"This is a waste of time, like I said, Jon." Roman Byers gripped the frame of the car, swung his legs out, levered himself once, twice, then gave up and sat leaning against the door, his jaw set, like a truculent toddler.

Gideon walked closer, extending his hand again, this time as an offer of assistance. "Hello, Mr. Byers. I'm Gideon Low. May I help you out?"

Wincing, Roman stiffly pulled himself to his feet, ignoring Gideon's kindness. "I'm fine. If that girl's serious about wanting Chaos, she can have him. Bugger ate another pair of my shoes this morning."

"Dad." Jonathan glanced apologetically at Gideon. "You'll have to excuse my father. He's frustrated."

"Don't speak as if I'm not here," Roman snapped. "I'm not frustrated. I'm mad. Where's Jamie? Least she could do is be here to meet us."

Gideon understood now why Jamie had been concerned about the pup's home. Roman wasn't up to dealing with the energetic animal.

"I'm sure she's around somewhere. I know she's excited to see you. Why don't you come in to the main house and I'll introduce you to the cook. She makes a mean cup of coffee. And if you're very lucky, she may find something to go with it."

Roman grumbled, but acquiesced at Jonathan's urging. Gideon led them into the front room, where Daphne immediately set about making them comfortable. Then he strode out to the kennel area. Jamie wasn't in the grooming room, or with the boarders, but when he went around back to the covered training ring, he found her running Haylee's poodle.

No longer the pathetic, filthy creature she'd been on arrival, the dog was now white and clipped clean. She moved with an elegant, even gait, her keen eyes fixed adoringly on Jamie. The transformation was nothing short of amazing.

From the way the animal watched her, Gideon guessed he'd discovered where Jamie had been hiding out lately.

He waved her over to the fence. "Roman Byers and his son are here. He's annoyed that he got stuck with me for a greeter. He's quite something."

Jamie's eyes widened, and a smile blossomed on her face. "Did they bring Chaos?"

Gideon nodded. "The old dog, too."

"Good." She patted the poodle, led her inside, then walked past Gideon to the main house. "Roman's a piece of work, but Jonathan's great, isn't he? Looking after a man like that can't be easy."

Her approval rankled. He hadn't pegged Jamie as someone who'd be swayed by preppy good looks and an easy smile.

"How often have you gone out to see them, Jamie?"

She shrugged. "A few times. Why?"

Good question. Her spare time was her own. She didn't owe anyone any explanations, least of all him.

She hurried ahead of him, her black boots leaving little tufts of dust in her wake, and he couldn't help watching that tight behind twitch in those tattered blue jeans, imagining Jonathan admiring the same view.

"No reason," he said.

It was the most they'd spoken in several days, and he didn't want it to end. But she was already on the porch and didn't hear him.

* * *

Jamie glanced at her phone. She still had five minutes before Jonathan was picking her up, and she'd left her favorite denim jacket in the stables. She couldn't decide whether to go get it and risk running into Gideon, or take a sweater instead.

The meeting with Roman had gone well, and they'd settled on dates and times for him to join her and Gideon in the barn with Apollo, after which he and Chaos would have a lesson with Haylee.

Gideon had been disturbingly unreactive to the plan, leaving without comment, as if aware of Gayle and Olivia's secondary plan to draw him out.

She glanced out the window of her cabin again and bit her lip. Maybe she should have gone after Gideon, tried harder to make him talk.

Then she sighed. Horses, thirst, troughs. It wasn't personal. He was preoccupied with Blake. As he should be.

So, today, she was going out to have some fun. There was nothing wrong with that.

Jonathan was a sweetheart, the way he worried about his father. When she found out that he'd never taken time to visit the town of Sunset Bay on his trips out, she'd immediately offered to take him to see a few sights on her next day off.

She'd spoken, as usual, without thinking, but now was glad for the opportunity to get away from the ranch for a few hours. Watching Gideon's torture as he waited to meet his son was killing her.

She stepped out of her cabin and headed for the stables. It got chilly on the water, even in summer. She needed her jacket. She hoped she could avoid running into Gideon. She didn't want to explain what she was doing.

Or with whom.

Though it would be infinitely good for him to see her with a life outside the ranch.

Outside *him*.

She nearly bumped into him as she rounded the corner. Cursing inwardly, she stepped back, smoothing a strand of hair away from her eyes. She wasn't used to it being styled like this.

"Where are you off to?" Gideon paused, the saddle on his hip sagging. He looked her up and down. He blinked; then his expression darkened. "Are you wearing makeup?"

Jamie felt her cheeks grow warm under the unfamiliar foundation and blusher. Abby had helped her; Abby, who understood hair and cosmetics and fashion, who was effortlessly feminine and endlessly generous, and who intimidated the hell out of Jamie.

"What business is it of yours? It's my day off." She started to walk past him, but he shifted to stand in her way.

His eyebrows rose. "No offense meant. You look good, is all."

"Oh. Thanks." She tugged at the pastel-colored top that Abby called peach and said brought out her creamy complexion. To Jamie it was orange, and made her feel like a traffic cone.

Black was her color. It had always been her color.

You could hide in black.

"Special plans?" Gideon's tone suggested that they were office cube-mates who exchanged the same words every week. Monday: Did you have a good weekend? Thursday: Can't wait for the weekend. Friday: Have a good weekend. Add a few Nice-day-todays and We-need-more-coffee-to-get-through-this-meetings and you had the basic structure of a one-hundred-percent meaningless relationship.

Which pissed her off.

"I," she said, tossing her head breezily, "am going to be a tourist for a few hours."

"What?" Gideon set the saddle down on his boot, pommel-down, leaning it against his leg to keep the padding clean. He crossed his arms. "With who?"

She shrugged. "With Jon."

"Jon. You mean Jonathan Byers?"

The incredulity in his tone tweaked a nerve. "Why not? He needs something to do while his dad's working with Haylee. And I could use a break."

Just then, they heard the sound of car tires on gravel as Jon pulled up to Olivia's flower bed near the corrals.

"You're dating Jonathan." Gideon's voice landed like a fresh cowpat.

"Terminology is so confining," she responded. "We're just spending some time together. Neighborly. You know."

"Neighborly." Gideon made a strange noise in the back of his throat. "Good. Great. Have fun."

Add that to the list of cube-mate-conversation material. She wanted to punch him.

"Thanks!" She grinned until she felt her cheeks might crack and fall off. "I thought it was time I turned over a new leaf. You know what they say. If you keep doing what you've always done, you'll keep getting what you've always gotten. Maybe I'm tired of what I keep getting, Gideon. Maybe I want more."

Oops. It wasn't her cheeks that cracked. It was her voice.

She hadn't intended for the words to come out with such intensity. Damn it, why did he always trigger her like this?

"Jamie," began Gideon.

"No, no." She held up both hands. "Forget it. I am going to have a great day. Now, be quiet. He's here."

Jonathan Byers got out of his car and *oh, mama*. Outside the context of his father, she was suddenly aware that the man was, well, beautiful. His hair glinted gold in the sunlight, matching the finish on the aviator sunglasses that set off his chiselled cheekbones. He wore faded jeans and a turquoise-blue long-sleeved T-shirt that would bring out the color of his eyes. His mouth curved into a smile as he walked toward her.

She ought to be all aflutter. Instead, she felt every molecule in her being straining toward the man beside her, instead.

"Gideon." Jonathan nodded in greeting, then turned to her. "You look great, Jamie. Are you ready to go?"

Heat rose in her cheeks at the unexpected pleasure Jonathan's words triggered. She'd taken pains with her appearance, but she chafed at her pleasure in his approval.

She didn't want to care what anyone thought about her.

"Just getting my jacket." She pushed past Gideon into the darkness of the stable and went to Apollo's stall, where she'd last seen it.

Maybe this was a date and that's why it felt so wrong. Adjusting her appearance to meet some hideously sexist standard of beauty was part of the deal, and she'd made a point, her entire life, of going out of her way not to impress others.

The old stallion whinnied, making her jump.

"Not you, too," she said. "I've had enough male commentary already today."

But when he reached his head over the stall door, she gave him a quick rub on his broad, scarred face. He nodded and whuffed, nudging her for a treat.

"Sorry, buddy."

She pulled her jacket from where it was hanging on a nail, and went back to join the men outside.

But as she approached the doorway, she slowed. From the depths of the barn, she was invisible to them, but they were both illuminated, framed by the stable doors. Gideon stood on firmly planted legs, the saddle still at his side, his hands on his hips, deceptively casual.

Next to Jonathan, he was dark and rough, brooding and unpolished. A strange, dangerous energy flowed off him. If he'd been a dog, Jamie would have distracted him with a toy while someone else whisked the intruder away to forestall bloodshed.

But Gideon never lost his temper. It was one of the things she loved about him, how measured and controlled he was. When everyone else was losing their shit, Gideon took stock and made plans. He didn't get angry.

But he was angry now.

Good.

"Found it," she said, letting her hips sway as she walked past Gideon, and took Jonathan by the elbow. "Let's go find us some whales. This is going to be a fun afternoon. See you later, Gideon."

The chill wafting off his body made her shiver.

"Come back during the migration," the boat captain said at the end of their trip. "That's the time to see them."

Jamie waved at him, wobbling off the boat on legs that felt like cooked spaghetti. Behind her, Jonathan carried the basket Daphne had sent with them. Jamie's portion of their snack was now feeding the fishes off the coast of Bandon.

"How are you doing?" asked Jonathan for the tenth time. He'd been clearly confused as to his role during the whole puke-a-thon, first patting her back gingerly, then bringing her tissues, then finally opting to leave her alone in her misery, which was what she preferred anyway.

Actually, she'd considered throwing herself overboard, but figured it would have an adverse effect on the boat owner's insurance. It wasn't his fault she was seasick.

Nor was it his fault they hadn't seen any whales. Each year, nearly twenty thousand gray whales migrated up the Oregon coast to Alaska, then down again to the warm lagoons of Baja, Mexico. But late summer wasn't optimal viewing time, as they'd learned in that blissful half-hour before the wind had picked up.

"I'm fine." She gripped her elbows and made her way to Jon's car, waiting for the unlock beep.

"Are you . . . done?" he asked, opening the passenger door for her. What a gentleman.

"Trust me," she said, "there's nothing left. Don't worry. I won't ralph on the upholstery."

"It's you I'm worried about," he corrected.

Jamie leaned her head back and closed her eyes. Her throat was on fire. "I know. You're a prince. I'm being a bitch. My mouth tastes like the inside of a Mexican toilet so if you don't mind, I'll just lie here and try not to make things worse, okay?"

He started the car, then put on some music, a soothing instrumental melody that made her want to cry. Today hadn't been about having fun. It had been about punishing Gideon, making him see what he was missing. She deserved this.

But Jonathan didn't.

"The inside of a Mexican toilet, huh?" There was a smile in his tone.

"Or worse."

She liked him. He was a perfectly nice guy. Really nice, actually.

"For what it's worth," he said, "I had a good time."

Captain Remmy hadn't been able to find any whales, but he'd taken them to a variety of reefs, islands, and headland areas where they'd seen seals, sea lions, and birds of all kinds. Jamie had begun to feel ill around the tufted puffin mark. By the pelagic cormorants, she was sitting inside, staring at her hands. But the trip really went downhill when Remmy pointed out a couple of western gulls feeding on some unknown bloated thing bobbing on the water.

"I'm sure you're a barrel of laughs," Jamie replied, "on a date with less vomiting."

"You should see me on a date with no vomiting." He reached over and patted her arm. "But it's okay. I can tell you're not into me."

She opened her eyes. "What do you mean?"

He turned onto the highway between Bandon and Sunset Bay and hit the gas pedal. "Come on, Jamie. A guy can tell when a girl's not feeling it."

"I'm totally into you." She braced her hand against the door as they rounded a curve. "Don't take the nausea personally."

"It's hard not to." He laughed. "But don't worry, I'm okay with friendship."

"Thanks." He and Gideon could start a club. The Friends of Jamie Club.

They went over a bump in the road, and her stomach lurched again. Jonathan seemed to consider the speed limit more of a guideline than an actual law.

"You're good company," Jonathan said. "I can see why Dad likes you."

She pressed her left foot against the imaginary brake pedal. "You're delusional."

"Nope." He threw her a quick smile. "He talks about you. That's a dead giveaway. I mean, he's complaining, don't get me wrong; after you showed up, I couldn't do anything right, especially with the dog. It's a real pain in the ass. What's with you and the cowboy?"

She jerked her head at the subject change. "Gideon? What do you mean?"

He arched his eyebrows. "Come on. While you were in the barn, he was practically frothing at the mouth that you were going out with me."

"I doubt that." But her pulse spiked anyway, sending a warm glow down her forearms. She'd wanted him to notice her as a woman. Maybe he had.

Then the warmth faded and she broke out in gooseflesh. How the hell was it any business of his who she went out with? Or when? Or what she did? If he wanted to stay in the friend zone, then he could stay the hell out of her fun zone. Not that anyone else was going there but still. It was the principle of the thing.

"Oh, ho," Jonathan said, peering at her over the top of his sunglasses. "Touched a nerve, did I?"

Jamie blew a raspberry. "Nerve, schmerve. He's an asshat."

"Sorry to hear it. You deserve better."

His kindness sent a wave of disappointment and sadness over her, surprising her with its strength. She turned to the window, hugging her elbows. She wasn't being fair to Gideon. She wished she could stay mad at him, but he was just a guy who'd lost too much and was afraid to lose more and didn't want to hurt anyone, and was too blind to see that he was biting off his nose to spite his face.

"That's where you're wrong." She cleared her throat. "You see, I'm something of an asshat, myself."

"Asshattery aside," Jonathan said, "I like you. You're a nice person."

"As a judge of character," she said, her voice still hoarse, "you suck."

But his words brought tears back to her eyes. Why, oh why couldn't she fall in love with someone simple? Jonathan was handsome. He was kind, as evidenced by the way he looked after Roman. He was pleasant and a good conversationalist and easygoing. He liked her.

But when she was with Gideon, she felt lit up on the inside, like the sheer fact of his presence made her better, stronger, faster, more than she'd been before he entered the room. And not just that, but safe.

Though she wasn't safe with him, was she? She was the

exact opposite of safe. He had the ability to hurt her like no one ever had. She'd put her heart in his hands, and he'd gently but firmly given it back. Now it lay inside her, throbbing and raw, like a hermit crab in need of a shell might lie in the hot sun, while gulls wheeled and dove overhead.

"It's none of my business, but"—Jonathan leaned toward her as he took another corner far too fast—"men can be stupid. Are you sure he knows how you feel?"

How much clearer could she be? She wasn't exactly the mysterious sort, and she didn't play games.

"I'm sure." Jamie pressed her foot against the floor, hard. "Listen, Mario Andretti, we're about to take flight here. I'd like to make it home alive, if it's all the same to you."

Chapter Twenty

*The Sun and Mars are in perfect sync. Now's the
time to make your dreams come true.*

—Gideon's horoscope

After a week that passed with both blinding speed and
agonizing slowness, Saturday arrived. Gideon gave up
trying to sleep at 4 AM, made coffee in his cabin, cleaned up
yet again, fed the horses, then went to the tack room to work
on the saddle for Jamie.

He worked carefully, loving the idea of taking something
so old and worn and bringing it back to life. The dry, cracked
leather drank in the restoring compound, turning supple and
bright again beneath his cloth. A couple of rivets needed replacing, as well as the wool under the padded seat, but he
knew a professional in town who could do this. He hoped
that, when they were finished, the saddle would be revived
for many more years of riding.

He swiped leather cream over a rough area on the
pommel, wishing everything could be fixed so easily. Unfortunately, he had no idea what Blake needed from him.
Worse was the fear, barely acknowledged within himself,
that his insistence on rejoining his son's life was creating
damage where none had been.

Something crunched beneath his palm and he dropped the cloth.

"Damn it." A flake of leather peeled off, like sunburned flesh, ruined by his thoughtless distraction.

And Jamie was dating Jonathan.

What did he expect? He'd pushed her away, after all. He knew how she felt about him, felt an answering attraction, and denied it, for them both.

He should be grateful. Jon seemed like a nice guy.

Another layer of skin cracked open.

Gideon threw down the cloth in disgust and checked the time. He might as well go back to his cabin and take a nap. He wasn't doing anyone any good out here.

But he only lay there, dry-eyed and nerve-wracked, until it was time to sit on the front porch and wait for Lana and Blake to arrive.

When he finally heard the sound of tires on gravel, however, and saw the face of the driver, he got to his feet in surprise, a knife twisting in his gut.

The man got out, eyeing him cautiously. "Gideon."

To see the man who'd been raising Blake in Gideon's place, the man who'd clumsily attempted to investigate him, sent his hackles rising.

But really, would it have been less bad if she'd dropped Blake off herself? Not likely. This first meeting was always going to be difficult, no matter how it happened.

"Hudson."

"Let's make this as painless as possible, okay?" Hudson's voice was gruff.

"Of course." He managed to keep his tone even, but a muscle he couldn't control twitched beneath his eye. He forced his shoulders down and the corners of his mouth up, not wanting to frighten his son.

Hudson went to the backseat and began unbuckling what appeared to be a complicated collection of straps.

A car seat, Gideon realized, with a stab. He hadn't realized six-year-olds needed them. He'd have to get his truck fitted with one.

Hudson helped Blake out, set him on the ground in front of the car, and straightened up, one hand on the boy's shoulder.

"Hey, Blake." Gideon took a step forward and put out his hand. His throat felt like it was coated with sawdust. "I'm very pleased to meet you."

Hudson nudged him gently.

"Hi." Blake blinked up at Gideon, his voice small and high and wavering, his small hand clutching Hudson's pant leg.

"Okay." Hudson exhaled sharply. "I'll be in town, waiting for your call. Have . . . fun."

He got into the car and drove off quickly, as if afraid the boy would come racing after him.

But he didn't. Blake stood motionless, watching as the vehicle left the yard, little swirls of dust settling on his sneakers. He gripped the backpack tight in his little fists, as if it alone held the power to protect him in this vast, unknown, and dangerous environment.

Gideon searched for words and came up empty, waiting for some genetic component to kick in that would tell him what to do and how to do it, what this child needed from him, the words that would unlock some latent bond.

"I wanna go home." Now the small, high voice wavered with tears.

"Hey, now. It'll be fine." Gideon patted his son's shoulder, thin beneath the plain T-shirt. Shouldn't he be meatier at this age? "You're going to love this place."

Blake shifted away. Gideon removed his hand and shoved it deep into his pocket, his fingers tingling as if they'd been burned.

Minutes ticked by as if attached to a bomb, the sough of

the wind deafening, the endless space between man and boy a yawning echo of nothingness.

Do something, he commanded himself. This was what he'd fought for, after all. This was what he'd been battling Lana for, a chance to be a father, to show their son that there was another whole side to his life.

But the tension in the small body beside him held Gideon captive, paralyzed, terrified to do the wrong thing, incapable of remembering the words he'd practiced, the tones and touches he'd intended.

He'd ruin this. Blake would tell Lana he never wanted to come back, and would Gideon have the strength to insist, despite his son's tears? Was this an end that justified the means? He didn't want Blake to hate him. But if he forced the issue, isn't that what he'd be asking for?

Blake's big shining eyes met Gideon's. He blinked, terrifying in his vulnerability. "I wanna go home." It was a whisper this time.

Gideon felt his heart flop over in his chest. Ah, hell. What was he doing?

He should have arranged someone else to meet Blake with him. He suspected the boy would be more comfortable if a woman was around, but he'd been afraid of overwhelming the boy with too many new faces. He'd told everyone, in no uncertain terms, to stay away.

What had he been thinking?

"How about I show you around?" He cleared his throat. "Do you like horses?"

All kids liked horses, right?

"I don't know. I told you."

"Right." He took Blake's small hand in his, and this time the boy did not pull away. "I ride one called Rosie. She's very friendly. She'll take carrots from your hand. And we've got one called Apollo too. He's very old."

The boy walked beside him without speaking, taking two

quick strides for every one of Gideon's. He forced himself
to slow down.

"When's Mommy coming back?"

Gideon made himself smile, then let his face relax again.
No point faking things. The kid would come around. It
would just take time. "After supper."

"Oh."

It took forever to walk to the stables. He hadn't appre-
ciated how large the yard was. But silence had a way of
enlarging the smallest spaces until they felt like the Grand
Canyon.

Several dogs were out in the yard including Jewel, Chaos,
and the new poodle. Chaos and the poodle immediately ran
up to the fence, leaping and barking, with the older dog
following at a more sedate pace.

Blake cried out and cringed behind Gideon's leg.

"Hey, buddy," he told the boy. "It's okay. They're friendly."

He tried to peel the kid off him, but Blake wasn't having
it. The boy whimpered and clung to him, his eyes squeezed
shut.

"Are they going to bite me?" Blake asked.

"Bite you?" Gideon managed to get Blake in front of him,
and then lifted him so he could see the dogs from higher up,
where he might feel less intimidated. "Nah. They love kids.
You want to meet them?"

"Uh-uh." Blake shook his head, eyeing Chaos, who was
yapping like he'd never seen a kid before.

Which he probably hadn't.

Footsteps sounded, and to Gideon's immense relief,
Jamie appeared around the corner. She stopped in her tracks
when she saw them, a wary expression coming over her face.
They stared at each other for a moment, and then Jamie's
face softened.

Gideon set Blake back on his feet.

"Hey, kiddo." She strode toward them, scooped Chaos

into her arms, and slipped through the gate. She wiped one hand on her jeans and then stuck it out toward Blake. "I'm Jamie. What's your name?"

Blake let her shake his hand, watching the pup closely. "Blake."

"It's very nice to meet you, Blake. This little guy's name is Chaos. You want to pet him?"

He shook his head again.

"Gotcha. He's a little wild." She put Chaos back into the fenced area and let the poodle out instead. "Much better to start with this one. Her name is Honey. She's a poodle. Do you know what's great about poodles?"

Blake shook his head, whether in answer to her question or as a general response to the situation, Gideon wasn't sure.

Blake was quivering and clinging to him again. The dog walked up to them calmly, sniffed, then circled around to stand at Jamie's left side. It was impressive. Had Haylee been training the dog? Or had Jamie achieved this?

"They can do tricks," Jamie said. "Watch this. Honey, sit."

The dog folded her back legs and sat.

"High-five."

Honey lifted a paw and tapped Jamie's outstretched palm. "Good girl!"

Blake giggled. "She high-fived you."

Gideon could have kissed her. The boy stuck close, but he'd stopped shaking. This was exactly what he needed. Something to break the ice.

"She's super smart," Jamie said. "Here's another one."

She took a treat, told Honey to stay, then carefully set it onto her nose. The dog held position, waiting, waiting.

"Okay, eat it."

In an instant, the treat was gone, flipped and snatched out of the air before it hit the ground.

"Whoa!" Blake said.

"You like that?" Jamie asked.

The boy nodded.

"You want to see another one?"

He nodded again.

"I need help for this one, though." Jamie looked solemnly at him, ignoring Gideon entirely. "Would you like to help me? You'd have to come inside the fence. Can you do that?"

Gideon felt Blake tense up again. "I don't know, Jamie," he said.

"Will the other doggies bite me?" Blake asked.

Jamie gave a snort of laughter. "These guys? No way. Come on. It'll be fun."

Chaos had lost interest and was digging at the corner of the fence, so Gideon walked through the gate with Blake, a little envious at how easily she'd earned the boy's cooperation. At Jewel's approach, Blake shuddered and pulled away, but the big dog had had years of experience with kids and knew to lie down on the grass and wait for him to come to her.

She might be waiting for a while, he thought.

"You know how to make a gun with your fingers, right? Like this?" Jamie held her thumb and forefinger out like a pistol.

Blake made a tiny gun with his right hand.

"Perfect!" Jamie crowed. "I love it. Now. Point your gun at Honey and say, 'Bang!'"

Blake blinked, then looked at the dog. He lifted his hand and pointed his index finger at the dog. "Bang," he said in his little voice.

Behind Blake's back, Jamie mirrored the boy's hand gesture. Honey sank to the ground, then flopped over on her side.

Blake laughed in delight. Honey immediately leaped to her feet and came over for her treat.

Blake huddled away from her, grasping at Gideon's hand again.

"You made her do the trick," Jamie said, "so you get to give her the reward. Here."

She pressed a piece of jerky into his little hand, then held it out to Honey, allowing the dog to take it from them both.

"See? She didn't bite you."

"She licked me," Blake said. "She's got a soft tongue."

"That's our Honey." Jamie looked at Gideon, then back at Blake. "You want to try a trick with Jewel?"

Blake shook his head and buried his face against Gideon's leg, shy now. He let his hand hover over his son's head, then gently stroked his hair, golden like Lana's, with a cowlick at the front.

He could feel Jamie's eyes on him, and he looked over at her. But she was looking at Blake, an expression of wonder on her face.

"Right there," she said on a breath. "The way he turned his head. He looked just like you."

She caught her lower lip between her teeth, blinked hard a few times, then shook herself. "Okay, I gotta get back to work. See you boys later."

"Jamie?" he called, suddenly desperate for her to stay.

She paused on her way to the kennel and looked over her shoulder. A ray of sun shone across her face and spilled over her body, and it was as if a light turned on inside him, illuminating the lie he'd been telling himself.

She was beautiful. Inside and out.

And he loved her.

"Yeah?"

He swallowed and stroked Blake's hair again. "Thanks," he managed to say around the lump in his throat. "For everything."

Her face softened again and the shine returned to her eyes. "Anytime, Gideon."

Then, surrounded by the dogs, she disappeared.

* * *

An hour or two later, Jamie left the kennel and went to check in on Gideon and Blake.

Watching him meet his son for the first time had been painful. He had obviously been nervous, smiling too hard, his face brittle, his movements uncertain and jerky, like someone using ice skates for the first time.

Seeing such a strong man brought to his knees by a small boy made her chest ache. He didn't let himself love easily, as she knew all too well. Seeing a piece of himself standing there in little red sneakers, frightened and confused, must have torn him up inside.

She found them in the stables.

"Hey, guys," she said. "How's it going?"

"Great."

"Geez, that bad, huh?"

He shot her a filthy look.

She turned to Blake. "You having fun meeting the horses?"

"I guess," said the boy.

Then she noticed he was moving restlessly from foot to foot.

"Uh, Gideon," she said from the side of her mouth. "I think we've got a bladder situation here."

His eyes widened. "Blake? Do you need to go to the washroom?"

Blake nodded quickly.

Gideon looked at Jamie. "Thank you again."

"No skin off my nose." She focused on Blake. "Do you need help?"

Blake shook his head from side to side.

"Come on." She motioned for Gideon and the boy to follow her. "The kennel bathrooms are closest. You staying for supper, kiddo?"

Blake nodded.

"Good," she said. "We'll sit together. Would that be okay?"

He nodded again, then darted toward the open door.

"All right. I'll see you then. Have fun with your dad."

Blake stopped in his tracks, and whirled around, his urgent business forgotten. "My dad's here?"

Jamie heard Gideon's inhalation like a slice through the air.

"She means me, Blake," he said gently.

"Oh." The boy's face fell. He closed the bathroom door.

Gideon sagged against the wall. "James, what the hell am I doing? Why did I think this would be a good idea?"

She turned on him, her voice low and harsh. "You're doing the right thing, and you're going to keep on doing the right thing. If you chicken out now, I swear, Gideon, I'll break you. Of course the kid's confused. That's natural. He doesn't know you, you don't know him. But it'll come. As long as you keep trying."

Gideon nodded. "Sure. I know."

She heard the whoosh of the toilet flushing, and the tap running, then the door opened.

Jamie squatted down to be at his level. "I want to tell you something, bud. You are one lucky dude, did you know that?"

Blake blinked at her. "No."

"You are. I didn't have one single dad when I was your age. And you've got two. Two whole dads! That's pretty darn lucky, the way I see it."

The boy frowned and looked hesitantly at Gideon.

Jamie snapped her fingers. "Eyes here, short stuff. I mean it. You've got the dad you and your mom live with, what's-his-name, Elliot, right?"

Her top lip wanted to curl up when she said the name, but she forced it to remain in place. The turd deserved a pounding for presuming he had the right to judge Gideon and the ranch, and she'd be happy to provide it, but right now, right here, they had to play nice.

Blake nodded.

"And he's a great guy, right?" She deserved one of the awards sitting on Roman's mantel, for this performance.

Another quick nod.

"And, now you've got Gideon, who's the dad who helped make you. You don't know him yet so it's weird." She made a face and Blake smiled. "But trust me. He's a great guy, too. You'll see." Then she leaned closer and lowered her voice. "Can I tell you a secret?"

Gideon adopted a hurt expression and opened his hands, palm out. "Hey, can't I hear it too?"

"No. It's just for Blake."

Blake brightened and moved closer. "What is it?"

She cupped her hand next to his ear. "He's scared of you," she whispered.

"Who is?" Blake whispered back.

She grinned. "Gideon."

Blake's mouth formed an O. "He is? Why?"

She shrugged. "Why are you scared?"

"'Cause I never met him before."

"Probably the same with him."

"But he's a grown-up."

"You think grown-ups don't get scared? Buddy, I've got news for you. Big people get scared just like little people do."

"Really?" Blake's eyes were saucer wide.

"Really-really. But don't tell him, okay?"

Blake giggled. "Okay."

His breath was warm and smelled faintly sweet, like oranges.

She stood up.

"If you two are finished with all your whispering and giggling," Gideon said, "maybe we can visit the horses now?"

Blake tugged on Jamie's arm. "I'm scared of horses."

Gideon opened his mouth, but she held up one finger before he could speak. "How about," she said, lowering her voice with a conspiratorial air, "some baby kittens?"

"Kittens?" Blake said.

Jamie nodded. "Gideon found them a few weeks ago

and rescued them. They were very sick. But they're fat and healthy now."

She was aware of Gideon watching her as she spoke. Could feel the energy changing, the tension abating between him and his son and, in its place, something else arising, the gentle hum of electricity arcing to her instead.

"Actually," Gideon said, his voice soft, "Jamie rescued them."

Blake looked back and forth between the two of them, his head tilting. "Is Gideon your boyfriend?"

Jamie jumped. The innocent assumption sent her heart racing even as the thought of Gideon's reaction scared the crap out of her. "Oh, no. We're just friends. We should find those kittens. Or, Gideon, you know where they are, right?"

He nodded. But his smile had faded, replaced by a quiz-zical expression, as if something familiar had become suddenly unrecognizable. Or vice versa.

"I'll see you later, Jamie," he said. Was there a slight upturn at the end of the phrase? Did he want to see her later? Or was it her imagination?

No, she decided. He was busy with Blake. They'd tabled anything that may have been between them.

But still, she couldn't help but hope.

Chapter Twenty-One

*Don't let the Venus–Saturn opposition cause a rift
between you and someone you love.*

—Gideon's horoscope

Blake hopped into Lana's black Audi without a backward glance. Lana buckled him in, then walked stiffly up to Gideon.

She glanced at Jamie and cleared her throat.

"We had a fun time." Jamie bared her teeth in a grin, as if she was determined to make Lana smile. "He's a great kid."

"You didn't mention you were in a relationship," Lana said to Gideon, cutting her eyes at Jamie.

"Oh, he's not," Jamie put in quickly. "Don't worry about that at all. We're just friends. You know. Good friends."

Another bright, wide-eyed smile.

Gideon didn't know what to say. His feelings for Jamie had changed, yes, but with Lana looking at Jamie like she had the mark of the beast tattooed on her forehead, he could hardly act on it.

"If you say so," Lana said. She quizzed Gideon then about what they'd done, what he'd eaten, if he'd been hurt or frightened.

"He had fun, Lana," Gideon told her, suddenly exhausted.

"He played with baby kittens and a poodle. We climbed a stack of hay bales, went for a tractor ride, ate meatloaf and mashed potatoes. We had a great time."

Lana narrowed her eyes as if unsure of whether or not to believe him. They confirmed the date for Blake's next visit, and she left.

As they watched the dust from behind her tires plume into the evening air, Jamie slipped her hand into his and squeezed lightly.

"You did good, Dad."

He pressed the back of his hand to his forehead. "That may be the hardest thing I've ever done in my life. You really think he had fun?"

She tipped her head sideways. "He was nervous, too. I think he's been pretty sheltered. But that means this is good for him. You're doing the right thing, Gideon."

He nodded.

She reached up, placed a soft kiss on his cheek, and then turned to go.

"Wait."

She looked up at him in surprise, and he felt as if he was on a steep precipice, about to take a step into thin air. He didn't deserve her and she certainly deserved better.

The least he could do was give her the truth.

"You want a cup of coffee?"

She lifted her eyebrows. "Gideon Low. Are you asking me back to your cabin?"

Her gentle teasing eased the roughness inside him, put them back onto familiar footing.

"Yes or no, Vaughn. I might rescind the offer at any moment."

"Well then," she said, linking her arm through his. "How could I refuse."

The last of the sunlight was filtering through the trees as they walked across the yard to the staff cabins, painting the path gold and red and orange. Birds settled above them, calling softly as they prepared to rest. Something sweet scented the air, lavender from Daphne's herb garden, maybe.

It felt completely natural for them to be walking together like this.

Inside the cabin, he spent several minutes moving dishes from place to place, heating water and grinding beans. Now that she was here, he wanted to call back the offer. He wanted to sit with her and hold her hand and touch her hair and put his cheek against hers.

He wanted much more than that, truth be told.

"Gideon," Jamie said, patting the couch seat beside her. "You're going to wear a hole in the floor. Just spit it out. I won't think worse of you."

He shook his head and looked down at his hands. "I told you I was in prison."

"Yup. It was a really short story. Is there more?"

So much more. "It's ugly, Jamie. I've spent a lot of time trying to forget it."

"And how's that worked for you?" Her voice was sharp now, the sympathy wiped out by alarm. "You've got peace like a river in your soul? Love like an ocean? No. You're sick inside. It's poison. I promise, it'll help to talk about it."

"I doubt that." He pressed his hands against his skull as if he could physically make the words start flowing in the right order.

Where, exactly, was the beginning, he wondered?

"I used to gamble," he said abruptly.

It wasn't the beginning, but it would do.

The second of two sons born to a thick-knuckled, bad-tempered tree-pruner of Malaysian descent and a stoic British seamstress, Gideon Low had learned early to watch for the subtle warning signs of trouble. The twitch of a throat muscle, the lines around the mouth that tightened almost imperceptibly, the slight increase in respiration or blinking.

Picking at a cuticle, biting a nail. Simple stillness could tell an epic story, if one was listening.

And Gideon had listened.

His brother, Josiah, had not. He'd inherited the simmering anger of their father but without the control of their mother, and seemed to take pleasure in running afoul of the older man's temper. Gideon had learned a great deal from watching their battles, even when they were fought in chilly silence. He'd seen the toll they'd taken on their mother, how she had been tortured between the love she had for her husband and that she had for her son and how she had been continually forced to choose sides in a war with no winners.

"I learned to stay quiet," he said.

Jamie reached over to squeeze his hand. "I like you better when you're talking. Go on."

When he was seventeen, he'd watched nineteen-year-old Josiah pack his bags, knowing it was probably best for everyone. The relief of a quiet house had quickly been dispelled by the weight of parental hope, laser-focused now on their second-born.

He'd spent as much time out of the house as possible, and he'd discovered blackjack.

The cards loved him and he loved them back. Every lunch hour and spare period at the exclusive Seattle high school his parents had moved him to at great personal sacrifice, he'd played cards with his friends, relieving most of them of their spending money, but losing just often enough that they'd continue to play with him. At night, he'd played online, honing his skill with cards, if not people. Although tall and strong, he hadn't been a jock or a nerd or a clown. He'd been a too-serious unidentifiably mixed-race kid who hadn't dressed quite as well as his classmates and had no car of his own.

After graduation from high school, he'd worked for his

parents for a few years, long enough to be certain it wasn't for him, then entered college, majoring in business. His parents, still believing he'd one day take over the landscaping company, had been pleased.

"I figured," he said, "that by the time I graduated, my parents would have let go of the idea."

Since he'd started talking, Jamie had moved closer to him and now the lengths of their thighs were touching. She kept his hand in hers, turning it over, stroking. He had to work to recall the threads of his story.

"In college," he went on, "I discovered poker."

Five-card stud and Texas Hold'em were becoming all the rage and he'd dived in. Again, the cards had loved him. He had a mind for patterns and numbers, and an excellent memory. He'd also discovered that the complicated family dynamic in the Low household had given him a gift for reading people.

By the end of his second year in college, he'd had no need for the money his parents sent, nor what they paid him to work in the summer. He'd tucked their money in a separate account, resolved to return it when the time was right.

But again, not wanting to rock the boat, or admit his newfound relative wealth, he'd cut sod and shovelled mulch and dragged hoses all day long throughout the summer, and spent his nights making his real money. He'd played mostly online, but dreamed of participating in real-life tournaments one day.

By his third year in college, he'd had the world by the tail. He'd had a healthy-enough bank balance that the idea of a nine-to-five job had lost its appeal. He'd learned to invest, and diversified the holdings in his parents' name also. He'd looked forward to paying them back, if not earning their gratitude, then at least assuaging the guilt he felt over not falling in with their plans.

At the end of third year, he'd returned to work in the nursery again, still unable to tell them that their plans for retirement would not involve him taking over the business. The secret had kept him up at night, but he'd spent the time playing and winning even more. He'd built an online persona that was so much better than reality.

"I wasn't that quiet kid no one noticed anymore," he said. "I was The Prophet."

He laughed at the absurdity of it.

"I bet the girls noticed you plenty." Jamie gave him a frankly appreciative look that accelerated his pulse.

He shrugged, not wanting to talk about that. The little affection he'd witnessed at home had made him distrust romantic entanglements. Relationships had been superficial and fleeting, another thing he wasn't proud of.

During his fourth year, he had been invited to a stag party for a classmate who was getting married. Delighted and somewhat shocked to be included, Gideon had joined the cohort in a Las Vegas guys weekend.

Within hours of landing on the strip, he'd discovered that his friends were interested in nothing but strippers and booze, so he'd wandered into the Bellagio and signed up for a tournament.

"I stayed a full week," he said. "I was hooked."

He'd come clean with his parents after graduation, but they couldn't forgive him for refusing his place in the business. They'd rejected the money, too, so he'd reinvested it and it had continued to grow.

He'd taken a job with a marketing firm in Vegas, so he could continue playing, and spent the next several years getting a master's degree in economics and building his portfolio.

"I basically coasted," he admitted. "And then I met Lana."

"Lana," Jamie echoed.

The air changed between them, grew heavier, laden with something that could be promise, could be dread.

"She was young, a junior at UNLV, dealing cards on the weekend." He exhaled through his mouth. "It was a classic whirlwind romance. And it nearly destroyed me."

At first, it had been good. She was beautiful, funny, smart, and always ready for sex. What twenty-eight-year-old male was going to argue with that?

Gideon looked up at Jamie and felt his cheeks heat up. "Sorry. You probably don't want to hear that."

"I could live without it."

"Don't worry, it didn't last long."

The end had begun in a fight about money, of course. His winnings. Their future. Where they were going to settle down. When they were going to settle down.

If they were going to settle down.

Lana had decided.

He had not.

He'd decided to quit his job for a year, play full-time, take time to travel, apart from Lana. Let her figure out her life, or at least finish her degree. Get some distance, some perspective. A little freedom.

Instead, she'd quit college, following him from tournament to tournament, then Reno and even Macau.

As the months went on, and his success had grown and his social world had expanded, Lana's world had shrunk. Her happiness had hinged more and more on what he said or how he treated her. The pressure had been too much.

"She was suffocating me," he said, determined to make a full confession. "I had a whole life, friends, travel plans, and she was always there, waiting for me, adjusting her plans, always expecting something more, growing unhappier by the minute."

"She didn't want to be left out," Jamie said. "She knew you were pulling away."

"Probably." He sighed again. "Twenty-twenty hindsight, and a lot of years to sharpen that vision."

He'd expected she'd give up and dump him. It had never occurred to him to end things himself.

But Lana had had no intention of letting him go.

"Let me guess." Jamie shifted in her seat. "She got pregnant."

"She chose to tell me just as I was on my way out to a big tournament. My reaction wasn't optimal."

It had been an awful scene. Lana had claimed she hadn't planned it, that she'd been on antibiotics for a sinus infection, that if he didn't want it, she'd get rid of it. But she'd begged him to decide right then, to change his plans, to give up the game that night and stay with her instead.

Instead, he'd grabbed another beer and gone to the balcony before he said something he would regret.

"She knew how important that game was to me," he said. "It was like I couldn't compute what was happening. All I knew was that I had to get out."

Get out of the room, get out of the house, get away from her, so he could breathe.

He forced himself to remember the events, now, determined not to let himself off the hook. If he was to tell Jamie, he'd have to do it bare bones, just the facts, no excusing himself or seeking her sympathy.

There were no excuses and he deserved no sympathy.

He'd insisted on going to the casino, but he'd spent too much time alternately arguing with and comforting Lana to walk there, as he'd planned. He had to drive, or risk a cabbie not getting him there on time.

He'd left the garage of their luxury condo, his only thought to get to the casino, sit down at the table, and lose himself in the cards, the numbers, the faces and tics and tells that he was so good at reading, even though he couldn't read his own girlfriend.

Instead, before he'd even made it out of the neighborhood, he'd looked down for a split second to adjust his satellite radio. A woman bending into the backseat of a car parked on the side of the road had straightened up at the same split second and then stumbled, right into the path of the vehicle.

All Gideon had seen before the crash was her wide-eyed terror.

And the toddler in her arms.

Chapter Twenty-Two

A continuing Sun–Mars merger will light your fire.
Enjoy the heat but don't get burned.

—Jamie's horoscope

"**O**h, Gideon."
Jamie pressed her fingertips against her lips to stem her reaction. Gideon was lost in the telling and he didn't need her bringing him back.

He'd moved to the upholstered chair next to the window, while she remained cross-legged on the couch that butted up against it in the small room.

Pulling away.

Protecting himself.

"I told you it was ugly."

The child had been bruised and frightened but intact. The mother had sustained two fractured vertebrae and a broken pelvis.

Gideon, of course, hadn't had a scratch on him.

Even his car had had only minor front end damage, a sickening insult, a mockery of the devastation that it had wrought under his thoughtless hands.

He hadn't been speeding. Witnesses had seen her turn her ankle and fall into his path.

But those two drinks he'd had earlier had been just enough, and that was that.

"My emotional state alone was enough to impair me," he said. "I should have known better."

Now she understood why he didn't drink.

He fell silent and she let the emptiness stretch out between them. Nothing in the year and a half she'd known him had prepared her for this. Polite, quiet Gideon, who treated everyone with such respect and kindness, who never raised his voice, let alone his hand, to even that nastiest of Olivia's horses.

"By the time I got out, my boy was four years old." He braced his elbows on his knees and hung his head, as if he was too tired to hold it up. "She stuck with me until I was sentenced, but once she realized I was actually going to prison, she cut bait. I couldn't blame her, didn't care one way or another, in fact. She sent me a card when the baby was born. Told me his name was Blake. I didn't feel a thing. You know, Jamie, I've always felt badly about that, that I didn't feel some kind of connection to him."

He shook his head, an expression of bewilderment on his face.

"But why would you?" Jamie worked to keep her tone even. Gideon didn't need her anger. "How could you feel connected to him? You hadn't even seen him."

"Whenever I thought about him, I pictured that other little boy, in his mother's arms. He had on a blue jacket and his cheeks were red, like apples."

He shuddered, then seemed to pull himself together. "I started an account for him, and set everything up for Lana before I went in, too. House, money. That much I could do."

Gideon had been out of prison for two years now. His son would be six years old, old enough to start asking questions, to wonder about his father, to want more than whatever story Lana had made up about him.

Her heart broke. She leaned forward, clasping his hands in hers. "I don't know what kind of mom Lana is, or what Elliot is like with Blake. But I know this. Neither of them is you. You're his father and you're amazing. He deserves to know you. You deserve to know him."

He gave her hands a squeeze, then patted them lightly. "That's nice of you to say, James."

She yanked her hands away, stung. Nice. It was about the worst response he could give her.

"I'm never nice, Gideon." She lifted her hand, ready to slap him to prove her point.

But he grabbed her hand, and before she realized what he was doing, he yanked her to his chest. Suddenly, he was kissing her, as if she were the only thing holding him together.

"Oh!" she gasped, as he settled her onto his lap and cupped his hands behind her head. "This is a surprise."

"Don't talk," he said, pulling her to him again.

His lips were as soft and full and perfect as she'd always known they would be. He tasted of fresh water with a hint of salt, the way their skin would taste if they went skinny-dipping where Driftwood Creek met the sea.

His hands roved over her back, pressing her to his chest, and she could feel the evidence of his arousal hot and hard beneath her.

She couldn't breathe. She felt like her heart was going to burst through her chest. Finally, after all this time.

She tugged at his shirt, pulling it up, over and out, desperate to be closer, to feel his skin against hers, to feel the weight of his body, to explore the planes of his belly, the lines of his back, those gorgeous shoulders.

"Jamie," he whispered, his lips moving over her neck. "We can't."

"Yes, yes, we can." They had to. If she didn't feel him inside her soon, she'd explode. She'd waited so long.

She shimmied out of her jeans, tore off her shirt, and was

tugging at the buttons of his fly when he captured her hands, stopping her.

"What?" She hardly recognized her own voice, it was so full of wanting. She was near tears, desperate that he was going to change his mind.

But that wasn't it.

"Don't hurry," was all he said.

And then he proceeded to, very slowly, slip one bra strap off her shoulder, then the other. He sighed, looking at her, and then he trailed his big hand, his big, dark hand, down her ribs, to her hips and hooked a finger under the elastic of her bikini panties.

She quivered so hard her teeth chattered together. "I'm not cold," she assured him.

He gave her a slow smile and glanced down at her nipples. "Parts of you are." His finger dipped lower. "But other parts are hot. Holy hell, Jamie, how can I resist you?"

"Why would you try?" she replied huskily. "I'm here for you, Gideon. I've always been here for you."

His expression clouded at that, and she knew she'd said something wrong.

She wrapped her arms around his neck, kissing him back with all the hurt fury that had been pent up inside her for so long. She lifted one leg and gripped him behind the knee.

He pulled her off the couch and lowered her to the floor, tossing a blanket down for her. It was still hard against her ass, but she didn't care. Finally, she'd show Gideon that they were meant to be together, that they were perfect together. That of all the people in the universe, there was only one of him and one of her and some wise God had put them on the planet at the same time, in the same place so that they could find one another and turn those dark empty spaces light with love and laughter.

They already shared so much laughter. It was one small step to love.

"Jamie," he muttered against her throat. With a calloused hand he kneaded her breast roughly but oh, so perfectly.

"Shh," she said. "Don't talk."

Her chest bared, he moved over it with his lips, sucking and biting gently at her nipples until jolts of fire raced down her body, settling into a throbbing heat between her legs.

He traced one finger up and down her torso again, making her quiver in the moonlight.

She almost wept. Her voice shook. "Don't make me beg."

His face softened then. He ran his finger down the side of her face, looking at her with something like amazement.

"You're so beautiful, my Jamie," he murmured.

Her heart soared at the words. "I am yours, Gideon. I always have been. Let me show you."

"I'm powerless against you. I should be stronger, but I'm not. God help me, I'm not."

And he lowered himself to her again, closing his mouth over hers, their tongues dancing back and forth, sharing breath.

Then the last of his clothes were off and they were skin to skin and she felt the length of him against her, finally, all the glorious, sleek, muscled hardness she'd craved. He lowered his head to her breast and suckled, at the same time dipping his fingers between her legs. He stroked her slick heat and she gasped. She'd been ready for him for so long.

He slid off to lie beside her while he touched and explored, kissing and fondling and nuzzling, driving her higher and higher until she exploded around him, arching her back, throwing her arms above her, crying out as waves of pleasure crested and broke.

When she regained her breath, she looked at him. He was gazing at her as if he couldn't get enough of her.

"What?" The world was still spinning. "What are you looking at?"

He smiled. "You."

"You're making me self-conscious. This is supposed to be a two-person game."

"I could do that all night."

"Said no man, ever."

He chuckled. "I'm not saying it's all I want to do."

"Then come here."

She reached for him, taking pleasure in his quick intake of air. He groaned as she stroked, slowly, then quicker.

Suddenly, he froze and rolled away from her.

"What?" she asked.

"Condom," he said, through gritted teeth. "I'm praying you have one."

"No need," she said. "IUD. I don't have any diseases. Do you?"

She took up the rhythm of stroking him again.

"No. Thank God."

"Shh."

She ran her finger over the moist tip, then shifted so that she was straddling him.

She lowered herself onto him, slowly, feeling her body expand to accept him. At that moment, she didn't care about anything other than joining herself with him, finally.

She felt her own passion rising again as they set up a rhythm. He gripped her hips, then reached up to capture her mouth again. They kissed endlessly, and she held his head, running her fingers through his hair. Then the waves began to crash over her again, and she threw back her head, crying out, clenching around him.

Suddenly, with a groan, he flipped her off him, put her on her back and drove himself into her again. Over and over, one hand beneath her to protect her from the wood floor, kissing and biting and suckling until with a hoarse cry, he stiffened and emptied himself into her.

Then, he collapsed beside her on the rumpled blanket, their naked bodies glistening with sweat.

She felt at that moment what everyone feels at one point in their lives when they dream of achieving the impossible, the need to be good, to be righteous, to be of service, dutiful and brave, to be trusted and commanded, and sent out to slay dragons. She believed, to her sudden amazement, in the cupid-bows of romance, that love could be not just a fairy tale but the truest truth, and the whole force and shaping passion of life.

"Gideon," she whispered, taking his hand. She loved him so much. Should she say it? Or would it drive him away?

Surely, he'd recognize now that what they had was special. He threw one arm over his forehead, panting hard. She felt her throat tighten, amazed that this had finally happened.

But as he caught his breath and the sweat cooled on their bodies and they grew chill, she felt him pulling away. She felt the change in him. She snuggled against his side, and he held her, but he hadn't said a word. A nameless dread came over her.

Chapter Twenty-Three

Uranus retrograde is a time to rethink old beliefs and free yourself from patterns that no longer work.

—Gideon's horoscope

Gideon spent the next morning in a haze, his extremities tingling, his senses heightened. He swore he could still taste the sweet sweat on Jamie's skin, but maybe it was just the salt breeze drifting in from the ocean.

Then Roman Byers arrived for a session with Apollo and jolted him back to normal.

"What's the matter with you?" snapped the man, when Gideon dropped a bucket of oats outside the horse's stall. "You're scaring him."

Roman left Sadie in the breezeway and entered the stall, lowering himself gingerly onto the straw bale, armed with carrots, apple slices, and a curry comb. He'd become protective of the old horse, but whether it improved his mood or not was anyone's guess.

It certainly hadn't improved Gideon's mood. Roman monopolized Jamie whenever they were together, which left Gideon feeling both left out and useless. If this was equine therapy, it didn't seem to be accomplishing anything.

Apollo approached from the back of the stall, his ears pricked forward, and Gideon was surprised to note that his step was a bit more confident. Perhaps his feet were starting to feel better. And his eyes seemed clearer, too.

He amended his opinion. If the extra attention from Roman had achieved this, then it was worthwhile after all.

Gideon went about his chores, staying nearby, just in case. With Roman's mumbling and grumbling in the background, he let his thoughts drift back to Jamie.

The sex was probably a mistake that would complicate things between them, but he didn't regret it. She'd caught him at a weak moment and truth be told, he'd needed what she'd offered.

Holy God, had he needed it. The physical connection had been a natural culmination to the emotional outpouring she'd triggered, and he'd been desperate for both, he realized. He'd been shut down for a long time, in every way, but she'd awakened him. No power on earth could have pulled him away from her unselfconscious enthusiasm, her generosity, her ability to give and receive pleasure.

All that tight, wet heat.

He gripped the pitchfork with restless fingers, remembering that second, spontaneous orgasm. She came so easily, had she any idea what that did to a man? To see a woman find pleasure so quickly, to feel her clamp around him like that?

He'd lost his mind, become crazed, fully, completely. Damn the consequences. He loved her. She loved him. It was perfect pleasure and nothing else mattered.

Wait. He straightened up and the tool slipped out of his fingers, clattering onto the concrete floor.

Roman's head appeared above Apollo's stall wall. "Damn it, man. Do you have to be so noisy?"

"Sorry," Gideon said, barely listening.

No one had said anything about love.

After that first, explosive bout on his living room floor, they'd taken a hot, soapy shower together, and made love a second time, in his bed, slowly and luxuriantly.

She'd stroked his face so tenderly and when she'd begun to shake and cry out again, he'd nearly shouted out with joy. She was right, they were good together.

But then she'd kissed him, put on her clothes, and disappeared into the night.

He hadn't seen her at all today, and every minute seemed to stretch longer and become more laden with suspense. Had he imagined the tenderness? He wanted her again, but what if she'd had time to think about his confession, consider the baggage he brought into the relationship and decided to protect herself? It's what he'd advise. Hell, he'd warned her away, hadn't he? He was a bad bet. But she'd played her hand anyway.

Then again, it was a busy time of year. Haylee'd been impressed with the bond Jamie had built with the poodle and was letting her work more with the puppy. They had livestock to move before winter, a full roster of guest activities coming up, and then, the autumn slaughter.

It was nothing personal.

Still, he wished he'd seen her at breakfast. Jamie didn't hide her feelings. He'd know immediately if she regretted last night, or if, like him, she wanted more.

A tiny part of him feared that once more, he'd thrown his heart onto the table without knowing for certain that he had the hand to back it.

Lana had nearly broken him when she'd deprived him of his son. He would let no woman do that to him again.

Fortunately, Jamie understood that Blake was his priority. Maybe one day, there could be something more between the two of them. Once he'd sorted out his life, become the father Blake needed.

She understood that whatever was happening between them would have to stay casual.

Settled in his mind, he went about his chores, then went to the tack room to do a bit more work on the saddle. Olivia had decided not to sell it to him, but instead to give it to Jamie for her birthday, as a lead-in for Gideon's gift.

He smiled, thinking of the mustang boarding at the farm. He couldn't wait to see Jamie's face when she learned that the horse was hers.

This, at least, he could give her, he thought with a twinge.

A sliding sound came from Apollo's stall, followed by a thump, then a moan.

Gideon left the wheelbarrow in the middle of the breezeway and rushed to the old horse's box, where Sadie was already on her feet, barking and pawing at the door.

Gideon was next to him in three strides. "What is it? What happened?"

Roman squeezed his eyes shut tight. He lay half on, half off the straw bale. "Goddamn it," he managed through gritted teeth. "Lock down. Can't move."

"How can I help?"

"You can't." Roman panted. His arms were shaking. "It'll pass."

Beside him, Sadie whined and pawed at his legs. Apollo, not bothered by the dog's presence, nudged Roman with his big muzzle.

"I'm getting you to the hospital."

"No." Roman shifted slightly, then jerked wildly, crying out. "Aw, hell. Fine."

Gideon ran outside, hoping someone would be within earshot. His heart leaped to see Jamie exiting the kennel.

"What?" she said, her eyes widening at his expression.

"It's Roman," he said. "He fell or something. I'm taking him to the hospital. Can you call Jonathan?"

"Of course. Do you need help?"

"Can you bring my truck to the front of the stables?"

She took the keys he handed her and ran off. Gideon jogged back to the stall, where he found the man hovering on the edge of the straw bale.

"I'm fine," Roman said. Perspiration shone on his forehead. "You're overreacting."

"Maybe," Gideon said. "Think of it as a liability issue."

Hoping he wasn't hurting the man, he positioned himself underneath him, to bear as much of his weight as possible.

"Okay?" he said. "Now stand up."

With a hoarse groan, Roman got upright. Sadie was beside herself, hovering so close they almost stepped on her. They made it to the truck and, with Jamie's help, they got the man settled into the passenger seat. He was sweating profusely now.

"Roman." Jamie bent over him. "Where are your pills?"

Roman squeezed his eyes shut and shook his head.

Sadie jumped up, trying to get in beside him. She missed, her claws scrabbling wildly against the upholstery and Roman's leg.

"God almighty, dog," Roman cried out. "Jamie, help her in, will you?"

"I can keep her here if you want." Jamie's eyes met Gideon's in a mute question.

"It's okay," Gideon said, lifting the dog into the car. "He needs her."

Gideon wheeled Roman into the emergency room with Sadie pacing anxiously beside them. He hadn't thought to grab a leash, but the dog stayed close.

When they took Roman into triage, he kept the dog with him. Obedient but unhappy, she danced from foot to foot, agitated and upset at the separation.

"Settle down, girl," Gideon said, patting her. Perhaps he should have left her with Jamie after all.

About twenty minutes after their arrival, a small Asian woman appeared.

"There she is. Sadie, you can come on in now. Your master is waiting."

Sadie limped over to her as fast as her feet could find purchase on the slippery tile floor.

"You know her?" Gideon asked.

The nurse looked up in surprise. "Mr. Byers is a regular, and we're all big fans of Sadie. Come on, girl."

They disappeared behind the double metal doors. Gideon sat in the waiting room, resting his forearms on his knees, his hands folded. *Where is Jonathan? He should be here.*

"Are you with Mr. Byers?" A different young woman came through the doors. She was wearing green scrubs and had a stethoscope around her neck.

"I am." He got to his feet. "How's he doing?"

"Are you family?"

Gideon blew out a breath. If he said no, they might not give him any information, might not even let him see the man. "Yes. A son."

Roman needed someone with him. As soon as Jonathan arrived, he'd relinquish the role.

"I'm Dr. Fairchild. Follow me. And thanks for bringing the dog. He does so much better when she's with him."

She brought him to a curtained-off area where the older man lay on a narrow bed, pillows wedged around his body. His color was better, Gideon noted, and he was breathing normally again. He appeared to be asleep. Sadie lay curled up on a layer of flannel sheets in the corner, her head on her paws, motionless except for her eyes.

"Is he going to be okay?" Gideon whispered.

"How much do you know about his condition?" the doctor asked.

Nothing, Gideon wanted to say. *Not one damn thing*. But that would get him evicted and wouldn't help Roman one bit.

He shrugged instead. "Not as much as I should. He's chintzy with the details. Doesn't like to talk about it, I guess."

"Sounds familiar." She smiled. "My dad's the same way. We're waiting on radiology, but I don't think he's broken anything. The degeneration already present, combined with soft-tissue injury and scarring results in massive, deep spasms like what you witnessed. Given his previous nerve damage, it's a complicated situation. The spasm will ease and we've medicated him so he's not in pain. As soon as Jonathan arrives, we'll discharge him. That's right." She leaned closer to him. "I know you're not his son. But I also know that Roman wouldn't have let you touch him unless he was in seriously rough shape. And since you brought him in, and you stayed, you obviously care about him. You're a good man."

Shows what you know, Gideon wanted to say. He regretted his impatience at the old man's grouchiness. Olivia often said that no one got up in the morning determined to be an asshole, but that enough pain, disappointment, or sorrow could make anyone behave badly.

In that case, Roman Byers must be dealing with a lot of heartache.

The doctor was looking at her watch and there was activity over by the nurses' station, so he thanked her and let her go.

He stepped closer to the man in the bed. "You asleep?"

"Nope," said Roman and smiled droopily.

Drugged. Good.

"I'm going to go find some coffee," Gideon said. "You okay if I leave for a few minutes?"

"Never wanted you here in the first place." He spoke deliberately, as if picking the words out of a hat and finding, to his delight, that they went together.

"I recall," Gideon said. "Can I get you anything?"

"Got everything I need right here." Roman tapped the IV taped to his hand. "Where's my dog?"

"On the floor."

Roman turned his head slowly, then blinked. "Good. Good girl. She's a very good girl. Be sad when she goes. Big shoes to fill. Chaos can't do it."

Gideon thought of how much emotional effort Jamie had already invested in the pup. How much of her own time she'd spent teaching him basic obedience, how far the little guy had come since she'd picked up the runaway at Driftwood Creek.

"Give him time," he said. "He's in good hands."

"Your girlfriend's a smart cookie." Roman was fading fast.

Girlfriend. The word caught him off guard. He let it roll around in his mind for a moment. It wasn't wrong, but it wasn't entirely right, either.

"Jamie's got a gift," he said.

He could have said a lot more. She had passion. She had skill. She had more patience than she gave herself credit for, she had the ability to see what others couldn't, to encourage, cajole, badger, whatever was necessary, to make someone believe in themselves again.

She'd made him believe in himself, he realized with a jolt.

"You love her." Roman's eyes were closed and his voice had taken on a singsong quality.

Gideon didn't know what to say. Maybe he should just leave. Roman probably wasn't completely aware of his presence and, with any luck, wouldn't remember this conversation tomorrow.

"You love her," he repeated, louder.

"Jamie's my friend," Gideon said, emphasizing the word. He looked around for someone, anyone. Nobody.

"A friend you want naked," Roman continued.

Heat rushed into Gideon's face. How on earth did Roman know that? "Yeah, I'm going to get that coffee now."

Roman blew a raspberry. Those drugs were doing a number on him. "Shoulda kissed her at the creek that day. She wanted it. You did too."

Gideon stopped. "You saw that?"

A rough laugh. "Pissed her off, too. Take her to a nice hotel, man. That's what I always did. Women appreciate a little effort."

"Well." Gideon shoved his hands deep into his pockets. "Okay then."

He nearly bumped into Jonathan as he rounded the corner to the vending machines.

The younger man grabbed his arm. "Gideon! Thank God. Where is he? Is he okay?"

Gideon reassured him, pointed the way and, relieved, made his way to the parking lot.

All the way home, Roman's words echoed in his mind. Did he love Jamie? Of course. She was easy to be around. They had a lot in common. The horses. Their need for solitude. They respected each other but also knew how to joke around.

But did he love her the way she wanted?

That moment beside the pool had been his first inkling that what he'd thought was a crush on her part might be more. After the battering his pride had taken over the past few years, to see a woman he cared about look at him with admiration and genuine interest, well, it did his soul good. Maybe, if it hadn't felt so good, he could have stopped things before they got to this stage, before the stakes had risen and words like love and girlfriend started to go around and people's hearts were on the line.

"Damn," he muttered, as he pulled his truck to a stop next to his cabin. He lay his forehead against the steering wheel.

Learning to love his son took all the emotional energy he had. Jamie deserved someone who could love her with his whole heart, and whatever beat inside his chest might have been a slab of frozen beef, for all the good it did anyone. All the soft, tender bits had been carved off long ago and what was left was hard and stringy, utilitarian only. It moved to bring blood throughout his body. There was nothing left over for anyone else.

If he really loved Jamie, the kindest thing he could do was to let her go.

Chapter Twenty-Four

With Venus in Cancer, don't be surprised if you
start crying at cat food commercials.

—Jamie's horoscope

"**I**'m done." Haylee waddled into the main house and flopped into the chair nearest the window. "Life's too short to deal with mean old men with attitude problems."

Jamie looked up from scraping carrots for Daphne's stew. There was only one person Haylee could be talking about: Roman Byers. Her pulse sped up. Since the day Gideon had taken the man to the hospital, he'd gone to his place to check up on him daily and driven him back to the ranch several times a week to visit the horse.

Every time Roman visited the horse, he had a training session with Haylee and unfortunately, his outlook on life hadn't been improved by recent events.

"Does that mean you want me to take over?" she asked. "I've got almost no mean old men with attitude problems in my life. Well, except for him."

She looked over at Huck, who stood leaning against the doorframe, cleaning under his nails with a pocket-knife. Except for the bright pink knitted beanie, he was the poster-boy image of a young, healthy, happy ranch hand.

"Thank you, ma'am." Huck tipped his head.

The only old man with an attitude problem in her life was Gideon, and he'd gone dark and distant again. Maybe it was about Blake, but she had a bad feeling he regretted telling her his story, regretted the intimacy they'd shared that night.

"I'm serious." Haylee let her forearm flop onto her face. "The SOB thinks he has nothing to learn from me."

"Language," chided Daphne. "Little pitchers have big ears."

She glanced to the other room, where Sage was playing with the baby.

"SOB?" said Haylee. "Seriously?"

Tyler hovered in the entrance. "Like we all haven't heard far worse." His eyes followed Sage's movements hungrily. Jamie figured he had a mad crush on Sage but was terrified of the baby. Or, more accurately, terrified of the whole breast-feeding business.

Jamie couldn't blame him. It was pretty gross.

Daphne slammed her cleaver into the pile of fresh parsley on the cutting board. "We have standards, young man. Haylee, do you require a reminder?"

Haylee huffed. "You know I'm part owner here, right, Daphne?"

"We all know who runs the place," the cook replied, running through the greens with frightening speed.

"Yeah, yeah, Olivia's the big cheese, I'm just the niece. Whatever." Haylee sat up, pursing her lips. "Anyway, I've had enough. Roman Byers is all yours, Jamie. I'm done with him. Best of luck, hope you survive, it was nice knowing you."

Jamie gathered the carrot peelings into a pile and tossed them into the compost pail, somehow managing not to leap into the air, pumping her fist. Things with Gideon might be on hold, but at least she had this.

"He's not so bad."

"Oh, he's that bad and worse," countered Haylee. "He called me little lady, today. Then, when he met Sage, he called me Granny."

Daphne let out a hoot of laughter. "Granny Haylee. It never gets old, does it?"

Haylee pulled a cushion over her face. "I'm fat and irritable, and I just want this to be over. I'm so jealous of you, Jamie. You've got the round-up tomorrow, while I'm stuck here, gestating, unable to see my feet."

"Aw," Jamie said. She went over and gave her friend a hug. "You're beautiful when you're full of self-pity, did you know that? And thank you, Haylee."

Haylee rolled her eyes. "You're such a liar. And you'll be singing a different tune soon enough, guaranteed. Daphne? Have you got a cinnamon bun around somewhere? Baby's got a craving."

Should have seen this coming, Gideon reflected, as he found himself handing a steaming bowl of mashed potatoes to Roman Byers.

Between Daphne's soft spot for hungry bellies and Olivia's eye for hungry souls, it was probably only a matter of time before the curmudgeon got added to the payroll. Though what he might have to offer remained a mystery.

Between the four guests Olivia and Huck had just brought in from the trails and the whole staff contingent, including Sage, Sal, Tyler, and Duke, the Byers men made it a full house.

"Help yourself and don't be stingy." Daphne set a container of chilled butter near Roman. "There's always plenty in Daffy's kitchen. You could use some fattening up."

Roman glanced across the table at Olivia. "Is she always like this?"

Olivia gave a bark of laughter. "That's nothing. But I suggest you clean your plate. I don't want to be around when someone insults her cooking."

Daphne lifted her chin. "That day will never come. Jonathan, pass your father the peas."

Jamie smiled warmly at Gideon, but sat next to Jonathan. The two seemed to have no end of conversation.

She was playing it cool, he realized. Smart. No need to let anyone else know about last night. It could be their little secret.

Or maybe it wasn't that. Maybe she was having second thoughts, too. Maybe she'd realized that he was a bad deal, that he came with too much baggage, that someone like Jon would be a much better bet.

He put down his fork, his appetite gone.

But wasn't that what he'd told her himself? If he really cared for her, he'd have pushed her to Jon and kept his own hands off her.

"How's parenthood, Gideon?" asked Sage.

She sat between Olivia and Haylee, little Sal on her lap. The baby was waving her arms, reaching for Sage's fork, making *mum-mum-mum* sounds. A string of drool hung from her lip and her eyes followed the food as it went from the plate to her mother's mouth.

"Great," he said.

"Yeah, it's a laugh riot, all right," Sage said, narrowly avoiding getting mashed potatoes smeared into her hair.

He'd missed so much with Blake.

"Here, let me take her so you can eat," said Haylee, scooping her granddaughter onto her lap.

She was younger than him, and a grandmother. Young motherhood ran in the family, apparently, except Haylee had mostly skipped her first stab at being a mother.

"Where's Aiden?" he asked. He liked the man. He was

good for Haylee, which was the one criteria that mattered to all of them. They'd each walked a lonely, rocky road to find peace on this ranch and now that they'd found it, they protected it, and each other.

If any of the rest of them found out about what he'd been up to with Jamie, they'd string him up.

"Working." Haylee caught the baby's hand as it was heading for her water glass. "Again."

"Here. Give her this." Daphne handed over a thigh bone, cleaned of meat and gristle.

"Daphne," Sage protested. "You can't give her that. She'll choke."

"Every generation thinks they've reinvented parenting. Trust me, honey. If you want to survive, you'll take advice from your betters. And before you ask, that means me. And anyone else who's been there before you."

Sage lifted her eyebrows, intercepting the bone. "I'll get her pacifier."

The baby, having caught a whiff of the savory toy, started wailing.

"Now look what you've done," Sage said. She took the child from Haylee's arms.

"At least you got to eat," Daphne pointed out, as Sage left the table.

"Kids," Roman said, slanting a look at Jonathan.

"Can't live with them, can't shoot them." Daphne shrugged. "My advice looks pretty good to her at two in the morning."

"A wise woman and an amazing cook," Roman said, lifting his half-glass of wine in her direction. "To Daphne."

Gideon clinked his water glass around as everyone joined the toast.

At the far end, with a loud scraping sound, Ezra shoved his chair back. He got to his feet and picked up his plate. His normally placid face was tight, with white spots at the sides of his mouth.

"Excuse me, ma'am." He nodded in Daphne's direction, but didn't make eye contact. "Thank you for another wonderful meal."

He stalked from the dining area, rinsed his plate at the sink, and put it into the industrial sized dishwasher.

Daphne got to her feet and bustled over to him. "Oh, hon, you don't have to do that. Huck and Jamie are on cleanup tonight."

Olivia said something to smooth over the moment and conversation resumed. But Gideon kept watching the two in the kitchen.

"It's no trouble." Ezra wouldn't look at the cook, but he shot a quick glance toward Roman. "That's what family does. We help each other out. It's the least I can do."

That's when Gideon saw it. Despite her fussy, grandmotherly behavior, the cook was an attractive woman, fit and strong from kickboxing, with lines on her face from smiling, sunshine, and the belief that time is a gift.

Ezra wasn't a forward man, though, and he knew Daphne was justifiably wary of romantic relationships.

He caught up with the older man on the porch steps.

"Dessert not to your taste?" Gideon said.

"Table was a little crowded," Ezra replied, pulling his car keys out of his pocket.

"Didn't have you pegged as a man who'd cut and run."

Ezra opened his car door, then turned to face Gideon. "You have something to say, say it."

"Roman Byers is an ass."

Ezra looked toward the porch, where muted laughter and conversation could be heard from inside. "He's a guest."

"He can be both. She's just being polite, you know that,

right? You're going to have to up your game if you want a shot at her."

For a long moment, Ezra was quiet. "Don't take this the wrong way, but I'll look elsewhere for advice on my love life." He exhaled softly. "Watch yourself, Gideon. Jamie's my friend, too."

Chapter Twenty-Five

*A Jupiter–Pluto square can have a negative
aspect on something of great value in your life.*

—Jamie's horoscope

In the corral farthest from the main house, separated from the rest of the outbuildings by a stand of vine maples, Jamie rubbed the head of a two-year-old caramel-colored steer with a white face.

The animal was one of three Blonde d'Aquitaines, a relatively uncommon breed with a reputation for easy birthing, good temperament, and excellent meat that Olivia had added to their small herd of Herefords and Black Angus. Both the Blonde heifers had freshened secretly and uneventfully one night early last spring, producing sturdy, healthy calves that nicely proved the first point.

Charley, the one now nuzzling her pocket for sugar lumps, proved the second.

And would, in about three weeks, prove the third, also. She knew it was stupid to get attached, that playing with him like this would only end up hurting later on, but she hated the thought of any creature living without affection. And since everyone else rotated through slaughterhouse duty, they couldn't be expected to treat the steer like a pet. It felt like a sacred duty to spoil Charley a little during his brief life.

"Jamie!" came a voice from the other side of the fence.

She looked up in surprise. Gideon was waving at her from atop Rosie. Her heart leaped into her throat. Finally, he was ready to talk.

"Come on," he said. "Everyone's waiting."

She glanced at her watch. "Damn," she muttered to Charley. She'd been here longer than she thought.

"We need to get the cattle in before the storm breaks," he added. Something was different about his voice. She couldn't place it exactly, but he sounded like he'd just received bad news.

"Be right there," she yelled back.

Ten minutes later, she was on Nash. Dust from a dozen bovine hooves billowed into the dry air, even though the clouds above were heavy, the air sluggish. A storm would be coming soon, and it would be dramatic, if the sky was any indication.

Good, thought Jamie, nudging her mount toward the left side, where a straggler was threatening to break free from the herd. She wanted some drama. Maybe Gideon thought they could go back to normal, or whatever passed for normal between them, but she couldn't. Everything had changed when they'd made love. She'd given him lots of time and space, but enough was enough.

"Yah!" She gently pressed her heel into Nash's flank and they went wide of the steer. They had two guests riding with them today, Maggie and Ed, a husband and wife who were competent enough in the saddle. Whatever they lacked in skill, they made up for in enthusiasm, and it didn't much matter because the horses did most of the work anyway.

At least, that's what she had thought at the beginning. Ed was riding up front with Gideon. Maggie was back with

Jamie, and even with the horse's help, it was becoming apparent that she was in over her head.

The steer was eyeing a low-lying bluff thick with brambles, and if he got in there, they'd have a hell of a time getting him out. Jamie motioned for Maggie, who was closer, to get between the steer and his target. Maggie waved back and continued on her way, oblivious to the path of the steer.

"James!" yelled Gideon, aware but unable to reach the steer. "You got him?"

"Yeah!" she yelled back, urging Nash hard. She could feel the horse's muscles bunch and gather as he raced toward the steer and she felt as if she were a part of him, and he a part of her, instead of two separate beings. There was a joy in that.

A branch caught her on the sleeve of her western shirt, nearly whipped her in the face. She ducked low in the saddle, urging Nash farther down the path, angling sideways to cut off the steer. Finally the steer got the hint and turned back toward the herd, bawling, eyes rolling dark in its white face, flecks of saliva dotting his red coat.

"Good boy." Jamie patted Nash's neck, staying between the steer and the path to relative freedom.

Don't be an outlier, little bovine. Stick to the herd. That's where it's safe.

Some people, at least, thought that was safe.

Not her.

She sucked in a breath and let Nash fall back to a gentle lope. They were almost within sight of the ranch.

"What a picture, right?" Maggie drew up beside her, her generous figure bouncing in the saddle, waving an arm toward the herd starting down the final leg of the valley that would pass the ranch and eventually edge out toward the ocean.

She had long golden hair pulled into a ponytail at the back of her head, under her white cowboy hat.

"Yeah," said Jamie.

"I'm a vegetarian myself," Maggie continued, "but there's something elemental about a cattle drive that makes me feel like I'm contributing to the survival of my homestead or something."

She laughed, a light tinkling sound. Her smile was genuine and Jamie felt bad about her earlier annoyance.

"I don't eat meat either," she said. "But I can live with this. They grew up out here, happy, safe, no forced weaning, no growth hormones, no feed lot or drugs. They spend their last few weeks in the north pasture, on the best grass with the best view. They're fat and happy before the slaughter."

Maggie shuddered. "Oh, I hate that word."

Jamie did too, but she forced herself to use it. "We use the most humane methods available, but it's still killing.

She'd promised Olivia that she'd be supportive. No more protests. No placards. No proselytizing. She didn't have to eat the meat, but if Jamie wanted to live here, she had to find a way to make peace with the fact that they grew animals for meat.

Just before they reached the creek, the steer darted away from the herd again.

"Jamie!" yelled Gideon.

"Got him!" She dug her heels into Nash's side, calling to Maggie over her shoulder. "Stay here. Hold the line here."

The horse needed no encouragement, his eye on the errant animal, his stride sure and strong.

Jamie felt Nash's power coursing through her, felt like she was flying. Maybe she wasn't polished like Lana or cute like Abby, but she was tough. She could handle shit. She'd handled a lot of crap that would have had other women rocking in a corner.

She could handle Gideon's shit, too. Nothing scared her. Whatever he'd done, he'd done because he had to. She trusted that. And now, he'd do whatever was necessary to get Blake back.

Because that's the kind of guy he was.

The best kind.

Then Nash jerked sideways. Suddenly there was air where the saddle had been, and she actually was flying.

She landed, hard. And everything went black.

Gideon saw Jamie fall. Nash had side-stepped something and Jamie, normally so in tune with the horse, had been caught off guard.

Like it so often happened, he watched the fall as if it were in slow motion. He saw the wind take Jamie's hat, saw her arms fly into the air, saw her legs flailing outwards, saw her bounce and settle on the ground, her limbs loose and flopping.

No, he prayed to a God he'd long ago stopped believing in. *Don't punish her. I'm to blame.*

He put his heels to Rosie and pounded to where Nash stood over Jamie, nudging her in the shoulder with his muzzle.

He slid off and fell to his knees. "Jamie!"

He touched her shoulders, then pulled back, afraid to move her. Panic raced up and down his spine. Every regular rider got thrown or fell off at some point. New horse, not paying attention, bad equipment. Mostly not paying attention. You rolled with it and moved on. Learned from the bruises. But this wasn't any rider.

This was Jamie.

Her eyelids fluttered. He saw her chest rise and fall, thank the sweet Lord, and he didn't see any blood or obvious injuries.

"Jamie, honey, talk to me."

She blinked slowly, then seemed to come back to herself. "Oops," she said. "I'm not s'posed to be down here, am I?"

Breath he didn't realize he'd been holding rushed back into Gideon's lungs. "Are you okay? Are you hurt? Can you move?"

She scrunched up her face, gave her head a shake, and pulled herself up onto her elbows.

Maggie and Ed trotted up to them.

"Is she okay?" Maggie asked. "Should we ride back for help?"

"I'm fine." The sharpness in her reply let Gideon know that the main damage had been done to her pride.

"Give us a minute." Gideon took her face in his hands, looking at her eyes, feeling for bumps and bruises.

She pulled away. "Nothing damaged but my dignity, and there wasn't much of that to start with. Come on, we're losing the herd." She struggled to her feet, using Gideon's arm for support only until she found her balance.

Gideon waved Maggie and Ed back to their corners, where the cattle were indeed beginning to break. "Let me look, Jamie. I think you lost consciousness for a moment. You could have a concussion."

"I do not have a concussion." She retied the bandana holding the hair back from her face. It was longer than it used to be, he noticed, and a softer color.

She stalked past him, whisked her hat off the ground, grabbed Nash's reins, and with one graceful movement, swung herself up into the saddle.

Gideon had no choice but to get back on Rosie and go after her. That was when he noticed that Nash was limping.

She was gonna have a bruise on her ass the size of a frying pan, and her head was starting to ache, but bruises healed and headaches went away.

Everyone knew what happened to horses that came up lame.

"It's probably just a sprain, Jamie. He's a tough horse. I'm more worried about you."

Now he was talking to her. He'd tried to make her ride Rosie home while he led Nash, but she'd refused. She'd tacked him up, she'd ridden him, she'd get him back to the stable.

Five days since he'd bared his soul to her and they'd barely seen each other. Yes, they'd been slammed with tasks, but seriously, sex like that was an opening act, to be followed by overtime, double encore, and standing ovation.

Right now, it felt like a failed audition.

She ran a trembling hand over Nash's broad neck. "Hey, boy, you're going to be okay."

She didn't give a good goddamn about falling off. But Nash's limping gait filled her with dread.

Tears blurred her vision and she leaned into the horse, her boots dragging over the tufted grass.

A thump and then Gideon was beside her.

He took Nash's reins from her and pushed her toward the mare. "Please. Get on Rosie. Do it for me."

She whirled on him. "For you? Why? What do you care?" The tears were flowing freely now and she rushed at him, her fists out. "It's your fault this happened. If I hadn't been so distracted, wondering what was going on between us, I would have been paying attention. I wouldn't have fallen, Nash wouldn't be hurt, Huck wouldn't have had to come help Maggie and Ed bring the cattle in."

He caught her forearms and pulled him to his chest. "He's going to be okay, Jamie. Ice and rest will put him right."

But she pushed back. "You don't know that! He's a trail horse, Gideon. If he's not fit for riding, what'll happen to him? He's such a good horse."

As she looked up at him, fat rain droplets started spattering the earth, one here, another there, making blades of grass jump and dance in her peripheral vision.

One struck her cheek, then another on his forehead. He looked the way he'd looked the night he'd told her about the accident, like he was bracing for a blow. Without thinking, she reached up to smooth the rain drop away from his eye.

"Oh, Gideon," she said. "Please don't break my heart. You know I love you."

His face collapsed, fell in on itself, and this time when he pulled her to his chest, she let him.

"Jamie," he whispered into her hair. "I wish I could be the man you deserve."

"You are! I deserve you. And you deserve me. Why can't you believe that? Why can't you trust that what we have is good and right?"

He shook his head, but his hand still tenderly stroked her hair. "It's not about that."

"Well then, what is it about?" She lifted her face, searching for clues that would explain his ambivalence. He loved her too. She knew it. She knew it! What was he afraid of?

He tightened his grip on her and she could feel him shaking.

"Gideon? You're scaring me."

"I'm so sorry, Jamie." His voice was broken, utterly shattered. "I let things go too far. Lana is pushing hard. If I want to have Blake in my life . . ."

She gripped the front of his denim shirt. "What? Tell me?"

"I might have to leave."

"Leave?" She didn't understand. "Go where? For how long?"

Water dripped down his face. "Wherever Lana and Elliot take Blake."

"But . . . can she do that?"

He lifted one shoulder, let it fall. "She can do whatever she wants. She mentioned moving back to Las Vegas. The drive now is one thing, but I can't fly my son back and forth from Vegas. I can't do that to him. If she moves, I have to go, too."

She touched his cheek again. Was some of it tears? She couldn't tell. "I'll move too, then."

He shook his head. "Jamie, this is your home. I couldn't

ask that of you, and anyway I don't know what's going to happen. I'm sorry. I didn't know how to tell you."

She swallowed. "I love you, Gideon."

He lowered his face, pressed his forehead against hers. Then, with a sigh, he moved to kiss her. She met him, pulling him close, taking his lips between her teeth, sucking his tongue into her mouth, greedy, desperate, starving for him.

They stood in the rain, sheltered from the wind by the horses, and she kissed him as if she might never get the chance again.

For all she knew, it was the truth.

Chapter Twenty-Six

The Jupiter–Pluto square has the potential to be
productive—if you can resist the urge to use
force.

—Jamie's horoscope

Lana had brought Blake for another visit, and according to Gideon, she hadn't made any further demands. Olivia gave both Jamie and Gideon time off to spend with the boy, and during the visit, they'd gotten him into the corral and onto Rosie.

Gideon had led them around while Jamie took pictures and video on his phone. They looked so good together, Gideon tall and dark, Blake small and fair, but with the same tilt to his head when he asked a question, the same quirk of his lips when he smiled.

Only, when they'd led Rosie into the field, the boy had started rubbing his nose. By the time they'd reached the ridge with the view of the ocean, his eyes had turned red and he'd begun complaining. When they'd gotten back to the ranch, poor Blake had been crying for Lana, begging to go home.

Now, Jamie watched while Gideon stood next to the kitchen counter, one hand protectively on his son's leg while

Aiden examined the boy. Blake's wails had subsided to low, hiccupping sobs.

"An allergic reaction?" Gideon sounded relieved, annoyed, and bewildered all at the same time. "Are you sure?"

"He should be seen by his pediatrician when he gets home," Aiden said, holding a cool compress against Blake's eyes, "but from the way he's responded to the antihistamine, I'd hang my hat on it. A lot of people are allergic to horses."

"What?" Gideon's mouth dropped open, then slammed shut. He looked away.

Jamie's heart ached for him. They were just starting to connect. She'd seen the excitement in the boy's eyes, his pride at wearing the new boots Gideon had purchased for him. The triumph at sitting astride Rosie's back.

Not being able to share his love of horses with Blake would hurt, bad.

"We don't know the extent of his reactivity," Aiden said. "It might not be horses at all, either, since he's seen them once before. It's ragweed season, after all. Or it's horses, but it's dose-dependent. Maybe a bit of dander or hair got directly in his eye and that's what caused the acute swelling and tearing. Don't panic just yet, Gideon. You might still be able to teach Blake to ride."

Aiden stood up and gathered his supplies, this examination over, the drama overrated.

"I don' wanna ride Rosie anymore," Blake said in a hitching voice. "I wanna go home."

"Your mom's not coming for two hours." Gideon's bleak announcement triggered a fresh bout of tears from Blake.

"I want my mommy." He was somewhat subdued from the medication but not enough for him to forget the trauma.

Jamie couldn't hang back any longer. "Hey, hey," she said, muscling in beside Gideon. She took Blake's hands in hers. "Thank goodness we've got two more hours with you. This is the time of day when the fairies come out to play."

Blake looked up. "Fairies?" he said in a small voice.

Gideon made a noise in the back of his throat, but Jamie threw him a look that shut him up.

"Work with me, cowboy," she whispered.

He opened his mouth, then closed it and gestured for her to continue.

"Fairies, leprechauns, elves, we've got all kinds. They're super-shy, so I can't guarantee we'll see them, but if you want, I can show you the place where we've got the best chance. Gideon, do you want to come along?"

He looked around himself as if evidence against the existence of fairies was just at his fingertips, if only he could find it. Then he shrugged. "Sure. Why not?"

"Hey, Daff," Jamie called.

The cook had been hovering in the background during the crisis, but popped out from the baker's pantry now and rushed to Blake's side. "How's our boy? Is everything okay? Oh, the poor lamb."

"He's fine, Daphne," Gideon said. "It's just an allergic reaction."

"You don't know what Blake is going through." Daphne put her hands on her hips, irritation spiking her words.

"My eyes hurt," Blake said, his voice wobbling again.

Jamie wanted to smack sense into Gideon and understood that Daphne felt the same way. But she knew, better than most, how sensitive children were to the emotions around them, how much they hated and feared conflict among adults, especially when they had no one familiar to cling to.

"Can you get us a snack, Daphne?" Jamie asked. "We're going fairy hunting in the apple orchard, and I think Blake might be hungry."

"Ah, fairy hunting." Daphne assumed an Irish brogue. "'Tis a lovely time to be hunting the wee folk. Watch the shadows, young Blake. That's where they dance."

She hurried out to the walk-in fridge, muttering over

256   *Roxanne Snopek*

her shoulder about men who didn't have the sense God gave them.

"Two hours of fairy hunting, huh?" said Gideon, hoisting Blake onto his hip. The boy laid his head against Gideon's broad shoulder. "You think that's wise?"

"You got a better idea?"

"There's a TV right there. He's probably going to fall asleep anyway."

"Uh-huh. And when his mom asks what you did with him, is that what you want to report?"

"Fine." He walked out the door.

Jamie found a blanket in the closet and then waited at the counter while Daphne put together a basket of snacks.

"What's his problem?" Jamie said. "He's acting like Blake did this on purpose. The kid needs comfort, not whatever that was."

"Be careful now, my girl." Daphne spoke mildly, but it was enough to still Jamie's tongue. Daphne could call down all manner of curses upon the heads of those who wronged her, but no one trash-talked those she loved in her presence.

"He's afraid, you know. He could probably use a little encouragement from his best friend."

Jamie swallowed. "Yeah. That's me. The best friend."

Daphne squeezed her arm. "Hang in there, my girl. He's in a tough place right now. He needs you to believe in him."

"But—"

"No buts." She pushed the basket into Jamie's hands. "Here. Banana muffins. Men are always more cooperative when you feed them."

Gideon sat down with his back against the trunk of a tree heavy with fruit just beginning to ripen and settled the boy between his knees. Blake wasn't asleep, but he was drowsy enough to allow himself to be carried without protest.

"Is this where the fairies are?" he asked.

"This is an apple orchard." Lana was going to freak out when she got a look at Blake.

"Have you seen fairies?" Blake persisted.

"Nope. Sorry, bud."

"But Jamie has?"

"I guess you'll have to ask her."

Blake thought for a moment. "Don't you like her anymore?"

Gideon started. "Jamie? Of course I still like her. She's . . . she's my best friend."

And so much more. But he turned his mind away from that. If he had to leave, it would be painful enough already, without them giving in to the attraction simmering between them.

Giving in more, he amended. *Giving in again*.

Though every night, before he fell asleep, his thoughts went to the taste of her lips and the warmth and softness of her body and how he'd give anything to bury himself inside her again and hear her tell him she loved him.

His breath caught in his throat.

Not anything. Not if the price was Blake.

Blake snuggled closer to him. "You shouldn't use your mad voice with her, then."

"I have a mad voice?"

Jamie arrived then, set the basket onto the grass, and spread out the blanket.

"Everyone has a mad voice," she said. "Sounds like I walked in on an interesting conversation. What did I miss?"

"Gideon used his mad voice, so I thought he didn't like you," Blake explained. "But he said he did. I like you, Jamie. I think he should talk nice to you."

"I agree." Jamie's eyes twinkled. "Here, have a muffin."

Blake scrambled off Gideon's lap and onto the blanket

next to Jamie. He carefully peeled the wrapper off a muffin, folded it, and handed it to Jamie before taking a bite.

He was so tidy. Too tidy for a kid. Kids should be messy and wild.

"Gideon says he never sees fairies."

"Oh, they only show themselves to people who believe," Jamie responded. She stroked the boy's hair lightly. "It's very important to believe, you know. But it's a lot easier for kids. Gideon's a very responsible grown-up, and sometimes responsible grown-ups have the hardest time believing in things they can't see."

"So they can't see them, if they don't believe?"

Jamie nodded. "But maybe if you see one, he'll believe."

They chattered back and forth, with Jamie pointing into the sunshine as the rays lengthened and lowered. Dust motes danced in the air. Between the kid's swollen eyes and the drugs, he'd probably go home saying he saw purple elephants flying through the trees. What would Lana think of that?

Blake giggled, pointed at something with his tiny fingers, and then tucked his head under Jamie's arm.

A few minutes later, he was asleep.

Jamie laid him onto the blanket, bunching up a corner for a pillow.

"So," Gideon asked, "did he see a fairy?"

"Don't know. You can ask him when he wakes up. But he had fun looking. That's the main thing."

"Kids need to know the real world, the sooner the better."

Jamie took a breath. "That's exactly why they need to chase fantasies, because the real world will intrude all too soon. You're pulling away from me, Gideon. I feel it and I understand. But don't pull away from Blake, okay? You're a good dad. He needs you."

A piece of muffin broke off and fell to the blanket.

He was deeply touched. Her opinion meant more to him than anyone's. And probably no one else understood how badly he wanted to make a good impression on Blake. And to show Lana that he could be trusted with their son.

"James," he said softly.

She looked away, squinting against the scarlet light. "It's okay. You don't have to say anything."

Chapter Twenty-Seven

*The Aquarius Full Moon is time to wind down
projects that have to do with friends and
charitable concerns.*

—Jamie's horoscope

Jamie was in the kitchen nursing a cup of coffee when
Haylee walked in.

"Whoa," she said, taking in Haylee's rumpled demeanor.
"You look like something the cat yarked up."

"Good morning to you, too." Haylee groaned. "My back
is killing me. I couldn't sleep, and the very idea of bacon
and eggs makes me nauseous. I thought I'd get some tea and
toast before I head down the hill. Ezra and Gideon want to
get this done as soon as possible, and I don't blame them."

Haylee wasn't the only one who'd been restless last night,
Jamie thought. They were slaughtering the spring steer
today, and it wasn't anyone's favorite day. She didn't par-
ticipate, but knowing what was happening in the far shed
distracted her all day.

"I'd have thought being fourteen months pregnant would
have gotten you a pass," she commented.

"I don't want a pass." Haylee curled her lip. "I hate being

treated like I'm made of glass. I'll be off twiddling my thumbs soon enough. Until then, I'll pull my weight."

They sipped their beverages quietly. Haylee had handed over the training of Honey and Chaos, and Jamie knew how hard that had been for her. She watched, provided commentary and advice, and she still took Jewel to visit the school kids and seniors. But other than that, Jamie ran the kennel.

If Gideon left, how could Jamie not go with him? But how could she leave all this behind?

Sage and Daphne were in the kitchen, the cook rolling out dough for her famous cinnamon buns, not listening to one of her reading group podcasts, or so it seemed since her earbuds dangled over her chest. Sage was poring over a stack of pages.

She lifted her head, noticing her mother's arrival.

"Hey, Ma, can you watch Sal tomorrow morning for me? I've got a meeting."

Haylee blinked and her fair cheeks went pink. "Sure." The tips of her lips tilted as if she was trying to hide a smile. "What meeting?"

Sage usually addressed her as Haylee. Ma was an upgrade, and clearly, she liked it.

Sage tilted her head toward the papers in front of her and rolled her eyes. "You know. Getting those last credits so I can brag about graduating high school before twenty."

Jamie lifted her hand, and she and Sage exchanged air high-fives. "You go, girl."

"You bet, honey." Haylee twisted sideways, and an audible pop sounded from her low back. "Oh, that's better. Where is the munchkin anyway? Sleeping?"

Sage shook her head. "She was fussing so Huck took her outside for a walk. With any luck, she'll fill her diaper while they're out and he'll change it for me."

Jamie smiled. Huck had a massive crush on Sage, the

poor, sweet, deluded soul, ignoring her proclamations about being off men, maybe forever.

As to Sal's paternity, Sage kept the lid securely shut on that intel, claiming Sal had no father.

It made her sad. Oh, little Sal had no lack of love and attention. But there was no replacing a father.

If Gideon learned to trust himself, Blake would know more love than most kids could dream about. He was such a good man.

Haylee went to lift the kettle off the stove, then buckled over, gripping the edge of the stove for balance.

"Ma? Haylee!" Sage said, the stud in her eyebrow twinkling in the morning light. "You okay?"

"Of course." She put a hand to her side, then dropped it quickly. "What time is your appointment tomorrow?"

"Forget it," Sage said. "I'll find someone else."

"For what it's worth," Jamie said, eyeing Haylee's midriff, "I suggest you clear your calendar. If Aiden was here, you'd get a spanking. And not the good kind."

"Bite me," Haylee said. "I'm fine." She straightened up, raised both arms and did jazz hands. "See?"

"Whatever." Jamie refilled her coffee and opened the paper. What about pregnancy, she wondered, turned previously normal human beings into irrational aliens?

But when Haylee stroked her belly in that casual gesture so full of love, Jamie's ribs contracted. She swallowed. She'd seen it in Sage, too. Haylee would fight to the death for her child. For either of them. As would Sage for Sal.

Was that how Lana felt about Blake? Was that what Gideon was up against?

But what about his fatherly passion? Didn't that count, too?

It made her head hurt, to think about the meaning of family and of all the ways that caring and fear and jealousy and ignorance and love made people hurt each other so badly.

Yet, she still wished she was part of it, that someone felt about her the way Aiden felt for Haylee, or Haylee for Sage.

She imagined what it might be like, if Gideon fought for her like he was fighting for Blake. If he placed her inside the circle of his life, instead of keeping her on the outside.

In the background, Haylee and Sage discussed their plans for the next day and Daphne kept working behind them, deep in the rhythm of kneading the mound of dough in front of her.

The yeasty, slightly sweet aroma coming from Daphne's workstation, combined with the toasting bread, made her stomach growl.

Huck came in, Sal bouncing on his hip. The little girl had apples in her cheeks, and a string of drool shining between her lip and the front of her sweater.

"Here's your mama, little angel," Huck crooned, handing the baby over. He wore a bright fuchsia beanie this morning.

"Huck!" called Daphne, her voice overloud thanks to the earbuds now back in her ears. "Did you bring in the eggs?"

"Just about to do so, ma'am." He tipped his head and exited the kitchen.

Olivia wandered into the kitchen then, her hair still wet from the shower. "Is Daphne making cinnamon buns?"

Haylee nodded.

Sage swirled her finger in Haylee's direction. "Haylee look a little off to you, Liv?"

"Hm. I don't know." She tilted her head, evaluating her niece. "You feel okay, Haylee?"

In the office, the phone rang. Everyone ignored it.

"I'm fine. Tired, that's all." Haylee spread peanut butter on her toast, then stared at it, as if it had suddenly lost its appeal.

"Well, Jamie and I think she looks like crap." Sage plopped

the baby into a nearby playpen and handed her a toy to chew on, then went back to poring over her syllabus.

"Very helpful." Haylee nibbled a corner of toast, massaging her side again. Then, she set her mug down on the table and bent over again. A low moan came from her.

The phone kept ringing.

"Does this not bug anyone else?" Jamie said, getting to her feet.

Olivia waved a hand. "Let it go to voice mail. Haylee? Oh, my. Either you just peed yourself . . ."

"Holy shit!" Sage hollered. "Daphne!"

Haylee looked at the floor with horror. "But I've got three weeks left. This isn't supposed to happen yet. I'm not ready. I'm working!" She sounded utterly outraged.

"Too bad, missy." Daphne smoothed Haylee's curls away from her neck and took her other arm. "Babies come when they come and we welcome them. Got it?"

She'd said something similar when Sal had arrived.

"Ahhhh!" Haylee moaned.

Olivia tossed Haylee's cell phone to Sage. "Call Aiden. Tell him to meet us at the hospital. His baby's coming."

Jamie stood there, not sure what to do, as a flurry of activity erupted around her.

She heard the phone click over and then, from the office, a tinny voice, someone leaving a message.

It was Lana.

She ran to the room and played the message.

Lana couldn't reach Gideon on his cell and she needed to talk to him. Immediately.

Ezra and Gideon looked up together at the knock on the slaughterhouse doorframe.

"Jamie," Gideon said. "What are you doing here?"

She looked around the room and swallowed. "Lana called. She wants to meet you in town today. She's on her way, now."

"What? Today?" He glanced down at himself, the plastic apron, the rubber boots. "I can't see Blake today. Did she say what it's about?"

"No. You didn't answer your phone so she called the house. Go on." She nodded and took a breath. "I'll find someone to cover for you."

"Who?"

"Doesn't matter," she said, pulling the ties at his back and slipping the apron over his head.

He glanced at Ezra.

"Go on," the man said. "Your boy is more important. Haylee's on her way anyway, right, Jamie?"

Jamie folded the apron and hung it on a hook. "Yeah. And I think Liv or Daphne will come down, too."

He didn't like the way Jamie wasn't meeting his eyes. Something was up, but he'd figure it out later. Trust Lana to pull something like this, just to put him off his game.

He returned her call while changing his clothes. She and Elliot were coming to Sunset Bay and thought he'd like the chance to see Blake while they ran their errands. As expected, she'd been very unhappy about Blake's last visit to the ranch but was trying to be reasonable. He could see the boy now, at the time and place of her choosing. If it wasn't convenient, she said, that was fine.

But Gideon understood. It was this or nothing. "I'll see you in thirty minutes," he said.

He got in his truck and headed for town, to the small park on the beach where Jamie taught her classes in the summertime, got himself a coffee, and sat down to wait. This was what the next ten years of his life might be: trailing along after Lana, taking the crumbs of time with Blake she offered, never sure when it might be revoked.

How could he possibly expect Jamie to live like this? It

wasn't fair to her. Gideon could do it, but eventually, she'd want a life of her own. A life of their own. And what would that look like?

He couldn't imagine.

Their vehicle arrived, with Hudson at the wheel. Gideon watched as Lana got out to help Blake with the seat belt. Today she wore jeans and boots, and her hair was pulled back in a simple tail.

Gideon waved a greeting from his seat but didn't approach, unsure of his reception, unwilling to do anything that might jeopardize the tenuous cease-fire.

He watched as Lana knelt down and pulled Blake to her tightly, pressing her cheek against his golden hair for a long moment. She kissed him three times in quick succession, then stood up. Her boot caught on a stone and she nearly stumbled backwards, but Hudson caught her elbow. She held on to him and even from the distance, Gideon could see her shaking.

She was afraid, he understood that now. Everyone was afraid. Fear was one of the biggest drivers of human behavior. He'd learned that in prison. As a motivator, ambition paled in comparison to the primitive need to cover your plate, to guard your possessions, to protect what you have, who you love. Loss was the big equalizer.

Hudson kept hold of her, patting her hand, putting his face close to hers. Blake said something up to them, and they both squatted down to the child's level, each with an arm around him, making a circle, a triumvirate, a closed unit with him squarely on the outside.

Then they rose, and stepped back, finally returning Gideon's wave.

Lana was still shaking and her cheeks sparkled in the sun. Elliot's shoulders were slumped, his hand slightly outstretched, as if he wanted to snatch the child back but knew he couldn't.

"Hey, Blake," Gideon called out in a voice like a rasp.

The left side of his chest felt hot and itchy, and the muscle beneath his eye was twitching again. He didn't want to feel sympathy for them. If Lana hadn't shut him out six years ago, none of this would be happening. He was justified in feeling angry. He was Blake's rightful father. He wasn't the bad guy here.

It was easier, cleaner, to stay angry.

But he couldn't. They loved Blake. Both of them. Lana and Elliot.

It would definitely be easier to remain angry at Hudson, but Gideon knew, from the way the boy talked about him, that he treated them well, that Lana was happy with him, and that all three of them were excited about the upcoming marriage.

And he could read it in the man's body language, how much love he had for them. And how afraid he was of losing them.

They were—all of them—working from a fear of loss, he realized. Right or wrong, he'd triggered this, by finally dealing with his own loss.

Blake held his backpack against his chest and curled over it protectively as he walked to the picnic table, and that's when Gideon saw the hitch in the boy's gait, the way he rose onto his toes at the end of each step. It was exactly how he himself walked. Jamie was right—the boy did have something of his father in him.

"Hi, Gideon," he said without a hint of a smile.

He cleared his throat. "You ready to have some fun on the beach with your old man?"

He gave Gideon a cautious glance, his eyes wide and watchful. His knuckles white where he gripped his bag. "Okay."

A bubble of pride welled into the itchy place in his chest. His blood flowed in those small veins, his DNA in every tiny cell. They were alike in ways that couldn't be taught or untaught, but simply were.

He'd find common ground. He'd build a relationship with his son. He'd earn Blake's love and a place in his heart and finally ease the ache of failure.

Then Blake turned to wave at the couple still holding each other beside the car. In his small, thin voice, he called out, "Bye, Mom. Bye, Dad."

Dad.

After Gideon left, Jamie stood in the stainless-steel room, listening to the reverberation of the metal door echo off the stinky walls. He was heading to town, for an impromptu meeting with Lana. Whatever it was about, she guessed it wasn't good.

As soon as he was out of earshot, she turned to Ezra. He wore the same long, white waterproof apron and heavy rubber boots that Gideon had just removed.

"Are Haylee and Olivia on their way?" he asked. "I want to get it over with."

She cleared her throat. "They're not coming. Liv and Sage just took Haylee to the hospital. She's in labor. Daphne's looking after Sal. I'm it today, Ezra. Sorry about that."

While she spoke, his gentle features went from confused to concerned to excited and finally landed on what she could only interpret as sorrowful kindness. "You didn't want Gideon to know."

"He needs to see Blake."

"He would have stayed. He would never have asked you to do this."

"Of course he wouldn't." Her throat was tight. "I hope I'll be helpful."

"Jamie."

"I can handle it." Tears dripped off her chin and she wiped them with her shoulder. "Let's just do it, okay?"

Ezra looked at her for a long moment. "It'll be fast."

"I know," she said, her voice thick with dread.

"He won't feel a thing."

She nodded, squeezing her eyes shut. Then she lifted her head, inhaled deeply, and pulled up to her full height and met Ezra's concerned gaze. "I'm ready."

Outside the shed, the rest of the cattle grazed calmly, their big brown eyes untroubled. They led the animal to an area out of sight of the herd, around a corner and into the stainless steel room, where a stanchion stood at the ready. The steer walked in without complaint, having been acclimated to the device often for routine procedures, always accompanied by copious positive reinforcements and treats.

"Good man," Jamie said in a shaky voice. "Good boy, Charley." He slapped a thick pink tongue against her arm, leaving a clear trail of drool, like a baby.

Ezra patted Charley on the head, gave him an alfalfa pellet, then applied two electrodes to his head and sent two hundred volts of electricity into his brain.

The steer died without ever knowing what hit him.

Afterwards, Jamie walked back to the main house without so much as a drop of blood on her to provide evidence of her activity. Her arms ached, her legs felt numb, her chest hollow, empty.

She wandered into the kitchen, sank onto a stool, and rested her head on her arms.

"It's done?" Daphne asked. She, more than anyone, knew what it had cost Jamie to do this.

Jamie didn't eat meat, but most people did and she understood that. An animal like Charley would feed them and their guests for most of a season. It was an annual procedure that no one looked forward to, but the solemnity with which they approached it seemed somehow appropriate. Respectful of the earth and the creatures on it.

Jamie had seen guests fall apart at the sight of a two-day old chick found squashed by the automatic feeder, people who would, that same night, tuck into Daphne's roast chicken, their minds seeing no connection between the two. She had lived with kids whose bones and flesh were built on the tidy, grocery-store wrapped packages of other animals, and because they saw no blood, they were able to perpetuate the disconnect.

The privileged ones were, in some ways, worse off than the street kids, whom she'd also known, because they were unaware that death was a part of life. They weren't allowed to attend funerals, for fear of trauma. They weren't given pets, too much mess and work. And then, when someone they cared about actually died, they fell apart.

They never learned to handle the devastation of loss because they were never allowed to discover that they could. That life went on. That we all have a time and a purpose and that they, too, could survive and embrace what time they had.

"It's done," she told Daphne. "Any news on Haylee?"

The cook shook her head. "No. Could be a long day." She exhaled. "It changes you, doesn't it?"

Jamie nodded. "It's only right."

Taking a life *should* change a person. She thought of the old hunting traditions of thanking the creature that had given its life for the survival of the tribe. She'd borne witness. She'd been with Charley at the end; she knew the animal had suffered neither pain nor fear. She'd honored the animal's sacrifice by facing it with him.

This did not make it easier, but it was honest, at least.

"A good life and a humane death," Daphne reminded her. "It's the best we can do in a fallen world."

"I guess." She wanted to go to bed and sleep for days.

"It was a good thing you did."

Jamie made a sound in the back of her throat that could have been a laugh or a sob.

"You really love that man, don't you?"

She pressed her eyes closed, feeling the tears behind them. "I wish I didn't. It would be so much easier."

"Nah. You've never been one for easy. Here." Daphne slid a large slice of pie her way. "You look like you could use it."

Chapter Twenty-Eight

*An intense alignment today. Keep calm and
    carry on.*

—Gideon's horoscope

When they came to retrieve Blake, Gideon immediately saw the anger in Lana's stride. Elliot stood beside the car, the rear door open, as if he couldn't wait to get Blake safely back into his care.

Lana hugged her son and sent him off.

"Bye, Gideon," Blake said.

They'd had a nice walk, collecting sea glass and chasing birds. But the boy's face lit up now as he scampered to Elliot.

"How could you, Gideon," Lana said, standing with her back to Blake. Her voice shook with fury. "I trusted you with him."

Gideon took a step backward. "What?"

She threw a newspaper onto the picnic table. It was open to the Letters to the Editor page.

"That woman of yours," she said, her words ending in a hiss. "She hurt a kid. Right here, on the beach. There were witnesses! She's being charged with child abuse, Gideon. And you let my son be with her."

The bottom fell out of his stomach. He grabbed the paper and scanned the entry she'd circled.

It was the mother whose children had been nearly pulled in by the rogue wave. Red flames edged the periphery of his vision. "These are lies, Lana. There were no charges. I was there. I saw what happened. Jamie saved those kids. If she hadn't been there, that little girl might have been hurt a whole lot worse than a dislocated elbow."

"Maybe. Maybe not. But I won't have her around my son."

The breath left his lungs. His knees buckled and he sat down heavily on the concrete bench. He had no words.

Lana had plenty. "I gave you a chance, Gideon. But I have to put Blake first. Did you know he's having nightmares? He's starting school in a few weeks and he's not sleeping properly. He's asking me if Elliot will still be his dad, if we're still getting married, if he did something bad to make me cry."

Her voice broke. She looked away and hugged her arms to her chest. "Please, Gideon, let him go. Let us go. You're trying to be something you're not. How many people are you willing to hurt before you give up?"

Jamie walked along the shoreline, kicking at random rocks, listening to the surf, letting the crisp briny flavors of the air flood her senses. She couldn't bear to be on the ranch right now. Not only was she dreading the news Gideon might bring, but she was still shaken by the image of Charley sinking to his knees, a sentient creature gone in an instant.

Like Eve in the garden of Eden, she felt unclean, the shiny placard of her soul tarnished with knowledge she'd never wanted to have and now couldn't erase.

She'd made Ezra promise not to tell Gideon that she'd covered for him. It would only add another layer of guilt to his already overloaded sense of responsibility. Later, when the situation with Blake was settled, then she'd tell him.

If he was still here.

No. Don't think about that. One day at a time. One crisis per day. One heartache to rule them all.

Gideon was the gold ring on her quest, but the carousel was moving too fast for her to catch it and hold fast.

"Pick a metaphor, Vaughn," she muttered to herself. "Actually, don't. This isn't about you, so pull your head out and grow up."

She took a look around, wondering if anyone had heard her. She never felt weird talking to herself when she was on Nash. She often worked her way through problems while talking to him, his swivelling ears and soft grunts like advice from a thoughtful, wise friend.

"You're losing it," she told herself. "Get a grip."

She was meeting Jonathan and Roman shortly for a session with Chaos, and unless she got her act together, she'd never have patience for the old man's complaints.

Of course, now, thanks to Gideon's intervention, they knew more about his injuries, and everyone had grown more tolerant of him. He wasn't mean or angry. He loved his dogs, even Chaos, though you had to watch closely to see it.

Pain and immobility had become a vicious circle, leading to isolation and the anger and depression she'd witnessed at their first meeting. It was encouraging to see how quickly the gentle interactions with Apollo, grooming and walking with him, had improved his outlook.

Thinking of Apollo made her miss Nash more. She wanted, more than anything, to be in the saddle, to let out the reins, ride full out across the foothills until they were deep into the forest, with nothing around them but dense, thick green and muted bird calls.

He wasn't ready to return to full activity yet. Olivia assured her he'd be fine, but had also suggested that she choose a different horse for her extracurricular riding.

There was no other horse.

How would Gideon manage if he had to move back to the city? He loved riding as much as she did and would never be satisfied with rented horses on groomed paths. Above all else, he needed open space, solitude, freedom.

She lifted her face to the grey sky, letting the mist settle on her skin. The season would change soon, returning to the moody tones of steel and stone that was the Oregon coast's backdrop for much of the year.

Everything was changing.

If Gideon lost his son, he'd be devastated.

And it would be her fault.

Oh, he'd never blame her outright. He was too kind for that. He knew Jamie never meant to make things worse. But that's what she did. She leaped, as always, without thinking. She'd pushed him and Blake, so determined to help forge the father-son bond Gideon craved so badly.

She'd meant so well, and now, everything was spinning out of control.

Lana was angry. Blake was afraid. And Gideon was fighting a battle inside himself that had no winner. She saw the torment etched in the lines around his eyes, heard it in his voice, read it in his posture.

He could continue to fight for his boy and maybe damage him in the process or he could let him go peacefully and find a way to live with it. Just as she always chose to barge ahead, heedless of who got hurt, Gideon would go the opposite direction, overthinking and ultimately taking the route that would cause the least pain. For everyone but himself.

He never chose himself.

And that meant he couldn't choose her, either.

She bent down, picked up a rock, and threw it into the retreating surf, as hard as she could.

Gideon was Blake's father, not Elliot. Look what the child would be missing out on, if Gideon didn't fight for him. And one day, there would be a reckoning. Blake would wonder. He'd ask. He'd learn that his father hadn't wanted him.

Could Gideon live with that?

She knew he couldn't. Letting Blake go would break his heart. Finding him one day five, ten or twenty years from now and accepting the inevitable blame that would accompany a reunion would destroy him.

She thought of everything Haylee had gone through, reuniting with Sage and then watching Sage negotiate a tentative reconciliation with her adoptive parents.

Family wasn't easy, no matter how you sliced it. But children didn't suffer from having too many people who loved them. They suffered from having too few.

She shoved her hands deep into the pockets of her fleece jacket, wishing there was a way to fix things for Gideon.

She kicked hard at a piece of driftwood. The sodden remnant of long-dead tree didn't move.

Chapter Twenty-Nine

*A good day for lovers and seekers. Keep your eyes
and your hearts open.*

—Gideon's horoscope

"What's going on around here?" Roman demanded as
he walked into the barn.

Sadie was at his side, as usual, though her pace had slowed
since their last visit. Gideon was surprised to see that Roman
had the pup on a leash with him, too.

"We've had a little excitement here," he replied. "Make
yourself at home with Apollo. Let me know if you need
anything."

Haylee and Aiden's baby had been born in the middle of
the previous night, a little boy, and in the turmoil, with Olivia
still at the hospital with them, Gideon hadn't realized that
Roman was scheduled for today. He'd just finished covering
chores for everyone, and the last thing he needed was the old
man's running commentary on what all he was doing wrong.

"I'm not here for the horse," Roman said crossly. He
pointed to Chaos. "I'm here for Jamie. Where is she? She
wanted to work with him on the beach today."

Gideon hadn't seen Jamie since she'd given him Lana's

message yesterday. He pulled out his cell phone. "I'll call her for you."

She picked up immediately. "Gideon?"

"Where are you?" he said. "Roman's here, looking for you."

"I'm here, looking for him," she replied. He could hear gulls calling in the background. "Jonathan was supposed to bring him and the pup out to meet me here."

He relayed the message to Roman.

The older man gave a disgusted snort. "Jon must have gotten his wires crossed. You'll have to give us a ride."

"What, me?" Gideon said. "I'm working."

Jamie, who'd heard the conversation added, "Please, Gideon. It'll take too long for me to come back again. Besides, it's going to start raining soon. You should enjoy the beach while you can."

He ended the call, glanced around at the stalls, and decided to do it.

Roman sat uncomfortably in Gideon's truck, adjusting the position of the seat several times until he finally gave up. The dogs were in the backseat, the puppy curled up next to Sadie and yawning before they left the yard.

"He's improving then, is he?" Gideon asked, nodding toward the sleepy puppy.

"He's a different dog," Roman admitted. "Never thought someone could get him under control. She's a smart cookie, that Jamie of yours."

Not mine. He didn't say the words aloud, but something alerted Roman.

"You're a stubborn bastard, aren't you? What's your problem? You should lock that down while you can, man. Women like her don't come around every day, you know."

Gideon gritted his teeth and drove without responding. Roman didn't know what he was talking about.

"You better have a damn good reason," the man went on. "She's something special. She wouldn't hurt a fly, that girl, but she took your shift on the killing floor, just so you could see your kid. Didn't know that, did you? Right. That's because she wouldn't let anyone tell you. I caught the cook crying this morning, and she told me. Good woman, that Daphne. Heart of gold. And she loves that girl. Not happy with you though, I'll tell you that. Got your head pretty far up your ass, from what I can see. Trying to be a good guy to everyone but yourself and you're hurting her in the process. Unless I'm wrong."

He paused for breath and looked sharply at Gideon.

Gideon's head was reeling.

Jamie, in the slaughterhouse? With Charley, the steer she'd named and tamed and treated like a pet?

For *him?*

"Am I wrong?" Roman demanded.

"Uh . . ." he struggled to catch up. "About what?"

"You being in love with her, you asshole." He made a guttural sound in the back of his throat and turned back to the passenger window. "Her heart's on her sleeve, big as life. It's up to you. And I hope you choose right or there'll be a whole heap of people ready to rain down holy hell on your head."

Gideon couldn't take it any longer. "It's never been a question of love, damn it. Of course I love her. But love isn't always enough. What if loving me ends up hurting her? Then what kind of man am I to encourage her? And that's the only thing that's going to happen here. You think that's what I want? Of course not. I'd give anything to be with her. But it's not that simple. No matter what I choose, someone's going to get hurt."

"Asshole," Roman said again. "She's better off without you if that's your attitude."

Gideon bit his tongue, trying not to let the man's badgering get to him. His relationship with Jamie was no one else's business, not Lana's, not Elliot's, and certainly not some meddlesome neighbor they barely knew.

But Roman continued making comments, digging and probing until Gideon finally snapped.

"Look. I'm involved in a custody battle. It's about to get ugly, and I mean for Jamie, not me. Love isn't always simple, old man. Sometimes the only way to show someone you love them is to walk away."

Walking away from Jamie would be the hardest thing he'd ever do in his life. But regardless of what happened with his fight for Blake, he couldn't let Lana use her against him.

"You're so full of bullshit." Roman's eyes narrowed. "Wait. A custody battle? Tell me more."

And for some reason, fatigue, despair, or being worn down by the man's crotchety persistence, Gideon found himself telling him everything. How Jamie's heroism had led to her being unfairly accused of child abuse, how Lana was threatening to use the slanderous rumors to keep her away from Blake, to keep Blake off the ranch, how he might have to move in order to stay near his son, how he couldn't possibly choose between the two of them and yet he was being forced to do so and it was tearing himself up on the inside, but ultimately a man looked after those who needed him the most. No matter what he'd tried to convince himself, a child abandoned by his father was more vulnerable than a woman abandoned by her lover.

He slid into the gravel parking lot at the beach and slammed on the brake, breathing hard. His knuckles were white where he gripped the steering wheel and he forced himself to unclench them.

"There's no good outcome here, Byers," he said. "So will you shut up about it, please?"

"Young people," Roman said dismissively. "You give up so easily. I've got my own experience in the area of slander. Here's what we're going to do."

And he proceeded to give Gideon something he hadn't felt for weeks.

Hope.

Jamie saw Gideon's truck pull up and jogged to the lot to meet them.

She desperately wanted to ask what the meeting with Lana had been about, but not in front of Roman.

So, instead, she bent down and scratched Sadie behind the ears. "How's our old girl doing?"

"Slower every day," Roman said. "Like me. Gideon's going to join us. Hope you don't mind."

She looked up sharply. Something was different about the old man. He had a sparkle in his eye, like he was scheming. It was a heck of a lot better than the misery and self-pity that had characterized him so far.

"Fine," she said. "He can help carry you if you fall down."

Roman gave a rough bark of laughter.

They found a long, secluded stretch of sand and let the dogs off leash. It was a good place to work on Chaos's recall. He had a strong play drive, and he loved the water, which made this both an exercise and a reward for him.

While Jamie sent the pup running back and forth, reinforcing every quick response, Gideon got Roman settled on an enormous piece of driftwood that lay, like a beached humpback, on the sand.

"I heard about your PR problems," Roman said, when she stopped for a break.

"My what?"

"Sorry, James," Gideon said. "I should have told you first."

He held out a folded sheet of newsprint from the local paper.

She took the page, scanned it. Her face grew warm, then hot. "I thought Olivia took care of this."

"Anyone can write an Internet post," Gideon said. "It's all lies. Everyone knows it. The woman can't face the fact that her kids got hurt because she wasn't paying attention, so she's blaming you. For what it's worth, you've had lots of people write in on your behalf."

"That's worth nothing if Lana catches wind of it." She looked at him. "She already knows, doesn't she?"

He nodded.

"I'm so sorry." She glanced at Roman.

"Don't worry," Roman said. "He told me about all that, too."

"It was a long drive," Gideon said, the ghost of a smile on his mouth. "He beat it out of me."

"Bad people are everywhere," the older man continued. "I ought to know. I'm a crusty old codger with no friends, and I like it like that. But here's the thing. When you two trespassed on my land, stole my dog, broke into my house—yes, I know about that, girl—forced me to work in your stables and keep this useless dog, you forced me to start living again, out of sheer self-defense. You just wouldn't leave me alone. Now I have this irrational sense of obligation to you. I'm pissed that this woman is spreading lies about you, Jamie. I'm pissed that Gideon's ex is giving him grief. I don't have energy to be this annoyed, so for my own peace of mind, I'm going to help you out. I still have a few tricks up my sleeve."

She sent Gideon a skeptical look. "Did he fall on his head? What's he talking about?"

"I was a film agent for many years," Roman said, "but before that, I was an attorney. So I'm going to write a few letters and you're going to let me. It's the least you can do, for all the trouble you've caused me. Now go take this brat for another run before we head back to the ranch." He held out Chaos's leash and nudged her toward Gideon. "Also, you two have been mooning at each other long enough and

I'm royally pissed that nothing's come of it. It's time you had a fucking conversation. Or just a good—"

"Got it," Gideon said, putting his hand up.

Jamie bit back the urge to laugh.

"At least kiss her, then." Roman shook his head like they were beyond help. "Put me out of my misery."

Gideon shaded his eyes with his hand, searching for the best place for them to let Chaos off leash, where they'd be least likely to be interrupted.

Despite the overcast day, the beach had begun to fill up with people, families with children and dogs and sand toys. No one wanted to waste a day near the water. Once autumn arrived, these days would become few and far between.

"I had no idea he was a lawyer." Jamie kept her free hand stuffed deeply in her pocket. "Makes sense, though. But I thought you didn't want to involve lawyers with Lana."

She should be furious, but she wasn't upset on her own behalf. Instead, her immediate concern was how it would affect his battle with Lana.

"She went there first. Dragging you into it was the wrong move. Hell if I'm going to back down now." He kicked a strand of dried bull kelp out of their path. "You helped Ezra in the slaughterhouse. Why?"

Jamie stopped, turned to look at him. Her face was pale, her eyes a perfect match to the roiling sea being her. "Would you have gone if you knew there was no one else to cover?"

"Of course not! Jamie, you don't even eat meat. I can't imagine what that did to you, doing what you did in there."

"I've done worse."

He saw her throat move as she swallowed, and that tiny movement shifted something inside him.

"You did it for me." He took her hand, nearly overcome. "Thank you."

Her eyes shone with tears. "Is Roman right, Gideon? I mean, nothing's changed with me. I love you. I think I always have. I can't help myself. But if you don't feel the same about me, tell me and I'm gone. You've been at the ranch longer than me, and it means more to you. And it's a good place for Blake. You'll have help building your relationship with him."

"Jamie," he began.

"Don't worry about me. I'll find a new job, new place to live. It'll be a fresh start. Isn't that everyone's fantasy, after all? A do-over? I've been feeling restless anyway. And now that Nash—" Tears were flowing down her cheeks now and dripping off her chin.

The puppy was jumping up against the leash, excited by an overly confident gull. He stooped down and unclipped him, then took Jamie into his arms, bent his head, and pressed his lips to hers. "Nash is fine. You talk too much, has anyone ever mentioned that?"

She had her hands on either side of his head, holding him to her as if he was the substance keeping her alive. "Gideon," she whispered in a broken voice.

"Stop. Look at my face." She pulled back slightly, her eyes roaming over his features. "This is the face of a man too stupid to recognize what's been in front of him all along. Of course I love you, James."

She sucked in a deep, shuddering breath and then leaned against him and buried her face in his shoulder. "How many times have I told you," she said in a muffled voice. "Don't call me James."

"James," he whispered against her hair, drawing out the word. "Ah, James, what you do to me."

She shuddered again, and this time, she hooked her knee around his thigh and pulled their bodies together tightly. "I'm doing this for Roman," she whispered.

Then she seemed to come to her senses. She stepped back,

blinked several times, and pressed her lips together. "Lana. What's happening? Can she use that mess of mine to keep Blake from you?"

"She'll try." He ran his hands down her upper arms, barely restraining himself from pulling her close again. "But she won't succeed. I'm done being the nice guy. You made me see that love isn't supposed to be easy or convenient, at least not all the time. Love takes work. It will between you and me. It will between us and Blake. It will as we work with Lana and Elliot to provide a stable life for our child. But you also showed me that people are tougher than I give them credit for. Blake is my kid, which means he's tough enough to handle the upheaval as we negotiate the next steps. We all want the best for the boy. We'll make it work."

"I made you see all that?" she said.

"Roman helped." He gave a quiet laugh. "It was a lucky day when that pup of his escaped."

Jamie's eyes widened. She stepped away and scanned the horizon, searching for the flash of yellow fur.

"There," she said, letting out a gust of air. They quickly followed his tracks to where he was running after gulls and frothy waves, heading toward the small stretch of beach where Driftwood Creek emptied into the sea.

"Chaos! Come on back, boy." Then she pointed toward the little beach beyond the black rocks. "Hey. Isn't that Blake?"

He followed her gaze and yes, it was. Blake and Elliot were climbing among the tide pools while Lana sat at a picnic table out of reach of the surf.

"The tide's coming in," Jamie said, scanning the water.

"They'll come back," Gideon said. "Let's get Chaos and head back. I don't want to confront them here."

Jamie reached for the pup, but just then, someone kicked a red beach ball in the direction of the tide pools. In a flurry of sandy paws, he dashed off after it, barking with delight.

From the driftwood log where they'd left Roman, he heard a hoarse shout along with some cursing. The man was struggling to his feet so Gideon turned toward him, gesturing for him to stay put. "Jamie will get him, don't worry."

Fatigue and pain had made the older man's movements unsteady, and Gideon hurried up the beach to help support him. He should have insisted Roman bring his cane, though on the sand, it wouldn't have been much help anyway.

He glanced over his shoulder just as Chaos climbed the rocks, following Elliot and Blake. Lana had noticed them now and even from here, he could see the frown on her face. Perfect. Now she'd have this to use against him, too.

The puppy was having a blast, chasing the same waves Blake was playing in, the red ball forgotten, easily staying out of Jamie's reach.

Just as she rounded a bend and disappeared from sight, he realized that Jamie wasn't going after the puppy, anymore.

She was chasing Blake.

Chapter Thirty

It's an unfavorable day to schedule a major event.
Tread carefully.

—Jamie's horoscope

Blake and Elliot, not hearing her or seeing the coming danger, continued around the bend in the cove, no doubt attracted by the sheltered warmth provided by those jagged black arms.

But the tide was coming in fast and that pocket beach was the perfect place to get trapped.

"Blake!" she called, waving. "Elliot!"

But they didn't hear. The puppy had circled around and was now making his way back to Roman and Gideon, but Jamie didn't go back.

She kept watching Blake, willing the boy to turn around, to come back this way, to notice the water edging closer. But he saw nothing but the little birds running just in front of the surf.

Elliot held one hand at his ear, the other arm shading his face against the light from the gunmetal sky. He waved to Blake, then found a spot in the lee of the rock, sat down, and stretched out his legs.

He was sheltered from the wind but perfectly positioned to take a huge hit, should a sneaker wave attack.

Jamie slowed her steps. Was she being paranoid? This was near where she'd grabbed those two kids and look at the trouble that had caused. Maybe the mother was right, maybe they'd never been in danger and Jamie had run in and grabbed them and that little girl had been hurt for no reason.

Still, she knew the sea. And this was Gideon's son. She looked out at the choppy water offshore. Though it could change direction at any moment, it didn't appear to be heading for the shallow stretch where Blake played.

Elliot's perch, however, was directly in its path.

"Hey, Elliot," she called. "Wave's gonna get you. You need to move."

But the crashing surf muffled her words and the wind scattered them to the sky.

Farther down the beach, away from the rocks, children danced among the tide pools, while parents watched and chatted, all of them seemingly oblivious to the tide, expecting that it would continue its regular, gentle ebb and flow.

The wave was churning closer now, a big one, its path unchanging, heading straight for the spot where Elliot sat talking on his phone.

"Hey! Watch out!" she yelled and redoubled her pace.

Damn it, another sneaker wave. She should have trusted her instincts.

"Elliot!" she screamed, already knowing she'd be too late.

The man looked up about one second before it landed. Instantly he was engulfed in a mini-tsunami, a surging wall of water dark with sand that swept him off his feet and tumbled him like clothes in a washing machine.

The group on the beach looked over; then the women scrambled to their feet, racing for the children. One of the husbands took off toward Elliot, but Jamie reached him first and grabbed his arm.

"No," she gasped. "Get back. Get the kids."

From the corner of her eye, she saw Blake, standing out of harm's way, watching. Not him, then. Thank God, he was safe.

She ran, calculating the waves, dancing in and out of the worst of them. Elliot tried to get onto his feet, but the churning froth knocked him down again. His movements were clumsy and slow, weighed down by clothing saturated with a mixture of water and sand that probably felt like liquid cement.

"Hang on," Jamie called, evading another wave. If she could reach him, help him to his feet, he'd be able to get out. It didn't look like he'd been injured, but he was awfully close to the rocks.

The damn wave just wouldn't stop although she knew only seconds had passed.

Get up, Elliot, you idiot. Get up!

"Help him!" screamed a woman from the rocks above. Lana. "He's drowning!"

Elliot was prone now, his arms clawing at the sand, but then more water crashed over his head.

Then a smaller voice sounded.

"Elliot?"

Blake, too, had clambered the rocky edge separated from his mother by a series of tide pools.

"Get back, Blake!" Lana yelled.

But the boy started to cry. "Elliot!" He scrambled down. He was going to run to the man, and then, he might be swept out himself.

"Blake, stay back!" she hollered. "Someone, get that kid!"

Jamie gauged the rhythm of the water as best she could, and ran into the surf, grabbing for Elliot. His body slammed against her legs and she nearly went down herself. She reached for him, caught his sleeve, but the water retreated, snatching him away, then returned with fury, tipping him end over end, his neck bending grotesquely.

Holy fuck, he was going to be smashed to pieces, right in front of her.

In that split second of rest between the ocean's inhale and exhale, Jamie grabbed hold of the man's jacket, so full of sand it may have been an anchor, a death shroud.

"Get up, Elliot, damn it!" she shrieked. "Get up!"

She crouched in preparation for the next wave to hit and managed to stay on her feet. By some miracle, Elliot got his own legs under him and they clung to each other as the murky sea battered them.

"You okay?" she yelled, trying to step to higher ground. Her running shoes felt like bricks, and they dug into the sand as if wanting to bury her.

He didn't speak, but managed to stumble out of the water's grasp, pulling away from Jamie.

As his weight disappeared, she fell to her knees and that's when she felt the rip grab her legs and suck her under.

Shit, she thought as the water closed over her head and the world turned upside down.

I didn't see that coming.

Chapter Thirty-One

*If something in your life's not working, now's the
time to change it.*

—Gideon's horoscope

Gideon saw it unfold like a nightmare, and by the time he
realized what was happening, he was too far away to
help and the beach might as well have been quicksand.

By the time he reached Elliot, the man was sitting up,
coughing. "I'm fine, I'm fine," he said, waving the strangers
away. Sand and seaweed clung to his face and hair. His skin
was grey, his teeth were chattering, and his cheek was bleeding. "Where's Blake?"

"He's here." Lana fell to her knees beside him, gathering
Blake onto her lap, trying to hug them both at the same time.
"What happened?"

Elliot bent over, gagged, spat, and braced his hands on his
legs, panting. "I don't know, exactly. I was talking to my
brother, and then all of a sudden I was under water."

"Where's Jamie?" Gideon demanded.

"Jamie?" Lana drew back. "What do you mean?"

"She was here—where is she?" He gripped her shoulders
and shoved his face toward her. His throat was almost closed,

his voice strangled. "She saved him, Lana. The woman you say is a danger to Blake just saved your fiancé's life."

He shoved her away and staggered to his feet. "Jamie!"

"I saw her," Blake said in his clear little voice. "She pulled him out."

Gideon turned to his son. "She did?" He forced his voice down out of the panic zone. "Where is she now, son? Where did she go?"

Blake frowned. "They were in the water. And then Elliot was out. I don't know where Jamie went."

Oh, God. Gideon stood up and took several stumbling steps toward the surf, scanning the horizon.

"There!" Someone yelled, pointing. "I think that's her! Someone call 911!"

Gideon shielded his eyes against the sunlight glittering fiercely off the water.

There. A sleek head, just above the surface, now there, now gone.

"She got pulled in." He pointed, kicked off his shoes, threw off his jacket, and waded into the water.

He kept his eyes on the brief glimpses of Jamie, her head again, then what he guessed was her shoulder. When he had her location burned into his brain, he dove into the surf and swam hard, feeling the pounding white water over his head.

The riptide pulled viciously at him and he let it, swimming with the water, not fighting it, though every instinct screamed otherwise. His head broke the surface and he sucked in a deep breath before diving under again.

He could reach her. She wasn't far offshore and the ferocity of the wave had calmed now that they were away from the rocky beach.

But was she hurt? Was she conscious?

Was she alive?

No. He couldn't think like that. His muscles burned as he

pressed them against the frigid water, over and over, pushing himself hard, kicking and breathing, stroke after stroke.

Then she was in his arms.

"Jamie." He rolled onto his back, pulling her against him to keep her face out of the water.

She sputtered but didn't speak. Her eyes were closed.

She was breathing. Thank God.

He hiked her tighter under his arm and made a diagonal course for the beach, his heart thundering in his chest. She was a small woman, but the weight of her clothing and the sand she'd taken on made her body a hard haul.

Oh, Jamie.

She'd thrown herself into the sea for Elliot, a man she barely knew and had no reason to care about, without a thought for herself or her safety, without even taking off her jacket.

He could feel the pull of the water lessening, but it would get rough again when he reached the surf, unless he could make it to that long, sandy stretch.

Gideon sucked in another big breath, hoping for more buoyancy, and kicked hard. He was weakening.

"Jamie, can you kick?"

She moaned and twisted in his arms, immediately slipping below the water.

Never mind that.

He tightened his grip on her and swam for all he was worth, as his body grew colder and the water began to feel warm, as his ears began to sing in time with the slap-slap of the sea against his face, as his strokes shortened and his legs struggled against the heavy denim shackles.

Then, he could hear screaming, coming in spurts as his ears were under water, then above. People, on shore, reaching for them. Lights, flashing red and blue. Two men, running halfway in, dressed in wetsuits.

He pulled his arm through water that felt like mud, thick

and cloying. Suddenly, his foot hit something, turning his ankle, tripping him. Sand.

He'd made it. He tried to stand, missed, dunked them both in the surf. Tried again. The sand was gone, he'd lost it. Then he hit again, a dull underwater whack that bent back his toes. Someone grabbed Jamie from his arms, and he fell forward hard.

Careful, he wanted to say, but his mouth wasn't working. His lips didn't form the words, and his throat was tight and sore, too busy sucking in air to verbalize his thoughts. He pulled himself from the water on hands and knees, step by impossible step and finally he was out. He collapsed to the wet sand on shaking arms, unable to move. It took everything in him to lift his head to watch where they'd taken Jamie.

Someone was standing in his way. He shook his head, or tried to. He needed to see Jamie. Where was she? What were they doing?

Hands under his arms, lifting, pulling, dragging him like so much dead weight, and him letting them, powerless to assist.

"She's okay," said a voice. "She's going to be fine. Let me look at you, all right? You took a real shit kicking out there."

A light shone in his eyes and he squinted away from it. "Jamie," he croaked. "She's . . . okay?"

"Is that her name?" the paramedic asked. "Jamie?"

He nodded. "Jamie . . . Vaughn. From . . . Sanctuary Ranch."

"And you are . . . ?"

He coughed, spat out saliva bitter with salt water. "Gideon Low. Where are you taking her?"

The paramedic lifted him to his feet. "Same place we're taking you, Gideon. To the hospital."

Chapter Thirty-Two

*A sizzling Sun–Uranus trine means things are
finally looking up.*

—Jamie's horoscope

Voices, sharp with worry, drifted around Jamie, pulling
her up from a warm, easy sleep. Footsteps squeaking.
Metal creaking. Doors sliding, bells dinging.

She turned her head slightly, away from the sounds. She
didn't want to wake up. She was so cozy. Everything was
good in her dreams. Something bad was up there, in the
cold, not-sleeping world. Whatever it was, she wasn't ready
for it.

She drifted down, down into the warm, happy nothingness where she didn't have to worry about anything. Didn't
have to do anything. She was safe, completely and totally.

Yes.

"They're calling her a hero, you know."

No.

The voices were back, closer this time, tugging her
upward.

"That idiot would have drowned without her. I'd like to
smack him upside the head. Never turn your back on the
ocean. How many times do people have to hear it?"

Jamie knew that voice, even ragged and rough as it was. *Daphne.*

Who was the idiot? A thought slipped in, then out, before the fingers of her mind could catch hold.

"They're both okay, and that's the main thing."

Olivia, her boss. If Olivia was here, it must be serious.

"Jamie? Wake up, Jamie." Olivia touched her shoulder, and with Herculean effort, Jamie peeled open her eyes.

"Hey," she said. Her throat felt like she'd swallowed a cheese grater. She cleared it and tried again. "What . . . happened?"

"There she is. There's my girl." Daphne came closer and stroked her calloused fingers over Jamie's cheek. It felt like heaven. "He's okay, honey. You're both going to be just fine."

Wait.

"Gideon?" she rasped. She struggled to her elbows, then fell back against the pillows. Something bad, it was something bad. She knew it was something bad.

She smelled seawater in her hair, tasted salt on her lips.

Bright lights started to pulsate at the edges of her vision. Her fingers tingled, her eyes were hot, a sizzling sound filled her ears.

Something bad, something bad.

"Breathe, Jamie, breathe." Olivia pressed firm hands against her shoulders. "She's hyperventilating. Get the nurse."

Footsteps floated above the sizzling, she could see them, all sparkly pink and purple and gold.

Warm weight settled near her hip.

"James. Stay with me."

The voice came from far away.

Then someone gripped her upper arms, tight. Too tight. Bruising tight. But the spangles receded.

"Everyone's okay, Jamie." Olivia, smelling of mint and oregano.

She was falling backward, unable to stop herself, unable

to stop the dread pulling at her, to shut out the evil laughter just around the corner.

"You went in to save someone caught in a rip," Olivia said in slow careful tones.

A boy, a sweet towheaded boy with Gideon's smile.

The laughter roared like a freight train, like a mighty wave, crashing, destroying, nothing sneaky about it now, no need to hide.

No! She squeezed her eyes shut, but the images kept coming. The sensations wouldn't stop.

Cold water filling her eyes, her ears, her mouth. Reaching, reaching, the sleeve slipping out of her grasp, a body, heavy as a coffin filled with sand.

Something hot and wet spilled over Jamie's cheeks. She opened her mouth, but no sound came out. Her chest was in a vise.

"Do you remember Elliot? You got him out. He's okay. You did great, James. We're all so proud of you."

At Olivia's comforting tones, the vise cracked and air rushed into her lungs. Then a horrible noise filled her ears, the wracking, dreadful screech of an engine in need of oiling, a horse panicking in a storm, an old door slammed on a dark cellar with a child crying in its spidery depths.

It was coming from her.

More footsteps.

Daphne's hands on her brow. The smell of alcohol, the snap of plastic, the rustle of packaging.

"You're okay, honey, it's okay. You let it out. Daffy's here."

Something warm in her arm. A soft, spreading heat like oil spilling over her skin from the inside out. Her chest opened, the horrid sound stopped, and a great gust of air entered her body.

Yes. Better.

And she slipped back into the warm, happy nothingness.

Chapter Thirty-Three

Never underestimate the ability of a Venus–Jupiter
square to transform your relationships.

—Jamie's horoscope

A rustling sound at the curtain of her ER cubicle made
Jamie open her eyes again. In the opening, holding the
thin green curtain fabric against her like a shield, stood Lana.
Beside her was a man in a wheelchair, with a black eye and
several stitches on his cheek.

Elliot.

Her head spun, but she forced herself to sit up straight.
"Is Blake okay?" They kept telling her he was fine, but then
things went fuzzy again and she wasn't sure if she'd dreamed
it or not.

Lana nodded, tears spilling from her eyes. "Your cook
took him back to the ranch."

"Oh." Thank God. Jamie allowed herself to fall back
against the sheets.

"We had to come and thank you in person." Lana spoke
haltingly, her voice thick with emotion. "If it hadn't been for
you, Elliot could have drowned. Maybe Blake, too, if he'd
gone after him. Someone caught the whole thing on video.

Apparently it's already a social media hit. You're a hero, Jamie. You and Gideon both."

Lana gripped Elliot's hand so tightly that Jamie guessed he was hurting. The man's hair was standing up on end and she could see sand in his ear. He was lucky not to have broken his neck.

"Anyone would have done it." Jamie's throat hurt. Puking up seawater did that. Her knees were abraded from the sand, and they'd put twelve stitches into her shin, where she must have banged it on a rock. "I need to see Gideon. Where is he?"

Lana and Elliot exchanged a glance. "They're still working on him."

Jamie's brain stuttered. "What?"

"He's fine," Lana assured her quickly. "Banged up pretty good though. He wouldn't let them do anything until they'd tended to you."

Jamie swung her legs off the side of the narrow cot, then gripped the mattress as the world tilted. She may or may not have saved Elliot.

But Gideon had most definitely saved her.

Elliot reached for her. "You're not supposed to get up."

"Get your hands off me." She pushed past him. "Gideon!"

When her bare feet hit the floor, somehow her knees didn't work the way they were supposed to.

"Jamie!" Lana caught her under her arms and managed to get her onto the edge of the bed.

"Take me to Gideon," Jamie demanded. "Now."

She was shaking. Tears were next up, and the hell if she was going to cry in front of Lana.

Then, hell or not, it was happening. Man, one near-death experience and she turned into a goddamn faucet. "I need to see Gideon. If you're lying and he's dead or hurt or—"

"He's okay, I promise." Lana lowered her into the metal chair next to the bed. "I'll take you to him in a second, I swear. Just listen to me. We have to tell you something. He made me promise, and you know Gideon. Once he decides something, there's no turning him around."

She gave a half-strangled laugh and squatted next to Jamie. "There's a bunch of people out there waiting to talk to you. Your ranch friends and someone from the local paper and a very angry old man who had a lot of things to say to me. I don't know who he is, but boy does he care about you."

She glanced at Elliot, who took her hand and pressed it to his lips. She gave him a wobbly smile and then continued.

"But this is more important." She cleared her throat. "I don't know how to say this, but . . . I'm so sorry, Jamie. I let my fears and my prejudices cloud my judgment. I was afraid to share my son, and I guess I wanted to punish Gideon a little, too. That was wrong of me. He loves you, you know. He only held back because of me."

She stopped to collect herself. All the bright brittle composure was gone, and now Jamie could see that she was just a woman trying to look after the ones she cared about the best way she could.

"I get it. Tats and piercings don't exactly give off a wholesome, milk-fed babysitter vibe."

"But then you threw yourself into the ocean to save Elliot." She shook her head wonderingly.

"It's not about me, Lana," she said. "Gideon and Blake need each other. Are you going to let that happen?"

She nodded vigorously. "I am."

Jamie looked at Elliot. "Is she telling the truth?"

"She is." She read sorrow in his expression, but acceptance too.

"You're still getting married?"

"We are." Elliot nodded. "And we're staying in Gold Beach, so we're close by."

Lana pressed Elliot's hand between hers. "We'll share custody equally. And, he doesn't know it yet, but I'm putting Gideon on the birth certificate. He should have been there from the beginning, but I was young and angry and scared and I don't want to be that person anymore."

Jamie's heart soared. "He's going to be so happy."

"That's everything I promised Gideon I'd tell you." Lana took in a deep breath and let it out through her nose. "Now I want you to promise to tell him something."

Jamie blinked. "Okay. What?"

"Blake calls you the Fairy Lady. He asked me if you were going to be his other mother, since Gideon was his other father. I want you to make an honest man out of Gideon." Lana dabbed at her eyes. "I don't care if you get married or not, but for heaven's sake, you two love each other. It's time to go public. You tell him that for me. Okay?"

Jamie reached out and covered their clasped hands with hers. "You guys are a little bossy, but I can work with that." Then she pulled them forward and gave each of them a kiss on the cheek. All three were wet with tears.

And all three of them were smiling.

Epilogue

This week, Venus moves from Cancer to Leo.
Prepare for the dramatic side of love.

—Jamie's horoscope

Gideon backed against the wall to make way for Daphne and the gigantic cake plate she held out in front of her.

"Coming through, people. It's a big day. I hope you've got your eatin' pants on."

The cook set the plate on the long table, where it joined an enormous assortment of crackers, cheese, cold cuts, cut-up vegetables, appetizers, and other goodies. Beer, wine, and soft drinks waited on the side table. "This one's carrot spice with cream cheese. That one's double chocolate with mocha filling, and the other one is lemon chiffon."

Jamie's birthday was still two weeks away, so they'd gathered everyone together under the guise of celebrating the arrival of their newest member.

In fact, they had much to celebrate.

Gideon was watching the door, waiting for Jamie to arrive. She'd gone to pick up Roman and Jonathan, and now they, plus old Sadie, entered the room.

Greetings sounded, but it was background noise to Gideon. Now that there was nothing standing in the way of their love, he couldn't get enough of looking at her. It was like his heart had been beating inside an iron cage that was now broken open and everything he felt for her was pouring out, every moment of every day. He could gaze at her all he wanted, he could touch her, he could kiss her. . . .

She looked across the room at him, a sultry, intimate glance, and instantly desire flared inside him. She'd always been more open about her feelings for him, but now he realized that she'd held much back, too.

She wound through the people, threw herself into his arms, and smacked him on the mouth. "Gideon. I love doing that. My goal," she said, planting another kiss on him, "is to embarrass you to death with public displays of affection. How am I doing?"

He kissed her neck. "I think I'm building up an immunity. You'll have to try harder."

"Uh, some of us are eating here." Tyler mimed gagging. "Get a room, will ya?"

Then Gideon saw Olivia waving at him. "Gotta go for a second," he said. "Get me some carrot cake?"

Jamie aimed a pretty pout at him. "And just like that, the magic is gone."

Olivia led him around the corner to the porch, where the antique saddle sat on a sawhorse, a big blue bow attached to the horn. "What do you think?" she asked in a low voice.

"It's perfect," he said.

Life was perfect, right now. The paper had not only printed numerous letters of support for Jamie, to counteract the one claiming child abuse, but they'd also done a feature on her and Gideon, focusing on how the event had made them realize their love for each other.

The headline: A SUNSET BAY HAPPILY EVER AFTER.

Cheesy, but Daphne had had it enlarged, framed, and hung in the entrance to the main house. They loved it.

"Is the Altman truck arriving soon?" he asked Olivia.

"Any minute now."

Gideon had spent some time getting to know the mustang in the past few days. She would be a challenge for Jamie, certainly. But that was part of the gift.

Blake, who'd been playing on the floor with Sage and Sal, pressed against Gideon's legs and slipped little fingers into his hand. "Where's Jamie? Is she playing with the fairies again?"

The boy still wasn't entirely comfortable without Lana and Elliot, but he'd come a long way. And Jamie was a huge part of that.

Jamie was a huge part of everything good in his life.

"She's in the kitchen, son. Shall we go find her?"

He clapped his hands. "Yes, let's!"

They found her by the table, and joined her in loading up plates of goodies.

Then Roman Byers shouted, "Quiet, everyone! They're here."

The room went silent. They heard the slam of a truck door, and then Haylee and Aiden walked in from the porch.

"Welcome home!" they all yelled together.

Haylee stood up at the front of the room, holding the infant close. Her hair was mussed, her face was puffy, and there were circles under her eyes, but she'd never looked happier or more beautiful.

Aiden, too, was rumpled and creased and glowing. "May we present our son, Matthew Liam Hansen McCall."

A cheer went up, which triggered a lusty wail from the newborn.

"Thanks a lot everyone," Haylee said, smiling. She patted the baby until he quieted. "No seriously, thanks a lot. This means so much to have you all here, welcoming us home. And . . ."

Gideon's pulse sped up as Haylee turned her attention to Jamie, standing next to him.

"Thank you for coming to celebrate the birthday of one of my favorite people in the entire world, Jamie Vaughn."

Jamie gasped. "You . . ." She whipped around to look at Gideon. Then Daphne. And Olivia. "Oh, man. You got me."

"Happy Birthday, Jamie!" they all yelled together.

She jumped up and down and clapped her hands in front of her. "You got me! I can't believe you surprised me!"

A horn sounded outside.

Gideon took her arm. "Follow me."

Her eyes grew round with excitement. "What? What is it?"

"You'll see."

Roman stood beside the trailer, talking with Mrs. Altman, and he stepped away immediately. The horse stomped and whinnied.

"James," Gideon said, "meet Hacer el Jaimito. Also known as Bonita."

She turned on him, her eyes even wider, if possible, than before. She blinked, as if afraid to believe.

"She's yours," he said. "Aren't you going to say anything?"

"You bought me a . . . a horse?"

"He bought you a project," Roman grumbled. "Good luck with that beast."

She walked to the front of the trailer, where she could see the mare's face. The horse eyed her nervously, but accepted her touch.

Gideon felt a tug on his leg. "When's she going to see my present," whispered Blake.

"Hang on, buddy. Anytime now."

"What's this?" Jamie said, noticing a small bag attached to the mustang's halter. "Easy, Bonita, girl. It's okay."

Gideon's heart swelled. She was going to do great with the horse.

Jamie pulled out the bag and tugged open the small drawstring. Inside was a small box.

Written on it was, *To Jamy, Frm Blake. Happy Berthday.*

She opened the lid and pulled out a silver chain with a heart on the end.

Blake got down on one knee. "Jamie, will you be my other mom? Because Gideon's my dad too now and he's got a ring for you, like Elliot got for my mom, so I'll have a mom and dad at home and a mom and dad here, too. Oh!" He clapped his hands over his mouth. "I wasn't supposed to say that part about the ring."

Gideon couldn't help but laugh. He loved that his son had come up with the idea, all on his own. They'd be a family. Gideon, Jamie, Blake. Everyone at Sanctuary Ranch. Roman and his dogs.

And Lana and Elliot, too. In fact, they were on their way over now, to have cake with everyone and begin the process of getting acquainted.

Jamie dropped to her knees and pulled the boy into a huge hug. "Of course I'll be your other mom."

Then she stood up slowly and walked to Gideon. "Just when I thought you couldn't surprise me anymore, Gideon Low. I love you so much."

"And I love you, Jamie Vaughn."

In front of everyone they cared about in the world, she lifted to her tiptoes, planted a deep kiss on his mouth.

With his forehead pressed against hers, he asked, "Is that public enough for you?"

She grinned and whispered back, "Yeah. It'll do."

Then she leaned away, punched her fist into the air and yelled, "Yes!"

*Two thumbs up for Sanctuary Ranch: go for the
horses. Stay for the food. Best week ever.*

—DanandJan

There was a lot to love about ranch life, and as Haylee
Hansen breathed in the aromas coming through the open
sliding doors to the main house, and listened to the cook and
her assistant bantering in the kitchen, she agreed with Dan
and Jan's Trip Advisor review.

Horses, *dogs*, and food, she amended.

Best *life* ever.

"Come on Ju-Jube," she said to the elderly dog at her
side. "Let's see what Daphne's got for us tonight."

The dog, who was actually called Jewel but responded
to a variety of names including *Jay, Sweetie-bear, treat,
walkies, car-ride* and anything to do with food—perked her
ears and wagged her beaver-fat tail, her tongue lolling sideways from her grinning jaw. Jewel was the unwanted
product of a classic princess/stable boy romance between a
champion pedigreed Labrador retriever and an unknown op-
portunist, but her accidental life had brought immeasurable
joy to dozens of people over the years.

Haylee loved her like a child.

"I hope that animal's feet are clean." Daphne took one hand off a generous hip and pointed at Jewel. "You know where your bed is, Miss Ju-Jube-Bear. No getting in the way, you hear me?"

Jewel ambled to the large pillow in the corner and flopped onto it with a grunt, wagging her tail the whole time. She knew the drill.

Haylee stood on her tiptoes and peeked at the oven. "Is that pot roast I smell?"

"It's the smell of murder." Jamie, the kitchen assistant, stood at the prep station, her pierced eyebrows furrowed, up to her elbows in greens. She'd gone vegetarian three weeks ago and considered it her sacred duty to convert everyone else, as well. A month before that, she'd been all about coconut oil, which Daphne had been surprisingly open to. This, however, was a battle doomed to failure.

"It's pork shoulder and root vegetables roasted in pan drippings." Daphne donned oven mitts, opened the door, and lifted the enormous roasting pan onto the stovetop. "Kale salad, too. If Jamie can chop and complain at the same time."

Haylee's stomach growled at the rich, fragrant steam that wafted into the room.

"It smells amazing," she said. "Where are the guys? Still out on the trail?"

The wranglers had taken the foster boys plus a group of horseback riders out that morning.

Daphne nodded. "Olivia suggested they might want to top the day off with a wiener roast at the lookout, so I packed them a basket."

Haylee busied herself pouring a drink, grateful for Olivia's thoughtfulness. Of course, her aunt would be doing it for herself, as much as Haylee. It was a tough day for both of them.

"It's just you, me, Liv, and Gayle tonight," Daphne said. "And plenty of leftovers for tomorrow's lunch."

Haylee looked at Jamie. "You're not eating with us?"

The girl lifted her chin with a martyred air. "I'll be enjoying my salad in my quarters."

Jamie Vaughn was twenty-five, with the life experience of a forty-year-old and the attitude of a teen. She had arrived on Olivia's doorstep from Los Angeles several years ago like an oil-slicked seabird, all gawky limbs and tufted, greasy black hair, only tolerating their kindness because exhaustion and misery outweighed her ability to fight it off.

She'd been back and forth a few times but this time she seemed to want to stay. Haylee hoped she would. The ranch was good for Jamie. There was something healing about the Oregon coast. The air had a fresh, stinging bite. Food tasted better. With all the quiet, sound seemed purer, clearer, especially after busy city streets.

The ranch was good for all of them, in different ways.

"Your choice," Daphne said pitilessly. "Everyone's welcome at my table, but I set the menu. Take it or leave it."

"I choose life." Jamie plunked the enormous wooden bowl onto the long wooden dining room table. The salad was gorgeous, fresh curly leaves of kale mixed with sliced red cabbage, shaved Brussels sprouts, slivered almonds and chewy cranberries, all covered with a sweet, tangy poppy-seed dressing.

She served herself a large portion and then looked at Daphne. "Enjoy your flesh."

Daphne gave a low chuckle. "I've always enjoyed my flesh, honey."

Jamie made a face. "Gross. I'm outta here. Oh!" She stopped and turned to Haylee. "Before I forget, there's someone I want you to meet at the shelter. You have time in the next day or two to come with me?"

Haylee winced. Jamie's probation included community service at a variety of animal shelters, and Haylee's intake of potential service dogs had gone up dramatically since

Jamie's arrival. She loved the young woman's enthusiasm, and had to admit she had great natural ability with dogs, but Sanctuary Ranch had only so much space.

She sighed. "Sure. Let's talk tomorrow, okay?"

Jamie grinned and bounced out with her plate, the argument with Daphne forgotten.

Olivia and Gayle arrived in time to hold the screen door for Jamie, and managed to hold back their laughter until they got into the kitchen.

"I understand we've arrived at the scene of a crime," Gayle said, giving Haylee a one-armed side hug.

"That girl." Olivia took her usual seat nearest the window, her long, grey-blond braid slipping over her wiry shoulder. "I can't wait until she finds herself. But she's entertaining, no doubt about that."

Daphne glanced out the window. "Don't tell her, but I'm experimenting with some meatless dishes."

Haylee gave a bark of laughter and nearly dropped her water glass. "Seriously? This is going to be awesome." Then she thought for a moment. "The guys are going to hate that."

"So what? We could all do with a little less cholesterol. It's not like I'm going to quit cooking meat entirely." Daphne set the platter of sliced meat and crispy skinned vegetables onto the table. "I was already thinking about it before she went all Tibetan monk on us. Now, she's going to think it was all her idea. She'll never let me hear the end of it."

She surveyed the table. "What am I forgetting? Oh yes, applesauce."

Daphne went back to the kitchen and Haylee watched from the corner of her eye as the cook casually glanced over her shoulder, then set a small plate in front of Jewel. Haylee pretended not to notice.

No one went hungry in Daphne's kitchen. Period. It was an inarguable precept. If Jewel came in, she got fed. Haylee didn't believe Daphne would enforce the ban, but she also didn't want to test it. The compromise was lean meat, vegetables, and equivocation. Jewel certainly wasn't complaining.

"Applesauce?" Haylee said.

Daphne laughed. "Behind the bread basket. I guess we're both blind today."

They passed the dishes around family style, laughing and chatting in a way they couldn't quite do when the whole motley staff was present.

Yes, besides the animals, the best part of life on the ranch was the joy of coming together at the end of the day to share food, stories, news, gossip, the little things that make up a day, a week, a life.

Meat or no meat.

"Have you heard?" Gayle was saying. "There's a new doctor in town. I met him today at the department meeting. He comes from Portland with a rock-star reputation. He's also single, gorgeous, and let's just say, if I wasn't batting for the other team, I'd be checking him out."

"Hey," Olivia protested. "I've got feelings, you know."

"Your feelings are as fragile as a bull moose," Gayle said with an affectionate smile.

Olivia tilted her head and looked at the ceiling. "True. So tell us more."

"Maybe we could set him up with Haylee," Daphne said, her eyes alight.

"Ooh, good idea," Olivia said. "It's high time."

"They'd look good together," Gayle said. "He's got dark hair and eyes, almost Mediterranean looking."

Daphne put a hand to her chest and sighed. "With Haylee's fair coloring and curls."

"Hello." Haylee waved her fork at them. "I'm right here."

"He's heading up the emergency room," Gayle continued, ignoring her. "Maybe she'll get kicked by a steer again."

"She's awful clumsy," Daphne added thoughtfully. "Just

yesterday she stumbled bringing in a bagful of groceries. She could have fallen off the porch and broken her arm."

"I am not clumsy," Haylee said. No one even looked at her.

"Gideon's got that new skittish horse," Olivia said. "Maybe she could help him. That's an accident waiting to happen."

"While I appreciate your good wishes," Haylee broke in, "I'm not in the market for a rock-star boyfriend and have no intention of injuring myself for an introduction."

"Oh, honey," Daphne said with a laugh, "you stick to your animals and leave matters of the heart to the experts."

She lifted a palm and Olivia and Gayle returned air high-fives to her from across the table.

"A lesbian couple and a happily divorced middle-age cook?" Haylee said. "I question your credentials."

"Evil child. I'm in my prime." She got to her feet, her smile gone. "Who wants pie?"

Too late Haylee remembered that Daphne referred to herself as a divorcee but was, in fact, happily *widowed*, the end of her marriage and the end of her husband occurring around the same time, under circumstances that would have felled a lesser woman.

Haylee carried her plate to the sink, and gave the cook a hug. "Sorry, Daffy," she whispered. Then she straightened and raised her voice. "Dinner was great. I'll have pie later. Right now, Jewel and I need a walk. Come on, baby-girl."

The dog lurched to her feet, casting a longing glance at the plate beside her, licked glistening white, as if nothing had ever besmirched the pristine surface.

Not many people were on the beach, which suited Haylee's mood perfectly. She walked near the shining edge where the sand was surf-hardened and damp, enjoying the solid crunching shift of each footstep and the briny bite of ocean air. Occasionally she landed on a soft spot and her feet sank an inch or two but she didn't care. There were worse things than wet feet.

A lot worse.

There was no point lingering in the past, but memory was cyclical and the calendar didn't lie, so one day a year, she allowed herself to test the heaviness, like a tongue seeking a sore tooth, to see if it was still there, if it still hurt.

It was, and it did.

But a little better each year. And she'd feel better tomorrow.

Jewel gave a muffled woof and Haylee jumped. She lifted her gaze to see the dog loping awkwardly on dysplastic hips to greet a man approaching from the opposite direction.

"Jewel," she called, but the dog ignored her.

By sight, or by the dog they were with, she knew most of the people who frequented the stretch of sand between the town and the ranch property. But this man, she'd never seen before.

He lifted his head and pulled his hands from his pockets as Jewel came nearer, and reached out to pat her. He was tall and broad, his dark hair a fiery halo in the waning light.

"Hey there. This your dog?" His voice was espresso rich, deep and smooth as cream. "She's a real sweetheart."

If this was the rock-star doctor, Gayle hadn't been kidding.

"Yeah." She cleared her throat and swallowed. "Sorry about that. Jewel, come on back. She's very friendly."

"So I see. It's nice." The man squatted on his haunches to give Jewel a good scrubbing on her ribs. The dog groaned, her entire body wagging in delight.

A rock-star doctor who liked dogs.

"Sorry to interrupt your walk," she said, coming close enough to clip the leash onto Jewel's collar. He stood up as she did and she felt the full force of his presence.

There were lines around his eyes and mouth, laugh lines,

she guessed, though the shadows dancing across his sculpted features suggested he hadn't been laughing much lately. Her stomach gave a little flip.

Maybe he was just tired.

"Don't apologize." His gaze was direct and appreciative. "A friendly face is just what I needed today."

Haylee looked away, fumbling with the leash. "Good. I'm glad. Well. See you around, I guess."

She tugged gently and led the dog away. He may or may not be the person Gayle described but she had enough sense to know that chatting with a strange man on a nearly deserted beach as the sun went down was a bad idea. Dog lover or not.

Even though she really wanted to stay.

Especially since she wanted to stay.

She angled her path upward so she could keep an eye on him as he walked away and before long, he'd disappeared around a rise of black rock.

"He seemed nice," she told Jewel. "Though I could be biased by pretty packaging and a very nice voice. I'd ask your opinion but you're as subtle as a freight train. You'd snuggle up to Jeffrey Dahmer if you thought he'd feed you."

The dog kept looking behind them, as if hoping the man would reappear. And he hadn't given Jewel any food whatsoever.

"I don't have time for a man," she said. "Or interest."

She'd blown through her share of relationships—if you could call them that—years ago and wasn't interested in revisiting that minefield.

Fine. She was a coward.

"On the off chance I read the vibe correctly," she continued, "I'm doing him a favor by shutting this down before it gets started. Trust me."

Jewel wagged her tail, panted, and licked her lips.

"Enough arguing," she said. "Time to head on home."

As they retraced their steps to the area where she'd last seen the man, a sound wafted over the water. A voice, calling out. Calling *her*?

"Did you hear something?"

Haylee squinted against the last rays of gold and scarlet painting the smooth ripples of the bay, in the universal human belief that by straining her eyes she'd be able to hear better.

She glanced at her dog, ambling across the vast, lonely stretch of sand ahead of her.

Of course the dog had heard it. The lapping Pacific surf that muffled sound to human ears was nothing to a dog.

His voice?

She was probably imagining the distress.

Most likely, she was hearing some kids horsing around up by the cabins, in which case, they'd say hello and call it a night.

But what if it was someone in trouble?

"Find it, Jewel."

Immediately, the dog put her nose to the ground.

Haylee picked up her pace, watching Jewel's tail sweep back and forth, a flesh-and-blood metronome, the *tick-tick-tick* measuring out a life lived in the moment, anticipation unmarred by dimming vision and arthritic hips, joy untarnished by worry or regret.

She thought of her current fosters: the little terrier cross, so full of attitude. Another Lab–pit bull, who was almost ready to move to his forever home. The Border collie with the thousand-yard stare. None of them compared to Jewel.

She pulled salt air deep into her lungs following as the dog moved upward, scrambling over the surf-scoured rocks gleaming against the fading citrus sky, absorbed, Haylee imagined, not so much in the object at the end of the search, as the search itself. The journey, not the destination.

Jewel glanced back as if to say *Pay attention!*

"Right behind you, girl."

She'd heard no more calls, but the old dog's zeal was a joy to see. And you never knew.

Like freshwater pearls on a loose string, the Oregon coastline was dotted with beaches, each one a glowing gem nestled against the velvety silhouette of black rock. The wind-and-surf-pounded outcroppings, with their hidden caves and mussel-laden tide pools, all gloriously inviting in the light of day, told a different story when darkness fell.

It wouldn't be the first time an unsuspecting beach-comber or sunbather had miscalculated the tides and spent a chilly night waiting for the ocean to recede.

Newcomers and visitors were especially vulnerable.

She cupped her hands around her mouth. "Hello? Is someone there?"

In the silent suspension between waves, Haylee listened for the voice, but caught only the *pad-pad-swish* of foot and paw on sand, empty nothingness.

Not the tall stranger then, with his piercing eyes and soft dog-patting hands who may or may not be Gayle's handsome doctor.

"Ju-Jube, honey, I think we're SOL on this one."

But Jewel bunched her shoulders and clambered ahead. Haylee knew when she was being ignored. She ought to be firmer. She ought to reassert her position as alpha.

Being and doing as she ought to got old. It wasn't as if Jewel sought domination of their little pack, after all. She knew on which side of the pantry door her kibble was buttered.

Just then the ocean paused its breathing and the sound came again, a voice, certainly, *his* voice, maybe, carried gently over the evening air, but landing not so much like distress as . . . the sounds you made when you banged your head getting into your car, cussing yourself out for stupidity. *Dumb-ass noises,* she thought.

"Woof," said Jewel, breaking into a stiff old lady's run.

"Please don't throw yourself at him this time," she cautioned. "He could be hurt." More likely a loss of dignity, which did not preclude the need for assistance; however, she knew from experience that where dignity was concerned, the need for assistance was often inversely proportional to its welcome.

"Hello?" she called again. "Is everything okay?"

No answer.

Haylee pulled herself up onto a ledge of rock, the top still dry, but not for long, as evidenced by growing splotches of foam where the incoming tide marked it. Already across, the dog splashed through a tide pool still warm from the sun, and disappeared around a corner. Haylee hissed as her knee grazed a section of mussel-encrusted rock, glad she'd switched her flip-flops for sturdy-soled ankle boots after supper. She'd have to check Jewel's paws carefully when they got back.

A watery crash sounded, large-dog loud.

"Jewel!" Haylee hauled herself over boulders slippery with algae and bits of kelp. The Labrador retriever in Jewel gave her a great love of the water, but the Y chromosome could have come from a hippo, for all the grace she had.

Another splash, then a storm of sloshing and splattering, and then the voice again, clearer now. Her pulse sped up a notch.

It was definitely him. Didn't sound like he was in trouble. Though he could certainly *be* trouble. And now, there wasn't a single other soul to be seen on the peaceful beach.

"Are you okay? Be careful with my dog. She's old."

More squelching slips, accompanied by grunts and indeterminate half shouts. Haylee wide-stepped over a shallow pool and clambered around another section of rock, peering frantically for Jewel's form among the shadows beneath her.

"It's the friendly dog," came the voice. "That's a relief."

She looked down onto the rocky landing from where she heard the voice and saw a figure sitting on the dark slab of rock next to a glittering pool, the sharp edges worn smooth by surf and wind. A white T-shirt clung to his upper body, cargo shorts below, both darkened by water. Jewel draped over him like a bad fur coat, half-on, half-off, her tail slapping wetly on the rock.

The man sounded neither surprised nor irritated but, since Jewel's sudden appearance would most certainly be cause for such reaction, this in itself was disconcerting.

"We heard you calling," she said. "Thought you might need help."

"Way better than an amorous sea lion, at least, which was my first impression," continued the man, as if she hadn't spoken.

That nice crisp voice had a note of desperate calm running through it now.

Haylee half climbed, half slid down the rock separating them.

There he was, the same handsome stranger, in the flesh.

"So, you're okay, then?" she asked, slipping down the last bit, until she was standing just above where he sat with Jewel.

"Oh, absolutely. I'm more than okay. I'm fantastic." He gestured to the dog. "I can't feel my legs, though. Do you mind?"

"Right." Haylee motioned for Jewel to climb off.

He winced as the dog's nails dug into his thighs. "You sure she's not a sea lion? Ow! Or possibly a walrus? Wait. No tusks."

Haylee gave Jewel a hug. "Good girl, you found him. What a smart girl you are." The dog was wet, happy, and whole. She'd definitely earned her cookies tonight.

The guy rubbed his legs and got to his feet, keeping a hand on the rock. Yes, still tall. Still big. And all muscle, despite the unsteadiness.

Her pulse jumped another notch. The vibe coming off him was clangy, discordant, like an orchestra in warm-up, after the long summer break. The scattered light reflecting off waves and wet rock cast stark shadows across the rugged planes of his face. No laugh lines now.

"She was looking for me? Not to appear ungrateful, but I can't imagine why. If she's a sniffer dog, the cigarettes are oregano, I swear. I'm holding them for a friend. I've never even inhaled."

She took a step back and put a hand on Jewel's warm back.

There was no scent of tobacco, let alone weed, but he was speaking too quickly. Something definitely had him rattled and it was more than indignity.

"I'm joking. Badly, I see. Don't worry, I'll keep my distance. I bet you wish you'd taken a different path tonight."

"What are you doing out here?" Someone needed to get this conversation on track.

He wiped his face with his forearm. A tattoo ran along the underside but she couldn't make out details. His strong jaw was liberally covered in a two-day growth of dark whiskers.

You expected such a man to growl or roar or paw the ground, yet he talked like he had a beer in one hand and a pair of aces in the other.

Bluffing?

"It went something like this. I was watching the sunset, minding my own business, when a large, sea lion-esque creature"—he indicated the dog nudging her pocket—"belly-flopped into the tide pool at my feet. She seemed to not want to be there, so I helped haul her out. That's when she took our relationship to the next level. You arrived. The end."

"*You* hauled *her* out?"

"What can I say?" he answered. "I'm a helper."

"In that case . . . thanks." She hesitated, then thought what the hell. "I'm Haylee Hansen. I work at Sanctuary Ranch, about a mile inland. You're the new doctor, aren't you?"

He looked a little taken aback but then he caught himself and said, "Guilty as charged. Aiden McCall. Nice to meet you, Haylee. And Jewel, the friendly dog."

"Why were you yelling?" Haylee asked. "I thought you were hurt."

"Would you believe I was practicing for an audition?"

"No."

"Right. My stand-up routine sucks. Oh well, worth a try."

He kept both hands on the rocky outcropping at his hip, as if he expected the earth to fall out from beneath his feet.

"You're going to be trapped," she said. "The tide's coming in."

He glanced down, as if only now noticing that his once-dry perch had an inch of water covering it.

"Huh. What do you know? I guess we'll be trapped together, then."

"Nah, that's a rookie mistake." She hesitated a moment, then sighed and held out her hand. "Come on. I'll help you out."

But just then, a chunk of mussel-shell broke under her boot. She stumbled forward and would have slipped into the water below, but he caught her, one hand on her arm, the other around her waist, and pulled her away from the edge.

His hands were cold from the water, his grip like icy steel but instead of a chill, heat rushed across her skin where he touched her. His scent enveloped her, a light, woodsy cologne overlaid with kelp and brine and wind and sweat.

She'd misinterpreted his body language, she realized. Tight, tense, alert, this man was *on*, the same way she remembered her father and brother being, as all firefighters, soldiers, and surgeons were, even on weekends. Life-and-death situations demanded and honed a kind of raw energy, a costly undercurrent that didn't disappear at the end of a shift.

"God, I'm so sorry," she said with a gasp. Daphne would love this story, if she ever got wind of it.

"Don't be." His breath was warm on her neck. "My male ego is vastly improved."

He stepped away the second she found her feet, then slapped wet sand from his thighs and butt.

Lean. Muscled. Nice.

Oh dear.

"Follow me," she told him, hoping it was too dark for him to see the blush she felt on her cheeks.

"What about your sea lion?"

"Jewel?" Haylee gave a little laugh. The dog had given up on extra treats and was now trotting down the rocks back to the sandy beach above the waterline. "She's way ahead of us. You okay to get back to . . . to get back?"

He lifted his chin and looked at the horizon, his eyes narrow, his full lips set tight with thin lines slicing deep on both sides, as if in pain.

"You bet," he said. "I'm great."

Sunset colors splashed over the stark planes of his face, warmth meeting chill, light and shadow flickering and dancing. Haylee shivered.

He looked, she thought, like a man walking through fire.

As the last of the light faded, Aiden McCall walked the half hour across the beach, angling upward until the smooth sand became interspersed with the rough brush and tall, spiky grasses growing roadside. How much of his rant, he wondered, had that dog-walker caught?

A million miles of empty beach and he had to pick the one spot where someone could hear him.

And not just anyone.

A cute blonde with long curly hair, toned arms, and

the kind of no-nonsense attitude that belonged behind a triage desk.

Had she really thought he'd been stranded? Her dog—Jewel?—seemed to consider him the prize at the bottom of the Cracker Jack box. How long had he been sitting there? Surely not that long. But he wasn't the most reliable witness, was he?

One second he'd been watching the sun move down toward the sea and the next he was wrestling a dog in the semi-dark, up to his ass in seawater.

He swiped at his face, recalling the animal's warm tongue, ripe with the stink of life. Bacteria too numerous to count, certainly. Nothing dangerous, hopefully. Pet lovers always told him that living with animals strengthened the immune system; he preferred the soap-and-water method himself.

Still, the creature had shocked him with its fleshy closeness. The heavy body leaning against him without boundaries, judgment, awkward courtesy, or worst of all, sympathy, had been oddly intimate.

If only the woman hadn't been there to witness it all.

He kicked at a piece of driftwood. With his luck, she'd turn out to be pals with the head ER nurse, and before he'd even set foot in the hospital, everyone would know that the new trauma doc spent his evenings yelling into the sunset.

Let it out. Yell. Scream. Be angry. Find a place where no one can hear you and get it all out. Psychobabble bullshit.

What a load. Letting it out wasn't his style, but good old-fashioned denial wasn't working, so he had to try, didn't he?

Aiden preferred joking. He teased. He laughed. He prattled in true idiot savant fashion. Because, contrary to the board-mandated therapist's belief, he was already plenty angry and well aware of it. But open that can of worms? Let it out? Who would that serve?

Still, he'd tried, as he'd tried everything. He'd yelled into the setting sun and not only did he not feel better, but by tomorrow, they'd be calling him Crazy Eyes and monitoring his scalpel blades.

If he had the energy, he'd feel mortified. Or at least, embarrassed. But once you've self-diagnosed a heart attack in your own ER and been convinced you were dying, only to be informed that you were one hundred percent A-Okay, just suffering from anxiety, well, it was tough to beat that low.

His ward clerk finding him hyperventilating in the mop closet had done it, though.

That's when he knew he had to leave Portland. Two hundred and ten pounds of raw, quivering panic caused by a little car accident? He'd faced down whacked out meth-heads, calmed an armed man in full paranoid delusion, leaped into codes, led his team, handled everything, seen everything.

But the memories intruded, as they always did.

Tires squealing, metal screeching against metal, "*Mommy-Mommy-Mommy . . .*"

Then, silence.

The silence was the worst.

Aiden could hear his breath over the soft sounds of night. Slow down. Don't think about it.

Don't think at all.

But like avalanches, thoughts once started aren't easily stopped. They tumbled in, over, through, gaining momentum until now, after thirteen years running a Level 1 emergency facility in one of the biggest hospitals in the Pacific Northwest, he was falling apart.

It was the damnedest thing.

His chest hurt. He couldn't catch his breath. He needed to get inside. To sit down. To lie down.

It was almost full dark now as he wound through the rabbit warren of Beachside Villas, looking for the one he'd rented for the summer, trying not to violate the privacy of those who hadn't drawn their curtains.

But the eye naturally follows light and every window seemed to frame people sitting around tables or moving about kitchens. Ordinary people. Ordinary meals. Not take-out in soggy cardboard containers, eaten alone in front of the TV, but real food. Eaten on dishes, at tables. Families. Friends. Husbands and wives.

Children.

Babies.

He couldn't resist looking, even though the sight of one towheaded youngster in a high chair brought Garret to mind so clearly his knees nearly buckled and he had to stop walking. This, years after the memory of his young son's face had faded, after making peace with Michelle's remarriage, being happy for her, even.

The vise grip banding his ribs tightened but he stumbled on, tearing his gaze away from the window frames.

Almost there. You can make it.

Rich smells spiked the air, piercing his mind, giving his fragmented concentration something to grab on to but it made things worse: spicy tomato sauce spilled thick and red, garlic bit like acid, grill-seared flesh smoked, choking him.

He gripped the back of his neck, then brought his hand up over his head, crushing his cap, as if he could physically squeeze the negative thoughts from his brain.

He was over this! He was strong, fine, great. So why was he gasping like an asthmatic in a dust storm?

He bent over, bracing his hands on his knees.

He'd probably forgotten to eat again. That was a mistake. There was a bagel left in the cabin, he thought. In a bag on the counter. He'd eat that. That would help.

Right. A bagel. That'll fix everything.

He half straightened, stumbling Quasimodo-style to the

small playground adjacent to his unit. He grabbed at the lamppost that cast a soft light over the swings and teeter-totter, swallowed hard, then forced his ribs to expand and contract.

Garret was gone. It was no one's fault. But that little boy six months ago, well. Aiden, of all people, should have known to check.

The lights from the windows started to dance in pairs, then triplets. He couldn't get enough air.

Rough gasps tore raggedly from his throat, littering the serene night air.

In-one-two-three. Out-one-two-three.

Nope. The lights stopped dancing and coalesced into one small pinpoint, disappearing down a long tunnel, far away, like a subway train.

You're catastrophizing again, called a little voice from way off on the subway train. Mountains, molehills. Tempests, teacups. Crazy eyes, yes, a result of adrenal overload caused by living in the worst-case scenario, of which he had endless templates.

It was entirely possible that he'd pull himself together, get a full night's sleep, and walk into the office tomorrow morning bright and competent, prepared to become the new emergency physician in the smallest trauma center he'd ever seen. It would be perfect. Bug bites. Food poisoning. Cuts and scrapes.

Yeah. He could do that.

Except that he was going to die first. His heart was exploding. The roar of the ocean pulsated all around him, thump-thump-rushing like blood from an aortic dissection. Just because he hadn't been having a cardiac event last month didn't mean he wasn't having one now.

He pushed his back against the lamppost and slid down until he plopped hard into the dirt. He was fine. He just couldn't breathe, that's all. No one died of panic. Of course not. That was silly.

They died of cardiac arrest. Which followed respiratory arrest. Which was happening to him.

Right. Goddamn. Now.

He pushed his head between his knees, hoping to hell that he'd get over this spell before someone came by and found him. He imagined that big friendly dog leaping on him, body-slamming him to the ground, knocking the dead air out and resetting his lungs.

He remembered the woman, Haylee, when she'd fallen into him, her warmth bleeding into his cold flesh, hearing the steady, normal rhythm of her heart, the weight of her slender body like a blanket on a cold night, or a brick on a sheaf of papers, keeping them from flying away in the wind.

Slowly, slowly, the tunnel shortened.

The steel band around his chest loosened and he gulped in desperate lungfuls of cool night air. He was drenched all over again with icy sweat, as if he really had been trapped by the tide, like Haylee, the pretty dog-walker had warned. His limbs quaked and he couldn't have gotten to his feet for anything, but he could breathe again.

"You all right there, young man?"

Aiden lifted his head with a jerk. A figure stood in the lane beneath a large oak tree, her hair glowing white in the lamplight. Thin, knobby fingers gripped the slack leash attached to an equally small and elderly terrier.

"It's just, you look a little frayed around the edges," she added. "I recognize the signs, being a little frayed at times myself. Only you being young and strong, well. Seems a little out of place."

He got to his feet, keeping his back to the post in case the dizziness returned. It was too late for anonymity anyway, if such a thing was even possible in a small town.

"I'm . . . fine, thank you," he managed. "It's been a . . . fraying . . . kind of day."

"Ah, yes. Those happen, don't they? Is there anything I can do to help?"

Her gentle smile eased the embarrassment that welled up in him at being caught. "You already have." He glanced around the deserted play area. "It's late. Would you like an escort home?"

She hesitated and he realized he'd overstepped. She was right to be cautious. He started to speak, but she interrupted him with a laugh, a crinkly, tinkling sound that danced over the night air. "My name is Elsie. My husband—Anton—and I are in cabin three. You're the new doctor, I believe, yes? In cabin four?"

He held out his hand. "I see word's gotten around. Aiden McCall. I'm very pleased to meet you, Elsie."

Her small bones felt like twigs. The dog eyed him suspiciously and took a couple of steps sideways.

"Be nice," Elsie said to the dog. "Her name's Bette Davis. She'll be fine once she gets to know you. I've got apple pie in the cabin. Would you care for a piece?"

A short stand of shrubs blocked his view of the cabins on either side, a factor that had played into his decision to rent here. He wanted privacy, not company. Still, her easy generosity drew him.

"I appreciate the offer, Elsie. But I've got an early morning tomorrow."

"Young people, always so busy," she said with a sigh. "We'll be off, then. But the offer stands if you find yourself at loose ends another time. I love to bake and pies are my specialty. We're here year-round and always enjoy meeting the summer people."

He waved at her. His hands were steadier now, his vision clearer.

"See you, Bette Davis," he called.

The dog glanced over her shoulder and gave a low *woof*.
Elsie waved again and disappeared around the corner.

Aiden leaned against the lamppost. Elsie and Anton, he thought. They sounded nice. He hoped they had a dozen pie-loving grandchildren.

He waited a minute or two to let his new friends get a head start, then followed the trail back to his cabin. What would he do if a dozen children suddenly showed up next door?

He'd have to find a new place.

No. He couldn't keep running. He had to be okay. He *was* okay.

He could breathe.

Some days, that was the best you could get.